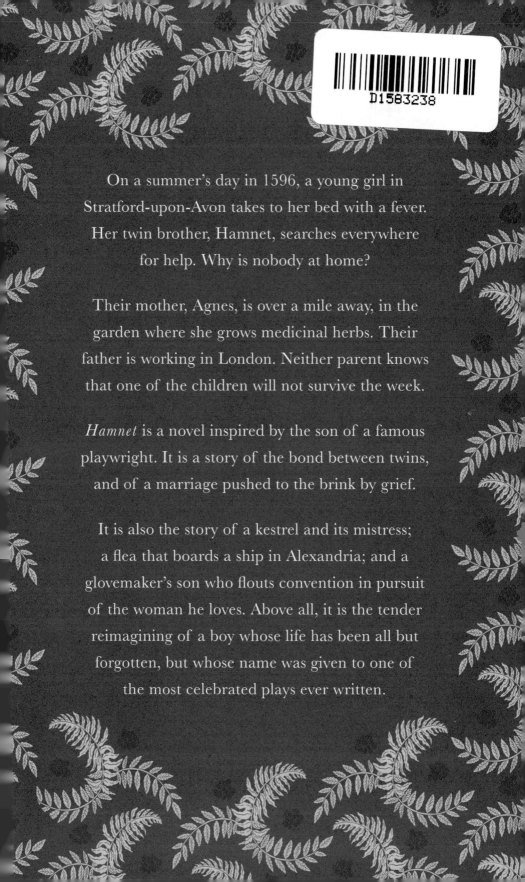

On a summer's day in 1596, a young girl in
Stratford-upon-Avon takes to her bed with a fever.
Her twin brother, Hamnet, searches everywhere
for help. Why is nobody at home?

Their mother, Agnes, is over a mile away, in the
garden where she grows medicinal herbs. Their
father is working in London. Neither parent knows
that one of the children will not survive the week.

Hamnet is a novel inspired by the son of a famous
playwright. It is a story of the bond between twins,
and of a marriage pushed to the brink by grief.

It is also the story of a kestrel and its mistress;
a flea that boards a ship in Alexandria; and a
glovemaker's son who flouts convention in pursuit
of the woman he loves. Above all, it is the tender
reimagining of a boy whose life has been all but
forgotten, but whose name was given to one of
the most celebrated plays ever written.

HAMNET

By Maggie O'Farrell

Fiction
After You'd Gone
My Lover's Lover
The Distance Between Us
The Vanishing Act of Esme Lennox
The Hand That First Held Mine
Instructions For a Heatwave
This Must Be the Place
Hamnet

Non-Fiction
I Am, I Am, I Am

H A M N E T

Maggie O'Farrell

TINDER
PRESS

First published in Great Britain in 2020 by Tinder Press
An imprint of HEADLINE PUBLISHING GROUP

2

Cataloguing in Publication Data is available from the British Library

Hardback ISBN 978 1 4722 8552 2

Typeset in Scala 11/15 pt by Palimpsest Book Production Limited, Falkirk, Stirlingshire
Printed and bound in Great Britain by Clays Ltd, Elcograf S.p.A.

Jacket Illustration © Cally Conway
Design © Yeti Lambregts & Patrick Insole

HEADLINE PUBLISHING GROUP
An Hachette UK Company
Carmelite House
50 Victoria Embankment
London EC4Y 0DZ

www.tinderpress.co.uk
www.headline.co.uk
www.hachette.co.uk

For Will

Historical note

In the 1580s, a couple living in Henley Street, Stratford, had three children: Susanna, then Hamnet and Judith, who were twins.

The boy, Hamnet, died in 1596, aged eleven.

Four years or so later, the father wrote a play called *Hamlet*.

He is dead and gone, lady,
He is dead and gone;
At his head a grass-green turf,
At his heels a stone.

Hamlet, Act IV, scene v

Hamnet and Hamlet are in fact the same name, entirely interchangeable in Stratford records in the late sixteenth and early seventeenth centuries.

Stephen Greenblatt, 'The death of Hamnet and the making of *Hamlet*', *New York Review of Books* (21 October 2004)

I

A boy is coming down a flight of stairs.

The passage is narrow and twists back on itself. He takes each step slowly, sliding himself along the wall, his boots meeting each tread with a thud.

Near the bottom, he pauses for a moment, looking back the way he has come. Then, suddenly resolute, he leaps the final three stairs, as is his habit. He stumbles as he lands, falling to his knees on the flagstone floor.

It is a close, windless day in late summer, and the down-stairs room is slashed by long strips of light. The sun glowers at him from outside, the windows latticed slabs of yellow, set into the plaster.

He gets up, rubbing his legs. He looks one way, up the stairs; he looks the other, unable to decide which way he should turn.

The room is empty, the fire ruminating in its grate, orange embers below soft, spiralling smoke. His injured kneecaps throb in time with his heartbeat. He stands with one hand resting on the latch of the door to the stairs, the scuffed leather tip of his boot raised, poised for motion, for flight. His hair, light-coloured, almost gold, rises up from his brow in tufts.

There is no one here.

He sighs, drawing in the warm, dusty air and moves through the room, out of the front door and on to the street. The noise of barrows, horses, vendors, people calling to each other, a man hurling a sack from an upper window doesn't reach him. He wanders along the front of the house and into the neigh-bouring doorway.

The smell of his grandparents' home is always the same: a mix of woodsmoke, polish, leather, wool. It is similar yet indefinably different from the adjoining two-roomed apartment, built by his grandfather in a narrow gap next to the larger house, where he lives with his mother and sisters. Sometimes he cannot understand why this might be. The two dwellings are, after all, separated by only a thin wattled wall but the air in each place is of a different ilk, a different scent, a different temperature.

This house whistles with draughts and eddies of air, with the tapping and hammering of his grandfather's workshop, with the raps and calls of customers at the window, with the noise and welter of the courtyard out the back, with the sound of his uncles coming and going.

But not today. The boy stands in the passageway, listening for signs of occupation. He can see from here that the workshop, to his right, is empty, the stools at the benches vacant, the tools idle on the counters, a tray of abandoned gloves, like handprints, left out for all to see. The vending window is shut and bolted tight. There is no one in the dining hall, to his left. A stack of napkins is piled on the long table, an unlit candle, a heap of feathers. Nothing more.

He calls out, a cry of greeting, a questioning sound. Once, twice, he makes this noise. Then he cocks his head, listening for a response.

Nothing. Just the creaking of beams expanding gently in the sun, the sigh of air passing under doors, between rooms, the swish of linen drapes, the crack of the fire, the indefinable noise of a house at rest, empty.

His fingers tighten around the iron of the door handle. The

heat of the day, even this late, causes sweat to express itself from the skin of his brow, down his back. The pain in his knees sharpens, twinges, then fades again.

The boy opens his mouth. He calls the names, one by one, of all the people who live here, in this house. His grandmother. The maid. His uncles. His aunt. The apprentice. His grandfather. The boy tries them all, one after another. For a moment, it crosses his mind to call his father's name, to shout for him, but his father is miles and hours and days away, in London, where the boy has never been.

But where, he would like to know, are his mother, his older sister, his grandmother, his uncles? Where is the maid? Where is his grandfather, who tends not to leave the house by day, who is usually to be found in the workshop, harrying his apprentice or reckoning his takings in a ledger? Where is everyone? How can both houses be empty?

He moves along the passageway. At the door to the workshop, he stops. He throws a quick glance over his shoulder, to make sure nobody is there, then steps inside.

His grandfather's glove workshop is a place he is rarely allowed to enter. Even to pause in the doorway is forbidden. Don't stand there idling, his grandfather will roar. Can't a man do an honest day's work without people stopping to gawk at him? Have you nothing better to do than loiter there catching flies?

Hamnet's mind is quick: he has no trouble understanding the schoolmasters' lessons. He can grasp the logic and sense of what he is being told, and he can memorise readily. Recalling verbs and grammar and tenses and rhetoric and numbers and calculations comes to him with an ease that can, on occasion, attract the envy of other boys. But his is a mind also easily

5

distracted. A cart going past in the street during a Greek lesson will draw his attention away from his slate to wonderings as to where the cart might be going and what it could be carrying and how about that time his uncle gave him and his sisters a ride on a haycart, how wonderful that was, the scent and prick of new-cut hay, the wheels tugged along to the rhythm of the tired mare's hoofs. More than twice in recent weeks he has been whipped at school for not paying attention (his grandmother has said if it happens once more, just once, she will send word of it to his father). The schoolmasters cannot understand it. Hamnet learns quickly, can recite by rote, but he will not keep his mind on his work.

The noise of a bird in the sky can make him cease speaking, mid-utterance, as if the very heavens have struck him deaf and dumb at a stroke. The sight of a person entering a room, out of the corner of his eye, can make him break off whatever he is doing – eating, reading, copying out his schoolwork – and gaze at them as if they have some important message just for him. He has a tendency to slip the bounds of the real, tangible world around him and enter another place. He will sit in a room in body, but in his head he is somewhere else, someone else, in a place known only to him. Wake up, child, his grandmother will shout, snapping her fingers at him. Come back, his older sister, Susanna, will hiss, flicking his ear. Pay attention, his schoolmasters will yell. Where did you go? Judith will be whispering to him, when he finally re-enters the world, when he comes to, when he glances around to find that he is back, in his house, at his table, surrounded by his family, his mother eyeing him, half smiling, as if she knows exactly where he's been.

In the same way, now, walking into the forbidden space of the glove workshop, Hamnet has lost track of what he is meant to be doing. He has momentarily slipped free of his moorings, of the fact that Judith is unwell and needs someone to care for her, that he is meant to be finding their mother or grandmother or anyone else who might know what to do.

Skins hang from a rail. Hamnet knows enough to recognise the rust-red spotted hide of a deer, the delicate and supple kidskin, the smaller pelts of squirrels, the coarse and bristling boarskin. As he moves nearer to them, the skins start to rustle and stir on their hangings, as if some life might yet be left in them, just a little, just enough for them to hear him coming. Hamnet extends a finger and touches the goat hide. It is unaccountably soft, like the brush of river weed against his legs when he swims on hot days. It sways gently to and fro, legs splayed, stretched out, as if in flight, like a bird or a ghoul.

Hamnet turns, surveys the two seats at the workbench: the padded leather one worn smooth by the rub of his grandfather's breeches, and the hard wooden stool for Ned, the apprentice. He sees the tools, suspended from hooks on the wall above the workbench. He is able to identify those for cutting, those for stretching, those for pinning and stitching. He sees that the narrower of the glove stretchers – used for women – is out of place, left on the bench where Ned works with bent head and curved shoulders and anxious, nimble fingers. Hamnet knows that his grandfather needs little provocation to yell at the boy, perhaps worse, so he picks up the glove stretcher, weighing its warm wooden heft, and replaces it on its hook.

He is just about to slide out the drawer where the twists of thread are kept, and the boxes of buttons – carefully, carefully, because he knows the drawer will squeak – when a noise, a slight shifting or scraping, reaches his ears.

Within seconds, Hamnet has darted out, along the passageway and into the yard. His task returns to him. What is he doing, fiddling in the workshop? His sister is unwell: he is meant to be finding someone to help.

He bangs open, one by one, the doors to the cookhouse, the brewhouse, the washhouse. All of them empty, their interiors dark and cool. He calls out again, slightly hoarse this time, his throat scraped with the shouting. He leans against the cookhouse wall and kicks at a nutshell, sending it skittering across the yard. He is utterly confounded to be so alone. Someone ought to be here; someone always is here. Where can they be? What must he do? How can they all be out? How can his mother and grandmother not be in the house, as they usually are, heaving open the doors of the oven, stirring a pot over the fire? He stands in the yard, looking about himself, at the door to the passageway, at the door to the brewhouse, at the door to their apartment. Where should he go? Whom should he call on for help? And where is everyone?

Every life has its kernel, its hub, its epicentre, from which everything flows out, to which everything returns. This moment is the absent mother's: the boy, the empty house, the deserted yard, the unheard cry. Him standing here, at the back of the house, calling for the people who had fed him, swaddled him, rocked him to sleep, held his hand as he took his first steps, taught him to use a spoon, to blow on broth before he ate it, to take care crossing the street, to let sleeping dogs lie, to swill out a cup before drinking, to stay away from deep water.

It will lie at her very core, for the rest of her life.

Hamnet scuffs his boots in the grit of the yard. He can see the remains of a game he and Judith had been playing not long ago: the lengths of twine tied to pine cones to be pulled and swung for the kitchen cat's kittens. Small creatures they are, with faces like pansies and soft pads on their paws. The cat went into a barrel in the storeroom to have them and hid there for weeks. Hamnet's grandmother looked everywhere for the litter, intending to drown them all, as is her custom, but the cat thwarted her, keeping her babies secret, safe, and now they are half grown, two of them, running about the place, climbing up sacks, chasing feathers and wool scraps and stray leaves. Judith cannot be parted from them for long. She usually has one in her apron pocket, a tell-tale bulge, a pair of peaked ears giving her away, making their grandmother shout and threaten the waterbutt. Hamnet's mother, however, whispers to them that the kittens are too big for their grand-mother to drown. 'She couldn't do it, now,' she says to them, in private, wiping tears from Judith's horrified face. 'She wouldn't have the stomach for it – they would struggle, you see, they would fight.'

Hamnet wanders over to the abandoned pine cones, their strings trailed into the trodden earth of the yard. The kittens are nowhere to be seen. He nudges a pine cone with his toe and it rolls away from him in an uneven arch.

He looks up at the houses, the many windows of the big one and the dark doorway of his own. Normally, he and Judith would be delighted to find themselves alone. He would, this very moment, be trying to persuade her to climb on to the cookhouse roof with him, so that they might reach the boughs of the plum tree just over the neighbour's wall. They are filled, crammed, with plums, their red-gold jackets near to bursting with ripeness; Hamnet has eyed them from an upper window in his grandparents' house. If this were a normal day, he would be giving Judith a boost on to the roof so that she could fill her pockets with stolen fruit, despite her qualms and protestations. She doesn't like to do anything dishonest or forbidden, so guileless is her nature, but can usually be persuaded with a few words from Hamnet.

Today, though, as they played with the kittens who escaped an early demise, she said she had a headache, a pain in her throat, she felt cold, then she felt hot, and she has gone into the house to lie down.

Hamnet goes back through the door to the main house and along the passage. He is just about to go out into the street when he hears a noise. It is a click or a shift, a minute sound, but it is the definite noise of another human being.

'Hello?' Hamnet calls. He waits. Nothing. Silence presses back at him from the dining hall and the parlour beyond. 'Who's there?'

For a moment, and just for a moment, he entertains the notion that it might be his father, returned from London, to surprise them – it has happened before. His father will be there, beyond that door, perhaps hiding as a game, as a ruse. If Hamnet walks into the room, his father will leap out; he will have gifts stowed in his bag, in his purse; he will smell of horses, of hay, of many days on the road; he will put his arms around his son and Hamnet will press his cheek to the rough, chafing fastenings of his father's jerkin.

He knows it won't be his father. He knows it, he does. His father would respond to a repeated call, would never hide himself away in an empty house. Even so, when Hamnet walks into the parlour, he feels the falling, filtering sensation of disappointment to see his grandfather there, beside the low table.

The room is filled with gloom, coverings pulled over most of the windows. His grandfather is standing with his back towards him, in a crouched position, fumbling with something: papers, a cloth bag, counters of some sort. There is a pitcher on the table, and a cup. His grandfather's hand meanders through these objects, his head bent, his breath coming in wheezing bursts.

Hamnet gives a polite cough.

His grandfather wheels around, his face wild, furious, his arm flailing through the air, as if warding off an assailant. 'Who's there?' he cries. 'Who is that?'

'It's me.'

'Who?'

'Me.' Hamnet steps towards the narrow shaft of light slanting in through the window. 'Hamnet.'

His grandfather sits down with a thud. 'You scared the wits out of me, boy,' he cries. 'Whatever do you mean, creeping about like that?'

'I'm sorry,' Hamnet says. 'I was calling and calling but no one answered. Judith is—'

'They've gone out,' his grandfather speaks over him, with a curt flick of his wrist. 'What do you want with all those women anyway?' He seizes the neck of the pitcher and aims it towards the cup. The liquid – ale, Hamnet thinks – slops out precipitously, some into the cup and some on to the papers on the table, causing his grandfather to curse, then dab at them with his sleeve. For the first time, it occurs to Hamnet that his grandfather might be drunk.

'Do you know where they have gone?' Hamnet asks.

'Eh?' his grandfather says, still mopping his papers. His anger at their spoiling seems to unsheathe itself and stretch out from him, like a rapier. Hamnet can feel the tip of it wander about the room, seeking an opponent, and he thinks for a moment of his mother's hazel strip, and the way it pulls itself towards water, except he is not an underground stream and his grandfather's anger is not like the quivering divining rod at all. It is cutting, sharp, unpredictable. Hamnet has no idea what will happen next, or what he should do.

'Don't stand there gawping,' his grandfather hisses. 'Help me.'

Hamnet shuffles forward a step, then another. He is wary, his father's words circling his mind: Stay away from your grandfather when he is in one of his black humours. Be sure to stand clear of him. Stay well back, do you hear?

His father had said this to him on his last visit, when they had been helping unload a cart from the tannery. John, his grandfather, had dropped a bundle of skins into the mud and, in a sudden fit of temper, had hurled a paring-knife at the yard wall. His father had immediately pulled Hamnet back, behind him, out of the way, but John had barged past them into the house without a word. His father had taken Hamnet's face in both of his hands, fingers curled in at the nape of his neck, his gaze steady and searching. He'll not touch your sisters but it's you I worry for, he had muttered, his brow puckering. You know the humour I mean, don't you? Hamnet had nodded but wanted the moment to be prolonged, for his father to keep holding his head like that: it gave him a sensation of lightness, of safety, of being entirely known and treasured. At the same time, he was aware of a curdling unease swilling about inside him, like a meal his stomach didn't want. He thought of the snip and snap of words that punctured the air between his father and grandfather, the way his father continually reached to loosen his collar when seated at table with his parents. Swear to me, his father had said, as they stood in the yard, his voice hoarse. Swear it. I need to know you'll be safe when I'm not here to see to it.

Hamnet believes he is keeping his word. He is well back. He is at the other side of the fireplace. His grandfather couldn't reach him here, even if he tried.

His grandfather is draining his cup with one hand and shaking the drops off a sheet of paper with the other. 'Take this,' he orders, holding out the page.

Hamnet bends forward, not moving his feet, and takes it with the very tips of his fingers. His grandfather's eyes are slitted, watchful; his tongue pokes out of the side of his mouth. He sits in his chair, hunched: an old, sad toad on a stone.

'And this.' His grandfather holds out another paper.

Hamnet bends forward in the same way, keeping the necessary distance. He thinks of his father, how he would be proud of him, how he would be pleased.

Quick as a fox, his grandfather makes a lunge. Everything happens so fast that, afterwards, Hamnet won't be sure in what sequence it all occurred: the page swings to the floor between them, his grandfather's hand seizes him by the wrist, then the elbow, hauling him forward, into the gap, the space his father had told him to observe, and his other hand, which still holds the cup, is coming up, fast. Hamnet is aware of streaks in his vision – red, orange, the colours of fire, streaming in from the corner of his eye – before he feels the pain. It is a sharp, clubbed, jabbing pain. The rim of the cup has struck him just below the eyebrow.

'That'll teach you,' his grandfather is saying, in a calm voice, 'to creep up on people.'

Tears burst forth from Hamnet's eyes, both of them, not just the injured one.

'Crying are you? Like a little maid? You're as bad as your father,' his grandfather says, with disgust, releasing him. Hamnet springs backwards, thwacking his shin on the side of the parlour bed. 'Always crying and whining and complaining,' his grandfather mutters. 'No backbone. No sense. That was always his problem. Couldn't stick at anything.'

Hamnet is running back outside, along the street, wiping at his face, dabbing the blood with his sleeve. He lets himself in through his own front door, up the stairs, to the upper room, where a figure lies on the pallet next to their parents' big curtained bed. The figure is dressed – a brown smock, a white bonnet, the strings of which are untied and straggle down her neck – and is lying on top of the sheets. She has kicked off her shoes, which lie, inverted, like a pair of empty pods, beside her.

'Judith,' the boy says, and touches her hand. 'Are you feeling any better?'

The girl's lids lift. She stares at her brother, for a moment, as if from a great distance, then shuts her eyes again. 'I'm sleeping,' she murmurs.

She has the same heart-shaped face as him, the same peaked brow, where the same corn-coloured hair grows upwards. The eyes that fixed so briefly on his face are the same colour – a warm amber, flecked with gold – the same set as his own. There is a reason for this: they share a birthday, just as they shared their mother's womb. The boy and the girl are twins, born within minutes of each other. They are as alike as if they had been born in the same caul.

He closes his fingers about hers – the same nails, the same shaped knuckles, although his are bigger, wider, grimier – and he tries to flatten the thought that hers feel slick and hot.

'How are you?' he says. 'Better?'

She stirs. Her fingers curl into his. Her chin lifts, then dips. There is, the boy sees, a swelling at the base of her throat. And another where her shoulder meets her neck. He stares at them. A pair of quail's eggs, under Judith's skin. Pale, ovoid, nestled there, as if waiting to hatch. One at her neck, one at her shoulder.

She is saying something, her lips parting, her tongue moving inside her mouth.

'What did you say?' he asks, bending nearer.

'Your face,' she is saying. 'What happened to your face?'

He puts a hand to his brow, feeling the swelling there, the wet of new blood. 'Nothing,' he says. 'It was nothing. Listen,' he says, more urgently, 'I'm going to find the physician. I won't be long.'

She says something else.

'Mamma?' he repeats. 'She – she is coming. She is not far away.'

*

She is, in fact, more than a mile away.

Agnes has a patch of land at Hewlands, leased from her brother, stretching from the house where she was born to the forest. She keeps bees here, in hemp-woven skeps, which hum with industrious and absorbed life; there are rows of herbs, flowers, plants, stems that wind up supporting twigs. Agnes's witch garden, her stepmother calls it, with a roll of her eyes.

Agnes can be seen, most weeks, moving up and down the rows of these plants, pulling up weeds, laying her hand to the coils of her hives, pruning stems here and there, secreting certain blooms, leaves, pods, petals, seeds in a leather bag at her hip.

Today she has been called there by her brother, who dispatched the shepherd's boy to tell her that something was amiss with the bees – they have left the hive and are massing in the trees.

Agnes is circling the skeps, listening for whatever the bees are telling her; she is eyeing the swarm in the orchard, a blackish stain spread throughout the branches that vibrates and quivers with outrage. Something has upset them. The weather, a change in temperature, or has someone disturbed the hive? One of the children, some escaped sheep, her stepmother?

She slides her hand up and under, into the skep, past its lip, through the remaining coating of bees. She is cool in a shift, under the dark, river-coloured shade of the trees, her thick braid of hair pinned to the top of her head, hidden under a white coif. No bee-keeper veil covers her face – she never wears one. If you came close enough, you would see that her lips are moving, murmuring small sounds and clicks to the insects that circle her head, alight on her sleeve, blunder into her face.

She brings a honeycomb out of the skep and squats to

examine it. Its surface is covered, teeming, with something that appears to be one moving entity: brown, banded with gold, wings shaped like tiny hearts. It is hundreds of bees, crowded together, clinging to their comb, their prize, their work.

She lifts a bundle of smouldering rosemary and waves it gently over the comb, the smoke leaving a trail in the still August air. The bees lift, in unison, to swarm above her head, a cloud with no edges, an airborne net that keeps casting and casting itself.

The pale wax is scraped, carefully, carefully, into a basket; the honey leaves the comb with a cautious, near reluctant drop. Slow as sap, orange-gold, scented with the sharp tang of thyme and the floral sweetness of lavender, it falls into the pot Agnes holds out. A thread of honey stretches from comb to pot, widening, twisting.

There is a sensation of change, an agitation of air, as if a bird has passed silently overhead. Agnes, still crouching, looks up. The movement causes her hand to waver and honey drips to her wrist, trails over her fingers, down the side of the pot. Agnes frowns, puts down the honeycomb, and stands, licking her fingertips.

She takes in the thatched eaves of Hewlands, to her right, the white scree of cloud overhead, the restless branches of the forest, to her left, the swarm of bees in the apple trees. In the distance, her second-youngest brother is driving sheep along the bridle path, a switch in his hand, the dog darting towards and away from the flock. Everything is as it should be. Agnes stares for a moment at the jerky stream of sheep, the skitter of their feet, their draggled, mud-crusted fleeces. A bee lands on her cheek; she fans it away.

Later, and for the rest of her life, she will think that if she had left there and then, if she had gathered her bags, her plants, her honey, and taken the path home, if she had heeded her abrupt, nameless unease, she might have changed what happened next. If she had left her swarming bees to their own devices, their own ends, instead of working to coax them back into their hives, she might have headed off what was coming.

She doesn't, however. She dabs at the sweat on her brow, her neck, tells herself not to be foolish. She places a lid on the full pot, she wraps up the honeycomb in a leaf, she presses her hands to the next skep, to read it, to understand it. She leans against it, feeling its rumbling, vibrating interior; she senses its power, its potency, like an incoming storm.

The boy, Hamnet, is trotting along the street, around a corner, dodging a horse that stands, patient, between the shafts of a cart, around a group of men gathered outside the guildhall, leaning towards each other with serious faces. He passes a woman with a baby in her arms, imploring an older child to walk faster, to keep up, a man hitting the haunches of a donkey, a dog that glances up from whatever it is eating to watch Hamnet as he runs. The dog barks once, in sharp admonishment, then returns to its gnawing.

Hamnet arrives at the house of the physician – he has asked directions from the woman with the baby – and he bangs on the door. He registers, momentarily, the shape of his fingers, his nails, and looking at them brings Judith's to mind; he bangs harder. He thuds, he thunders, he shouts.

The door is swung open and the narrow, vexed face of a woman appears around it. 'Whatever are you doing?' she cries, shaking a cloth at him, as if to waft him away, like an insect. 'That's a racket loud enough to wake the dead. Be off with you.'

She goes to shut the door but Hamnet leaps forward. 'No,' he says. 'Please. I'm sorry, madam. I need the physician. We need him. My sister – she is unwell. Can he come to us? Can he come now?'

The woman holds the door firm in her reddened hand but looks at Hamnet with care, with attention, as if reading the seriousness of the problem in his features. 'He's not here,' she says eventually. 'He's with a patient.'

Hamnet has to swallow, hard. 'When will he be back, if you please?'

The pressure on the door is lessening. He steps one foot into the house, leaving the other behind him.

'I couldn't say.' She looks him up and down, at the encroaching foot in her hallway. 'What ails your sister?'

'I don't know.' He tries to think back to Judith, the way she looked as she lay on the blankets, her eyes closed, her skin flushed and yet pale. 'She has a fever. She has taken to her bed.'

The woman frowns. 'A fever? Has she buboes?'

'Buboes?'

'Lumps. Under the skin. On her neck, under her arms.'

Hamnet stares at her, at the small pleat of skin between her brows, at the rim of her cap, how it has rubbed a raw patch beside her ear, at the wiry coils of hair escaping at the back. He thinks of the word 'buboes', its vaguely vegetal over-tones, how its bulging sound mimics the thing it describes. A cold fear rinses down through his chest, encasing his heart in an instant, crackling frost.

The woman's frown deepens. She places her hand in the centre of Hamnet's chest and propels him back, out of her house.

'Go,' she says, her face pinched. 'Go home. Now. Leave.' She goes to close the door but then, through the narrowest crack, says, not unkindly, 'I will ask the physician to call. I know who you are. You're the glover's boy, aren't you? The grandson. From Henley Street. I will ask him to come by your house, when he returns. Go now. Don't stop on the way back.' As an afterthought, she adds, 'God speed to you.'

He runs back. The world seems more glaring, the people louder, the streets longer, the colour of the sky an invasive, glancing blue. The horse still stands at its cart; the dog is now curled up on a doorstep. Buboes, he thinks again. He has heard the word before. He knows what it means, what it denotes.

Surely not, he is thinking, as he turns into his street. It cannot be. It cannot. That – he will not name it, he will not allow the word to form, even inside his head – hasn't been known in this town for years.

Someone will be home, he knows, by the time he gets to the front door. By the time he opens it. By the time he crosses the threshold. By the time he calls out, to someone, anyone. There will be an answer. Someone will be there.

Unbeknown to him, he passed the maid, both his grandparents and his older sister on his trip to the physician's house.

His grandmother, Mary, had been coming along an alleyway, down near the river, making deliveries, her stick held out to ward off the advances of a particularly peevish cockerel, Susanna behind her. Susanna had been brought along to carry Mary's basket of gloves – deerskin, kidskin, squirrel-lined, wool-lined, embroidered, plain. 'I don't for the life of me know why,' Mary had been saying, as Hamnet flashed unseen past the end of the alley, 'you cannot at the very least look people in the eye when they greet you. These are some of your grandfather's highest paying customers and a shred of courtesy wouldn't go amiss. Now I do really believe that . . .' Susanna had trailed in her wake, rolling her eyes, lugging the basket filled with gloves. Like severed hands, she was thinking, as she let her grandmother's voice be blotted out by the sound of her own sigh, by the sight of a slice of sky cutting through the building tops.

John, Hamnet's grandfather, had been among the men outside the guildhall. He had left the parlour and his calculations while Hamnet had been upstairs with Judith, and had been standing with his back to Hamnet as the boy ran for the physician. If the boy had turned his head as he passed, he would have seen his grandfather pushing his way into this group, leaning towards the other men, gripping their reluctant arms, urging them, teasing them, exhorting them to come with him to a tavern.

John hadn't been invited to this meeting but had heard that it was happening so had come along in the hope of catching the men before they dispersed. He wants nothing more than to reinstate himself as a man of consequence and influence, to regain the status he once had. He can do it, he knows he can. All he needs is the ear of these men, whom he has known for years, who know him, who could vouch for his industry, his loyalty to this town. Or, if nothing else, a pardon or a blind eye from the guild and the town authorities. He was once bailiff, and then a high alderman; he used to sit in the front pew of the church and wear a scarlet robe. Have these men forgotten that? How can they not have invited him to this meeting? He used to have influence – he used to rule over them all. He used to be someone. And now he is reduced to living on whatever coin his eldest can send back from London (and what an infuriating youth he had been, hanging about the market square, squandering his time; who would have thought he would amount to anything?).

John's business still thrives, after a fashion, because people will always need gloves, and if these men know of his secret dealings in the wool trade, his summons for not attending church and fines for dumping waste in the street, so be it. John can take in his stride their disapproval, their fines and their demands, their snide mutterings about the ruination of his family, the exclusion from guild meetings. His house is one of the finest in the town: there is always that. What John cannot bear is that not one of them will take a drink with him, will break bread at his table, will warm themselves at his hearth. Outside the guildhall, the men avoid his eye, continue their conversation. They don't listen to his prepared speech about the reliability of the glove trade, about his successes, his triumphs, his invitations to a tavern, to eat dinner at his house. They nod distantly; they turn away. One pats his arm, says, aye, John, aye.

So he goes to the tavern alone. Just for a while. Nothing wrong with a man's own company. He will sit here, in the half-light, like that of dusk, a candle stub on the table before him, and watch as stray flies circle and circle in its light.

Judith is lying on the bed and the walls appear to be bulging inwards, then flexing back. In, out, in, out. The posts around her parents' bed, in the corner, writhe and twist like serpents; the ceiling above her ripples, like the surface of a lake; her hands seem at once too close and then very far away. The line where the white of the plasterwork meets the dark wood of the joists shimmers and refracts. Her face and chest are hot, burning, covered with slick sweat, but her feet are ice-cold. She shivers, once, twice, a full convulsion, and sees the walls bend towards her, closing in, then pulling away. To block out the walls, the serpentine bedposts, the moving ceiling, she shuts her eyes.

As soon as she does so, she is elsewhere. In many places at once. She is walking through a meadow, holding tight to a hand. The hand belongs to her sister, Susanna. It has long fingers and a mole on the fourth knuckle. It does not want to be held: the fingers aren't curled around Judith's, but kept stiff and straight. Judith has to grip with all her might for it not to slide from her. Susanna takes great steps through the long grass of the meadow and with each one her hand jerks in Judith's. If Judith lets go, she may sink beneath the surface of the grass. She may be lost, never to be found. It is important – crucial – for her to keep hold of this hand. She must never let go. Ahead of them, she knows, is her brother. Hamnet's head bobs in and out of the grass. His hair is the colour of ripe wheat. He bounds through the meadow, ahead of them, like a hare, like a comet.

Then Judith is in a crowd. It is night-time, cold; the glow of lanterns punctuates the freezing dark. She thinks it is the Candlemas fair. She is in and also above a crowd, on a pair of strong shoulders. Her father. Her legs grip his neck and he holds her by each ankle; she has buried her hands in his hair. Thick dark hair he has, like Susanna's. She uses the smallest of her fingers to tap the silver hoop in his left ear. He laughs at this – she feels the rumble of it, like thunder, pass from his body to hers – and shakes his head to make the earring rattle against her fingernail. Her mother is there, and Hamnet and Susanna, and her grandmother. Judith is the one her father has chosen to ride on his shoulders: just her.

There is a great flaring of light. Braziers are bright and fierce around a wooden platform, raised to the level of herself, there, on her father's shoulders. On the platform are two men, dressed in gold and red clothing, with many tassels and ribbons; they have tall hats on their heads and their faces are white as chalk with blackened eyebrows and reddened lips. One lets out a high, keening cry and hurls a golden ball at the other; he flips himself on to his hands and catches the ball in his feet. Her father lets go of her ankles to applaud and Judith clutches at his head. She is terrified she might fall, tip back, off his shoulders and into the seething, restive crowd that smells of potato peelings, of wet dog, of sweat and chestnuts. The man's cry has set fear in her heart. She doesn't like the braziers; she doesn't like the men's jagged eyebrows; she doesn't like any of this at all. She begins, quietly, to weep, the tears coursing from her cheeks to rest like pearls in her father's hair.

Susanna and her grandmother, Mary, are not yet home. Mary has stopped to talk to a woman of the parish: they barter compliments and demurrals, pat each other on the arm but Susanna isn't fooled. She knows the woman does not like her grandmother; the woman can't stop looking around, over her shoulder, wondering if anyone is observing her in conversation with Mary, wife of the disgraced glover. There are many in the town, Susanna knows, who were once their friends and now cross the street to avoid them. It has been going on for years, but ever since her grandfather was fined for not attending church, many of the townsfolk have dropped the pretence of civility and will walk past without acknowledging them. Susanna sees how her grandmother plants herself in the woman's way, so that she cannot get past, cannot avoid talking to them. She sees all of this. The knowledge of it burns the inside of her head, leaving black scorch marks.

Judith lies alone on her bed, opening and closing her eyes. She cannot comprehend what has happened to this day. One moment, she and Hamnet were pulling bits of thread for the cat's new kittens – keeping an eye open for their grandmother, because Judith had been told to chop the kindling and polish the table while Hamnet did his schoolwork – and then she had suddenly felt a weakness in her arms, an ache in her back, a prickling in her throat. I don't feel well, she'd said to her brother, and he had looked up from the kittens, at her, and his eyes had travelled all over her face. Now she is on this bed and she has no idea how she got here or where Hamnet has gone or when her mother is coming back or why no one is there.

The maid is taking a long time to make her selection from the late milking at the market, flirting with the dairyman behind his stall. Well, well, he is saying, not letting go of the pail. Oh, the maid is replying, tugging at the handle. Will you not let me have it? Have what? the dairyman says, raising his eyebrows.

*

Agnes has finished collecting her honey and has taken up a sack and the burning rosemary and is making for the swarm of bees. She will sweep them into the sack and return them to the hive, but gently, ever so gently.

The father is two days' ride away, in London, and is, at this very moment, striding through Bishopsgate towards the river, where he aims to buy one of the flat, unleavened griddle cakes that sell on stalls there. He has a terrible hunger in him today; he woke with it, and his breakfast of ale and porridge and his lunch of pie has not sated it. He is careful with his money, keeping it close to his person, never spending more than he has to. It is the subject of much ribbing from those he works with. People say of him that he has gold stored in bags under the boards of his lodging: he has heard this and smiled. It is, of course, not true: everything he earns he sends home to Stratford, or takes with him, wrapped and stowed in his saddle-bags, if he is making the journey. But, still, he doesn't spend a groat unless absolutely necessary. And this day the griddle cake, in mid-afternoon, is such a necessity.

Alongside him walks a man, the son-in-law of his landlord. This man has been talking since they left the house. Hamnet's father is listening only intermittently to what the man is saying – something about a grudge towards his father-in-law, a dowry unfulfilled, a promise not kept. He is thinking instead of the way the sun reaches down, like ladders, through the narrow gaps in buildings to illuminate the rain-glazed street, of the griddle cake that awaits him near the river, of the flap and soap-tang of laundry hanging above his head, of his wife, fleetingly, the way her twinned shoulder-blades flex together and apart as she pins up the weight of her hair, of the stitching in the toe of his boot that seems to have worked itself loose and how he must now pay a visit to the cobbler, perhaps after he has eaten his griddle cake, as soon as he has rid himself of the landlord's son-in-law and his querulous babbling.

And Hamnet? He is re-entering the narrow house, built in a gap, a vacancy. He is sure, now, that other people will be back. He and Judith will no longer be alone. There will be someone here now who will know what to do, someone to assume charge of this, someone who will tell him that all is well. He steps in, letting the door swing closed behind him. He calls, to say he is back, he is home. He pauses, waiting for an answer, but there is nothing: only silence.

f you were to stand at the window in Hewlands and crane your neck sideways, it would be possible to see the edge of the forest.

You might find it a restless, verdant, inconstant sight: the wind caresses, ruffles, disturbs the mass of leaves; each tree answers to the weather's ministrations at a slightly different tempo from its neighbour, bending and shuddering and tossing its branches, as if trying to get away from the air, from the very soil that nourishes it.

On a morning in early spring, fifteen years or so before Hamnet runs to the house of the physician, a Latin tutor is standing in this place at the window, absently tugging on the hoop through his left ear. He is watching the trees. Their collective presence, lined up as they are, fringing the edge of the farm, brings to his mind the backdrop of a theatre, the kind of painted trickery that is unrolled, quickly, into place to let the audience know they are now in a sylvan setting, that the city or streets of the previous scene are gone, that they are now on wooded, uncultivated, perhaps unstable ground.

A slight frown appears on his face. He remains at the window, the fingertips of one hand pressed white to the glass. The boys are behind him; they are conjugating verbs, temporarily unheard by the tutor, who is intent on the startling contrast between the sharply blue spring sky and the new-leaf green of the forest. The colours seem to fight, vying for supremacy, vibrancy: the green versus the blue, one against the other. The children's Latin verbs wash over him, through him, like the wind through the trees. Somewhere in the farm-house a bell is rung, first briefly and then more insistently. There are footfalls along the passage, the sound of a door banging into its frame. One of the boys – the younger one, James, the tutor knows, without turning – sighs, coughs, clears his throat, then rejoins the intoning. The tutor readjusts his collar, smooths his hair.

The Latin verbs roll on and on, around him, like a fenland fog, through his feet, up and over his shoulders, past his ears, to seep out of the cracks in the window lead. He allows the chanted words to merge into an aural blur that fills the room, right to its high, blackened rafters. It collects up there, along with the curls and veils of smoke from the chimneyless fire that smoulders in the grate. He has instructed the boys to conjugate the verb 'incarcerare': the repeated hard *c* sound seems to scrape at the walls of the room, as if the very words themselves are seeking escape.

The tutor is forced to come here twice a week by his father, the glover, who is in some manner of debt to Hewlands, after the souring of an agreement or deal with the yeoman who used to own the farm. The yeoman had been a broad-backed man who carried through his belt a sheep-hook shaped like a cudgel, and there was something about his open, candid face that the tutor had rather liked. But the yeoman had died suddenly last year, leaving all his acres and flocks, along with a wife and eight or nine children (the tutor is unsure exactly how many). It was an event his own father had greeted with barely concealed glee. Only he knew of the nature of the loan: the tutor had overheard his father crowing, late at night, when he thought no one could overhear (the tutor is very good at clandestine listening): Don't you see? The widow will not know or, if she does, will not dare to come and ask me to make good on it, or that overgrown dullard of an eldest son.

It appears, however, that the widow or son has done just that and this arrangement (the tutor has gleaned, from listening in to conversations going on behind the door of his parents' chamber) is something to do with what his father did with a consignment of the yeoman's sheepskins. His father had told the yeoman that the hides were to be sent for whit-tawing and the yeoman had believed him. But then his father had insisted that the wool should be left on, which had aroused the suspicion of the yeoman, which for some reason has caused all this trouble. The tutor is unclear on this last point as his mother was called away from the whispered conversation by the querulous, creaking cry of Edmond, her youngest child.

The tutor's glover father has some new, slightly illicit venture that none of them are supposed to know about: this much the tutor can tell. They were to make out, their parents told them, to anyone who asked, that the sheepskins were for gloves. He and his siblings had been baffled as it had not occurred to them that the skins were for anything other than gloves. Whatever else could his father, the most successful glover in town, possibly want them for?

There is a debt or a fine and their father cannot – will not? – pay, and the yeoman's widow or son will not let it drop so it appears that he himself is the payment. His time, his Latin grammar, his brain. Twice a week, his father told him, he must walk the mile or so out of town, along the stream, to this low-lying hall, surrounded by sheep, where he must run the younger boys through their lessons.

He had had no warning of this plan, this web being spun around him. His father had called him into the workshop one evening, as the household was preparing for bed, to tell him that he was to go to Hewlands to 'start drumming some education into the boys there'. The tutor had stood in the doorway and stared hard at his father. When, he asked, was this arranged? His father and mother had been wiping and polishing the tools in preparation for the next day. Doesn't concern you, his father said. All you need to know is that you are going. What, the son replied, if I don't care to? The father fitted a long knife back into its leather sleeve, seemingly without hearing this response. His mother had glanced at her husband, then at her son, giving him a minute shake of her head. You'll go, his father said eventually, laying down his rag, and there's an end to it.

The desire to push himself away from these two people, to stride out of the room, to wrench open the front door and run into the street rose in the son, like sap in a tree. And, yes, to strike his father, to do some harm to that body, to take his own fists and arms and fingers and give back to this man all that had been dealt to him. They had, all six of them, from time to time, received the blows and grips and slaps that resulted from the father's temper, but with nothing like the regularity and brutality of this eldest son. He didn't know why but something about him had always drawn his father's anger and frustration to him, like a horseshoe to a magnet. He carried within him, always, the sensation of his father's calloused hand enclosing the soft skin of his upper arm, the inescapable grip that kept him there so his father could rain down blows with his other, stronger, hand. The shock of a slap landing, sudden and sharp, from above; the flensing sting of a wooden instrument on the back of the legs. How hard were the bones in the hand of an adult, how tender and soft the flesh of a child, how easy to bend and strain those young, unfinished bones. The doused, drenched feeling of fury, of impotent humiliation, in the long minutes of a beating.

His father's rages arrived from nowhere, like a gale, then blew quickly on. There was no pattern, no warning, no rationale; it was never the same thing twice that tipped him over. The son learnt, at a young age, to sense the onset of these eruptions and a series of feints and dodges to avoid his father's fists. As an astronomer reads the minuscule shifts and alterations in the alignment of the planets and spheres, to see what lies in store, this eldest son became an expert in reading his father's moods and expressions. He could tell, from the sound the front door made when his father entered from the street, from the rhythm of his footsteps on the flag-stones, whether or not he was in for a beating. A spilt ladle of water, a boot left in the wrong place on the floor, a facial expression deemed insufficiently respectful – any of these might be the excuse the father sought.

In the last year or so, the son has grown tall, taller than the father: he is stronger, younger, faster. His walks to various local markets, to outlying farms, to and from the tannery, with sacks of skins or finished gloves on his back, have brought muscle and weight to his shoulders and neck. It has not eluded the son's notice that his father's blows have, of late, tailed off. There was a moment, several months ago, when the father came out of his workshop late in the evening and, finding the son in the passageway, without a word, bore down on him and, lifting the wineskin he was holding, lashed the son about the face. The pain was of the stinging sort, not aching, not bruising, not pressing: it had a sharp, whipped, lacerating quality. There would, the son knew, be a red, broken mark on his face. The sight of the mark seemed to enrage the father further because he lifted his arm again, for a second blow, but the son reached up. He seized his father's arm. He pushed, with all his might, against him and found, to his surprise, that his father's body yielded under his. He could push this man, this leviathan, this monster of his childhood, back against the wall with very little effort. He did so. He kept his father there with the point of his elbow. He shook his father's arm, like that of a puppet, and the wineskin dropped to the floor. He leant his face into his, noticing at the same time that he was looking down on him. That, he said to him, is the last time you will ever hit me.

As he stands at Hewlands' window, the need to leave, to rebel, to escape is so great it fills him to his very outer edge: he can eat nothing from the plate the farmer's widow left for him, so crammed is he with the urge to leave, to get away, to move his feet and legs to some other place, as far away from here as he can manage.

The Latin rolls on, the verbs coming around again, from pluperfect tense to present. He is just about to turn and face his pupils when he sees, from the trees, a figure emerge.

For a moment, the tutor believes it to be a young man. He is wearing a cap, a leather jerkin, gauntlets; he moves out of the trees with a brand of masculine insouciance or entitlement, covering the ground with booted strides. There is some kind of bird on his outstretched fist: chestnut-brown with a creamy white breast, its wings spotted with black. It sits hunched, subdued, its body swaying with the movement of its companion, its familiar.

The tutor is imagining this person, this hawk-taming youth, is some kind of factotum to the farm. Or a relative to the family, a visiting cousin perhaps. Then he registers the long plait, hanging over the shoulder, reaching past the waist, the jerkin laced tight around a form that curves suspiciously inwards around the middle. He sees the skirts, which had been bunched up, now hastily being dragged down around the stockings. He sees a pale, oval face under the cap, an arched brow, a full red mouth.

He moves closer to the glass, leaning on the sill, and watches as the woman moves from the right to the left of the window frame, her bird riding on her fist, her skirts swishing around her boots. Then she enters the farmyard, moves through the chickens and geese, around the side of the house, and is gone.

He straightens, his frown vanished, a smile forming under his scant beard. Behind him, the room has fallen silent. He recalls himself: the lesson, the boys, the verb conjugation.

He turns. He arches his fingers together, as he imagines a tutor ought to do, as his own masters did at school not so long ago.

'Excellent,' he says to them.

They look towards him, plants turning to the sun. He smiles at their soft, unformed faces, pale as unrisen dough in the light from the window. He pretends not to see that the younger brother is being poked under the table with a peeled stick, that the elder has filled his slate with a pattern of repeated loops.

'Now,' he says to them, 'I would like you to work on a translation of the following sentence: "I thank you, sir, for your kind letter."'

They begin to labour over their slates, the elder (and stupidest, the tutor knows) breathing through his mouth, the younger laying his head down on his arm. And, really, what sense is there in giving the boys these lessons? Aren't they destined to be farmers, like their father and older brothers? But, then, what use has it been to him? Years and years at the grammar school and look where it has got him – a smoke-hazed hall, coaxing the sons of a sheep farmer to learn conjugation and word order.

He waits until the boys have half finished this exercise before he says: 'What is the name of that serving girl? The one with the bird?'

The younger brother looks at him with a direct, frank gaze. The tutor smiles back. He is, he prides himself, adept at dissembling, at reading the thoughts of others, at guessing which way they will jump, what they will do next. Life with a quick-tempered parent will hone these skills at an early age. The tutor knows the elder will not guess the intent behind his question but that the younger one, all of nine years old, will.

'Bird?' the elder one says. 'She doesn't have a bird.' He glances at his brother. 'Does she?'

'No?' The tutor gathers their blank looks. He sees again, for a moment, the mottled tawny feathers of the hawk. 'Perhaps I am mistaken.'

The younger brother says, in a rush, 'There's Hettie, who looks after the pigs and hens.' He creases his brow. 'Hens are birds, aren't they?'

The tutor nods at him. 'Indeed they are.'

He turns again to the window. Looks out. All is as before. The wind, the trees, the leaves, the filthy ewes in a huddle, the stretch of tamed, cultivated land meeting the hem of the forest. No girl to be seen. Could it have been a hen on her outstretched arm? He doubts it.

Later that day, after the lesson is finished, the tutor steps around the back of the house. He ought to be taking the path to town, beginning the long walk home, but he wants to see the girl one more time, wants to observe her, perhaps exchange some words with her. He has an urge to examine that bird up close, to hear what kind of voice will emerge from that mouth. He would like to weigh that plait in his hand, feel the silken ridged weave of it slip between his fingers. He glances up at the house's windows as he makes his way around the walls. There is, of course, no excuse for him being here in the farmyard. The boys' mother might divine in an instant what he is seeking and send him off. He might lose his position here, might jeopardise whatever tenuous agreement his father has brokered with the yeoman's widow. Not even this thought gives the tutor pause.

He steps through the farmyard, avoiding puddles and clods of dung. It rained earlier, as he was trying to teach the subjunctive: he heard the tick-tick of it on the high thatch of the hall. The sky is beginning to drain of light; the sun is fading for the day; there is still the chill grip of winter in the air. A chicken scratches diligently in the earth, groaning quietly to itself.

He is thinking of the girl, her braid, her hawk. A way to

lighten the load of these indentured visits now presents itself to him. This position, with these children, in this drear and awful place, might become tolerable after all. He is imagining liaisons after tutoring, a walk in the woods, a meeting behind one of these sheds or outhouses.

He does not, even for one moment, entertain the idea that the woman he saw is in fact the eldest daughter of the house.

She has a certain notoriety in these parts. It is said that she is strange, touched, peculiar, perhaps mad. He has heard that she wanders the back roads and forest at will, unaccompanied, collecting plants to make dubious potions. It is wise not to cross her for people say she learnt her crafts from an old crone who used to make medicines and spin, and could kill a baby with a single glance. It is said that the stepmother lives in terror of the girl putting hexes on her, especially now the yeoman is dead. Her father must have loved her, though, because he left her a sizeable dowry in his will. Not that anyone, of course, would want to wed her. She is said to be too wild for any man. Her mother, God rest her soul, had been a gypsy or a sorceress or a forest sprite: the tutor has heard many of these fanciful tales about her. His own mother shakes her head and tuts when this girl comes up in conversation.

The tutor has never seen her but he pictures a half-woman, half-animal: thick-browed, hobbling, hair streaked with grey, clothing clotted with mud and foliage. The daughter of a dead forest witch. She will walk with a limp, muttering to herself as she fumbles in her bag of curses and cures.

He casts a glance around him, at the shadow in the lee of the pig-pen, at the bare branches of apple trees bending over the fence at the perimeter of the farmyard. He wouldn't want to come across this daughter unawares. He goes through a gate in the fence and out along a track. He glances over his shoulder at the windows of the house, into the doors of the barn, where cattle chew and nod in their stalls. Where might she be?

He is distracted from thinking about the mad, witchy sister by a movement to his left: a door opening, the swirl of skirts, the squeal of a hinge. It is the girl with the bird! The very same. Emerging from some roughly built outhouse, closing the door behind her. Right here, in front of him, as if he had summoned her presence by thought alone.

He coughs into his fist.

'Good day to you,' he says.

She turns. She looks at him for a moment, raises her eyebrows, very slightly, as if she has seen the spool of his thoughts, as if his head is transparent as water. She looks all the way down to his boots and back again.

'Sir,' she replies, after a while, with the merest hint of a curtsy. 'What brings you to Hewlands?'

Her voice is clear, modulated, articulate. It has an instant effect upon him: a quickening of his pulse, a heat in his chest.

'I am tutoring the boys here,' he says. 'In Latin.'

He expects her to be impressed, to nod deferentially. A learned man is he; a man of letters, of education. No rustic stands before you, madam, he wishes he could say, no mere peasant.

But the girl's expression is unchanged. 'Ah,' she says. 'The Latin tutor. Of course.'

He is puzzled by the flatness of her reply. She is an altogether confusing person: her age is hard to guess, as is her standing in the household. She is perhaps a little older than him. She is dressed like a servant, in coarse and dirty clothes, but speaks like a lady. She is erect in stature, almost of a height with him, her hair dark as his own. She meets his eye as a man would, but her figure and form fill out that jerkin in a manner that is distinctly female.

The tutor decides that boldness is the best course of action here. 'May I see your . . . your bird?'

She frowns. 'My bird?'

'I saw you earlier, emerging from the forest, did I not? With a bird on your arm? A hawk. A most intriguing—'

For the first time, her face betrays an emotion: concern, worry, an element of fear. 'You won't tell them,' she gestures towards the farm, 'will you? I was forbidden to take her out today, you see, but she was so restless, so hungry, I couldn't bear to shut her up all afternoon. You won't say, will you, that you saw me? That I was out?'

The tutor smiles. He steps towards her. 'I shall never speak of it,' he is able to say, grandly, consolingly. He puts his hand on her arm. 'Do not concern yourself.'

She flicks her gaze up to meet his. They regard each other at close quarters. He sees eyes almost gold in colour, with a deep amber ring around their centres. Flecks of green. Long dark lashes. Pale skin with freckles over the nose and along the cheekbones. She does a strange thing: she puts her hand to his, where it is resting on her forearm. She takes hold of the skin and muscle between his thumb and forefinger and presses. The grip is firm, insistent, oddly intimate, on the edge of painful. It makes him draw in his breath. It makes his head swim. The certainty of it. He doesn't think anyone has ever touched him there, in that way, before. He could not take his hand away without a sharp tug, even if he wanted to. Her strength is surprising and, he finds, peculiarly arousing.

'I . . .' he begins, without any idea where that sentence will go, what he wants to say. 'Do you . . .'

All at once, she drops his hand; she moves her arm away from him. His hand, where she gripped him, feels hot and very naked. He rubs at his forehead with it, as if to make it right again.

'You wanted to see my bird,' she said, all business and competence now, taking a key from a chain hidden in her skirts, unlocking the door and pushing it open. She steps inside and, dazed, he follows.

It is a small, dim, narrow space, with a desiccated and familiar smell to it. He inhales: the aroma of wood, of lime, of something sweet and fibrous. Also a chalky, musky undertone. And the woman beside him: he can smell her hair and skin, one of which carries the faint scent of rosemary. He is just about to reach out for her again – her shoulder, her waist are tantalisingly close to him, and why else would she bring him in here, really, if she didn't also have in mind—

'There she is,' she whispers, urgent and low. 'Can you see her?'

'Who?' he says, distracted by the waist, the rosemary, the shelves around him, which are becoming clearer in the gloom, as his eyes adjust to the dark. 'What?'

'My falcon,' she says, and steps forward, and the tutor sees, at the far end of the outhouse, a tall wooden stake on which perches a bird of prey.

It is hooded, wings folded back on themselves, scaled ochre talons gripping the stand. Its stance is hunched, shrugged, as if assailed by rain. The feathers of its wings are dark but its breast is pale and rippled like the bark of a tree. It seems extraordinary to him to be in such close proximity to a creature which is so emphatically from another element, from wind or sky or perhaps even myth.

'Good God,' he hears himself say, and she turns and, for the first time, she smiles.

'She's a kestrel,' she murmurs. 'A friend of my father's, a priest, gave her to me as a chick. I take her out to fly most days. I won't take her hood off now but she knows you're here. She'll remember you.'

The tutor doesn't doubt it. Although the bird's eyes and beak are covered with a miniature hood, fashioned from leather – sheep or perhaps kid leather, he catches himself wondering, to his irritation – its head twitches and swivels with every word they speak, every movement they make. He would like, he finds, to look into the bird's face, to see that eye, to know what lies behind that hood.

'She caught two mice today,' the woman says. 'And a vole. She flies,' she says, turning to him, 'entirely in silence. They cannot hear her come.'

The tutor, emboldened by her stare, puts out a hand. He encounters her sleeve, her jerkin and, finally, her waist. He curves his hand around it, as firmly as she had touched him, attempting to draw her towards him.

'What's your name?' he says.

She pulls away but he grips her more tightly.

'I shan't tell you.'

'You shall.'

'Let me go.'

'Tell me first.'

'And then will you let me go?'

'Yes.'

'How do I know you'll keep your promise, Master Tutor?'

'I always keep my promises. I am a man of my word.'

'As well as a man of hands. Let me go, I tell you.'

'Your name, first.'

'And then you will release me?'

'Yes.'

'Very well.'

'You will tell me?'

'Yes, it's . . .'

'What is it?'

'Anne,' she says, or seems to say, at the same time as he is saying: 'I must know.'

'Anne?' he repeats, thrown, the word at once familiar yet queer in his mouth. It was the name of his sister, who died not quite two years ago. He has not, he realises, spoken the name since the day she was buried. He sees again, and for a moment, the wet churchyard, the dripping yew trees, the dark maw of the ground, ripped open to accept the white-wrapped body, so slight and small. Too small, it seemed, to go into the earth like that, alone.

The falconer girl takes advantage of his momentary confusion to push him away from her; he topples into the shelves that run around the walls. There is a strange, echoey sound, like a thousand game counters or balls finding their place. He gropes around himself and finds several round objects, tight-skinned, cool, a spike at their centre. Suddenly he realises what the familiar smell in here is.

'Apples,' he says.

She gives a short laugh, across the space from him, her hands resting on the shelf behind her, the falcon beside her. 'It's the apple store.'

He brings one up to his face and inhales the scent, sharp, specific, acidic. It brings a slew of distant images to mind: fallen leaves, sodden grass, woodsmoke, his mother's kitchen.

'Anne,' he says, biting into the apple's flesh.

She smiles, her lips curving in a way that maddens and delights him, all at the same time. 'That is not my name,' she says.

He lowers the apple, in mock-outrage, in partial relief. 'You told me it was.'

'I didn't.'

'You did.'

'You weren't listening, then.'

He flings aside the half-eaten apple and comes towards her. 'Tell me now.'

'I won't.'

'You will.'

He puts his hands to her shoulders, then lets his fingertips skip down her arms, watching her shiver at his touch.

'You'll tell me,' he says, 'when we kiss.'

She puts her head to one side. 'Presumptuous,' she says. 'What if we never kiss?'

'But we shall.'

Again, her hand finds his; her fingers grip the flesh between his thumb and forefinger. He raises his brows and looks into her face. She has the expression of a woman reading a particularly hard piece of text, a woman trying to decipher something, to work something out.

'Hmm,' she says.

'What are you doing?' he asks. 'Why do you hold my hand like that?'

She frowns; she looks at him directly, searchingly.

'What is it?' he says, suddenly disquieted by her, her silence, her concentration, her grip on his hand. The apples rest in their grooves around them. The bird sits immobile on its perch, listening in.

The woman leans towards him. She releases his hand, which again feels raw, peeled, ravaged. Without warning, she presses her mouth to his. He feels the twin plushness of her lips, the hard press of her teeth, the impossible smoothness of the skin of her face. Then she pulls back.

'It's Agnes,' she says. And this name, too, he knows, although he has never met anyone with it. Agnes. Said differently from how it might be written on a page, with that near-hidden, secret *g*. The tongue curls towards it yet barely touches it. Ann-yis. Agn-yez. One must lean into the first syllable, then skip over the next.

She is slipping out of the space between his body and the shelves. She opens the door and the light beyond is dazzling white, overwhelming. Then the door bangs behind her and he is alone, with the falcon, with the apples, with the smell of wood and autumn, and the dry, feathered, meaty smell of the bird.

He is so stupefied, by the kiss, by the apple store, by the remembered feel of her shoulders, by plans of what he will do next time he is sent to Hewlands, schemes to get that maid on her own again, that he is halfway back to town before a thought hits him. Isn't it said that the household's eldest daughter keeps a hawk?

There used to be a story in these parts about a girl who lived at the edge of a forest.

People would say these words, to each other, Did you ever hear about the girl who lived at the edge of a forest? as they sat around the fire at night, as they kneaded dough, as they carded wool for spinning. Such stories, of course, make the night pass more quickly, soothe a fractious child, distract others from their cares.

At the edge of a forest, a girl.

There is a promise, from teller to listener, concealed in that opening, like a note tucked into a pocket, a hint that something is about to happen. Anyone in the vicinity would turn their head and prick their ears, their mind already forming a picture of the girl, perhaps picking her way through trees, or standing beside the green wall of a forest.

And what a forest it was. Dense, verdant, crazily cross-stitched with brambles and ivy, the trees so closely packed that there were whole swathes, it was said, that received no light at all. Not a place to get lost, then. There were paths that went round and back on themselves, paths that led travellers from their route, their intentions. Breezes that whipped up from nowhere. Certain clearings where you might hear music or whispers or murmurs of your name, saying, *Here, come here, come this way.*

The children who lived near the forest were instructed from

the cradle never to venture in alone. Maidens were exhorted to stay away, warned of what might lurk in those green and brambled depths. There were creatures in there who resembled humans – wood-dwellers, they were called – who walked and talked, but had never set foot outside the forest, had lived all their lives in its leafish light, its encircling branches, its wet and tangled interior. It was said that a hunting hound, a marvellous creature it was, with sleek flanks and gleaming fangs, had dived into the bushes in pursuit of a deer, and was not seen again. It followed the white flash of the animal and the forest closed around it, never to release it.

People who needed to go through the forest would stop to pray; there was an altar, a cross, where you could pause and put your safety in the hands of the Lord, hope that He had heard you, trust that He would watch for you, that He wouldn't let your path intersect with those of the wood-dwellers or the forest sprites or the creatures of the leaves. The cross became covered, choked, some said, with tight skeins of ivy. Other travellers put their faith in darker powers: all around the fringes of the forest there were shrines where people tied shreds of their clothing to branches, left cups of ale, loaves of bread, scraps of crackling, strings of bright beads in the hope that the spirits of the trees might be appeased and give them safe passage.

So, in a house right at the edge of the forest, dwelt the girl and her little brother. The trees could be seen from the back windows, tossing their restless heads on windy days, shaking their bare and twisted fists in winter. The girl and her brother were born feeling the pull of the forest, its beckoning power.

People who had lived in the village a long time believed

that the girl's mother had come out of this wood. From where, no one knew. She might have been a wood-dweller who got lost, who became separated from those of her kind, or she might have been something other.

Nobody knew. The story went that she had appeared one day, parting the brambles, stepping out of the green, twilit world, and from then on the farmer, who happened to be standing there, watching his sheep, could never look away from her. He picked the leaves from her hair and the snails from her skirts. He brushed the twigs and moss from her sleeves, bathed the mud from her feet. He took her into his house, fed her, clothed her, married her and, not long after, a baby girl was born to them.

At this point in the story, the tellers would usually make it clear that no woman had ever doted on a child like this one. She bound the baby to her back and carried it wherever she went, walking about the farmhouse on her bare feet, even on the coldest winter days. She would not lay the child in a cradle, even at night, but kept her close, the way an animal might. She disappeared for hours on end into the forest, with the baby, coming home after dark, with perhaps an apronful of unpeeled chestnuts, to a house with no fire, no food, nothing ready for her husband to eat. The wives in neighbouring houses began to whisper, asking each other how the man put up with it. And, knowing the new mother was herself mother-less, or appeared so, those women came to the farm, to give her their wisdom on housekeeping, weaning, the avoidance of illness, the best way to stitch cloth, how the woman must wear a coif to cover her hair, now that she was married.

The woman nodded at them all, with a distant smile. She

was frequently seen in the road with her hair uncovered and loose about her shoulders. She had dug a patch of ground outside the farmhouse and was growing strange plants in it – woodland ferns and clambering worts, peppery flowers and ugly, low-lying bushes. The only person she seemed to talk to was an old widow-woman who lived at the far end of the village. They could often be seen in conversation in the widow's small walled garden, the older woman leaning on her stick as the younger, baby bound to her back, still barefoot, still with her hair on display, stooped to tend the widow's herbs.

It wasn't long before the woman was brought to bed again, this time giving birth to a boy, who was strong from the moment he drew breath. He was an enormous child, with wide hands and feet big enough to walk on. The woman did as before, tying the baby to her, but a day or two after he was born, she took off into the forest, the girl child toddling beside her.

When her belly was swollen for the third time, the woman's luck ran out. She took to bed, to birth her third child, but this time, she did not rise up from it again. The village women came to wash and lay her out, prepare her for the next world. They wept as they did so, not because they had been fond of the woman, who had appeared out of the forest and married one of their own, who went by the name of a tree, who had so little to say to them, who had rebuffed their attempts at companionship, but because her death reminded them of the possibility of their own. They cried together as they cleaned and combed her hair, as they peeled the dirt from under her fingernails, as they pulled a white shift over her head, as they wrapped up the tiny pod of the stillborn child and placed it in the corpse's arms.

The little girl sat watching, her back to the wall, legs crossed under her, not uttering a sound. She did not sob, she did not weep; she said not a word. Her gaze did not waver from the body of her mother. In her lap, she held her little brother, who sobbed and snivelled and wiped his eyes on her dress. If any of those well-meaning neighbours approached, the girl would spit and claw, like a cat. She would not let go of her brother, no matter how many people tried to prise him from her. Hard to help a child like that, they said, hard to feel anything for her.

The only person she would let near her was the widow-woman, who had been a particular friend of her mother's. The widow sat on a chair near the children, quite motionless, a bowl of meal in her lap. Every now and again, the girl would permit the woman to spoon some pap into the boy's mouth.

One of the neighbours remembered her unmarried sister, Joan, who was young but had had care of many smaller siblings, as well as pigs, and was used to hard work. Why not engage her at the farmer's place? Someone would have to keep house, to mind the children, to tend the fire and stir the pot. Who knew what might ensue? The farmer was, everyone knew, a man of means, with a fine hall and acres of land; the children could be brought to heel, with the right handling.

Now, it may or may not be true that before Joan had passed a month at the farm she was complaining about the girl to anyone who would listen. The child was driving her to distraction. She had twice woken in the night to find the girl standing above her, gripping her hand. She had caught her sliding into her pocket something which, on inspection, appeared to be twigs bound up with a chicken's feather. She had discovered ivy leaves under her pillow, and who else would have put them there?

The women of the village didn't know what to say or whether to believe her, but it was noticed by many that Joan's skin became spotted and pocked. That her hands grew warts. That her spinning was tangled and frayed, that her bread refused to rise. But the girl was only a child, a very young child, so how could it be that she was capable of such deeds?

You might think that Joan would be put off, would leave the farm and return home to her family. Joan was not so easily deterred by a naughty, wayward child. She held on grimly, rubbing pig fat into her warts, scrubbing her face with a cloth dipped in ash.

In time, as is often the way of these things, Joan's persistence was rewarded. The farmer took her for his wife and she went on to bear him six children, all of them fair and rosy and round, like herself, like the father.

After her wedding, Joan stopped complaining to people about the girl, as abruptly as if someone had sewn up her mouth. There was nothing unusual about her, she would say tartly. Nothing at all. It was nonsense and gossip to say that the girl could see into people's souls. There was nothing amiss in her family, in her farmhouse, nothing at all.

Word spread, of course, about the girl's unusual abilities. People came under cover of darkness. The girl, as she grew older, found a way for her path to coincide with those of the people who needed her. It was known, in the area, that she walked the perimeter of the forest, the fringes of the trees, in late afternoon, in early evening, her falcon swooping into the branches and back to land on her leather gauntlet. She took out this bird at dusk so, if you were of a mind, you could arrange to be walking in the area.

If asked, the girl – a woman, now – would remove the falconer's glove and hold your hand, just for a moment, pressing the flesh between thumb and forefinger where all your hand's strength lay, and tell you what she felt. The sensation, some said, was dizzying, draining, as if she was drawing all the strength out of you; others said it was invigorating, enlivening, like a shower of rain. Her bird circled the sky above, feathers spread, calling out, as if in warning.

People said the girl's name was Agnes.

This is the story, the myth of Agnes's childhood. She herself might tell a different story.

Outside were the sheep and they must be fed, watered, cared for, no matter what. They must be brought in and out and from one field to another.

Inside was the fire and it must never be left to go out. It must be fed and fed and tended and poked, and sometimes her mother must blow on it, with pursed lips.

And the mother herself was a slippery thing, because there had been a mother, and she'd had slender, strong ankles above bare feet. Those feet had blackened soles and walked one way then the other over the patterns of the flagstones, and sometimes they walked out of the house and past the sheep and into the forest, where they stepped through leaves and twigs and mosses. There was a hand, too, that held Agnes's, to stop her falling, and it was warm and firm. If Agnes was lifted from the forest floor to that mother's back, she could nestle under the cloak of hair. The trees appeared then, to her, through the dark skeins, like a lantern show. Look, the mother said, a squirrel, and a reddish flourish of tail disappeared up a trunk, as if she herself had conjured it from the bark. Look, a king-fisher: a jewel-backed arrow piercing the silver skin of a brook. Look, hazelnuts: the mother clambering into the boughs, shaking them with her strong arms and down came clusters of dun-jacketed pearls.

Her brother, Bartholomew, with the wide, surprised eyes and fingers that opened into white stars, rode on their mother's front and the two of them could stare into each other's faces as they went along, interlace their fingers over the round bones of their mother's shoulders. Their mother cut green rushes for them, which she dried, then wove into dolls. The dolls were identical, and Agnes and Bartholomew tucked them side by side into a box, their blank green faces gazing trustingly up at the roof.

Then this mother was gone and another was there in her place beside the fire, stoking it with wood, blowing at the flames, hauling the pot from hearthstone to grating, saying, Don't touch, mind, hot. This second mother was wider, her hair pale, screwed up in a knot, hidden under a coif grimed by sweat. She smelt of mutton and oil. She had reddened skin covered with freckles, as if splashed by a cart going through mud. She had a name, 'Joan', that made Agnes think of a howling dog. She took a knife and lopped off Agnes's hair, saying she hadn't the time to be attending to that every day. She picked up the rush babies, declared them devilish poppets, and fed them to the fire. When Agnes burnt her fingers trying to pull out their scorched forms, she laughed and said Agnes had got what she deserved. She had shoes tied over her feet.

Those feet never went from farm to forest. If Agnes went alone, without asking, this mother removed one of the shoes and lifted Agnes's skirt and brought the shoe down on the back of her legs, whack, crack, and the pain was so surprising, so unfamiliar that Agnes forgot to cry out. She stared instead at the beams, high above, where the other mother had tied a bundle of herbs to a stone with a hole at its centre. To keep away bad luck, she had said. Agnes remembered her doing this. She bit her lip. She ordered herself not to cry. She looked at the black eye of the stone. She wondered when this mother would come back. She did not weep.

This new mother would also remove her shoe if Agnes said, You are not my mother, or if Bartholomew trod on the dog's tail, or if Agnes spilt the soup, or let the geese out into the road, or didn't lift the pig-pail all the way to the slop trough. Agnes learnt to be agile, quick. She learnt the advantages of invisibility, how to pass through a room without drawing notice. She learnt that what is hidden within a person may be brought forth if, say, a sprinkling of bladderwort were to find its way into that person's cup. She learnt that creepers disentangled from an oak trunk, brushed against bed linen, will ensure no sleep for whoever lies there. She learnt that if she took her father by the hand and led him to the back door, where Joan had uprooted all the forest plants, her father would go silent, and then Joan would wail and tell him she hadn't meant any harm, she'd taken them for weeds. And she learnt that, afterwards, Joan would reach under the table and pinch her, leaving purple blotches on her skin.

It was a time of confusion, of the seasons following hard upon each other. Of rooms dim with smoke. Of the constant bleat and groan of sheep. Of her father away from the hearth for most of the day, tending the animals. Of trying to stop the mud of the outside reaching the clean inside. Of keeping Bartholomew away from the fire, away from Joan, away from the millpond and the carts in the road and the trampling hoofs of horses and the stream and the swinge of the scythe. Ailing lambs were put in a basket by the fire, fed from milk-soaked rags, their reedy cries sawing through the room. Her father in the yard, ewes gripped between his knees, their eyes rolling heavenwards in terror, him guiding the shears through their wool. The fleeces fell like storm clouds to the ground and out of each rose quite a different creature – thin, milk-skinned, gaunt.

Everyone told Agnes that there had been no other mother. Whatever are you talking about? they cried. When she insisted, they changed tack. You won't remember your real mother – you couldn't possibly remember. She told them this wasn't true; she stamped her foot; she banged her fists against the table; she screeched at them like a fowl. What did it mean? Why did they persist with these lies, these falsehoods? She remembered. She remembered everything. She said this to the apothecary's widow who lived at the edge of the village, a woman who took in wool for spinning; she continued to work her treadle, as if Agnes hadn't spoken, but then had nodded. Your mother, she said, was pure of heart. There was more kindness in her little finger – and she held up her own gnarled hand – than in the whole of any of those others.

She remembered everything. Everything except where she had gone, why she had left.

At night, Agnes whispered to Bartholomew about the woman

who liked to walk with them through the forest, who tied a stone with a hole to herbs, who made them rush babies, who had a garden of plants at the back door. She remembered it all. Almost all.

Then one day she came upon her father behind the pig-pen, his knee on the neck of a lamb, bringing down his knife. The smell, the sight, the colour took her back to a bed soaked red and a room of carnage, of violence, of appalling crimson. She stared at her father, stared and stared, yet did not see him at all. Instead, she saw a bed with a red bloom at its centre and then a narrow box. In it, she knew, was her mother, but not as she had been. This mother was different again. She was waxy and chill and silent, and in her arms was a wrapped bundle with the sad, wizened face of a doll. The priest had had to come at night because it was a secret, and he was a priest Agnes had never seen before. He had long robes and a burning bowl that he swung over the box, muttering strange, song-like words. Agnes must never tell, her father had said, between sobs, never tell the neighbours or anyone that the priest came and spoke magic words over the wax woman and the sad baby. Before he left, the priest had touched Agnes once, lightly, on the head, his thumb pressing into her brow, and he had said, looking straight into her eyes, in language familiar to her, Poor lamb.

Agnes says all this to her father, as he kneels there on this other lamb, red pumping from the line drawn in its neck. She shouts it – she yells it from the base of her lungs, the core of her heart. She says, I remember, I know all that.

Hush, maidy, he says, turning to her. You cannot remember. Hush, now. Don't say these things. There was no priest in the night. He did not touch your head. Don't ever let anyone hear you say that. Don't let your mother hear.

Agnes doesn't know if he means Joan, the woman in the house, or her own mother, up in Heaven. It feels to her as though the world has cracked open, like an egg. The sky above her could, at any moment, split and rain down fire and ash upon them all. At the edges of her sight seem to hover dark, nebulous shapes. The farmhouse, the pig-pen, her brothers and sisters in the yard, all seem at once far away and unbearably close. She knows there had been a priest. How can her father pretend otherwise? She remembers the cross around his neck that he brought to his lips to kiss, the way his bowl left feather smoke in the air over her mother and the baby, that he spoke her mother's name, over and over, in the middle of his mysterious prayers: Rowan, Rowan. She remembers. Poor lamb, he had said to her. Her father says, Hush, never say that, so she runs from him, from the lamb, slack and empty of blood now, little more than a sack of gizzard and bone, and into the forest where she screams these things to the trees, to the leaves, to the branches, where no one can hear. She grips the thorned stems of brambles until they pierce her skin and she shouts to the God of the church they walk to every Sunday, in neat formation, carrying the babies on their backs, where there is no smoke, no bowls, no speaking in tongues. She calls on him, she bawls his name. You, she says, you, do you hear me, I am finished with you. After this time, I will go to your church because I must but I shan't say a word there because there is nothing after you die. There is the soil and there is the body and it all comes to nothing.

She tells this to the apothecary's widow and these words

make the old woman look up. The wheel whirs more slowly, winding down, as the woman stares at the child. Never say this to anyone else, she says to Agnes, in her creaking voice. Never. You'll bring seven kinds of trouble down on your head, otherwise.

She grows up watching the mother with the shoes hug and pet her fair, chubby children. She watches her place the freshest breads, the choicest meat on their plates. Agnes must live with a sense of herself as second-tier, deficient in some way, unwanted. She is the one who must sweep the floors, change the babies' napkins, rock them to sleep, rake out the grate and coax the fire to life. She sees, she recognises, that any accident or misfortune – a dropped platter, a broken jug, some ravelled knitting, unrisen bread – will somehow be her fault. She grows up knowing that she must protect and defend Bartholomew from all of life's blows, because no one else will. He is of her blood, wholly and completely, in a way that no one else is. She grows up with a hidden, private flame inside her: it licks at her, warms her, warns her. You need to get away, the flame tells her. You must.

Agnes will rarely – if ever – be touched. She will grow up craving just that: a hand on hers, on her hair, on her shoulder, the brush of fingers on her arm. A human print of kindness, of fellow feeling. Her stepmother never comes near her. Her siblings paw and claw at her but that doesn't count.

She grows up fascinated by the hands of others, drawn always to touch them, to feel them in hers. That muscle between thumb and forefinger is, to her, irresistible. It can be shut and opened like the beak of a bird and all the strength of the grip can be found there, all the power of the grasp. A person's ability, their reach, their essence can be gleaned. All that they have held, kept, and all they long to grip is there in that place. It is possible, she realises, to find out everything you need to know about a person just by pressing it.

When she is no more than seven or eight, a visitor lets Agnes hold her hand in this way and Agnes says, You will meet your death within the month, and doesn't it come true, just like that, the visitor being struck down with an ague the very next week? She says that the shepherd will be knocked off his feet and hurt his leg, that her father will be caught in a storm, that the baby will fall ill on its second birthday, that the man offering to buy her father's sheepskins is a liar, that the pedlar at the back door has intentions towards the kitchen maid.

Joan and the father worry. It is not Christian, this ability. They beg her to stop, not to touch people's hands, to hide this odd gift. No good will come of it, her father says, standing over Agnes as she crouches by the fire, no good at all. When she reaches up to take his hand, he snatches it away.

She grows up feeling wrong, out of place, too dark, too tall, too unruly, too opinionated, too silent, too strange. She grows up with the awareness that she is merely tolerated, an irritant, useless, that she does not deserve love, that she will need to change herself substantially, crush herself down if she is to be married. She grows up, too, with the memory of what it meant to be properly loved, for what you are, not what you ought to be.

There is just enough of this recollection alive, she hopes, to enable her to recognise it if she meets it again. And if she does, she won't hesitate. She will seize it with both hands, as a means of escape, a means of survival. She won't listen to the protestations of others, their objections, their reasoning. This will be her chance, her way through the narrow hole at the heart of the stone, and nothing will stand in her way.

amnet climbs the stairs, breathing hard after his run through the town. It seems to drain his strength, putting one leg in front of the other, lifting each foot to each stair. He uses the handrail to haul himself along.

He is sure, he is certain, that when he reaches the upper floor, he will see his mother. She will be leaning over the bed where Judith is lying, her body curved like a bow. Judith will be tucked into fresh sheets; her face will be pale but awake, alert, trusting. Agnes will be giving her a tincture; Judith will be wincing at its bitterness but swallowing it all the same. His mother's potions can cure anything – everyone knows that. People come from all over town, all over Warwickshire and beyond, to speak with his mother through the window of the narrow cottage, to describe their symptoms, to tell her what they suffer, what they endure. Some of these people she invites in. They are women, mostly, and she seats them by the fire, in the good chair, while she takes their hands and holds them in her own, while she grinds some roots, some plant leaves, a sprinkling of petals. They leave with a cloth parcel or a tiny bottle, stoppered with paper and beeswax, their faces easier, lightened.

His mother will be here. She will bring Judith back to health. She can drive away any illness, any malady. She will know what to do.

Hamnet comes into the top room. There is just his sister, alone, on the bed.

She has, he sees, as he steps towards her, become paler,

weaker, in the time it took him to go for the physician. The skin around her eyes is bluish-grey, as if bruised. Her breaths are shallow and quick, her eyes, beneath their lids, flick back and forth, as if she is seeing something he cannot.

Hamnet's legs fold under him. He sits down on the side of the pallet. He can hear the suck and draw of her breath. There is, for him, some comfort in this. He hooks his smallest finger into the corresponding one of hers. A single tear leaks from his eye and drops onto the sheet, then into the rushes beneath.

Another tear falls. Hamnet has failed. He sees this. He needed to summon someone, a parent, a grandparent, a grown-up, a physician. He has failed on all counts. He shuts his eyes, to keep the tears in, and lets his head fall to his knees.

Half an hour or so later, Susanna comes in through the back door. She dumps her basket on a chair and slumps down at the table. She looks one way, disconsolately, she looks the other. The fire is out; no one is here. Her mother had promised she'd be back and she isn't. Her mother is never where she says she will be.

Susanna removes her cap and tosses it to the bench beside her. It slides off and on to the floor. Susanna thinks about bending to retrieve it but doesn't. Instead, she finds it with her toe and kicks it further away. She sighs. She is nearly fourteen. Everything – the sight of the pots stacked on the table, the herbs and flowers tied to the rafters, her sister's corn doll on a cushion, the jug set by the hearth – provokes in her a profound and fathomless irritation.

She gets up. She pushes open a window, to let in a little air, but the street smells of horse, of ordure, of something rank and rotting. She shuts it with a bang. Just for a moment, she believes she hears something from upstairs. Is someone here? She stands for a moment, listening. But no. There is no further sound.

She sits herself in the good chair, the one her mother's visitors use, the people who creep in at the door, usually late at night, to whisper about pains, bleeding, lack of bleeding, dreams, portents, aches, difficulties, loves inconvenient, loves importunate, augurs, moon cycles, a hare across their path, a bird inside the house, a loss of feeling in a limb, too much feeling elsewhere, a rash, a cough, a sore, a pain here or there or in the ear or the leg or the lungs or the heart. Their mother bends her head to listen, giving a nod, a sympathetic click of the tongue. Then she takes their hand and, as she does so, she lets her gaze float upwards, to the ceiling, to the air, her eyes unfocused, half closed.

Some have asked Susanna how her mother does it. They have sidled up to her in the market or out in the streets to demand how Agnes divines what a body needs or lacks or bursts with, how she can tell if a soul is restive or hankering, how she knows what a person or a heart hides.

It makes Susanna want to sigh and throw something. She can tell now if someone is about to enquire into her mother's unusual abilities and she tries to head them off, to excuse herself or begin to ask them questions about their family, the weather, the crops. There is, she has learnt, a certain hesitancy, a particular facial expression – half curiosity, half suspicion – which prefaces these conversations. Why do people not see that there is nothing Susanna is less happy to talk about? How can it not be plain that it is nothing to do with her – the herbs, the weeds, the jars and bottles of powders and roots and petals that make the room stink like a dung heap, the murmuring people, the weeping, the hand-holding? Susanna, when she was younger, used to answer truthfully: that she did not know, that it was like magic, that it was a gift. These days, however, she is curt: I have no idea, she will say, of what you speak, her head held high, her nose tipped up, as if sniffing the air.

And where is her mother now? Susanna crosses and recrosses her ankles over each other. Traipsing about the countryside, most likely, wading into ponds, gathering weeds, climbing over fences to reach some plant or other, tearing her clothes, muddying her boots. Other mothers of the town will be buttering bread or ladling out stew for their children. But Susanna's? She will be making a spectacle of herself, as ever, stopping to gaze up into the clouds, to whisper something in the ear of a mule, to gather dandelions in her skirts.

Susanna is startled by a knock at the window. She sits for a moment, frozen in the chair. There it comes again. She pushes herself to her feet and walks towards the pane. Through the criss-crossing lead and the blurred glass, she can make out the pale arch of a coif, a dark-red bodice: someone of means, then. The woman knocks again, seeing Susanna, with an imperious, commanding gesture.

Susanna makes no move to open the window. 'She's not here,' she calls instead, drawing herself up. 'You'll have to come back later.'

She turns on her heel and walks away, retreating to the

chair. The woman raps twice more on the pane and then Susanna hears her footsteps walk away.

People, people, always people, coming and going, arriving and departing. Susanna and the twins and her mother might sit down at table to take some broth and before they have lifted their spoons, there will be a knock and up her mother will start, putting aside her broth, as if Susanna hadn't taken a deal of trouble to make it, from chicken bones and carrots that required washing and more washing, and then peeling, not to mention the hours of stirring and straining in the heat of the cookhouse. Sometimes it seems to Susanna that Agnes isn't just mother to her – and the twins, of course – but mother to the whole town, the entire county. Will it ever end, this stream of people through their house? Will they ever just leave them in peace to live their lives? Susanna has overheard her grandmother say that she doesn't know why Agnes carries on with this business because it's not as if she has need of money, these days. Not, her grandmother added, that it ever brought in a great deal. Her mother had said nothing, not raising her head from her sewing.

Susanna curls her fingers around the carved ends of the chair arms, which are worn apple-smooth with the touch of a hundred palms. She shuffles her body backwards until her spine meets the chair's back. It is the chair her father likes to sit in, when he comes home. Twice, three, four, five times a year. Sometimes for a week, sometimes more. During the day, he will carry the chair upstairs, where he leans over a table to work; come the evening, he will carry it back downstairs, to sit by the fire. I come whenever I can, he told her, the last time he was here, touching the tips of his fingers to her cheek.

You know this to be true, he had said. He had been packing to leave, again – rolls of paper, close with writing, a spare shirt, a book he had bound with cat gut and a cover of pigskin. Her mother gone, vanished, off to wherever she went, for she hated to see him leave.

He writes them letters, which their mother reads, painstakingly, her finger moving from word to word, her lips forming the sounds. Their mother can read a little but is only able to write in a rudimentary fashion. Their aunt Eliza used to write their replies for them – she possesses a fine hand – but, these days, Hamnet does it. He goes to school, six days a week, from dawn until dusk; he can write as fast as you can speak, and read Latin and Greek, and make columns of figures. The scratch of the quill is like the sound of hens' feet in the dirt. Their grandfather says, with pride, that Hamnet will be the one to take over the glove business, when he is gone, that the boy has a fine head on his shoulders, that he is a scholar, a born businessman, the only one of them with any sense. Hamnet leans over his school books, gives no sign of having heard, the top of his head towards them all as they sit by the fire, the parting of his hair meandering like a stream over his scalp.

The letters from their father speak of contracts, of long days, of crowds who hurl rotten matter if they do not like what they hear, of the great river in London, of a rival playhouse owner who released a bag of rats at the climax of their new play, of memorising lines, lines, more lines, of the loss of costumes, of fire, of rehearsing a scene where the players are lowered to the stage on ropes, of the difficulty of finding food when they are out on the road, of scenery that falls, of props that are mislaid or stolen, of carts losing their wheels and pitching all into the mud, taverns that refuse them beds, of the money he has saved, of what he needs their mother to do, whom she must speak to in the town, about a tract of land he would like to purchase, a house he has heard is for sale, a field they should buy and then lease, of how he misses them, how he sends his love, how he wishes he could kiss their faces, one by one, how he cannot wait until he is home again.

If the plague comes to London, he can be back with them for months. The playhouses are all shut, by order of the Queen, and no one is allowed to gather in public. It is wrong to wish for plague, her mother has said, but Susanna has done this a few times under her breath, at night, after she has said her prayers. She always crosses herself afterwards. But still she wishes it. Her father home, for months, with them. She sometimes wonders if her mother secretly wishes it too.

The latch of the back door clatters open and into the room comes her grandmother, Mary. She is puffing, red in the face, dark half-circles of sweat under her arms.

'What are you doing, sitting there like that?' Mary says. There is no more serious affront to her than an idle person.

Susanna shrugs. She rubs her fingertips against the worn joints of the chair.

Mary casts her eyes about the room. 'Where are the twins?' she demands.

Susanna raises one shoulder, lets it drop.

'Haven't you seen them?' Mary says, mopping her brow with a handkerchief.

'No.'

'I told them,' Mary mutters, bending to pick up Susanna's fallen cap, placing it on the table, 'to chop the kindling and to light the fire in the cookhouse. And have they done it? No, they have not. They are both in for a hiding when they come in.'

She returns to stand in front of Susanna, hands on hips. 'And where's your mother?'

'Don't know.'

Mary sighs. Almost says something. But doesn't. Susanna sees this, senses the unsaid words rippling out like pennants into the air between them.

'Well, come on, then,' Mary says instead, flapping her apron at Susanna, 'stir yourself. The supper won't cook itself. Come and help us, girl, instead of sitting there like a brood hen.'

Mary takes Susanna's arm and hauls her to her feet. They go out of the back door, which slams shut behind them.

Upstairs, Hamnet wakes with a start.

here is suddenly nothing so excellent as teaching Latin. On the days he is due at Hewlands, the tutor is up at first call, folding his bedclothes and washing himself vigorously at the pail. He combs his hair and beard with careful strokes. He fills his breakfast plate but leaves the table before he has finished. He helps his brothers find their books and escorts them to the door, as they leave for school, waving them off. He has been known to hum, even to yield a polite nod to his father. His sister eyes him, sideways, as he whistles to himself, fastening his jerkin one way then the other, checking his reflection in the window pane before leaving, tucking and retucking his hair behind his ears, banging the door after him.

On the days when he is not at Hewlands, he lies in his bed until his father threatens to tan his hide unless he stirs himself. Once upright, he will slope about the house, sighing, not answering if spoken to, chewing absently on a crust of bread, picking things up, putting them down again. He is observed in the workshop, leaning on the counter, turning over pair after pair of ladies' gloves, as if searching for some meaning hidden in their seams, their inert fingers. He then sighs once more and pushes them all haphazardly back into their box. He stands over Ned, watching as he stitches a falconer's belt, so closely that the boy is quite put off his work, causing John to roar at the boy about how there's only the door between him and the street.

'And you,' John turns on his son, 'get out of here. Find

some useful occupation. If you can.' John shakes his head, turning his attention back to the cutting of a squirrel skin into useful, narrow strips. 'All that education,' he mutters, to himself, to the slippery lengths of pelt, 'and not an ounce of sense.'

His sister, Eliza, is sent later by her mother to find him. After wandering the ground floor, the yard, she takes the stairs and goes from the boys' chamber to hers, to her parents' and back; she calls his name.

The reply takes a while to come and, when it does, it is flat in tone, annoyed, displeased.

'Where are you?' she asks wonderingly, turning her head from side to side.

Again, the long, reluctant pause. Then: 'Up here.'

'Where?' she asks, mystified.

'Here.'

Eliza moves from her parents' chamber, to stand at the foot of the ladder to the attic. She calls his name again.

A sigh. A mysterious rustle. 'What do you want?'

For a moment, Eliza thinks he might be doing the thing that boys – young men – do sometimes. She has enough brothers to know that there is something that happens in private, and they are ill-tempered if interrupted. She hesitates at the bottom of the ladder, one hand on a rung.

'May I . . . come up?'

A silence.

'Are you sick?'

Another sigh. 'No.'

'Mother says, can you go to the tannery and then to the—'

There is a strangled, inarticulate cry from above, the sound of something weighty being thrown against the wall, a boot perhaps or a loaf of bread, a movement, then a thud, not unlike someone standing up and hitting their head on a rafter. 'Ow,' he screams, and lets out a volley of curses, some startling, some Eliza has never heard before but will ask him about later, when he is in a better humour.

'I'm coming up,' she says, and begins to climb the ladder.

She rises, head first, into a warm and dusty space, the only light coming from two candles propped on a bale. Her brother is sitting collapsed on the floor, his head cradled in his hands.

'Let me see,' she says.

He mutters something inaudible, possibly heretical, but the meaning is clear: he wants her to go away and leave him alone.

She puts her hands on his, peels back his fingers. With her other hand, she lifts the candle and examines the place of pain. There is a swelling, reddened and bruised, just under his hairline. She presses its outer edges, making him wince.

'Hmm,' she says. 'You've had worse.'

He lifts his eyes to hers and they regard each other for a moment. He gives a half-smile. 'That is true,' he says.

She lets her hand drop and, still holding the candle, sits herself down on one of the wool bales that are crammed into the space between floor and roof. They have been up here for several years. Once, last winter, in the yard, as they were wrapping gloves in linen, to be placed finger to wrist, finger to wrist, in baskets on a cart, her brother spoke up and asked why the attic was filled with wool bales, and what was their intended purpose? Their father leant across the cart and seized a fistful of his son's jerkin. There are no wool bales in this house, he said, giving his son a shake with each word. Is that clear? Eliza's brother had stared steadily back into his father's eyes, without blinking. Clear enough, he had replied, eventually. Their father had held on, fist clenched around his son's clothing, as if considering whether or not he was being insolent, then released him. Don't speak of what doesn't concern you, he had muttered, as he returned to his wrapping, and everyone in the yard let out the breath they had been holding.

Eliza allows herself to bounce up and down on the wool bale, the existence of which they are bound always to deny. Her brother watches her for a moment but says nothing. He tips his head back and stares at the rafters.

She wonders if he is recalling that this attic was always their space – hers and his, and also Anne's, before she died. The three of them would retreat here in the afternoons, when he got back from school, pulling the ladder up after them, despite the wails and entreaties of their younger siblings. It was mostly empty then, save for a few spoilt hides that their father was saving for some unspecified reason. Nobody could reach them there; it was just her and him and Anne, until they were called by their mother to perform some task or to take over the care of one of the younger children.

Eliza hadn't realised her brother still came up here; she hadn't known he still sought this place as a refuge from the household. She hasn't climbed the ladder since Anne died. She lets her gaze rove over the room: slanted ceilings, the undersides of the roof tiles, the bales and bales of wool, which are to be kept here, out of sight. She sees old candle stubs, a folding knife, a bottle of ink. There are, scattered over the floor, several curls of paper with words scrawled on them, crossed out, rewritten, crossed out again, then crumpled and tossed aside. Her brother's thumb and finger, the rims of his nails, she sees, are stained black. What can he be studying up here, in secret?

'What is the matter?' she says.

'Nothing,' he answers, without looking at her. 'Not a thing.'

'What is ailing you?'

'Nothing.'

'Then what are you doing up here?'

'Nothing.'

She looks at the curls of paper. She sees the words 'never' and 'fire', and something that might be 'fly' or 'try'. When she raises her eyes again, she sees that he is looking at her, eyebrows raised. She gives an involuntary quick smile. He is the only person in this house – indeed, this whole town – who knows that she has her letters, that she can read. And how does he know this? Because he is the one who taught her and Anne. Every afternoon, here, after he returned from school. He would trace a letter in the dust, on the floor, and say, Look, Eliza, look, Anne, this is a *d*, this is an *o*, and if you put a *g* at the end, it says 'dog'. Do you see that? You need to blend the sounds, run them together, until the sense of the word arrives in your head.

'Is "nothing" the only thing you're willing to say?' she says.

She sees his mouth twitch and knows that he is drawing on all his lessons in rhetoric and argument to find a way to answer this question with that very word.

'You can't do it,' she says, with glee. 'You can't find a way to reply "nothing", can you, however hard you try? You can't do it. Admit it.'

'I admit nothing,' he says triumphantly.

They sit for a moment, eyeing each other. Eliza balances the heel of one shoe on the toe of the other.

'People are saying,' she says carefully, 'that you've been seen with the girl from Hewlands.'

She doesn't say some of the coarser or more defamatory things she has heard against her brother, who is penniless and tradeless, not to mention rather young to be courting such a woman, who is of age and would come with a large dowry. What a way out it would be for the boy, she heard a woman at the market whisper, behind her back. You can see why he'd want to marry into money and get away from that father.

She tells herself to refrain from mentioning what people say of this girl. That she is fierce and savage, that she puts curses on people, that she can cure anything but also cause anything. Those wens on the stepmother's cheeks, she over-heard someone say the other day, she gave her those when the stepmother took away her falcon. She can sour the milk just by touching it with her fingers.

When Eliza hears these claims, made in her presence by people in the street, by neighbours, by those to whom she sells gloves, she doesn't pretend not to have heard. She stops in her tracks. She holds the eye of the gossip in question (she has an unnerving stare: this she knows – her brother has told her often enough; it is, he says, something to do with the purity of her eye-colour, the way she can open her eyes wide enough for the whole iris to be seen). She is only thirteen but she is tall for her age. She holds their gaze long enough for them to drop their stare, for them to shuffle off, chastised by her boldness, her silent severity. There is, she has found, great power to be had in silence. Which is something this brother of hers has never learnt.

'I've heard,' she continues, with great control, 'that you take walks together. After the lessons. Is that true?'

He doesn't look at her when he says, 'And what of it?'

'Into the woods?'

He shrugs, neither yes nor no.

'Does her mother know?'

'Yes,' he replies, quickly, too quickly, then amends this to 'I don't know.'

'But what if . . .?' Eliza finds the question she would like to put to him almost too unwieldy to ask; she has only the vaguest grasp of its content, the deeds involved, the matters at stake. She tries again: 'What if you are caught? While taking one of these walks?'

He lifts a shoulder, then lets it drop. 'Then we are caught.'

'Does the thought not give you pause?'

'Why would it?'

'The brother . . .' she begins '. . . the sheep farmer. Have you not seen him? He is a giant of a man. What if he were to—'

Eliza's brother waves his hand. 'You worry too much. He is always off with his sheep. I have never encountered him at Hewlands, in all the times I have been there.'

She folds her hands together, squints again at the curls of paper, but can make no sense of what is written there. 'I don't know if you know,' she says, timidly, 'what people say of her but—'

'I know what is said of her,' he snaps.

'There are many who claim she is—'

He straightens, his colour suddenly high. 'None of it is true. None of it. I'm surprised that you would attend to such idle gabble.'

'I'm sorry,' Eliza cries, crestfallen. 'I'm merely –'

'It is all falsehoods,' he continues, as if she hasn't spoken, 'spread by her stepmother. She is so jealous of her it twists her like a snake and—'

'– frightened for you!'

He regards her, taken aback. 'For me? Why?'

'Because . . .' Eliza tries to order her thoughts, to sift through all she has heard '. . . because our father will never agree to this. You must know that. We are in debt to that family. Father will never even speak their name. And because of what is said of her. I don't believe it,' she adds hastily, 'of course I don't. But, still, it is troubling. People are saying that no good can come of this attachment of yours.'

He slumps back to the wool bales, as if defeated, shutting his eyes. His whole body is quivering, with anger or something else. Eliza doesn't know. There is a long silence. Eliza folds the fabric of her smock into tiny tight pleats. Then she remembers something else she wanted to ask him, and leans forward.

'Does she really have a hawk?' she whispers, in a new voice.

He opens his eyes, lifts his head. Brother and sister regard each other for a moment.

'She does,' he says.

'Really? I had heard that but did not know if it was—'

'It's a kestrel, not a hawk,' he says, in a rush. 'She trained it herself. A priest taught her. She has a gauntlet and the bird takes off, like an arrow, up through the trees. You have never seen anything like it. It is so different when it flies – it is almost, you might think, two creatures. One on the ground and another in the air. When she calls, it returns to her, circling in these great wheels in the sky, and it lands with such force upon the glove, such determination.'

'She has let you do this? Wear her glove and catch the hawk?'

'Kestrel,' he corrects, then nods, and the pride of it makes him almost glow. 'She has.'

'I should love,' Eliza breathes, 'to see that.'

He looks at her, rubs his chin with his stained fingertips. 'Maybe,' he says, almost to himself, 'I'll take you with me one day.'

Eliza lets go of her dress, the pleats falling from the fabric. She is thrilled and terrified, all at once. 'You will?'

'Of course.'

'And you think she will let me fly the hawk? The kestrel?'

'I see no reason why not.' He considers his sister for a moment. 'You will like her, I think. You and she are not dissimilar, in some ways.'

Eliza is shocked by this revelation. She is not dissimilar to the woman of whom people say such terrible things? Only the other day, at church, she had an opportunity to observe the complexion of the mistress of Hewlands – those boils and blotches and wens – and the idea that a person might be able to do that to another is deeply disturbing to her. She doesn't say this to her brother, though, and, in truth, there is a part of her that longs to see the girl up close, to look into her eyes. So Eliza says nothing. Her brother does not appreciate being pressed or rushed. He is someone who must be approached sideways, with caution, as with a restive horse.

She must gently probe him and, in that way, she will likely find out more.

'What manner of person is she, then?' Eliza asks.

Her brother thinks before he answers. 'She is like no one you have ever met. She cares not what people may think of her. She follows entirely her own course.' He sits forward, placing his elbows on his knees, dropping his voice to a whisper. 'She can look at a person and see right into their very soul. There is not a drop of harshness in her. She will take a person for who they are, not what they are not or ought to be.' He glances at Eliza. 'Those are rare qualities, are they not?'

Eliza feels her head nodding and nodding. She is amazed at the detail in this speech, honoured at being its recipient. 'She sounds . . .' she gropes for the right word, recalling one he taught her himself, a few weeks ago '. . . peerless.'

He smiles and she knows he remembers teaching it to her. 'That's exactly what she is, Eliza. Peerless.'

'It also sounds,' she begins carefully, ever so carefully, so as not to alarm him, not to make him retreat into silence again – she cannot believe he has already said as much as he has, 'as though you are . . . decided. That you are fixed. On her.'

He doesn't say anything, just stretches out to tap his palm against the wool bale next to him. For a moment, she believes she has gone too far, that he will refuse to be drawn any further, that he will get up and leave, with no more confidences.

'Have you spoken to her family?' she ventures.

He shakes his head and shrugs.

'Are you going to speak to them?'

'I would,' he mutters, head lowered, 'but I am in no doubt

that my case would be refused. They would not view me as a good prospect for her.'

'Perhaps if you – waited,' Eliza says, faltering, laying a hand on his sleeve, 'a year or so. Then you'd be of age. And more established in your position. Maybe Father's business will have seen some improvement and he might regain some of his standing in the town, and perhaps he could be persuaded to stop this wool—'

He jerks his arm away, pulling himself upright. 'And when,' he demands, 'have you ever known him to listen to persuasion, to sense? When has he ever changed his mind, even when he was wrong?'

Eliza stands up from the bale. 'I just think—'

'When,' continues her brother, 'has he ever exerted himself to give me something I want or need? When have you known him to act in my favour? When have you known him not to go deliberately out of his way to thwart me?'

Eliza clears her throat. 'Perhaps if you waited, then—'

'The problem is,' her brother says, striding through the attic, through the words scattered on the floor, making the curls of paper skitter and swirl around his boots, 'that I have no talent for it. I cannot abide waiting.'

He turns, steps on to the ladder and disappears from view. She watches the two points of the ladder judder with his every step, then fall still.

The lines and lines of apples are moving, jolting, rocking on their shelves. Each apple is centred in a special groove, carved into the wooden racks that run around the walls of this small storeroom.

Rock, rock, jolt, jolt.

The fruit has been placed with care, just so: the woody stem down and the star of the calyx up. The skin mustn't touch that of its neighbour. They must sit like this, lightly held by the wooden groove, a finger width from each other, over the winter or they will spoil. If they touch each other, they will brown and sag and moulder and rot. They must be preserved in rows, like this, separate, stems down, in airy isolation.

The children of the house were given this duty: to pluck the apples from the twisted branches of the trees, to stack them together in baskets, then bring them here, to the apple store, and line them up on these racks, spaced evenly and carefully, to air, to preserve, to last the winter and spring, until the trees bring forth fruit again.

Except that something is moving the apples. Again and again and again, over and over, with a shunting, nudging, insistent motion.

The kestrel, on her perch, is hooded but alert, always alert. Her head rotates within its ruff of flecked feathers, to ascertain the source of this repetitive, distracting noise. Her ears, tuned so acutely that they can, if required, discern the heartbeat of a mouse a hundred feet away, a stoat's footfall across the forest, the wingbeat of a wren over a field, pick up on the following: twenty score apples being nudged, jostled, bothered in their cradles. The breathing of mammals, of a size too large to elicit the interest of her appetite, increasing in pace. The hollow of a palm landing lightly on muscle and bone. The click and slither of a tongue against teeth. Two planes of fabric, of differing texture, moving over each other in obverse direction.

The apples are turning on their heads; stalks are appearing from undersides, calyxes are facing sideways, then back, then upwards, then down. The pace of the knocking varies: it pauses; it slows; it builds; it pulls back again.

Agnes's knees are raised, splayed open like butterfly wings. Her feet, still in their boots, rest on the opposite shelf; her hands brace against the whitewashed wall. Her back straightens and bows, seemingly of its own accord, and low, near-growls are being pulled out of her throat. This takes her by surprise: her body asserting itself in this way. How it knows what to do, how to react, how to be, where to put itself, her legs white and folded in the dim light, her rear resting on the shelf edge, her fingers gripping the stones of the wall.

In the narrow space between her and the opposite shelf is the Latin tutor. He stands in the pale V of her legs. His eyes are shut; his fingers grip the curve of her back. It was his hands that undid the bows at her neckline, that pulled down her shift, that brought out her breasts into the light – and how startled and how white they had looked, in the air like that, in daytime, in front of another; their pink-brown eyes stared back in shock. It was her hands, however, that lifted her skirts, that pushed herself back on to this shelf, that drew the body of the Latin tutor towards her. You, the hands said to him, I choose you.

And now there is this – this fit. It is altogether unlike anything she has felt before. It makes her think of a hand drawing on a glove, of a lamb slithering wet from a ewe, an axe splitting open a log, a key turning in an oiled lock. How, she wonders, as she looks into the face of the tutor, can anything fit so well, so exactly, with such a sense of rightness?

The apples, stretching away from her one way and the other, rotate and jostle in their grooves.

The Latin tutor opens his eyes for a moment, the black of his pupils wide, almost unseeing. He smiles, places his hands on either side of her face, murmurs something, she isn't sure what, but it doesn't matter at this particular moment. Their foreheads touch. Strange, she thinks, to have another at such proximity: the overwhelming scale of lash, of folded eyelid, of the hairs of the brow, all facing the same way. She doesn't take his hand, not even out of habit: she doesn't need to.

When she had taken his hand that day, the first time she had met him, she had felt – what? Something of which she had never known the like. Something she would never have expected to find in the hand of a clean-booted grammar-school boy from town. It was far-reaching: this much she knew. It had layers and strata, like a landscape. There were spaces and vacancies, dense patches, underground caves, rises and descents. There wasn't enough time for her to get a sense of it all – it was too big, too complex. It eluded her, mostly. She knew there was more of it than she could grasp, that it was bigger than both of them. A sense, too, that something was tethering him, holding him back; there was a tie somewhere, a bond, that needed to be loosened or broken, before he could fully inhabit this landscape, before he could take command.

She watches an apple turn its red-stained flesh towards her, then away, a pitted tree-mark appearing, then the flash of the navel-like end.

Last time he came to the farm, they had walked together after his lesson, up to the furthest field, as dusk settled on the land, dimming the trees to black, as the furrows of the new-cut hayfields seemed to deepen into valleys, and come upon Joan, stepping between the springy flanks of their flocks. She liked to check on Bartholomew's work, or liked Bartholomew to know she was checking. One of the two. She had seen them coming, Agnes knew. She had seen Joan's head turn towards them, take a long look at them, as they walked up the path together. She would have realised why they were coming, would have seen their joined hands. Agnes had sensed the anxiety of the tutor: all at once, his fingers were cold and she could feel them tremble. She pressed his hand once, twice, before releasing it and letting him go ahead of her, through the gate.

Never, was what Joan had said. You? Then she laughed, a harsh trill that startled the sheep around her, making them lift their blunt heads and shift their cloven feet. Never, she said again. What age are you? She didn't wait for a reply but answered herself: Not old enough. I know your family, Joan had said, screwing up her face into a contemptuous pout, pointing at the tutor. Everyone knows them. Your father and his shady dealings, his disgrace. He was bailiff, she said, spitting out the word 'was'. How he loved to lord it over us all, swanning about in his red robes. But not any more. Have you any idea how much your father owes around the town? How much he owes us? You could tutor my sons until they are all grown men and it wouldn't come close to clearing his debt here. So, no, she said, looking round him at her, you cannot marry her. Agnes will marry a farmer, by and by – someone with prospects, someone to provide for her. She's been brought up for that life. Her father left her a dowry in his will – I'm sure you know that, don't you? She'll not marry a feckless, tradeless boy like you.

And she had turned away, as if that had been an end to it. But I don't want to marry a farmer, Agnes had cried. Joan had laughed again. Is that so? You want to marry him? Yes, she said. I do. Very much. And Joan had laughed again, shaking her head.

But we are handfasted, the tutor said. I asked her and she answered and so we are bound.

No, you are not, said Joan. Not unless I say so.

The tutor had left the field, marched down the path and off through the woods, his face dark and thunderous, and Agnes was left with her stepmother, who told her to stop standing there like a simpleton, go back to the hall and mind the children. The next time he came to the farm, Agnes beckoned to him. I know a way, she said. I have an answer. We can, she said, take matters into our own hands. Come. Come with me.

Each apple, to her, at this moment, seems toweringly different, distinct, unique, each one streaked with variations of crimson, gold and green. All of them turning their single eye upon her, then away, then back. It is too much, all too much, it is overwhelming, how many of them there are, the noise they are all making, the tapping, rhythmic, rocking sound, on and on it goes, faster and faster. It steals her breath, makes her heart trip and race in her chest, she cannot take it much more, she cannot, she cannot. Some apples rock right out of their places, on to the floor, and perhaps the tutor has trodden on them because the air is filled with a sweetish, acrid smell and she grips his shoulders. She knows, she feels, that all will be well, that everything will go their way. He holds her to him and she can feel the breath leave him, enter him, leave him again.

*

Joan is not an idle woman. She has six children (eight, if you count the half-mad step-girl and the idiot brother she was forced to take on when she married). She is a widow, as of last year. The farmer left the farm to Bartholomew, of course, but the terms of the will allow her, Joan, to remain living here to oversee matters. And oversee she will. She doesn't trust that Bartholomew to look further than his nose. She has told him she will continue to run the kitchen, the yard and the orchard, with the help of the girls. Bartholomew will see to the flocks and the fields, with the help of the boys, and she will walk the land with him, once a week, to make sure all is as it should be. So Joan has the chickens and pigs to see to, the cows to milk, food for the men, the farmhand and the shepherd to prepare, day in, day out. Two younger boys to educate as best she can – and Lord knows they will need an education as the farm will not be coming down to them, more's the pity. She has three daughters (four, if you count the other, which Joan usually doesn't) to keep under her eye. She has bread to bake, cattle to milk, berries to bottle, beer to brew, clothes to mend, stockings to darn, floors to scrub, dishes to wash, beds to air, carpets to beat, windows to polish, tables to scour, hair to brush, passages to sweep, steps to scrub.

Forgive her, then, if it is almost three months before she notices that a number of monthly cloths are missing from the wash.

At first, she believes she has made a mistake. The washing is done once a fortnight, early on a Monday morning, which allows time for airing and pressing. There is always a day with a small number of the monthly cloths; she and her daughters bleed at the same time; the other one keeps to her own time, of course, as she does with everything else. She and the girls all know the rhythm: there is the fortnight's wash with her and her daughters' cloths, heaps of them, dried to rust, and there is the wash with the smaller number of Agnes's. Joan tends to toss them into the pot with wooden tongs, holding her breath, covering them with salt.

On a morning in late October, Joan is sifting through the mounds of laundry in the washhouse. A pile of shifts and cuffs and caps, ready for a dousing in scalding water and salt; a pile of stockings, for a cooler tub; breeches, caked with filth and mud, a spattered kirtle, a cloak that had borne the brunt of a puddle. The pile Joan thinks of as 'the dirties' is smaller than usual.

Joan lifts a piece of soiled cloth, one hand over her nose, a bedsheet with the tang of urine (her youngest son, William, is still not wholly reliable in that respect, despite threats and cajolings, though he is only three, bless him). A shirt smeared with some manner of dung is stuck to a cap. Joan frowns, looks about her. She stands for a moment, considering.

She goes outside, where her daughters, Caterina, Joanie and Margaret, are twisting a sheet between them. Caterina has tied a rope around William's middle, the end of which is looped around her waist. He strains and tugs at the end, grumbling in a low murmur, holding fistfuls of grass. He is trying to get to the pig-pen but Joan has heard too many stories about swine trampling children or eating them or crushing them. She will not let her young ones wander at will.

'Where are the monthlies?' she says, standing in the doorway.

They turn to look at her, her daughters, separated and linked by the tortured sheet, which is dripping water to the ground. They shrug, their faces blank and innocent.

Joan goes back into the washhouse. She must have made a mistake. They must be here somewhere. She lifts pile after pile from the floor. She sifts through shifts and caps and stockings. She marches out, past her daughters, into the house and straight to the cupboard. There, she counts the thick cloths, folded and laundered, on the upper shelf. She knows how many there are in this house and that exact number is right there in front of her.

Joan stamps down the passage, out through the door and slams it behind her. She stands for a moment on the step, her breath streaming in and out of her nostrils. The air is cool, with the crisp edge that denotes the tipping of autumn into winter. A chicken struts up the ladder into the henhouse; the goat, at the end of its rope, chews ruminatively on a mouthful of grass, eyeing her. Joan's mind is clear, tolling with one single thought: which one, which one, which one?

Perhaps she already knows but, still, she marches down the steps, across the farmyard and up to the washhouse where her girls are still twisting wet sheets, giggling together about something. She seizes Caterina, first, by the arm and presses her hand to the girl's belly, looking into her eyes, ignoring her cries. The sheet falls to the wet, leafy ground, trodden on by her and the frightened girl. Joan feels: a flat stomach, the nudge of a hipbone, an empty pod. She lets Caterina go and gets hold of Joanie who is young, still a girl, for pity's sake, and if it is her, if someone has done this to her, Joan will, she will, do something terrible, something bad and fearful and vengeful, and that man will rue the day he ever set foot in

Hewlands, ever took her daughter wherever it was he took her and she will—

Joan lets her hand drop. Joanie's belly is flat, almost hollow. Perhaps, she finds herself thinking, she should feed up these girls of hers a bit more, encourage them to take a larger share of meat. Is she underfeeding them? Is she? Is she allowing the boys to take more than their due?

She shakes her head to banish that line of thought. Margaret, she thinks, surveying her youngest daughter's smooth and anxious face. No. It cannot be. She is still a child.

'Where is Agnes?' she says.

Joanie is staring at her, aghast, glancing down at the muddied sheet beneath their feet; Caterina, Joan notes, looks away, looks sideways, as if she understands what this means.

'I don't know,' says Caterina, stooping to pick up the sheet. 'She may have—'

'She's milking the cow,' blurts out Margaret.

Joan is screeching even before she reaches the byre. The words fly out of her mouth, like hornets, words she didn't even know she knew, words that dart and crackle and maim, words that twist and mangle her tongue.

'You,' she is yelling, as she comes into the warmth of the byre, 'where are you?'

Agnes's head is pressed against the smooth flank of the cow as she milks. Joan hears the psht-psht-u-psht of milk jetting into the pail. At the sound of Joan's cry, the cow shifts and Agnes lifts her cheek and turns to look at her stepmother, a wary expression on her face. Here it comes now, she seems to be thinking.

Joan grabs her by the arm, yanks her off the milking stool,

and pushes her up against the stall partition. Too late, she sees her son James standing in the next stall: he must have been helping Agnes with the milking. Joan has to fumble through the girl's kirtle, the fastenings of her gown, and the girl is struggling, pushing her fingers away, trying to break free, but Joan gets her hand through, just for a moment, and feels – what? A swelling, hard in texture, and hot. A quickening mound, risen like a loaf.

'Whore,' Joan spits, as Agnes pushes her away. 'Slut.'

Joan is propelled backwards, towards the cow, which is tossing its head now, uneasy at this change in atmosphere, at this unexplained hiatus in the milking. She falls against the cow's rump and stumbles slightly and Agnes is off, away, running through the byre, past the dozing ewes, through the door, and Joan is not going to let her get away. She rights herself, goes after her stepdaughter, and her fury propels her to a new speed because she catches up with her easily.

Her hand reaches out, closes over a lock of Agnes's hair. So simple to yank it, to pull the girl to a stop, to feel her head jerked back by her grip, as if pulled up by a bridle. The ease of it astonishes and fuels her: Agnes drops to the ground, falling awkwardly on her back and Joan can keep her there by winding the hair round and round her fist.

In this way, the two of them by the fence to the farmyard, Joan can get Agnes to listen to anything she says.

'Who,' she screams at the girl, 'did this? Who put that child in your belly?'

Joan is running through the not inconsiderable number of suitors who have sought Agnes's hand, ever since the details of the dowry in her father's will became known. Could it have been one of them? There was the wheelwright, the farmer from the other side of Shottery, that blacksmith's apprentice. But the girl hadn't seemed to take to any of them. Who else? Agnes is reaching round, trying to prise Joan's fingers off her hair. Her face – that haughty, high-cheekboned pale face of hers of which she is so proud – is contorted by pain, by thwarted anger. There are tears streaking down her cheeks, pooling in her eye sockets.

'Tell me,' Joan says, into this face, which she has had to see, every day, looking back at her with indifference, with insolence, since the day she came here. This face, which Joan knows resembles that of the first wife, the beloved wife, the woman her husband would never speak of, whose hair he had kept pressed in a kerchief in a shirt pocket, next to his heart – she had discovered this as she was laying him out for burial. It must have been there all along, all the years she had washed and cleaned for him, fed him, borne his children, and there it was, the hair of the first wife. She, Joan, will never get over the smart and sting of that insult.

'Was it the shepherd?' Joan says and she sees that, despite everything, this suggestion makes Agnes grin.

'No,' Agnes gets out, 'not the shepherd.'

'Who, then?' Joan demands and is just about to name the son at the neighbouring farm when Agnes twists around and lands a kick on her shin, a kick of such force that Joan staggers backwards, her hands springing open.

Agnes is up, off, away, scrambling to her feet, gathering her skirts. Joan gets up unsteadily, and goes after her. They are in the farmyard when Joan catches up with her. She grabs her by the wrist, swings her round, lands a slap on the girl's face.

'You will tell me who—' she begins, but never finishes the sentence because there is a noise at the left side of her head: a deafening explosion, like a clap of thunder. For a moment, she cannot comprehend what has happened, what the noise means. Then she feels the pain, the smart of skin, the deeper ache of bone, and she realises that Agnes has struck her.

Joan puts a hand to her face, aghast. 'How dare you?' she shrieks. 'How dare you hit me? A girl raising a hand to her mother, someone who—'

Agnes's lip is swollen, bleeding, so her words are slurred, indistinct, but Joan still manages to hear her say: 'You are not my mother.'

Enraged, Joan slaps her again. Agnes, unbelievably and without hesitation, slaps her back. Joan lifts her hand again but it is seized from behind. Someone has her around the waist – it is that great brute Bartholomew and he is lifting her up and away, forcing down her hands and holding them fast with the effortless grip of his fingers. Her son, Thomas, is there too, standing now between her and Agnes, holding up a sheep crook, and Bartholomew is telling her to stop, to calm herself. Her other children stand by the henhouse, open-mouthed, amazed. Caterina has her arms around Joanie, who is crying. Margaret holds little William, who is burying his face in her neck.

Joan feels herself carried to the other side of the yard and Bartholomew is restraining her, asking what is amiss, what has brought this on, and she is telling him, pointing a finger at Agnes, now being helped to her feet by Thomas.

Bartholomew's face falls as he listens. He closes his eyes, breathes in, breathes out. He rubs a hand over the bristles of his beard and examines his feet for a moment.

'The Latin tutor,' he says, and looks across at Agnes.

Agnes doesn't reply but lifts her chin a notch.

Joan looks from stepson to stepdaughter, to sons, to daughters. All of them, save the stepdaughter, drop their gaze and she realises that they all, every one of them, saw what she did not. 'The Latin tutor?' she repeats. She pictures him suddenly, standing at a gate in the furthest field, asking her for Agnes's hand, in a faltering voice. She had almost forgotten. '*Him?* That – that *boy?* That wastrel? That wageless, useless, beardless—' She breaks off to laugh, a harsh, mirthless sound that leaves her chest feeling emptied and hot. She remembers it all, now, the lad standing there as she told him no; she remembers feeling a brief stab of pity for him, that young lad, his face so crestfallen, and with such a father, too. But Joan had dismissed the thought of him, as soon as he had left her sight.

Joan shakes off Bartholomew's hand. She becomes focused, ruthless. She marches into the house, past Agnes, past her children, past the chickens. She bangs open the door and, once inside, is fast and thorough. She moves through the room, collecting anything that belongs to her stepdaughter. A pair of shifts, a spare cap, an apron. A wooden comb, a stone with a hole, a belt.

The family is still gathered in the farmyard when Joan comes out of the house and hurls a bundle at Agnes's feet.

'You,' she cries, 'are banished from this house for ever more.'

Bartholomew shifts his gaze from Agnes to Joan and back again. He folds his arms and steps forward. 'This is my house,' he says, 'left to me, in my father's will. And I say that Agnes may stay.'

Joan stares at him, wordless, the colour rising in her cheeks.

'But . . .' she blusters, trying to rally her thoughts '. . . but . . . the terms of the will stated that I may stay in the house until such time—'

'You may stay,' Bartholomew says, 'but the house is mine.'

'But I was given the running of the house!' She seizes upon this triumphantly, desperately. 'And you the care of the farm. So by that fact, I am within my rights to send her away, for this is a matter of the house, not of the farm and—'

'The house is mine,' Bartholomew repeats softly. 'And she stays.'

'She cannot stay,' Joan shrieks, infuriated, powerless. 'You need to think about – about your brothers and sisters, this family's reputation, not to mention your own, our standing in—'

'She stays,' Bartholomew says.

'She has to go, she must.' Joan tries to think fast, scrabbling about for something to make him change his mind. 'Think of your father. What would he have said? It would have broken his heart. He would never—'

'She will stay. Unless it comes to pass that—'

Agnes puts a hand on her brother's sleeve. They look at each other for a long moment, without speaking. Then Bartholomew spits into the dirt and lifts a hand to her shoulder. Agnes smiles at him crookedly, with her split and bleeding mouth. Bartholomew nods in reply. She sweeps a sleeve up and over her face; she unpicks the knot of the bundle, ties and reties it.

Bartholomew watches as she shoulders the bundle. 'I'll see to it,' he says, to her, touching her hand. 'Not to worry.'

'I shan't,' Agnes says.

She walks, only a little unsteadily, across the farmyard. She enters the apple store and, after a few moments, emerges with her kestrel on her glove. The bird is hooded, wings folded, but its head pivots and twitches, as if it is acquainting itself with its new circumstances.

Agnes shoulders her pack and, without saying goodbye, exits the farmyard, taking the path around the side of the house, and is gone.

He is behind his father's stall in the market, lounging against the counter. The day is crisp, with the startling metallic cold of early winter. He is watching his breath leave his body in a visible, vanishing stream, half listening to a woman debate squirrel-lined versus rabbit-trimmed gloves, when Eliza materialises beside him.

She gives him an odd, wide-eyed, teeth-gritted smile.

'You need to go home,' she says, in a low voice, without letting her fixed expression falter. She then turns to the browsing woman and says, 'Yes, madam?'

He pushes himself upright. 'Why do I need to go home? Father told me I should—'

'Just go,' she hisses, 'now,' and addresses the customer, in a louder tone: 'I believe the rabbit trim to be the very warmest.'

He lopes across the market, weaving in and out of the stalls, dodging a cart laden with cabbages, a boy carrying a bundle of thatch. He is in no hurry: it will be some complaint of his father's about his conduct or his chores or his forgetfulness or his laziness or his inability to remember important things or his reluctance to put in what his father has the temerity to call 'an honest day's work'. He will have forgotten to take an order or to pick up skin from the tanners or omitted to chop the wood for his mother. He wends his way up the wide thoroughfare of Henley Street, stopping to pass remarks with various neighbours, to pat a child on the head and, finally, he turns into the door of his house.

He wipes his boots against the matting, letting the door close behind him, and casts a glance into his father's workshop. His father's chair is empty, pushed back, as if in haste. The thin shoulders of the apprentice are bent over something at the workbench. At the sound of the latch hooking into itself, the boy turns his head and looks at him, with round, frightened eyes.

'Hello, Ned,' he says. 'How goes it?'

Ned looks as if he might speak but closes his mouth. He gives a gesture with his head that is halfway between a nod and a shake, then points towards the parlour.

He smiles at the apprentice, then steps through the door from the passage, across the squared flags of the hall, past the dining table, past the empty grate, and into the parlour.

The scene that greets him is so unaccountable, so confusing, that it takes him a moment to catch up, to assess what is happening. He stops in his tracks, framed by the doorway. What is immediately clear to him is that his life has taken a new turn.

Agnes is sitting on a low stool, a ragged bundle at her feet, his mother opposite her, next to the fire; his father is at the window, his back to the room. The kestrel is perched on the topmost rung of a ladderback chair, claws curled around the wood, its jesses and bell hanging down. Part of him wants to turn and run. The other part wants to burst into laughter:

the idea of a falcon, of Agnes, in his mother's parlour, surrounded by the curlicued and painted wall hangings of which she is so proud.

'Ah,' he says, attempting to gather himself, and all three turn towards him. 'Now . . .'

The words shrivel in his mouth because he catches sight of Agnes's face. Her left eye is swollen shut, reddened, bruised; the skin under the brow is split and bleeding.

He steps towards her, closing the gap between them. 'Good God,' he says, placing a hand on her shoulder, feeling the flex and pull of her shoulder-blade, as if she might fly, take to the air, like her bird, if only she could. 'What happened? Who did this to you?'

There are vivid marks on her cheek, a cut on her lip, the tracks of fingernails, raw patches on her wrist.

Mary clears her throat. 'Her mother,' she says, 'has banished her from the house.'

Agnes shakes her head. 'Stepmother,' she says.

'Joan,' he puts in, 'is Agnes's stepmother, not—'

'I know that,' Mary snaps. 'I used the word merely as a—'

'And she didn't banish me,' Agnes says. 'It isn't her house. It's Bartholomew's. I chose to leave.'

Mary inhales, shutting her eyes for a moment, as if mustering the final shreds of her patience. 'Agnes,' she says, opening her eyes and fixing them on her son, 'is with child. Says it's yours.'

He gives a nod and a shrug, all at the same time, eyeing the broad back of his father, who looms behind his mother, still facing the street. He is, despite himself, despite the fact that he is clutching the hand of the woman he has vowed to marry, despite everything, working out which way he will have to duck to avoid the inevitable fist, to feint, to parry, and to shield Agnes from the blows he knows will come. Such a thing has no precedent in their family. He can only imagine what his father will do, what is fermenting in that balding, lumpen head of his. And then he realises, with a deep undertow of shame, Agnes will see how matters stand between him and his father; she will see the tumult and struggle of it all; she will see him for what he is, a man with his leg caught in the jaws of a trap; she will see and know all, in only a moment.

'Is it?' his mother says, her face white, stretched.

'Is it what?' he says, feeling skittish and a little mad, therefore unable to keep himself from lapsing into verbal sparring.

'Yours.'

'Is what mine?' he returns, almost gleefully.

Mary presses her lips together. 'Did you put it there?'

'Did I put what where?'

At this point he is aware of Agnes turning her head to look at him – he can imagine her dark eyes on him, assessing, gathering information, like a spool gathers thread – but he still can't stop. He wants whatever is coming his way to come soon: he wants to goad, to tip his father into action; he wants to have done with it, once and for all. Enough creeping around the matter. Let the truth of who his father is come out. Let Agnes see.

'The child.' Mary speaks in a slow, loud voice, as if to someone simple-headed. 'In her belly. Did you put it there?'

He feels his face curling into a smile. A child. Made by him and Agnes, among the apples in the storehouse. How can they not be married now? Nothing can be done to stop it, in such circumstances. It will be, just as she said it would. They will be married. He will be a husband and a father, and his life will begin and he can leave behind this, all of this, this house, this father, this mother, the workshop, the gloves, this life as their son, the drudgery and tedium of working in the business. What a thought, what a thing. This child, in Agnes's belly, will change everything for him, will free him from the life he hates, from the father he cannot live with, from the house he can no longer bear. He and Agnes will take flight: to another house, another town, another life.

'I did,' he says, feeling a smile broaden across his face.

Several things happen at once. His mother launches herself from her seat, towards him, peppering him with her fists; he feels the blows make contact with his chest and shoulders, like taps on a drum. He hears Agnes's voice, saying, Enough, stop, and another voice, his own, saying that they are hand-fasted, that there is no sin in it, they will wed, they must. His mother is shrieking that he is not of age, that he will need their consent and they will never give it, something about how he has been bewitched, what ruination this is, she will send him away, she would rather he went to sea than marry this wench, what a catastrophe. Behind him, he is aware of the bird shifting uneasily on its chair, shrugging its feathers, the flap and flutter of its open wings, the jangling of its bell. And then the dark broad shape of his father is near, and where is Agnes in all this chaos, is she behind him, is she safely out of his father's reach because, by God, he will kill him, he will, if the man so much as lays a finger on her.

His father is stretching out an arm and he is ready, muscles tensed, but the meaty hand doesn't strike him, doesn't curl into a ball, doesn't injure him. Instead, it lands on his shoulder. He can feel all five fingertips denting his flesh, through the cloth of his shirt, can catch the familiar whiff of leather, of whittawing – acrid, smarting, uric – off them.

There is the unfamiliar sensation of his father's hand pressing him down, into a chair. 'Sit,' his father says, his voice even. He gestures to Agnes, who is behind them, soothing her bird. 'Sit down, lass.'

After a moment, he complies. Agnes comes to stand beside him, smoothing the feathers on the kestrel's neck with the back of her fingers. He sees his mother examining her with an expression of disbelief, of naked amazement. It makes him want to laugh, again. Then his father speaks and his attention is pulled back.

'I'm in no doubt,' his father is saying, 'we can . . . come to an arrangement.'

The expression on his father's face is an odd one. He stares at it, struck by its peculiarity. John's lips are pulled back from his teeth, his eyes strangely alight. It takes him several seconds to realise that John is, in fact, smiling.

'But, John,' his mother is exclaiming, 'there is no possible way that we can agree to such—'

'Hush, woman,' John says. 'The boy said they were hand-fasted. Did you not hear him? No son of mine will go back on his promises, will shirk his responsibilities. The lad has got this girl with child. He has a responsibility, a—'

'He's eighteen years of age! He has no trade! How can you think—'

'I told you to hush.' His father speaks with his accustomed rough fury, just for a moment, before reassuming the odd, almost wheedling tone. 'My son made you a promise, did he?' he says, looking at Agnes. 'Before he took you to the woods?'

Agnes strokes her bird. She looks at John, with a level gaze. 'We made a promise to each other.'

'And what does your mother – your, ah, stepmother – say to the match?'

'She . . . was not in favour. Before. And now,' she gestures towards her belly, 'I cannot say.'

'I see.' His father pauses for a moment, his mind working. And there is, to the son, something familiar in this silence of his father's, and just as he is staring at him, frowning, wondering, he realises what it is. This is the face his father wears when he is contemplating a business deal, an advantageous one. The expression is the same as when a cheap lot of skins has come his way, or a couple of extra bales of wool, to be hidden in the attic, or an inexperienced merchant has been sent to barter with him. It is the expression he assumes when he is trying not to let on to the other party that he will come out of the deal better off.

It is covetous. It is gleeful. It is suppressed. It chills the son, right down to the marrow of his bones. It makes him clutch the edges of the chair beneath him with both hands.

This marriage, the son suddenly sees, with a choking sensation of disbelief, will be beneficial to his father, to whatever dealings he has with the sheep farmer's widow. His father is about to turn all this – Agnes's bleeding face, her arrival here, the kestrel, the baby growing in her belly – to his own good.

He cannot believe it. He cannot. That he and Agnes have, unwittingly, played into his father's hands. The thought makes him want to run from the room. That what happened between them both at Hewlands, in the forest, the kestrel diving like a needle through the fabric of leaves above them, can be twisted into a rope with which his father will tether him ever more closely to this house, to this place. It is insupportable. It cannot be borne. Will he never get away? Will he never be free of this man, this house, this trade?

John begins to talk again, in the same honeyed voice, saying how he will go out to Hewlands directly, to talk to the yeoman's widow, to Agnes's brother. He is sure, he tells them, he can broker an agreement, can draw up terms beneficial to all. The boy wants to marry the girl, he says to his wife, the girl wants to marry the boy: who are they to forbid this union? The baby must be born in wedlock, cannot be delivered into this world on the wrong side of the sheet. It is their grandchild, is it not? Many weddings are brought about thus. It is nature's way.

At this point, he turns to his wife and gives a laugh, reaches out a hand to grab at her hip, and the son must look at the floor, so queasy does he feel.

John leaps to his feet, his face flushed, all eagerness and fervour. 'It is settled, then. I will go out to Hewlands, to set out my terms . . . our terms . . . to . . . to seal this most . . . sudden . . . and, it must be said, blessed union between our families. The girl will remain here.' He beckons to his son. 'A word with you, in private, if you please.'

Out in the passage, John lets the pretence at geniality drop. He grips his son by the collar, his fingers cold against his skin; he pushes his face right up to his.

'Tell me,' he says, with low, grizzled menace, 'there are no more.'

'No more what?'

'Say it. There are no more. Are there?'

The son feels the wall pressing into his back, his shoulder.

The fingers grip his collar with such force that they stop the air in his throat.

'Are there?' his father hisses into his face. His breath is vaguely fishy, loamy. 'Will there be other Warwickshire doxies lolloping up to my door to tell me that you swelled their bellies with a child? Must I be dealing with others? Tell me the truth, now. Because, by God, if there are others and her family hear of it, there'll be trouble. For you and for all of us. Understand?'

He gasps, pushes back against his father but there is an elbow pressed into his shoulder, a forearm across his throat. He tries to say, no, never, there is only her, she is no doxy, how dare you say such a thing, but the words cannot make it to his mouth.

'Because if you have ploughed and planted another one – just one – I'll kill you. And if I don't, her brother will. Do you hear me? I swear I will part you from your life, with God as my witness. Remember that.'

His father gives one final shove to his windpipe, then moves off, out of the door, letting it clang shut behind him.

The son bends over, drawing in air, rubbing at his neck. As he draws himself upright, he sees Ned, the apprentice, looking at him. The two stare at each other for a moment, then Ned turns away, back to the bench, leaning in to examine his work.

John walks directly to Hewlands. He doesn't stop at his stall to chivvy Eliza, to mete out criticisms and judgements, or to check on the stock. He doesn't pause to exchange words with a guildsman he meets on Rother Street. He takes the path to Shottery and hurries along it, almost as if the girl might have the baby at any minute and somehow nullify this opportunity.

His steps are quick and, he is pleased to think, sprightly, especially for a man of his years. He feels the anticipation of a good deal ahead of him, senses that particular pleasure run through his veins, like a cup of wine. John knows this is the moment, that a deal must be struck without delay, lest things change and the advantage slip away from him, as well it might. He has the upper hand, yes, he does. He has possession of the girl, in his house; he has the boy, who will require a special licence to wed because of his youth, the signed permission of his parents. There is the matter of the old debt between them, but their most pressing issue will be the girl. They need her to be married, in her state, and no marriage can take place unless he, John, agrees to it. It is the perfect position. He holds every card. He allows himself, as he walks the path, to whistle out loud, an old dancing tune from his youth.

He finds the brother in a distant field; he must pick his way through the filth to reach him, the brother leaning on his crook, watching him approach, without moving.

Groups of sheep shift around him, turning their bulging eyes on him, veering from him, as if he is a large and terrifying predator. Gloves, he mutters to them, under his breath, without letting his smile drop, you'll all be gloves before ye know it. You'll be worn on the hands of the Warwickshire gentry before the year is out, if I have anything to do with it. It is difficult, as he steps over the field, to prevent the glee from showing on his face.

The puddles, beneath his town boots, are frozen white clouds, solidified into the ridges and furrows of mud.

John reaches the sheep-farming brother. He holds out his hand. The brother looks at it for a moment. He is a huge man, with a look of Agnes about the eyes, with black hair tied back from his face. He is dressed in a sheepskin cape, like the father used to wear, and carries a carved cudgel. Another fairer, younger lad, also with a crook, hovers in the background, watchful, and for a moment, John feels a slight qualm. What if these men, these brothers, these people, mean to harm him, to wreak vengeance on him for his wastrel son who has taken the maidenhead of their sister? What if he has misread the situation and it is not, after all, to his advantage, and he has made a grave mistake in coming? He sees, for a fleeting moment, death coming for him, here, in a frosty Shottery field. Sees his corpse, the head stoved in by a shepherd's crook, his brain spattered and spent, steaming in the frozen earth. His Mary a widow, his young children, little Edmond and Richard, fatherless. All the fault of his errant son.

The farmer shifts his cudgel to his opposite hand, spits emphatically on the ground, and takes John's fingers, giving them a painfully strong squeeze. John hears himself give a high, almost girlish cry.

'Well,' John says, with the deepest, manliest chuckle he can muster, 'I believe, Bartholomew, we have matters to discuss.'

The brother looks at him for a long moment. Then he nods, looking past him at something over John's shoulder.

'That we do,' he says and, points. 'Here comes Joan. She will want to have her say, I'll warrant.'

Joan comes hurrying over the fields, flanked by daughters, a small boy perched on her hip.

'You,' she calls, as though he were one of her farm-boys. 'A word with you, if you please.'

John waves his hand at her cordially, then turns to include

Bartholomew in a smile and a head tilt. It is a knowing, side-ways, male nod that John offers him, one that says, Women, eh? Always wanting their way. We men must let them feel included.

Bartholomew holds his gaze for a moment, his flecked eyes so like his sister's, but expressionless, cold. Then he drops his gaze and, with an imperceptible gesture, bids his brother to leave, to open the gate for Joan, whistling for the dogs to go with them.

They stand in the field for a long time, Bartholomew, Joan and John. The other children watch, unseen, hidden behind a wall. After a while, they begin to ask each other, Is it settled, is it done, has Agnes gone to their house, will she be wed, is she never to come back? The smallest brother tires of this game of standing at a wall and whines to be put down. The sisters' eyes never leave the three figures standing among the sheep. The dogs scuffle and yawn, dropping their heads on to their paws, raising them, every now and again, to check with Thomas, awaiting his orders.

Their brother is seen to shake his head, to turn sideways, as if to leave the talk. The glover seems to make an entreaty, uncurling first one hand, then the other. He counts something off on the fingers of his right hand. Joan speaks animatedly for a long time, waving her arms, pointing towards the house, gripping her apron. Bartholomew looks long and hard at the sheep, before reaching out to touch the back of one, turning his face to look at the glover, as if proving a point about the animal to the other man. The glover nods vigorously, gives a long speech, then smiles as if in triumph. Bartholomew taps his cudgel against his boot, a sure sign that he is unhappy.

The glover steps closer; Joan holds her ground. The glover puts a hand on Bartholomew's shoulder; the farmer lets it remain.

Then they shake hands. The glover with Joan, and then with Bartholomew. Oh, says one of the girls. The sons let out their breath. It is done, whispers Caterina.

amnet starts awake, the mattress rustling beneath him. Something has woken him – a noise, a bang, a shout – but he doesn't know what. He can tell, by the long reaches of the sun into the room, it must be near evening. What is he doing here, asleep on the bed?

He twists his head and then he remembers everything. A form lies flat, next to him, head twisted to one side. Judith's face is waxen and still, a sheen of sweat making it glimmer like glass. Her chest rises and falls at uneven intervals.

Hamnet swallows, his throat closed and tight. His tongue feels furred, ungainly, too large to fit in his mouth. He scrambles upright, the room blurring around him. A pain enters the back of his head and crouches there, snarling, like a cornered rat.

Downstairs, humming to herself, Agnes comes through the front door. She places upon the table the following items: two bundles of rosemary, her leather bag, the jar of honey, a hunk of beeswax, wrapped in a leaf, her straw hat, a tied posy of comfrey, which she intends to pluck and dry, then steep in warmed oil.

She walks through the room, straightening the chair by the hearth, moving a cap of Susanna's from the table to a hook behind the door. She opens the window to the street, in case any customers come for her. She unties her kirtle and shrugs it off. Then she opens the back door and goes down the path towards the cookhouse.

The heat can be felt from the distance of several paces.

Inside, she sees Mary, stirring water in a pot, and beside her Susanna, seated on a stool, rubbing mud from some onions.

'There you are,' Mary says, turning, her face reddened by heat. 'You took your time.'

Agnes gives a noncommittal smile. 'The bees were swarming in the orchard. I had to coax them back.'

'Hmm,' Mary says, hurling a handful of meal into the water. She hasn't the patience for bees. Tricky creatures. 'And how are all at Hewlands?'

'Well, I believe,' replies Agnes, touching the hair of her daughter's head briefly in greeting, taking up a loaf of bread she made that morning and putting it on to the counter. 'Bartholomew's leg is still troubling him, I'm afraid, although he will not admit it. I see him limping. He says it aches in damp weather and that is all but I told him he needs—' Agnes breaks off, bread knife in hand. 'Where are the twins?'

Neither Mary nor Susanna looks up from her task.

'Hamnet and Judith,' Agnes says. 'Where are they?'

'No idea,' Mary says, lifting a spoon to her lips to taste, 'but when I find them, they're in for a hiding. None of my kindling chopped. The table not laid. The pair of them off, God knows where. It'll be supper time soon and still no sign of either of them.'

Agnes guides the serrated edge of the knife down through the loaf of bread, once, twice, the slices falling on to each other. She is about to make an incision in the crust for the third time when she lets the knife slide from her hand.

'I'll just go and . . .' She trails away, moving through the cookhouse door, up the path and into the big house. She checks the workshop, where John is leaning over the bench in a do-not-bother-me posture. She walks through the dining hall and the parlour. She calls their names up the stairs. Nothing. She comes out of the front door, into Henley Street. The heat of the day is passing, the dust of the street settling, people retreating back into their homes to take their supper.

Agnes goes in at the front door of her own house, for the second time that evening.

And she sees, standing at the foot of the stair, her son. He is stock still, his face white, his fingers gripping the stair rail. He has a swelling, a cut on his brow that she is sure wasn't there this morning.

She moves towards him swiftly, covering the room in a few paces.

'What?' she says, taking him by the shoulders. 'What is it? What happened to your face?'

He does not speak. He shakes his head. He points towards the stairs. Agnes takes them, two at a time.

liza says to Agnes that she will make the wedding crown. If, she adds, that is what Agnes would like.

It is an offer made shyly, in a tentative voice, early one morning. Eliza is lying back to back with the woman who has come into their house so unexpectedly, so dramatically. It is just after dawn and it is possible to hear the first carts and footfalls out on the street.

Eliza must, Mary has said, share her bed with Agnes, until such time as the wedding can be arranged. Her mother told her this with tight, rigid lips, not meeting Eliza's eye, flapping out an extra blanket over the bed. Eliza had looked down at the half of the pallet nearest the window, which has remained empty since her sister Anne died. She had glanced up to see that her mother was doing the same and she wanted to say, Do you think of her, do you still catch yourself listening for her footsteps, for her voice, for the sound of her breathing at night, because I do, all the time. I still think that one day I might wake and she will be there, next to me, again; there will have been some wrinkle or pleat in time and we will be back to where we were, when she was living and breathing.

Instead, though, Eliza wakes alone in the bed, every day.

But now here is this woman who will marry her brother: an Agnes instead of an Anne. It has all been a rush and a bother to arrange, with her brother needing a special licence and – Eliza isn't clear on this point – a protracted discussion (heated) about money. Some friends of Agnes's brother have put up surety: this much she knows. There is a baby in her belly, Eliza has heard, but only through doors. No one has explicitly told her this. Just as no one has thought to tell her that the wedding will be tomorrow, in the morning: her brother and Agnes will walk to the church in Temple Grafton, where a priest has agreed to marry them. It is not their priest, and it is not the church they attend every Sunday. Agnes says she knows this priest well. He is a particular friend of her family. It was him, in fact, who gave her the kestrel. He reared it himself, from an egg, and he once taught her how to cure lung rot in a falcon; he will marry them, she said airily, as she worked the treadle of Mary's spinning wheel, because he has known her since she was a child and has always been kind to her. She once traded some jesses for a barrel of ale with him. He is, she explained, gathering wool in her spare hand, an expert in matters of falconry and brewing and bee-keeping, and has shared with her his great knowledge of all three.

When Agnes made this speech, from her place at the spinning, by the fire in the parlour, Eliza's mother let her knitting needles fall, as if she could not believe what she was hearing, which had made Eliza's brother laugh immoderately into his cup, which in turn had made their father angry. Eliza, however, had listened, rapt, to every word. Never had she heard such things said, never had anyone spoken in such a way in their house before, with such unselfconscious flow, such frank cheer.

Either way, the wedding is set. The hawking, honey-producing, ale-trading priest will marry them early the next day, in a ceremony arranged quickly, furtively, secretively.

When Eliza gets married, she wants to walk down Henley

Street in a crown of flowers, in bright sunshine, so that all may see her. She does not want some ceremony miles from town, in a small church with a strange priest sneaking her and her groom in through the door; she will hold her head high and marry in town. She is sure of it. She will have her banns read loudly at the church door. But her father and Agnes's brother cooked this up between them so nothing more can be said.

She would, however, like to make the flower crown for Agnes. Who else will do it? Not Agnes's stepmother, Eliza is sure, or her sisters: they are keeping themselves to themselves, back in Shottery. They may come to the wedding, Agnes has shrugged, or they may not.

But Agnes must have a crown. She cannot be married without one, baby or no baby. So Eliza asks her. She clears her throat. She laces her fingers together, as if about to pray.

'May I . . .' she begins, speaking into the icy air of the room '. . . I wondered if you would like it if I . . . made your flower crown? For tomorrow?'

She feels Agnes behind her, listening. Eliza hears her inhale and she thinks for a moment that she will refuse, she will say no, that Eliza has spoken out of turn.

The pallet rustles and judders as Agnes turns over to face her.

'A crown?' Agnes says, and Eliza can hear in her voice that she is smiling. 'I would like that very much indeed. Thank you.'

Eliza rolls over and the two of them stare into each other's faces, sudden conspirators.

'I don't know,' Eliza says, 'what flowers we will find, this time of year. Maybe some berries or—'

'Juniper,' Agnes cuts in. 'Or holly. Some fern. Or pine.'

'There's ivy.'

'Or hazel flowers. We could go down to the river, you and I,' Agnes says, catching hold of Eliza's hand, 'later today, and see what we can find.'

'I saw some monkshood there last week. Maybe—'

'Poisonous,' Agnes says, turning on to her back, keeping hold of Eliza's hand and placing it square on her belly. 'Do you want to feel the baby? She moves about in the early morning. She'll be needing her breakfast.'

'She?' says Eliza, amazed at this abrupt intimacy, the heat of the woman's taut, hard skin, the strong grip of her hand.

'I think it will be a girl,' Agnes says, with a yawn, neat and quick.

Eliza's hand is being pressed between Agnes's fingers. It is the oddest sensation, as if something is being drawn from her, like a splinter in the skin or infection from a wound, at the same time as something else is being poured into her. She cannot work out if she is being made to give or receive something. She wants to withdraw her hand, at the same time as wanting it to remain.

'Your sister,' Agnes says softly. 'She was younger than you?'

Eliza stares at the smooth brow, the white temples and black hair of her soon-to-be sister-in-law. How does she know that Eliza had been thinking of Anne?

'Yes,' Eliza says. 'By almost two years.'

'And she was how old when she died?'

'Eight.'

Agnes clicks her tongue in sympathy. 'I am sorry,' she murmurs, 'for this loss.'

Eliza doesn't say that she worries about Anne, all alone, so young, without her, wherever she may be. That for a long time she lay awake at night, whispering her name, just in case she was listening, from wherever she was, in case the sound of Eliza's voice was a comfort to her. The pain of wondering if Anne was distressed somewhere and that she, Eliza, was unable to hear her, unable to reach her.

Agnes pats the back of Eliza's hand and speaks in a rush: 'She has her other sisters with her, remember. The two who died before you were born. They all look after each other. She doesn't want you to worry. She wants you . . .' Agnes pauses, looks at Eliza, who is shivering with the cold or the shock or both. 'I mean,' she says, in a new, careful voice, 'I expect that she wouldn't want you to worry. She would want you to rest easy.'

They are silent for a moment. The clop-clop of a horse's hoofs passes by the window, heading north up the street.

'How did you know,' Eliza whispers, 'about the other two girls who died?'

Agnes seems to think for a moment. 'Your brother told me,' she says, without looking at Eliza.

'One of them,' Eliza breathes, 'was called Eliza. The first child. Did you know that?'

Agnes starts to nod and then shrugs.

'Gilbert says sometimes that . . .' Eliza has to cast a look over her shoulder before she speaks '. . . that she might come, in the middle of the night, to stand at my bed, wanting her name back from me. That she'll be angry because I took it.'

'Nonsense,' Agnes says crisply. 'Gilbert's talking nonsense. Don't you listen to him. Your sister is happy for you to have her name, for you to carry it on. Remember that. If I hear Gilbert saying that to you, again, ever, I'll put nettles in his breeches.'

Eliza bursts out laughing. 'You will not.'

'I most certainly will. And that will teach him not to go about frightening people.' Agnes releases Eliza's hand and pushes herself upright. 'Now then. Time to start the day.'

Eliza looks down at her hand. There is a dent in her skin, from the press of Agnes's thumbnail, a rose-red bloom all around it. She rubs at it with her opposite hand, surprised at its heat, as if it has been held near a candle.

The crown Eliza makes is of fern, larch and Michaelmas daisies. She sits at the dining table to do it. She has been given the task of minding her youngest brother, Edmond, as she works, so she gives him some larch leaves and daisy petals. He sits on the floor, legs outstretched, and drops the leaves, one by one, solemnly, into a wooden bowl, where he stirs them with a spoon. She listens to the string of sounds that comes from his mouth breathily, as he stirs: 'eef' is in there, for 'leaf', and 'ize', for 'Eliza', and 'oop', for 'soup'. The words exist, if you know how to listen.

Her fingers – strong, slender, more used to the stitching of leather – weave the stems together in a circlet. Edmond gets to his feet. He toddles to the window, then back, then to the fireplace, admonishing himself as he gets closer: 'Na-na-na-na-na.' Eliza smiles and says, 'Nay, Edmond, not the fire.' He turns a delighted face towards her, thrilled at being understood. The fire, the heat, no, don't touch. He knows he is not allowed near it but it fills him with a great and irresistible longing, the bright, leaping colour, the blast of warmth to his face, the array of fascinating implements to stoke and poke and grip.

She can hear, at the back of the house, her mother banging pots and pans in the cookhouse. She is in a filthy temper and has already caused the maid to cry. Mary is pouring all her ire and fury into the food. The joint won't cook. The pastry for the pie will crumble. The dough hasn't risen fast enough. The sweetmeats taste grainy. It seems to Eliza that the cookhouse is at the centre of a whirlwind and she must stay here, away from it, with Edmond, where they are safe.

Tuck, tuck, go her fingertips, severed stem ends into the weave; the palm of the opposite hand turns the circle of the crown as she works.

Above her, she can hear the thud and clatter of her brothers' feet. They are wrestling at the top of the stair, by the sound of it. A grunt, a gust of laughter, Richard's plaintive plea to be let go, Gilbert's false reassurances, a thud, a creak of floorboard, then the smothered 'Ow!'

'Boys!' comes the roar from the glove shop. 'Stop that this instant! Or I'll come up there and give you something to wail about, wedding or no wedding.'

The three brothers appear in the doorway, jostling each other out of the way. Eliza's eldest brother, the bridegroom, skids across the room, seizes her, kisses the top of her head, then whirls around to lift Edmond high in the air. Edmond is still gripping his wooden spoon in one hand and a fistful of leaves in the other. His eldest brother spins him around, once, twice. Edmond quirks his eyebrows and smiles, the air lifting the hair from his forehead. He tries to cram the spoon sideways into his mouth. Then he is set down and all three bigger brothers promptly disappear out of the door into the street. Edmond lets his spoon drop, looking after them, forlorn, unable to understand this sudden desertion.

Eliza laughs. 'They'll be back, Ed,' she says. 'By and by. When he is wed. You'll see.'

Agnes appears in the doorway. Her hair is all unravelled and brushed. It spreads down her back and over her shoulders like black water. She is wearing a gown Eliza hasn't seen before, in a pale primrose, the front of which is ever so slightly pushed out.

'Oh,' says Eliza, clasping her hands together. 'The yellow will pick out the hearts of the daisies.' She leaps to her feet, holding out the crown. Agnes ducks down so that Eliza can place it on her head.

Frost has descended overnight. Each leaf, each blade, each twig on the road to the church has encased itself, replicated itself, in frost. The ground is crisp and hard underfoot. The groom and his men are up ahead: the noise from their group is of hooting, yelling, breaks of song, the trill of a pipe, played by a friend who skips half on, half off the verge. Bartholomew brings up the rear, his height obscuring those ahead of him, his head lowered.

The bride walks in a straight line, not looking left or right. With her are Eliza, Edmond riding on her hip, Mary, several of Agnes's friends, the baker's wife. Off to the side are Joan and her three daughters. Joan is pulling her youngest son by the hand. The sisters walk in tight formation, arm-in-arm, three abreast, giggling and whispering to each other. Eliza glances sideways at them, several times, before turning her head away.

Agnes sees this, sees Eliza's sadness gather about her, like fog. She sees everything. The rosehips on the hedgerow that are turning to brown at their tips; unpicked blackberries, too high to reach; the swoop and dip of a thrush from the branches of an oak by the side of the track; the white stream of breath from the mouth of her stepmother as she carries the youngest boy on her back, the strands of strangely colourless hair escaping from her kerchief, the wide swing of her hips. Agnes sees that Caterina has her mother's nose, flat and broad across the bridge, Joanie her mother's low hairline and Margaret the thick neck and elongated earlobes. She sees that Caterina has the gift or ability to make her life happy, and Margaret, to a lesser degree, but that Joanie does not. She sees her father in the youngest boy, walking now, and holding Caterina's hand: his fair hair, the squarish set of his head, the upturned ends of his mouth. She feels the ribbons tied about her stockings, tightening and releasing as the muscles of her legs work beneath her. She feels the prickle and shift of the herbs and berries and flowers of her crown, feels the minute trickle of water within the veins of their stems and leaves. She feels a corresponding motion within herself, in time with the plants, a flow or current or tide, the passage of blood from her to the child within. She is leaving one life; she is beginning another. Anything may happen.

She senses, too, somewhere off to the left, her own mother. She would be here with her had life taken a different turn. She would be the one holding her hand as Agnes walked to her wedding, her fingers encasing her daughter's. Her foot-steps would have followed her beat. They would be walking this path together, side by side. It would have been her making the crown, affixing it to Agnes's head, brushing the hair so that it hung all around her. She would have taken the blue ribbons and wound them around her stockings, woven them into the hanks of her hair. It would have been her.

So it follows, of course, that she will be here now, in whatever form she can manage. Agnes does not need to turn her head, does not want to frighten her away. It is enough to know that she is there, manifest, hovering, insubstantial. I see you, she thinks. I know you are here.

She looks ahead instead, along the road, where her father would have been, up ahead with the men, and sees her husband-to-be. The dark worsted wool of his cap, the motion of his walk, springier than that of the other men around him – his brothers, his father, his friends, her brothers. Look back, she wills him, as she walks, look back at me.

She is unsurprised when he does exactly that, his head turning, his face revealing itself to her as he pushes back his hair to look at her. He holds her gaze for a moment, pausing in the road, then smiles. He makes a gesture, holding up one hand and moving the other towards it. She tilts her head quizzically. He does it again, still smiling. She thinks he is miming a ring going on to a finger – something like that. Then one of his brothers, Gilbert, Agnes thinks, but can't be sure, launches himself at him sideways, seizing him around the shoulders and shoving him. He responds in kind, wrestling Gilbert into a headlock, making the boy howl in outrage.

The priest is waiting at the church door, his cassock a dark shape against the frost-whitened stone. The men and boys fall silent as they move up the path. They gather in a cluster near him, nervous, silent, their faces flushed in the morning air.

As Agnes comes up the church path, the priest smiles at her, then breathes in.

He closes his eyes and speaks: 'I declare the banns for this marriage between this man and this woman.' A stillness falls over all of them, even the children. But Agnes is making an internal plea of her own: If you are here, she thinks, show me now, make yourself known, now, please, I am waiting for you, I am here. 'If any of ye know of any cause or just impediment why these persons should not be joined together in holy matrimony, ye are to declare it. This is for the first time of asking.'

The lids of his eyes open and he looks around them all, one by one. Thomas is poking James's neck with a holly leaf; Bartholomew cuffs him quickly, efficiently, on the back of the head. Richard is jigging from foot to foot, looking very much as if he needs to relieve himself. Caterina and Margaret are covertly eyeing the groom's brothers, assessing their worth. John is grinning, thumbs slotted into the straining ties of his doublet. Mary stares at the ground, her face immobile, almost stricken.

The priest inhales again. He says his words for the second time. Agnes breathes in, once, twice, and the baby turns inside her, as if it has heard a noise, a cry, as if it has heard its name for the first time. Show me now, Agnes thinks again, forming the words in her head with deliberate, delicate care. Joan bends to hear something her son is mouthing; she shushes him with a finger at her lips. John shifts to the other foot and barges accidentally into his wife. Mary drops the gloves she is holding and must bend to retrieve them, but not before glaring at him.

The banns are said for the third time, the priest holding them all in his gaze, his hands parted, as if he would embrace them all. Before he has finished speaking the final words, the groom steps forward, into the church porch, taking up his place beside the priest, as if to say, Let's get this under way. There is a ripple of laughter throughout the group, a release of tension, and Agnes sees a flash to her right, in the corner of her eyes, a burst of colour, like the fall of a hair across her face, like the motion of a bird in flight. Something is dropping from a tree above them. It lands on Agnes's shoulder, on the yellow stuff of her gown, and then on her chest, to the gentle swell of her stomach. She catches it neatly, cupping it against her body. It is a spray of rowan berries, fire-red, still with several narrow silver-backed leaves attached.

She holds it in her fingers for a moment. Then her brother steps forward. He takes in the berries, held in Agnes's palm. He looks up at the tree above them. Brother and sister regard each other. Then Agnes reaches for Bartholomew's hand.

His grip is strong, perhaps too strong; he has never known or recognised his own extraordinary strength. His fingers are cold, the skin rough and grainy. He walks her towards the church door. The groom is already reaching out for her, his arm eagerly extended. Bartholomew pauses, pulling Agnes to a stop. The groom waits, hand outstretched, a smile on his face. Bartholomew leans forward, still holding Agnes back by the hand. He reaches out his other hand and grips the husband-to-be by the shoulder. Agnes knows he doesn't intend her to hear but she does: her hearing is sharp as a hawk's. Bartholomew leans in and whispers in her husband-to-be's ear: 'Take good care of her, Latin boy, very good care, and no harm will come to you.'

When Bartholomew leans back again, towards his sister, he is grinning, teeth bared, facing the crowd; he releases Agnes's hand and she steps towards her groom, who is looking a little pale.

The priest dips the ring in holy water, murmuring a blessing, and then the groom takes it. *In nomine Patris*, he says, in a clear voice, audible to all, even those at the back, sliding the ring on to her thumb and then off again, *in nomine Filii*, the ring is pushed on to her first finger, *in nomine Spiritus Sancti*, her middle finger. At *Amen*, the ring encircles her third finger where, the groom told her the other day, as they were hiding in the orchard, runs a vein that travels straight to her heart. It feels cold, for a moment, against her skin, and damp with holy water, but then the blood, flowing straight from her heart, warms it, brings it up to the temperature of her body.

She steps into the church, conscious of the three things she is holding. The ring on her finger, the spray of rowan berries, curled into her palm, the hand of her husband. They walk down the aisle together, a surge of people behind them, their feet clattering on the stone, taking their places in the pews. Agnes kneels at the altar, at the left side of her husband, to hear Mass. They bow their heads in unison and the priest places linen over them, to protect them from demons, from the devil, from all that is bad and undesirable in the world.

gnes moves across the upstairs room, through the converging shafts of light, where dust motes swarm and drift. Her daughter is lying on the rush pallet, still in her dress, her shoes shed beside her.

She is breathing, Agnes is telling herself, telling her fluttering heart, her thumping pulse, as she gets nearer, and that is good, is it not? There is her chest, going up and going down and, look, her cheeks are flushed, her hands resting beside her, fingers curled. All is not so bad. Surely. She is here and Hamnet is here.

Agnes reaches the bed and crouches down, her skirts inflating around her.

'Judith?' she says, and puts a hand to the girl's forehead, then to her wrist, then back to the cheek.

Aware that Hamnet is in the room, just behind her, Agnes bows her head while she thinks. Fever, she tells herself, in a silent voice that sounds so calm, so cool. Then she corrects herself: a high fever, the skin damp and fire-hot. Breathing rapid and shallow. Pulse weak, erratic and fast.

'How long has she been like this?' She speaks aloud, without turning.

'Since I returned from school,' says Hamnet, his voice pitched high. 'We were playing with the kittens and Jude said . . . that is, Grandmamma had asked us to chop the wood and we were about to start, on the wood, but we were having a game with the kittens and a bit of ribbon. The wood was there and I—'

'Never mind the wood,' she says, with control. 'It matters not. Tell me about Judith.'

'She said her throat was hurting her but we played a bit longer and then I said that I would chop the wood and she said that she was feeling ever so tired, so she came up here and lay down on the bed. So I did some of the wood – not all of it – and then I came up to see her and she wasn't at all well. And then I looked for you and Grandmamma and every-body,' his voice is rising now, 'but there was no one here. I went all over, looking for you and calling for you. And I ran for the physician but he wasn't there either and I didn't know what to do. I didn't know how to . . . I didn't know . . .'

Agnes straightens, comes towards her son. 'There now,' she says, reaching out for him. She tucks his smooth, fair head to her shoulder, feels the shake of his body, the shudder of his breaths. 'You did well. Very well. None of this is your—'

He wrenches away from her, his face stricken and wet. 'Where *were* you?' he yells, fear becoming anger, his voice wavering, as it has begun to do, of late, deepening on the second word, then rising again for the third. 'I looked every-where!'

She gazes at him steadily, then back at Judith. 'I was out at Hewlands. Bartholomew sent for me because the bees were swarming. I was longer than I'd planned. I'm sorry,' she says. 'I'm sorry I wasn't here.' She reaches out again for him, but he ducks away from her hand and moves towards the bed.

Together, they kneel next to the girl. Agnes takes her hand.

'She's got . . . it,' Hamnet says, in a hoarse whisper. 'Hasn't she?'

Agnes doesn't look at him. His is a mind so quick, so

attuned to others that she knows he can read her thoughts, like words written on a page. So she must keep them to herself, her head bowed. She is checking each fingertip for a change in colour, for a creeping tide of grey or black. Nothing. Each finger is rosy pink, each nail pale, with an emerging crescent moon. Agnes examines the feet, each toe, the round and vulnerable bones of the ankle.

'She's got . . . the pestilence,' Hamnet whispers. 'Hasn't she? Mamma? Hasn't she? That's what you think, isn't it?'

She is gripping Judith's wrist; the pulse is fluttering, inconstant, surging up and down, fading then galloping. Agnes's eye falls on the swelling at Judith's neck. The size of a hen's egg, newly laid. She reaches out and touches it gently, with the tip of her finger. It feels damp and watery, like marshy ground. She loosens the tie of Judith's shift and eases it down. There are other eggs, forming in her armpits, some small, some large and hideous, bulbous, straining at the skin.

She has seen these before; there are few in the town, or even the county, who haven't at some time or other in their lives. They are what people most dread, what everyone hopes they will never find, on their own bodies or on those of the people they love. They occupy such a potent place in everyone's fears that she cannot quite believe she is actually seeing them, that they are not some figment or spectre summoned by her imagination.

And yet here they are. Round swellings, pushing up from under her daughter's skin.

Agnes seems to split in two. Part of her gasps at the sight of the buboes. The other part hears the gasp, observes it, notes it: a gasp, very well. Tears spring into the eyes of the first

Agnes, and her heart gives a great thud in her chest, an animal hurling itself against its cage of bones. The other Agnes is ticking off the signs: buboes, fever, deep sleep. The first Agnes is kissing her daughter, on the forehead, on the cheeks, at the place where hair meets skin on her temple; the other is thinking, a poultice of crumbed bread and roasted onion and boiled milk and mutton fat, a cordial of hips and powdered rue, borage and woodbine.

She stands, she moves through the room and down the stairs. There is something strangely familiar, almost recognisable, about her movements. What she has always dreaded is here. It has come. The moment she has feared most, the event she has thought about, mulled over, turned this way and that, rehearsed and re-rehearsed in her mind, during the dark of sleepless nights, at moments of idleness, when she is alone. The pestilence has reached her house. It has made its mark around her child's neck.

She hears herself telling Hamnet to find his grandmother, his sister, yes, they are back, they are in the cookhouse, go and bid them come, go now, yes, directly. And then she is in front of her shelves and her hands are reaching out to find the stoppered pots. There is rue and there is cinnamon, and that is good for drawing out the heat, and here is bindweed root and thyme.

She drops her gaze to her shelves. Rhubarb? She holds the dried stalk in her hand for a moment. Yes, rhubarb, to purge the stomach, to drive out the pestilence.

At the word, she is aware of letting out a small noise, like the whimper of a dog. She leans her head into the plaster of the wall. She thinks: My daughter. She thinks: Those swellings.

She thinks: This cannot be, I will not have it, I will not permit it.

She seizes her pestle and brings it down with a thump into the mortar, scattering powders and leaves and roots over the table.

Hamnet is out, down the path, into the backyard and at the door of the cookhouse, where his grandmother is fossicking in a barrel of onions and the maid is standing beside her, apron held out, ready to receive whatever Mary will see fit to toss into it. The fire blasts and cracks in the grate, its flames reaching up to bait and caress the undersides of several pots. Susanna is standing by the butter churn, one listless hand curled around the handle.

She is the first to see him. Hamnet looks at her; she looks back, her mouth slightly open at the sight of him. She frowns, as if she might speak, might remonstrate with him about something. Then she turns her head towards her grand- mother, who is instructing the maid to peel the onions and chop them small. The heat in the room is unbearable to Hamnet – he can feel it, breathing at him, like fumes from the gates of Hell. It almost blocks the doorway, filling the space, pressing its fierce mass against the walls. He doesn't know how the women stand it. He passes a hand over his brow and its outer edges seem to shimmer and he sees, or seems to see, just for a moment, a thousand candles in the dark, their flames guttering and flaring, wisp lights, goblin candles. He blinks and they are gone; the scene before him is as before. His grandmother, the maid, the onions, his sister, the butter churn, the headless pheasant on the table, scaled legs fastidiously drawn up, as if the bird is worried about getting its feet muddy, even though it happens to be decapitated and very much dead.

'Grandmamma?' Susanna says uncertainly, still with her eyes on her brother. Later, this moment will return to Susanna, again and again, particularly in the early morning, when she wakes. Her brother, standing there, framed by the doorway. She will remember thinking that he looked white-faced, shocked, quite unlike himself, a cut under his eyebrow. Would it have made a difference if she had remarked upon this to her grandmother? If she had drawn the attention of her mother or grandmother to it? Would it have changed anything? She will never know because all she says at the time is: 'Grandmamma?'

Mary is in the middle of saying to the maid, 'And mind you don't burn them this time, not even a little at the edges – as soon as they begin to catch, you lift the pot off the fire, do you hear?' She turns, first towards her granddaughter, and then, following Susanna's gaze, towards the doorway and Hamnet.

She jumps, her hand travelling to her heart. 'Oh,' she says. 'You frightened me! Whatever are you doing, boy? You look like a ghost, standing there like that.'

Mary will tell herself, in the days and weeks to come, that she never said these words. She couldn't have done. She would never have said 'ghost' to him, would never have told him that there was anything frightening, anything amiss about his appearance. He had looked entirely well. She never said such a thing.

With trembling hands, Agnes is sweeping the scattered petals and roots back into the mortar and begins to grind, her wrist twisting, twisting, her knuckles whitening, her finger-nails gripping the wooden pestle. The dried rhubarb stalk, the rue, the cinnamon are mashed together, their scents mingling, the sweet, the sharp and the bitter.

As she grinds, she counts off to herself the people this mixture has saved. There was the wife of the miller, who had been raving and tearing at her clothes. The very next day, after drinking two draughts of this potion, she was sitting up in bed, quiet as a lamb, supping soup. There was the nephew of the landowner at Snitterfield: Agnes had been taken there in the middle of the night, after the landowner had sent for her. The lad had re-covered well with this medicine and a poultice. The blacksmith from Copton, the spinster from Bishopton. They had all recov-ered, hadn't they? It is not an impossibility.

She is concentrating so hard that she jumps when someone touches her elbow. The pestle falls from her fingers to the table. Her mother-in-law, Mary, is next to her, her cheeks red from the cookhouse, her sleeves rolled back, a frown pinching together her brow.

'Is it true?' she says.

Agnes takes a breath, her tongue registering the dusky tang of cinnamon, the acid of the powdered rhubarb and, realising she might cry if she speaks, she nods.

'She has buboes? A fever? It's true?'

Agnes nods again, once. Mary's face is clenched, her eyes blazing. You might think she was angry, but Agnes knows better. The two women look at one another and Agnes sees that Mary is thinking of her daughter, Anne, who died of the pestilence, aged eight, covered with swellings and hot with fever, her fingers black and odorous and rotting off her hands.

She knows this because Eliza told her once but, then, she knew it anyway. Agnes doesn't turn her head, doesn't break her gaze with Mary, but she knows that little Anne will be there in the room with them, over by the door, her winding sheet caught over her shoulder, her hair unravelled, her fingers sore and useless, her neck swollen and choking. Agnes makes herself form the thought, Anne, we know you are there, you are not forgotten. How frail, to Agnes, is the veil between their world and hers. For her, the worlds are indistinct from each other, rubbing up against each other, allowing passage between them. She will not let Judith cross over.

Mary mutters a string of words under her breath, a prayer, of sorts, an entreaty, then pulls Agnes to her. Her touch is almost rough, her fingers gripping Agnes's elbow, her forearm pressing down hard on Agnes's shoulder. Agnes's face is pressed to Mary's coif; she smells the soap in it, soap she herself made – with ashes and tallow and the narrow buds of lavender – she hears the rasp of hair against cloth, underneath. Before she shuts her eyes, submitting herself to the embrace, she sees Susanna and Hamnet step in through the back door.

Then Mary has released her and is turning, the moment between them over, done. She is all business now, brushing down her apron, inspecting the contents of the mortar, going to the fireplace, saying she will build it up, telling Hamnet to bring wood, quickly, boy, we shall build a great blaze for there is nothing so efficacious to the driving out of fever as a hot fire. She is clearing a space before the hearth and Agnes knows that Mary will bring down the rush mattress; she will bring clean blankets, she will make up a bed there, by the fire, and Judith will be brought down before the blaze.

Whatever differences Agnes and Mary have – and there are many, of course, living at such close quarters, with so much to do, so many children, so many mouths, the meals to cook and the clothes to wash and mend, the men to watch and assess, soothe and guide – dissolve in the face of tasks. The two of them can gripe and prickle and rub each other up the wrong way; they can argue and bicker and sigh; they can throw into the pig-pen food the other has cooked because it is too salted or not milled finely enough or too spiced; they can raise an eyebrow at each other's darning or stitching or embroidery. In a time such as this, however, they can operate like two hands of the same person.

Look. Agnes is pouring water into a pan and sprinkling the powder into it. Mary is working the bellows, taking the wood from Hamnet, instructing Susanna to go to the coffer next door and bring out sheets. She is lighting the candles now, the flames flaring and lengthening, spreading circles of light into the dark corners of the room. Agnes is handing the pan to Mary, who is setting it to warm over the flames. They are both climbing the stairs now, without conferring, and Agnes knows that Mary will greet Judith with a smiling face, will call out some rousing and unconcerned words. Together, they will see to the girl, lift down the pallet, give her the medicine. They will take this matter in hand.

t is past midnight on Agnes's wedding night; it might even be near dawn. It is cold enough for her breath to be visible with every exhalation, for it to collect in droplets on the blanket she has wrapped about her.

Henley Street, when she looks through the windows, is drenched in the darkest black. No one is abroad. An owl can be heard intermittently, from somewhere behind the house, sending its shivering cry out into the night.

Some, Agnes reflects, as she stands at the window, blanket clutched around her, might take this as a bad omen, the owl's cry being a sign of death. But Agnes isn't afraid of the creatures. She likes them, likes their eyes, which resemble the centre of marigolds, their overlapped, flecked feathers, their inscrutable expressions. They seem, to her, to exist in some doubled state, half spirit, half bird.

Agnes has risen from her marriage bed and is walking about the rooms of her new house. Because sleep won't seem to come for her and fold her in its plumes. Because the thoughts in her head are too many, too crowded, jostling for space. Because there is too much to take in, too much of the day to go over. Because this is the first time she has ever been expected to sleep either in a bed or on an upstairs floor.

And so she is drifting through the apartment, touching things as she goes: the back of a chair, an empty shelf, the fire irons, the door handle, the stair rail. She moves to the front of the house, to the back, and again to the front; she goes down the stairs, she comes up again. She runs a hand down the curtains surrounding the bed, given to them as a wedding gift by his parents. She pulls aside the curtain and contemplates the form of the man within, her husband, ocean-deep in sleep, sprawled in the middle of the bed, arms outstretched, as if drifting on a current. She looks up at the ceiling, beyond which is a small, slope-roofed attic.

This apartment, now her home, has been built on to the side of the family's house. It has two storeys: downstairs there is the fireplace and the settle, the table and the plate, up here the bed. John had been using it for storage – for what exactly has never been mentioned but Agnes, sniffing the air, the first time they came in here, caught the unmistakable scent of fleece, of baled wool, rolled up and left for several years. Whatever it was it has been removed and taken elsewhere.

Agnes has a strong sense that this arrangement has something to do with her brother, and was perhaps part of his terms for the marriage. Bartholomew had been there when they first came over the threshold. He had looked over the narrow rooms, going up the stairs and coming back down, walking from wall to wall, before nodding at John, who had remained standing at the door.

Bartholomew had had to nod at him twice before John turned over the key to his son. It had been an odd moment, interesting to Agnes. She had watched as father slowly, slowly, held out the key to son. The father's reluctance to relinquish it was matched – perhaps outdone – by the son's unwillingness to accept it. His fingers had been listless, slack; he hesitated, examining the iron key in his father's hand, as if unsure what it was. Then he plucked it from him with only finger and thumb, and held it, at arm's length, as if deciding whether or not it might harm him.

John had attempted to smooth over the awkwardness, making a remark about hearths and happiness and wives, reaching forward to slap the son on the back. It was a gesture intended to be kind, in a gruff, fatherly sort of way, but was there not, Agnes would think later, something uneasy about it? Something unnatural? The slap had had a little too much force, a little too much intent. The son wasn't expecting it and it made him stagger sideways, lose his balance. He had righted himself, quickly, almost too quickly, like a boxer or a fencer, raising himself on his toes. They looked for a moment, the pair of them, as if they might begin to exchange blows, not keys.

She and Bartholomew had observed this from either end of the room. When the son turned away and instead of putting the key into the purse at his waist, placed it on the tabletop, with a dull, metallic click, she and Bartholomew had looked at each other. Her brother's face was expressionless, except for a minor inflection of one eyebrow. To Agnes, this spoke a great deal. You see now, she knew her brother was saying, what you are marrying into? You see now, that eyebrow movement meant, why I insisted upon a separate dwelling?

Agnes leans towards the glass panes, allowing her breath to collect upon them. They remind her, these rooms, of the initial letter of her name, a letter her father taught her to recognise, scratching it into the mud with a sharpened stick: 'A'. (She can recall this so clearly, sitting with both her parents on the ground between her mother's shins, her head leaning against the muscle of her knee; she could reach down and grip her mother's feet. She can summon the sensation of the fall of her mother's hair on her shoulder as she leant forward to see the movements of Agnes's father's stick, saying, 'Here, Agnes, look.' The letter manifesting itself from under the blackened point, hardened to charcoal in the kitchen fire: 'A'. Her letter, always hers.)

The apartment is formed like the letter, sloping together at the top, with a floor across its middle. Agnes takes this as her sign – the letter etched in the dirt, the memory of her mother's strong feet, the brush of her hair – not the owl, not the long, pained looks of her mother-in-law, not the youth of her husband, not the narrow feel of this house, its atmosphere of emptiness and inertia, that hard back slap of her father-in-law, none of this.

She is untying a cloth bundle and laying out items on the floor when a voice from the bed makes her start.

'Where are you?' His voice, deep anyway, is made deeper still by sleep, by the muffled layer of curtain.

'Here,' she says, still crouched on the floor, holding a purse, a book, her crown – wilting now and dishevelled, but she will tie it up and dry the flowers and none will be lost.

'Come back.'

She stands and, still holding her possessions, moves towards the bed, pushes aside the curtains and looks down at him. 'You're awake,' she says.

'And you're very far away,' he says, squinting up at her. 'What are you doing all the way over there when you should be here?' He points at the space next to him.

'I can't sleep.'

'Why not?'

'The house is an A.'

There is a pause and she wonders if he heard her. 'Hmm?' he says, raising himself on one elbow.

'An A,' she repeats, shuffling everything she is holding into one hand so that she can inscribe the letter in the chill winter air between them. 'That is an A, is it not?'

He nods at her gravely. 'It is. But what has it to do with the house?'

She cannot believe he can't see it as she does. 'The house slopes together at the top and has a floor across its middle. I do not know that I shall ever be able to sleep up here.'

'Up where?' he asks.

'Here.' She gestures around them. 'In this room.'

'Why ever not?'

'Because the floor is floating in mid-air, like the cross stroke of the A. There is no ground underneath it. Just empty space and more empty space.'

His face breaks into a smile, his eyes examining her intently, and he flops back to the bed. 'Do you know,' he says, addressing the covering above him, 'that this is the foremost reason I love you?'

'That I cannot sleep in the air?'

'No. That you see the world as no one else does.' He holds out his arms. 'Come back to bed. Enough of this. I put it to you that we shall have no need of sleep for a while.'

'Is that so?'

'Yes, it is.'

He gets to his feet, lifts her and places her carefully in the bed. 'I shall have my Agnes,' he says, climbing in beside her, 'in our A. And I shall have her again and again and again.'

He is kissing her for emphasis, with each word and she is laughing and her hair is spilling all over them, between them, catching in his lips, his beard, his fingers.

'There shall not be much sleeping in this bed,' he is saying, 'not for a while.' And: 'Why in God's name are you holding all these things? What are they for? I don't think we need any of them at this moment.'

He is taking all the things, one by one – her gloves, her crown, her purse – out of her hands and placing them on the floor. He removes the Bible from her hand and then another book, but before he puts it down, he pauses, looking at it.

'What is this?' he asks, turning it over.

'I was left it by a neighbour when she died,' Agnes says, touching her fingertip to the frontispiece. 'She used to do spinning for us and I would take the wool to her, then collect it when she was done. She was always kind to me and wrote in her will that I was to have it. It had belonged to her husband, who had been an apothecary. I used to help her with her garden when I was a child. She told me once . . .' and here she pauses '. . . that she and my mother used to consult it together.'

He has taken his arm from around her and is holding the book in both hands, parting the pages. 'And you've had it since you were young?' he is saying, his eyes raking the closely printed words. 'It's in Latin,' he says, frowning. 'It's about plants. Their uses. How to recognise them. How they heal certain illnesses and distempers.'

Agnes looks over his shoulder. She sees the picture of a plant with tear-shaped petals and a long, dark tangle of roots, an illustration of a bough with heavy berries. 'I know that,' she says. 'I have looked through it often enough, although I cannot read it, of course. Will you read it to me?' she asks.

He seems to recall himself. He puts down the book; he looks her over. 'I will indeed,' he says, his fingers working at the ties on her shift. 'But not now.'

It seems strange to Agnes, during this time, that she has, in the space of a month, exchanged country for town, a farm for an apartment, a stepmother for a mother-in-law, one family for another.

One house, she is learning, runs very differently from another. Instead of the sprawl of generations, all working together to look after animals and land, the house in Henley Street has a distinct structure: there are the parents, then the sons, then the daughter, then the pigs in the pig-pen and the hens in the henhouse, then the apprentice and then, right at the bottom, the serving maids. Agnes believes her position, as new daughter-in-law, to be ambiguous, somewhere between apprentice and hen.

Agnes watches people come and people go. She is a gatherer, during this time, of information, of confidences, of the daily routines, of personalities and interactions. She is like a painting on the wall, eyes missing nothing. She has her own house, the small, narrow apartment, but she can go out of her back door and there is the communal yard: she and her husband will share the kitchen garden, the cookhouse, the piggery, the hens, the washhouse, the brewhouse. So she can withdraw into her own place but also mix and mingle with the others. She is at once observer and participant.

The maids rise early, as early as Agnes does: town people lie in their beds much longer than those of the country, and Agnes is accustomed to beginning the day before sunrise. These girls bring in the firewood, light the fires in the hall and the cookhouse. They let out the hens and scatter seed and grain for them in the yard. They take the slops to the pig-pen. They bring ale from the brewhouse. They take the dough, proved overnight in the cookhouse jar, and beat it into shape, leaving it beside the warming oven. It's a good hour or so before any of the family emerges from their chamber.

Here, in town, there are no fences to mend; there is no mud to clean off boots. Clothes do not acquire streaks of soil, hair, dung. No men return at midday, ravenous of appetite and cold of bone. There are no lambs to warm by the hearth, no beasts with colic or worm or foot-rot. There are no animals to feed, early in the morning, and no kestrel either: her bird has gone to live with the priest who conducted the wedding. Agnes can visit whenever she likes, he says. No sheep trying to escape through fences. No ravens or pigeons or woodcocks landing on the thatch and calling down the chimney.

Instead, there are carts going up and down outside all day, people shouting to each other in the street, crowds and groups passing by. There are deliveries, to be made and to receive. There is a storehouse at the back for the glove workshop, where the empty skins of forest creatures are stretched out like penitents on racks. There are the serving maids who skulk in and out of the hall, shoes flapping and slapping on the flags. They look Agnes up and down, as if assessing her worth and finding her lacking. They sigh, ever so slightly, if she happens to be standing in their way, but if Mary appears, they stand upright, straighten their caps and say, Yes, mistress, no, mistress, I do not know, mistress.

In the country, people are too taken up with their livestock and crops to make calls but in this house people come at all hours of the day, expecting to find company: Mary's relatives, John's business associates. The former are to be brought to the parlour; the latter are to be shown first into the workshop, where John will decide to which room they will be taken. Mary is mostly in the house, keeping her eye on the servants and the apprentice or sitting at her needlework, unless out on calls. John is often nowhere to be seen. The younger boys are at school. Agnes's husband is sometimes in, sometimes out: he teaches, he goes out to taverns in the evenings, he is sometimes sent on errands for his father. The remainder of the time, he skulks upstairs in their apartment, reading or staring out of the window.

Customers come at all hours to the workshop window, to peruse the gloves, to ask questions; sometimes John lets them in and they can look around the whole workshop and perhaps order a special pair to be made.

Agnes watches it all for three or four days. On the fifth day, she is up before the serving girls and out of the apartment's back door, which leads into the shared yard. By the time they appear, she has fired the oven in the cookhouse and coaxed the dough into rounds, adding a handful of ground herbs from the kitchen garden. The serving girls exchange worried looks.

At the breakfast table, the family seize the bread rolls, which seem softer, flatter, with a burnished glaze. The butter is arranged in a swirl. When broken, the bread gives off the hot fragrance of thyme, of marjoram. It brings, to the mind of John, a recollection of his grandmother, a woman who kept a posy of herbs tied to her belt. It makes Mary think of the squared, walled kitchen garden at the door of the farm where she grew up, of the time her mother had had to shoo away the geese with a broom because they had broken in and eaten the thyme bushes. She smiles at the recollection, at the memory of her mother's skirts, wet with dew and mud, at the offended honking of the geese, and takes another slice, dipping the knife into the butter.

Agnes glances at the face of her father-in-law and that of her mother-in-law and then her husband. He catches her eye and gives a barely perceptible nod towards the bread, raising his eyebrows.

It takes Mary a week or so to notice that the house is different. The candlewicks are trimmed, without Mary having to remind the maids. The table linens are changed, again without asking, the wall drapes free of dust. The plateware is spotless and shining. She sees these things individually, without adding them up. It's only when she smells the distinct, pollen-heavy scent of beeswax in the parlour one day when she is entertaining a neighbour that she begins to wonder.

After the neighbour has taken her leave, she walks through her house. There are holly branches in a jar in the hall. Cloves studded into sweetmeats in the cookhouse, a pot of fragrant leaves that Mary doesn't recognise. There are gnarled and soil-heavy roots drying in the eaves of the brewhouse, and berries in a tray. A pile of starched and pressed collars lies waiting on the landing. The pigs in their pen look suspiciously scrubbed and pink, the hens' trough is clean and filled with water.

At the sound of voices, Mary goes along the path towards the washhouse.

'Yes, like that,' she hears Agnes's low voice say, 'as if you were rubbing salt between your palms. Gently. Just the smallest movement. That way the flowerheads will be preserved.'

There is another voice – inaudible to Mary – and then a burst of laughter.

She pushes at the door: Agnes, Eliza and the two maids are all crammed into the washhouse, aprons tied around them, the air hot and filled with the acrid, stinging smell of lye. Edmond has been placed in a tub on the floor, with a number of pebbles.

'Ma,' he exclaims at the sight of her, 'Ma-ma-ma!'

'Oh,' says Eliza, turning, her face flushed with heat and laughter, 'we were . . . well, we were . . .' She dissolves into laughter again, brushing a hair from her face with her forearm. 'Agnes was showing us how to mix lavender into the soap and then she . . . then we . . .' Eliza begins to laugh again, setting off one of the maids into giggles most inappropriate for her station.

'You're making soap?' Mary asks.

Agnes glides forward. She is poised, unruffled, not at all flushed. She looks as if she has just raised herself from a parlour chair, not melted and stirred a batch of soap in a sweltering, moist washhouse. The front of her apron is dented outwards with the swell of her stomach. Mary looks, and looks away. Not for the first time, it strikes her that she will never feel that again, that it is an experience now closed to her, at her age, at her stage in life. The loss of that possibility sears her sometimes: it is hard for a woman to let go of; harder still if another woman in your household is just entering that state. The sight of this girl's stomach, every time, makes Mary think of the emptiness, the quiet of her own.

'We are,' Agnes says, revealing her small, sharpish teeth as she smiles. 'With lavender. I thought it might be a nice change. I hope that's agreeable to you?'

'Of course,' Mary snaps. She bends down and snatches Edmond out of the tub. He is so startled that he starts to sob. 'Agreeable indeed,' she says, and goes out, clutching her inconsolable son, letting the door slam behind her.

In the early weeks of her marriage, Agnes collects impressions as a wool-gatherer hoards wool: a tuft from here, a scrap from there, a few strands from a fence, a bit from a branch, until, until, until you have a whole armful, enough to spin into yarn.

She sees that John loves Gilbert the best of the boys – because he is strong and likes to set people against each other for sport – but that Mary favours Richard. Her head jerks up if he speaks; she shushes the others in order to hear him. Agnes sees that Mary harbours a deep love for Edmond but is resigned to the fact that most of his care falls to Eliza. Agnes sees that Edmond watches her husband, his eldest brother, all the time. His eyes follow him wherever he goes in the room; he reaches up for him when he passes. Edmond will, Agnes sees, grow up sanguine and happy; he will follow his eldest brother, inevitably, unasked, largely unnoticed. He won't live long but will live well: women will like him; he will father numerous children during his short life. The last person he will think of, just before he dies, will be Eliza. Agnes's husband will pay for his funeral and will weep at his graveside. Agnes sees this but doesn't say it.

She sees, too, that all six children flinch if John gets suddenly to his feet, like animals sensing the approach of a predator. She sees Mary blink slowly, as if closing her eyes to what might occur.

There is a dinner when Edmond is tired, fractious, hungry but somehow unable to eat, unable to see the connection between the food on the plate and the nameless discomfort in his belly. He grizzles and moans, thrashing his head from side to side. Agnes sits beside him, slipping morsels into his mouth. His gums are red and sore, the peaks of new teeth poking through, his cheeks livid and hot. He fusses, he squeezes pie between his fingers, he tips over his cup, he leans on Agnes's shoulder, he grabs at her napkin and drops it to the floor. Agnes's husband, on the other side of her, puts on a mock-rueful face and asks, Not happy today, eh? Their father, however, looks blacker and blacker, muttering, What ails the child, can't you take him away? When Edmond, losing patience with the meal, hurls a piecrust across the table, hitting John on the sleeve, leaving a brown stain, there is a long, stretched moment of silence. Mary bows her head, as if interested by something in her lap, Eliza's eyes begin to fill with tears, and John lurches from his stool, yelling, By God, that boy, I will—

Agnes's husband springs to his feet and is around the table before Agnes realises what is happening. He is putting himself between his father and the boy, who is wailing now, mouth wide, as if sensing the change in atmosphere. There is a scuffle, her husband holding back his father, some oaths, a shove of chest against chest, a restraining hand on an arm. Agnes can't quite see because she is lifting the child away from the table, easing his feet out of the bench, holding him to her as she runs with him from the room.

After a while, her husband comes and finds her. She has Edmond in the yard, her shawl wrapped twice around his short frame, and he is restored to good humour, feeding grain to the chickens. She holds the grain bowl for him, saying just a little, just enough, the hens dart-darting at the ground. Her husband comes to stand next to her, watching. Then he leans his head against hers, sliding his arms about her. She thinks, as she holds the grain, of that landscape of caverns and hollows she sensed within him. She thinks of the seams of a glove, running up and down and over each finger, keeping close the skin that does not belong to the wearer. How a glove covers and fits and restrains the hand. She thinks of the skins in the storeroom, pulled and stretched almost – but not quite – to tearing or breaking point. She thinks of the tools in the work-shop, for cutting and shaping, pinning and piercing. She thinks of what must be discarded and stolen from the animal in order to make it useful to a glove-maker: the heart, the bones, the soul, the spirit, the blood, the viscera. A glover will only ever want the skin, the surface, the outer layer. Everything else is useless, an inconvenience, an unnecessary mess. She thinks of the private cruelty behind something as beautiful and perfect as a glove. She thinks that if she took his hand now and pressed her fingers to it, she might see the landscape she found before but she would also see a dark and looming presence there, with tools to eviscerate and flay and thieve the essence of a creature. She thinks, as Edmond scatters food for the hens, that they will perhaps not live long in this apartment: soon it will be necessary for them to leave, to take flight, to find a different place.

Eliza comes out into the yard, signalling that the dinner is at an end. Her face is set, her eyes damp. She picks up Edmond and takes him back into the house. Agnes and her husband look at each other, then walk towards the back door of their apartment.

It is evident to Agnes now, as they enter the kitchen, as he stirs the fire and throws on a log, that her husband is split in two. He is one man in their house and quite another in that of his parents. In the apartment, he is the person she knows and recognises, the one she married.

Take him next door, to the big house, and he is sullen, sallow of face, irritable, tetchy. He is all tinder and flint, sending out sparks to ignite and kindle. Why? he challenges his mother. Whatever for? he snaps. I don't want to, he retorts to his father. She had never understood why this was so but the coiled fury she witnessed in John, as he raised himself from his stool, told her everything she needs to know.

In their apartment, he lets her take his hand, lets her lead him from the fire to a chair, lets his eyes lose focus, lets her rub her fingers through his hair, and she can feel him switch from one character to another; she can sense that other, big-house, self melt off him, like wax sliding from a lit candle, revealing the man within.

Three heavy knocks to the door of the apartment: boom, boom, boom.

Hamnet is closest so he goes to answer it. As it swings open, he cringes and yelps: on the doorstep is a terrifying sight, a creature from a nightmare, from Hell, from the devil. It is tall, cloaked in black, and in the place of a face is a hideous, featureless mask, pointed like the beak of a gigantic bird.

'No,' Hamnet cries, 'get away.' He tries to shut the door but the creature puts out a hand and presses it back, with horrible, preternatural strength. 'Get away,' Hamnet screams again, kicking out.

Then his grandmother is there, pushing him aside, apologising to the spectre, as if there is nothing out of the ordinary about it, inviting it to step into the house, to examine the patient.

The spectre is speaking without a mouth, saying he will not come in, he cannot, and they, the inhabitants, are hereby ordered not to go out, not to take to the streets, but to remain indoors until the pestilence is past.

Hamnet takes a step backwards and another. He collides with his mother, who is going to the window and opening her hatch to the street. She leans out to examine this person.

Hamnet darts to her side and, for the first time in years, takes her hand. His mother squeezes his fingers, without looking at him. 'Don't be afraid,' she whispers. 'It is only the physician.'

'The . . .?' Hamnet stares at him, still there on the doorstep, talking with his grandmother. 'But why is he . . .?' Hamnet gestures to his face, his nose.

'He wears that mask because he thinks it will protect him,' she says.

'From the pestilence?'

His mother nods.

'And will it?'

His mother purses her lips, then shakes her head. 'I don't think so. Not coming into the house, however, refusing to see or examine the patient, might,' she mutters.

Hamnet places his other hand inside the strong, long fingers of his mother, as if her touch might keep him safe. He sees the physician reach into a bag and hand his grandmother a wrapped parcel.

'Tie it to the stomach of the girl with linen,' he is intoning, accepting some coins from Mary in his pale hand, 'and leave it there for three days. Then you may take an onion and soak it in—'

'What is that?' his mother interrupts, leaning out of her hatch.

The physician turns to look at her, his horrible pointed beak swinging towards them. Hamnet shrinks into her side. He doesn't want this man to look at him; he doesn't want to fall into his sights. He is seized with the notion that to be seen by his eye, to be noted or recorded by him would be a terrible omen, that some dreadful fate will befall them all. He wants to run, to drag his mother away, to seal shut the doors and windows so that the man will not get in, so that his gaze will not fall on any of them.

But his mother is not in the least frightened. The physician and Hamnet's mother regard each other for a moment, through the hatch, from which his mother sells cures. Hamnet realises, he sees, with the cutting clarity of a child poised to enter manhood, that this man doesn't like his mother. He resents her: she sells cures, she grows her own medicines, she collects leaves and petals, bark and juices and knows how to help people. This man, Hamnet suddenly sees, wishes his mother ill. She takes his patients, trespasses on his revenue, his work. How baffling the adult world seems to Hamnet at that moment, how complex, how slippery. How can he ever navigate his way in it? How will he manage?

The physician inclines his beak, once, then turns back to Hamnet's grandmother, as if his mother hadn't spoken.

'Is it a dried toad?' Agnes says, in a clear, carrying voice. 'Because if it is, we don't want it.'

Hamnet fastens his arms around his mother's waist; he wishes to communicate to her the urgency, the necessity of ending this conversation, of getting away from this person. She doesn't move but brings a hand down to his wrist, as if to say, I acknowledge you, I am here.

'Madam,' the physician says, and again his beak swings towards them, 'you may trust that I know much more about these matters than you do. A dried toad, applied to the abdomen for several days, has proven to have great efficacy in cases such as these. If your daughter is suffering from the pestilence, I regret to say that there is very little that may—'

The rest of the speech is cut off, curtailed, lost because Agnes has banged the hatch shut. Hamnet watches as her fingers fumble to lock it. Her face is furious, desperate, flushed.

She is muttering something under her breath: he catches the word 'man', and 'dare' and 'fool'.

He unfastens his arms and watches as she walks across the room, agitatedly straightening a chair, picking up and putting down a bowl, then coming to crouch by the pallet where Judith has been placed, next to the fire.

'A toad, indeed,' his mother is murmuring, as she dabs Judith's brow with a wet cloth.

Across the room, his grandmother closes the front door and slides the bolt into place. Hamnet sees her place the parcel with the dried toad on a high shelf.

She mouths something incomprehensible to Hamnet, with a nod.

n a morning in the spring of 1583, if they had risen early enough, the residents of Henley Street would have seen the new daughter-in-law of John and Mary exit the door of the little narrow cottage where the newlywed couple live. They would have seen her shoulder a basket, straighten her kirtle, and set off in a north-westerly direction.

Upstairs, her young husband turns over in bed. He sleeps deeply, and always has. He does not notice that her side of the bed is vacant and rapidly cooling. His head presses further into the pillow, an arm is tucked about the coverlet, his hair fallen over most of his face. He is in the profound, untroubled slumber of the young; if undisturbed, he could sleep on for hours. His mouth opens slightly, drawing in air, and he begins, softly, to snore.

Agnes continues on her way across Rother Market, where stallholders are beginning to arrive. A man selling bundles of lavender; a woman with a cart of willow strips. Agnes pauses to speak to her friend, the baker's wife. They exchange words about the fairness of the day, the threat of rain, the heat of the ovens in the bakery, the progress of Agnes's pregnancy and how low the baby feels in her bones. The baker's wife tries to press a bun into Agnes's hand. Agnes refuses. The baker's wife insists, lifting the covering on Agnes's basket and pushing it inside. She catches sight of cloths, clean and neatly folded, a pair of scissors, a stoppered jar, but thinks nothing of it. Agnes nods to her, smiles, says she needs to go.

The baker's wife stands for a moment before her empty

market stall, watching her friend walk away. Agnes pauses momentarily, at the edge of the market, putting one hand up to the wall. The baker's wife frowns and is just about to call out, but Agnes straightens and continues on her way.

During the night, Agnes dreamt of her mother, as she does from time to time. Agnes had been standing in the farmyard at Hewlands and her skirts had been dragging in the dirt; there was a heavy feeling around her, as if her gown was waterlogged. When she looked down, there were birds standing and trampling on the hem of her dress: ducks, hens, partridges, doves, tiny wrens. They were struggling and pushing each other, wings unfolded and awkward, trying to remain standing on her skirts. Agnes was trying to shoo them away, trying to free herself, when she became aware of someone approaching. She turned and saw her mother passing by: her hair in a braid down her back, a red shawl knotted over a blue smock. Her mother smiled but didn't pause, her hips swaying as she walked past.

Agnes had felt an unravelling deep within her, a profound longing starting up, like the whir of a wheel. 'Mother,' she said, 'wait, wait for me.' She tried to step forward, to follow her mother, but the birds were still stepping on her skirt, their low-slung feathered bellies, their webbed and clawed feet trampling it down. 'Wait!' Agnes cried, in the dream, at her mother's receding back.

Her mother didn't stop but turned her head and said, or seemed to say: 'The branches of the forest are so dense you cannot feel the rain.' Then she continued to walk towards the forest.

Agnes called after her again, stumbling forward, tripping

over the massed bodies of the insistent, flapping birds, falling to the mud. Just as she hit the ground, she woke, with a start and a gasp, sitting up, and suddenly she was no longer at Hewlands, in the yard, calling to her mother. She was in her house, in bed, her shift slipping off her shoulder, the baby curled inside her skin, her husband next to her, reaching out in sleep to pincer her closer with his arm.

She had lain down, fitting herself into his form; he had nestled his face into her back. She had found a skein of his hair and smoothed it, twisting and twisting it between her fingers; she had pictured the thoughts in his head drawing upwards, along his hair, into her fingers, as a reed draws water up its hollow stem.

He was, she could sense, worrying about her, as men will when their wives approach childbirth. His mind circled and circled the thought, Will she survive? Will she come through? His limbs tightened about her, as if he wanted to keep her there, in the safety of their bed. She wished she could say to him, You must not fret. You and I are to have two children and they will live long lives. But she remained silent: people do not like to hear such things.

After a while she rose, parting the curtains around the bed, stepping out. She walked to the window, spread her hand to the glass. The branches are so dense, she thought. The branches. You cannot feel the rain.

She went to the small table by the fireplace, where her husband kept his papers and a quill. She lifted the lid of the ink pot and dipped the quill, its claw-like point holding the ink. She can write, after a fashion, the letters coming out small and cramped, and perhaps not in an order legible to most (unlike her husband, who has been to the grammar school, and oratory after that, and can produce a looping, continuous flow of letters, like a skein of embroidery, from the tip of his quill. He stays up late into the night, writing, at his desk. What, she does not know. He writes so fast and with such concentration that Agnes cannot keep up, cannot make it out). But she knows enough to be able to record an approximation of this sentence: The branches of the forest are so dense you cannot feel the rain.

Agnes has riddled the fire, thrown on logs to revive it, placed a jug of cream and a loaf of bread upon the table. She has taken up her basket and let herself out of the front door. She has spoken with her friend, the baker's wife, and now she is taking a path beside a stream, her basket straining her arm.

It is mid-May. Sunlight brightens the ground in glancing, shifting shapes; Agnes notices, despite everything, because she cannot not notice such things, what is flowering along the verges. Valerian, campion, dog rose, wood sorrel, wild garlic, river flags. Any other time, she would be on her hands and knees, plucking their heads and blooms. Not today.

Even though it is still early, she skirts the boundary fence of Hewlands. She doesn't want to risk meeting anyone along the way. Not Joan, not Bartholomew, not any of her brothers and sisters. If they saw her, they would raise the alarm, they would call someone, they would send for her husband, they would force her indoors, into the farmhouse. It is the very last place she would want to be for this. The branches of the forest, her mother had said to her.

She catches sight, in the distance, as she steps along the bridleway, of her brother Thomas, moving from house to yard, and she hears Bartholomew's piercing whistle to his dogs. There is the thatch of the hall; there the pig-pen; there the rear of the apple store, the sight of which makes her smile.

She enters the wood half a mile or so from Hewlands. By this time, the pains are coming regularly. She can just about catch her breath between them, ready herself, steady herself for the next. She has to wait by a huge elm, pressing her palm to its rough, ridged bark as the sensation begins in her lower back, deep between her legs, and surges upwards, seizing her in its grip, shaking her with its force.

Once she is able, she shoulders her burden and continues. She has reached the part of the forest she was aiming for. Fight through the dense tangle of branches and brambles and juniper bushes. Go over the stream, past a thicket of holly trees, which give the only colour in the winter months. And then there is a clearing, of sorts, where sunlight penetrates, creating a thick fleece of green grass, in circular patterns, the curved fronds of ferns. There is an almost horizontal tree here, an immense fir, felled like a giant in a story, its roots splayed out, its reddish trunk held up in the forked branches of other trees, supported by its lesser neighbours.

And underneath its end, where it once stood in the earth, is a hollow – dry, sheltered, big enough for several people. Agnes and Bartholomew used to come here when they were children, if Joan had been shouting or if she gave them too many tasks. They would bring a cloth sack of bread and cheese, crawling in under the tree roots and say to one another that they would stay there for ever, live in the forest like elves; they would never go back.

Agnes lowers herself to the ground. It is dry, in the lee of the uprooted tree, with a carpet of pine needles. She feels another pain coming, driving towards her, getting closer, like thunder over a landscape. She turns, she crouches, she pants through it, as she knows she must, holding tight to a tree root. Even in the throes of it, when it has her in its clutches, when it drives everything from her mind but the narrow focus of when it might end, she recognises that it is getting stronger. It means business, this pain. It will not leave her be. Soon it will not let her rest or gather herself. It means to force her out of herself, to turn what is inside outside.

She has seen women go through this. She remembers her mother's time: she saw it from the doorway; she heard it from outside the house, where she and Bartholomew were sent. She attended Joan at each of her labours, catching her brothers and sisters in her hands as they made their entry into the world, wiping the grease and blood from their mouths and noses. She has seen neighbouring women do it, has heard their cries rise into screams, smelt the rusty coin scent of new birth. She has seen the pig, the cow, the ewes birth their young; she has been the one called on by her father, by Bartholomew, when lambs were stuck. Her female fingers, slender, tapered, were required to enter that narrow, heated, slick canal, and hook out the soft hoofs, the gluey nose, the plastered-back ears. And she knows, in the way she always does, that she will reach the other side of birth, that she and this baby will live.

Nothing, however, could have prepared her for the relent-lessness of it. It is like trying to stand in a gale, like trying to swim against the current of a flooded river, like trying to lift a fallen tree. Never has she been more sensible of her weakness, of her inadequacy. She has always felt herself to be a strong person: she can push a cow into milking position, she can douse and stir a load of laundry, she can lift and carry her small siblings, a bale of skins, a bucket of water, an armful of firewood. Her body is one of resilience, of power: she is all muscle beneath smooth skin. But this is something else. Something other. It laughs at her attempts to master it, to subdue it, to rise above it. It will, Agnes fears, overtake her. It will seize her by the scruff of her neck and plunge her down, under the surface of the water.

She raises her head and sees, across the clearing, the silvery trunk and delicate leaves of a rowan tree. Despite everything, she smiles. She says the word to herself – rowan, rowan – pulling out the two syllables. Reddened berries in autumn, used for stomach pains, if boiled, and wheezing chests; if planted by the door of a house, it will repel evil spirits from the inhabitants. People say the first woman was made from its branches. It was her mother's name, although her father never let it past his lips; the shepherd had told her, when she'd asked him. The branches of the forest.

Agnes plants her hands in front of her, on all fours, like a wolf, and submits to another pain.

In Henley Street, he wakes. He spends a while staring up at the dark red curtain above him. Then he gets up, walks to the window and gazes down into the street, absently scratching at his beard. He has two Latin tutorials this afternoon, at houses in town; he is aware of the stifling boredom of them, as you might be of the stench of a nearby carcass. The drowsing boys, the squeal of slates, the flutter and crease of the primers, the intoning of verbs and conjunctions. This morning he is meant to be helping his father with deliveries and collections. He yawns, leans his head into the wood frame of the window, glares at a man yanking a donkey by its bridle, a woman pulling a wailing child by its jacket, a boy running in the opposite direction with a bundle of firewood under his arm.

Is it to be, he asks himself, that they remain here, in this town, for ever? Is he never to see any other place, never to live elsewhere? He wants nothing more than to take hold of Agnes and the baby and run with them, as far as they are able to go. When he married, he had thought that a larger, freer life might begin, the life of a man, and yet here he is, a mere wall separating him from his boyhood home, his family, his father, and the vagaries and flashes of his inconstant tempers. He knew, of course, that they had to wait for the baby, that nothing could be achieved until the safe arrival of their child. But now that time is near and he is no further on in his plan to leave. How can he ever get away? Are they to live like this, in a narrow appendage to his parents' house? Is there to be no escape for them? Agnes says that he must—

At the thought of Agnes, he straightens up. He looks at her side of the bed, where the straw still holds the indent, the shape of her. He calls her name. Nothing. He calls it again. Still nothing. His mind is traversed, for a moment, by an image of her body in its current astonishing shape, as he saw it last night: limbs, neat ribcage, the spine a long indent down the back, a cart-track through snow, and then this perfectly rounded sphere at the front. Like a woman who had swallowed the moon.

He lifts his clothes from the chair beside the window and shrugs himself into them. He makes his way across the room in his stockinged feet, shaking his hair out of his collar. Hunger growls in his stomach, low and menacing, like a dog crouched inside his body. Downstairs will be bread and milk, oats and eggs, if the hens have laid. He almost smiles to think this. As he passes his desk in the corner, it seems to him, from the corner of his eye, that something has altered about it. Something has changed. He pauses. The quill rests in the inkwell, point down, fronded feathers up. He frowns. This is something he never does: to leave a quill like that, overnight, in the damp dark of a well. What a waste, what profligacy. It will be quite spoilt.

He steps forward and lifts it out, giving it a gentle shake, so that the drops don't fall to the curled pages. He notices, then, that something has been added to what he had been writing the night before.

It is a string of letters, written in a slanted fashion; the words seem to slide down the page, as if they weigh more at the end of the sentence than at the beginning. He bends to look. There is no punctuation, no indication of the start or finish. He can make out the words 'branches' and 'rain' (written as 'rayne'); there is another word beginning with a capital B and another with an F or possibly an S.

The branches of the something are something something . . . rayne. He cannot follow it. His fingers hold flat the page. With his other hand, he scuffs the end of the quill against his cheek. The branches, the branches.

His wife has never done this before, taken up a quill and

written something at his desk. Is it a message for him? Is it important that he understand it? What does it mean?

He lays down the quill. He turns. He calls her name again, with a questioning lilt. He descends the narrow stairs.

She is not in the downstairs room or outside on the street. Could she have gone to the priest to fly her kestrel, as she does sometimes? But surely she wouldn't undertake to walk that far, so close to her confinement? He goes through the back door, into the yard, where he finds his mother standing over Eliza, who is dipping cloth in and out of red dye.

'Have you seen Agnes?'

'Not like that,' his mother is scolding. 'The way I showed you yesterday, with light fingers. Light, I said.' She raises her head to look at him. 'Agnes?' she repeats.

The baby is alive: Agnes doesn't realise, despite her intimations, how much she feared that this might not be until she sees it twist its head, scrunch up its features into a yell of outrage. Her daughter's face is wet, greyish, with an expression of dismay. She holds her fists up on either side of her head and lets out a cry – surprisingly loud and emphatic for so small a creature. Agnes turns her on to her side, as her father always did with lambs, and watches as the water – from that other place where she has been, these long months – leaks out of her mouth. Her lips become tinged with pink and then the colour spreads to her cheeks, her chin, her eyes, her forehead. She looks, suddenly and completely, human. No longer aquatic, a mer-child, as she did when she emerged, but a small person, very much herself, with her father's high forehead, his bottom lip, his swirl of hair at the crown of her head, and Agnes's sharp cheekbones and wide eyes.

She reaches out with her spare hand and brings the blanket and scissors out of the basket. She lays the baby on the blanket and works at the cord with the scissors. Who would ever think it could be so thick, so strong, still pulsing like a long, striped heart? The colours of birth assail Agnes: the red, the blue, the white.

She tugs on her shift, baring her breast, lifting the baby to it, watching in something close to awe as her daughter's mouth opens wide, as she clamps down and begins to suck. Agnes lets out a laugh. Everything works. The baby knows what to do, better than her.

In the house and, shortly afterwards, in the whole town, there follows an enormous hue and cry, a panic and a lament. Eliza is in tears; Mary is screeching, running up and down the stairs in the narrow apartment, as if Agnes has been hiding in a cupboard. I had it all ready for her, she keeps shouting, the birthing room, everything she needs, right here. John thunders in and out of the workshop, alternately roaring that he can't possibly work with all this racket, and then, where the devil has she got to?

Ned, the apprentice, is dispatched to Hewlands, to see if they have any news of her. No one can find Bartholomew, who went out early in the morning, but soon all the sisters and Joan, neighbours and villagers are out, searching for Agnes. Have you seen a woman, greatly with child, carrying a basket? The sisters have been up and down the lane, asking anyone they meet. But no one has seen her, save the wife of the baker, who said she went in the direction of the Shottery path. She wrung her hands, threw her apron over her head, saying, Why did I let her go, why, when I knew something wasn't right? Gilbert and Richard are sent out into the streets, to apprehend passers-by, to see if anyone has any news at all.

And the husband? He is the one to find Bartholomew.

When Bartholomew spies him on the path that runs along the outer edge of his land, he throws down the bale of straw he is holding and strides towards him. The lad – Bartholomew cannot think of him as anything other than a lad, soft-handed towns-boy that he is, hair all smoothed back, a ring through his ear – blanches to see him coming over the field. The dogs reach him first and they bound and bark around him.

'What?' Bartholomew demands, as he comes within earshot. 'Is she brought to bed? Is all well?'

'Eh,' the husband says, 'the situation, such as it is, if indeed one might call it that, is—'

Bartholomew's fingers seize the front of the husband's jerkin. 'Speak plainly,' he says. 'Now.'

'She's disappeared. We don't know where she is. Someone saw her, early this morning, heading in this direction. Have you seen her? Have you any clue as to where she—'

'You don't know where she is?' Bartholomew repeats. He stares at him for a long moment, his grip tightening on the jerkin, then speaks in a quiet, menacing voice: 'I thought I made myself very clear. I told you to look after her. Didn't I? I said that you were to take good care of her. The best of care.'

'I have! I do!' The husband struggles in his grasp but he is a good head and shoulders shorter than Bartholomew, who is a colossus of a man, with hands like bowls and shoulders like an oak tree.

From nowhere, and without warning, a bee drones between them; they feel the movement of it on their faces. Bartholomew reaches up instinctively, to flick it away, and the husband takes the opportunity to wrest himself from Bartholomew's grasp.

He darts sideways, agile, ready, up on his toes.

'Listen,' he says, from his new distance, holding up his hands, bouncing from foot to foot, 'I don't want to fight you—'

Despite everything, Bartholomew wants to laugh. The idea of this pasty-faced scholar engaging in bare-knuckled combat with him is preposterous. 'Damn right you don't,' he says.

'We have the same end in mind here,' the husband says, stepping back and forth, 'you and I. Wouldn't you say?'

'What end would that be?'

'We both want to find her. Don't we? To make sure she's safe. And the baby.'

At the thought of Agnes's safety – and the baby's – Bartholomew's anger rises again, like a pot left on the boil.

'You know,' he mutters, 'I have never really understood why my sister chose you, above all others. "What do you want to go marrying him for?" I said to her. "What use is he?"' Bartholomew takes his crook and places it squarely between his feet. 'You know what she said to me?'

The husband, standing straight as a reed now, arms folded, lips pressed together, shakes his head. 'What did she say?'

'That you had more hidden away inside you than anyone else she'd ever met.'

The husband stares, as if he can't believe what he is hearing. His face is anguished, pained, astonished. 'She said that?'

Bartholomew nods. 'Now, I can't pretend to understand her choice, in marrying you, but I do know one thing about my sister. You want to know what it is?'

'Yes.'

'She is rarely wrong. About anything. It's a gift or a curse, depending on who you ask. So if she thinks that about you, there's a possibility it's true.'

'I cannot divine,' the husband puts in, 'whether—'

Bartholomew continues, speaking over him, 'It is of no importance, either way, at this present moment. Our task now is to find her.'

The husband says nothing, but lowers himself to the ground, his head in his hands. When he speaks, his voice is muffled. 'She wrote something on a page before she left. It was perhaps some manner of message for me.'

'What did it say?'

'Something about rain. And branches. But I couldn't properly make it out.'

Bartholomew regards him for a second or two, turning these words over and over in his mind. Rain and branches. Branches. Rain. Then he lifts his crook and tucks it into his belt.

'Get up,' he says.

The husband is still speaking, more to himself than anyone else. 'She was there this morning and then she wasn't,' he is saying. 'The Fates have intervened and swept her away from me, as if on a tide, and I have no idea how to find her, no idea where to look and –'

'I do.'

'– I shall not rest until I find her, until we are—' The husband stops short and raises his head. 'You do?'

'Yes.'

'How?'' he demands. 'How can you know her mind so quickly and yet I, who am married to her, cannot begin—'

Bartholomew has had enough of this. He nudges the husband's leg with his boot. 'Up, I tell you,' he says. 'Come.'

The lad springs upright and regards Bartholomew with a wary air. 'Where?'

'The forest.'

Bartholomew puts two fingers into his mouth and, without taking his eyes off the lad's face, whistles for his dogs.

Agnes is dozing, somewhere between awake and asleep, with the baby tucked at her breast, when Bartholomew finds them.

He has walked over the fields, his dogs at his heels, the husband trailing in his wake, still moaning and whining, and he has found her, here, just where he suspected she might be.

'There now,' he says to her, bending to hoist her into his arms – the mess and stink and matter of birth are of no consequence to him. 'You cannot stay here.'

She protests, lightly, drowsily, but then leans her head into her brother's chest. The baby, he notices, is alive and its cheeks are drawing in and out. At suck, then. Bartholomew nods to himself.

The husband has caught up with them now, making a fuss and bother of the moment, gesturing, clutching his hair, his voice still churning away, throwing out words and words and more words into the greenery. He will carry her, he is saying, and what is the baby, a girl or a boy, and what was she thinking, running off like that, she's had them all frantic, he had no idea where she had gone. Bartholomew considers giving him a kick, to shut him up, to fell him to the fecund, leaf-damp ground, but resists. The husband tries to take Agnes from him, but Bartholomew brushes him off, as he might a bothersome fly.

'You get the basket,' he says to the lad. Then adds, over his shoulder, as he strides away: 'If it's not too heavy for you.'

or the pestilence to reach Warwickshire, England, in the summer of 1596, two events need to occur in the lives of two separate people, and then these people need to meet.

The first is a glassmaker on the island of Murano in the principality of Venice; the second is a cabin boy on a merchant ship sailing for Alexandria on an unseasonably warm morning with an easterly wind.

Several months before the day Judith takes to her bed, as the year is turning from 1595 to 1596, the master glassmaker, who is skilled in the layering of five or six colours to produce the star or flower-patterned glass beads known as *millefiori*, is momentarily distracted by a fight breaking out between the stokers across the glassworks. His hand slips and two of his fingers enter the roaring white flame that was, a moment earlier, heating the bulb of glass to stretchable, malleable gum. The pain is so severe that it goes beyond sensation and at first he cannot feel it at all; he cannot think what has happened, why everyone is staring, then running towards him. There is a smell of roasting meat, a yelling almost canine in its intensity, a flurry around him.

The result, later in the day, is two amputations.

One of his fellow workers, then, is the one to pack up the tiny red, yellow, blue, green and purple beads into boxes the following day. This man doesn't know that the master glass-maker – now at home, bandaged and dosed into a stupor with poppy syrup – usually pads and packs the beads with wood shavings and sand to prevent breakage. He grabs instead a handful of rags from the glassworks floor and tucks them in and around the beads, which look like hundreds of tiny, alert, accusing eyes staring up at him.

In Alexandria, at exactly the same moment, all the way across the Mediterranean Sea, the cabin boy must leave his ship, for Judith to contract the pestilence and for a tragedy to be set in motion, halfway across the world. He must receive orders to go ashore and find some victuals for his hungry and overworked shipmates.

So he does.

He goes down the gangplank, clutching the purse given to him by the midshipman, along with a short, sharp kick in the backside, which would explain the boy's listing, limping gait.

His crewmates are hauling crates of Malaysian cloves and Indian indigo off the ship, before taking on sacks of coffee beans and bales of textiles.

The dockside, under the cabin boy's feet, is disconcertingly firm and solid after weeks at sea. Nevertheless, he staggers off towards what looks to him like a tavern, passing a stall selling spiced nuts, a woman holding a snake about her neck. He pauses to look at a man with a monkey on a golden chain. Why? Because he has never seen a monkey before. Because he loves animals of all kinds. Because he is, after all, not much older than Hamnet, who is, at this very moment, sitting in a cold wintry schoolroom, watching the schoolmaster hand out horn books of Greek poetry.

The monkey at the port of Alexandria is wearing a little red jacket and a matching hat; its back is curved and soft, like that of a puppy, but its face is expressive, oddly human, as it peers up at the boy.

The cabin boy – a young lad from a Manx family – looks at the monkey and the monkey looks at the boy. The animal puts its head on one side, eyes bead-bright, and chatters softly, a slight judder of sound, its voice light and fluting. It reminds the boy of an instrument his uncle plays at gatherings on the Isle of Man, and for a moment he is back at his sister's churching, at his cousin's wedding, back in the safety of his kitchen at home, where his mother would be gutting a fish, telling him to mind his boots, to wipe his shirt front, to eat up now. Where his uncle would be playing his flute and everyone speaking the language he had grown up with, and no one would be yelling at him or kicking him or telling him what to do, and later on there might be dancing and singing.

Tears prick the eyes of the cabin boy and the monkey, still regarding him, with a sentient and understanding gaze, reaches out its hand.

The fingers on the monkey's hand are familiar and strange, to the boy, all at once. Black and shiny, like boot leather, with nails like apple pips. Its palm, though, is striated, just like the boy's and there passes between them, there, under the palm trees that line the wharf, the confluence of sympathy that can flow between human and beast. The boy feels the golden chain, as if it is around his own neck; the monkey sees the boy's sadness, his longing for his home, the bruises on his legs, the blisters and calluses on his fingers, the peeling skin on his shoulders from the relentless scorch of months in the ocean sun.

The boy holds out his hand to the monkey and the monkey

takes it. Its grip is surprisingly strong: it speaks of urgency, of maltreatment, of need, of craving for kind company. The monkey climbs up the boy's arm, using all four of its feet, across his shoulders and up on to his head, where it sits, paws buried in the boy's hair.

Laughing, the boy puts up a hand to be sure of what is happening. Yes, there is a monkey sitting on his head. He feels himself fill with numerous, warring urges: to run about the dockside, shouting to his crewmates, Look at me, look; to tell his little sister this, to say, You'll never guess what happened to me, a monkey sat on my head; to keep the monkey for himself, to dart away, to jerk the chain from the man's hand and sprint up the gangplank and disappear into the ship; and to cradle this creature in his arms, for ever, never let it go.

The man is getting to his feet, gesturing at the boy. He has skin that is pocked and scarred, a mouthful of blackened teeth, an eye that doesn't quite match its pair, in either direction or colour. He is rubbing the fingers of his hand together, in the universal language that means: money.

The boy shakes his head. The monkey clings tighter, curling its tail about the boy's neck.

The man with the scarred, pocked skin bears down, gripping the boy's arm. He repeats his gestures. Money, he is insisting, money. He points at the monkey, then makes the gesture again.

Again, the boy shakes his head, presses his lips together, puts a protective hand over the purse tied to his belt. He knows what will happen to him if he returns to the ship without food, without ale. He will carry the memory of the midshipman's lash – given to him twelve times in Malacca and seven times in Galle, ten in Mogadishu – for ever.

'No,' says the boy. 'No.'

The man lets out a stream of angry words, into the boy's face. The language they speak in this place called Alexandria is jabbing, nicking, like the point of a knife. The man reaches up to seize the monkey, which chatters and then shrieks, a piercing high cry of distress, gripping the boy's hair, the collar of his shirt, the tiny black nails scoring the skin of his neck.

The boy, almost sobbing now, tries to hold on to his new friend. For a moment, he has him, by the forelimb, the warm fur of the elbow fitted into his palm, but then the man jerks the chain and the monkey falls, screaming, from the boy's grasp, to the cobbled dock, where it rights itself and then, tugged again, scrambles after the man, whimpering.

Aghast, the boy watches the animal leave, the hunch of its back, the workings of its haunches, trying to keep up with its master. He swipes at his face, at his eyes, his head feeling bare and empty, wishing that he might bring the moment back, that he could have somehow persuaded the man to let him keep it. The monkey belonged to him: surely anyone could see that?

What the boy doesn't know – can't know – was that the monkey leaves part of itself behind. In the scuffle, it has shed three of its fleas.

One of these fleas falls, unseen, to the ground, where the boy will unwittingly crush it with the sole of his foot. The second stays for a while in the sandy hair of the boy, making its way to the front of his crown. When he is paying for a flagon of the local brew in the tavern, it will make a leap – an agile, arching spring – from his forehead to the shoulder of the innkeeper.

The third of the monkey's fleas will remain where it fell, in the fold of the red cloth tied around the boy's neck, given to him by his sweetheart at home.

Later, when the boy has returned to the ship for the night, having eaten a dinner of some of the spiced nuts and a curious patty of bread, shaped like a pancake, he will pick up his favourite of the ship's cats, an animal mostly white but with a striped tail, and nuzzle it against his neck. The flea, alert to the presence of a new host, will transfer itself from the boy's neckerchief, to the thick, milk-white fur of the cat's neck.

This cat, feeling unwell, and with the feline's unerring eye for those who dislike it, will take up residence, the next day, in the hammock of the midshipman. When he, that night, comes to his hammock, he will curse at the now-dead animal he finds there, turn it unceremoniously out, kicking it across the room.

Four or five fleas, one of which once belonged to the monkey, will remain where the cat lay. The monkey's flea is a clever one, intent on its survival and success in the world. It makes its way, by springing and leaping, to the fecund and damp armpit of the sleeping, snoring midshipman, there to gorge itself on rich, alcohol-laced sailor blood.

Three days out, past Damascus and heading for Aleppo, the quartermaster enters the captain's cabin to report that the midshipman is unwell and confined below. The captain nods, still examining his charts and sextant, and thinks nothing more of it.

The next day, he receives word, as he stands on the upper deck, that the midshipman is raving, foaming at the mouth, his head quite pushed sideways by a tumour in his neck. The captain frowns as the quartermaster speaks these words into his ear, then gives orders for the ship's physician to visit the man. Oh, the quartermaster then adds, and several of the ship's cats seem to have expired.

The captain turns his face to regard the quartermaster. The expression on his face is one of distaste, bafflement. Cats, you say? The quartermaster nods, respectfully, eyes cast down. How very peculiar.

The captain thinks for a moment longer, then flicks his fingers towards the sea. Throw 'em overboard.

The deceased cats, three in all, are taken by their striped tails and flung into the Mediterranean. The cabin boy watches, from a hatch in the deck, wiping his eyes with his red scarf.

Shortly afterwards, they dock at Aleppo, where they offload more of the cloves and a portion of the coffee and several score rats, which make a dash for the shore. The ship's physician knocks on the door of the captain's cabin, where he is conferring about weather and sails with his second officer.

'Ah,' says the captain, 'how is the man . . . the, well, midshipman?'

The physician scratches under his wig and smothers a belch. 'Dead, sir.'

The captain frowns, surveying the man, taking in his crooked wig, the potent smell of rum off him. 'By what cause?'

The physician, a man more suited to setting bones and extracting teeth, looks up, as if the answer might be found on the low, planked ceiling of the cabin. 'A fever, sir,' he says, with a drunkard's decisiveness.

'A fever?'

'An Afric fever would be,' the physician slurs, 'my opinion.

He's turned all black, you see, in patches, around the limbs and also in other places I will refrain from mentioning here, in this salubrious place, and so it is necessary for me to conclude that he must have taken ill and—'

'I see.' The captain cuts him off by turning away from him, towards his charts, the matter dealt with, as far as he is concerned.

The second officer clears his throat. 'We shall, sir,' he says, 'arrange a sea burial.'

The midshipman is wrapped in a sheet and brought up on deck. The sailors nearby cover their noses and mouths with cloth: the corpse is excessively odorous. The captain gives a short reading from the Bible; he, too, is struggling with the dead man's smell, despite twenty-five years at sea and more watery funerals than he can recall.

'In the name of the Father,' the captain enunciates, raising his voice above the sounds of discreet retching at the back, 'the Son and the Holy Ghost we commend this body unto the waves.

'You,' he gestures at the two sailors nearest him, 'take the . . . do the . . . ah . . . yes . . . overboard.'

They dart forward and, with green faces, lift the corpse up and over the side.

The choppy, pleated surface of the Mediterranean folds over the body of the midshipman.

By the time they reach Constantinople, with an order to collect a consignment of furs from the north, the cats are all dead and the rat population is becoming a problem. They are eating through the crates and getting at the dried-meat rations, the second officer tells the captain. There were fifteen or sixteen of them in the cook's quarters this morning. The men are demoralised, he says, keeping his eyes on the line of horizon out of the window, and several more have fallen ill overnight.

Two more men die, then a third, and a fourth. All with the same Afric fever that swells the neck and turns the skin red and blistered and black in places. The captain is forced to make an unscheduled stop in Ragusa, to take on more sailors, for whom he has no references or recommendations, which is the kind of hasty, slipshod seamanship he likes to avoid.

These new sailors are shifty-eyed, snaggle-toothed; they keep to themselves and speak very little, and only in some kind of Polack language. The Manx crew distrusts them on sight and will not communicate with them, or willingly share quarters.

The Polacks, however, are skilled at killing rats. They approach it as a sport, baiting a string with food, then lying in wait with an enormous shovel. When the creature appears – sleek, with drooping belly, gorged as it is on the sailors' rations – the Polacks leap on it, shouting, singing, and beat it to death, rat brains and entrails sprayed on the walls and ceilings. They then cut off the tails and string them to their belts, passing around a clear liquid in a bottle, from which they all drink.

Turns your stomach, one of the Manx sailors says to the cabin boy, watching from across the cabin. Doesn't it? Then he swats at his neck, his shoulder; the place is overrun with fleas. Damned rats, he growls to himself and turns over in his hammock.

At Venice, they don't plan to dock for long – the captain is keen to get his cargo back to England, to recoup his fee, to get this hellish voyage over with – but while the unloading and loading take place, he gives an order to the cabin boy to find some cats for the ship. The cabin boy leaps eagerly down to the dockside; he is more than keen to leave the ship, its cramped, low ceilings and stink of rat and fever and death. Today two more men are confined to their quarters with fever, one a Manxman, like himself, the other one of the Polacks, his rat-tail adorned belt hung up beside him.

The boy has been in Venice once before, on his first voyage, and it is as he remembers it: a strange, hybrid place, half of sea, half of land, where the steps of houses are lapped by jade-green waters, and windows are lit by the guttering flares of candles, where there are no streets but narrow alleyways, leading off each other in a dizzying labyrinth, and arch-backed bridges. A place where you might very easily lose your way among the fog and the angled squares and the high buildings and tolling church bells.

For a moment he watches the crew, who are hauling crates and sacks between them, shouting in a mixture of Manx and Polack and English. A Venetian man pushes a cart towards them, loaded with boxes; he too starts shouting, in Venetian. He is gesturing to the sailors, to his boxes, while gripping his cart, and the boy sees that the first two fingers of his hand are missing and the rest of the hand is of a strange, puckered texture, like melted candlewax. He is calling to the sailors, gesturing at the ship with his good hand, at his boxes, and the boy can see that the cart is about to lurch sideways, that the boxes will soon be spilt all over the dockside.

He leaps forward, rights the cart, grins at the surprised face of the man with the mangled hand, then darts away because he has seen, underneath a stall selling fish, the whiskered, triangular faces of several cats.

Unbeknown to them both, the flea that came from the Alexandrian monkey – which has, for the last week or so, been living on a rat, and before that the cook, who died near Aleppo – leaps from the boy to the sleeve of the master glassmaker, whereupon it makes its way up to his left ear, and it bites him there, behind the lobe. He doesn't feel it as the cool air of the misty canal has rendered his extremities sensationless, and he is intent only on getting these boxes of beads aboard the ship, receiving his payment, then returning to Murano, where he has many orders to fulfil and the fire stokers are sure to be fighting again, during his brief absence.

By the time the ship is rounding the heel of Sicily, the second officer has fallen ill with the Afric fever, his fingers purple and black, his body so hot that the sweat drips through the knots of his hammock to the floor below. They bury him at sea, along with two Polacks, outside Naples.

The Venetian cats, when not killing rats, stay true to their origins, choosing to sleep in the hold, on the boxes of beads from Murano. There is something about their wooden surfaces, their knotted ties, their chalked markings in Venetian on the side that evidently appeals to them.

Because not many people go into the hold during a voyage, when the cats die – and they do, in succession, one by one – their bodies remain unfound, on top of these boxes. The fleas that leapt from the dying rats into their striped fur crawl down into these boxes and take up residence in the rags padding the hundreds of tiny, multi-coloured *millefiori* beads (the same rags put there by the fellow worker of the master glassmaker; the same glassmaker who is now in Murano, where the glassworks is at a standstill, because so many of the workers are falling ill with a mysterious and virulent fever).

At Barcelona, the remaining Polacks jump ship, disappearing into the melee of the port. The captain sets his teeth and tells the men they will carry on, depleted as they are. They will deliver their crates of cloves and fabric and coffee and they will set sail.

The men do as they are told. The ship docks at Cádiz, then Porto, then La Rochelle, with more men lost along the way, then north, finally, to Cornwall. When they sail into London, they are down to a crew of five.

The cabin boy goes off to find a ship heading to the Isle of Man, the once-red scarf still tied around his neck, the sole surviving female Venetian cat tucked under his arm; the other three men head to a tavern at the furthest end of London Bridge; the captain orders a horse to take him home to his wife and family.

The cargo, unloaded and stacked in Custom House, is gradually distributed throughout London: the cloves and spices and textiles and coffee to merchants, to be sold on, the silks to the Palace, the glassware to a dealer in Bermondsey, the textile bales to clothworkers and haberdashers in Aldgate.

The boxes of glass beads, crafted by the glassmaker on the island of Murano, just before he injured his hand, lie on the shelf in a warehouse for almost a month. Then one is dispatched to a dressmaker in Shrewsbury, another in York, a jeweller in Oxford. The final box, the smallest of the lot, still wrapped in rags from the floor of the Venetian glassworks, is sent by messenger to an inn at the north edge of the city, where it remains for a week. It is then carried outside by the innkeeper and, along with a parcel of letters and a packet of lace, is given to a man heading into Warwickshire on horseback.

His leather saddlebag gives off a rhythmic click-click-click as he rides, the beads jostling together with the movement of the horse, turning their six colours around and around, rubbing against each other. For the two days of the journey, he idly wonders to himself what could be in the wrapped box: what could give off such a minute, clean sound?

Two of the beads break, crushed by the weight of their replicas. Five are scratched irreparably on their surfaces. The heavier ones work their way gradually, with each jolt of the horse, to the bottom.

The fleas in the rags crawl out, hungry and depleted by their hostless stay in the wharfhouse. Soon, however, they are recovered, rejuvenated, springing from horse to man and back again, then out on to the various people the rider encounters on the way – a woman who gives him a quart of milk, a child who comes to pat his horse, a young man at a roadside tavern.

By the time the rider reaches Stratford, the fleas have laid eggs: in the seams of his doublet, in the mane of the horse, in the stitching of the saddle, in the filigree and weave of the lace, in the rags surrounding the beads. These eggs are the great-grandchildren of the monkey flea.

He delivers the letters, the packet of lace and the box of beads into the hands of an innkeeper on the outskirts of the town. The letters are delivered, one by one, to their recipients, by a boy, in return for a penny (one, incidentally, arrives at Henley Street, for the husband in London has written to his family, telling them how he has sprained his wrist by falling down some steps, about a dog owned by his landlord, the play they are about to take on tour, all the way into Kent). The packet of lace is collected, after a day or two, by a woman from Evesham.

The rider turns his horse back towards London, noticing that the movement causes him some discomfort: there seems to be some painful, tender spot in his armpit. But he ignores it and continues on his way.

The box of beads is taken, by the same delivery boy, to a seamstress in Ely Street. She has an order for a new gown for the wife of a guildsman, who will wear it at the harvest fair. It is said that the wife has visited London and also Bath, in her time, so has refined ideas about dress. She told the seamstress that she must have a bodice decorated with Venetian beads, or else the dress will be worth nothing to her. Nothing.

And so the seamstress sent to London, who in turn sent to Venice, and they waited and they waited, and the wife of the guildsman fretted that the beads might not arrive in time, and they sent a second letter to London, and heard nothing back, but here they are.

The seamstress reaches through the hatch and takes the box from the boy. She is about to open it, when her neighbour's child, Judith, who helps with the stitching and the tidying of coloured twists and the cutting of cloth, comes through the door.

The seamstress holds aloft the box. 'Look,' she says to the girl, who is small for her age, and fair as an angel, with a nature to match.

The girl clasps her hands together. 'The beads from Venice? Are they here?'

The seamstress laughs. 'I believe so.'

'Can I look? Can I see? I cannot wait.'

The seamstress puts the box on her counter. 'You may do more than that. You may be the one to open them. You'll need to cut away all these nasty old rags. Take up the scissors there.'

She hands the girl the box of *millefiori* beads and Judith takes it, her hands eager and quick, her face lit with a smile.

O n an afternoon in the summer of Susanna's first year, Agnes notices a new smell in the house.

She is spooning meal into the waiting mouth of Susanna, saying, Here's one for you, here's another, the spoon going in laden with meal and coming out streaked and shining. Susanna is seated at the corner of the table on a chair piled high with cushions. Agnes has fastened her in place on this throne with a knotted shawl. The child is rapt, miniature hands scrolled into themselves, like the shells of snails, eyes fixed on the spoon as it travels from bowl to mouth and back again.

'Dat,' shouts Susanna, her mouth pitted with four blue-white teeth, in a row, on her lower gum.

Agnes repeats the sound back to her. She finds herself frequently unable to look away from her child, to remove her gaze from her daughter's face. Why would she ever want to behold anything else, when she could be taking in the sight of Susanna's ears, like the pale folds of roses, the winglike sweep of her tiny eyebrows, the dark hair, which clings to her crown as if painted there with a brush? There is nothing more exquisite to her than her child: the world could not possibly contain a more perfect being, anywhere, ever.

'Deet,' Susanna exclaims, and, with a deft and determined lunge, grabs at the spoon, causing meal to be splattered to the table, to her front, to her face, to Agnes's gown.

Agnes is finding a cloth, wiping the table, the chairs, Susanna's disbelieving face, trying to quell the outraged roaring, when she raises her head and sniffs the air.

It is a damp, heavy, acrid scent, like food gone off or unaired linen. She has never smelt it before. If it had a colour, it would be greyish green.

Cloth still in hand, she turns to look at her daughter. Susanna is gripping the spoon, banging it rhythmically on the table, blinking with each impact, her lips pursed together, as if this percussion is an act that requires the fullest concentration.

Agnes sniffs the cloth; she sniffs the air. She presses her nose to her sleeve, then to Susanna's smock. She walks about the room. What is it? It smells like dying flowers, like plants left too long in water, like a stagnant pond, like wet lichen. Is there something damp and rotting in the house?

She checks under the table, in case one of Gilbert's dogs has dragged in something. She kneels down to peer under the coffer. She puts her hands on her hips, standing in the middle of the room, and draws in a deep breath.

Suddenly she knows two things. She doesn't know how she knows them: she just does. Agnes never questions these moments of insight, the way information arrives in her head. She accepts them as a person might an unexpected gift, with a gracious smile and a feeling of benign surprise.

She is with child, she feels. There will be another baby in the house by the end of winter. Agnes has always known how many children she will have. She has foreknowledge of this: she knows there will be two children of hers standing at the bed where she dies. And here is the second child now, its first sign, its very beginning.

She also knows that this smell, this rotten scent, is not a physical thing. It means something. It is a sign of something

– something bad, something amiss, something out of kilter in her house. She can feel it somewhere, growing, burgeoning, like the black mould that creeps out of the plaster in winter.

The opposing natures of these two sensations perplex her. She feels herself stretching in two directions: the baby, good; the smell, bad.

Agnes walks back to the table. Her first and only thought is her daughter. Is this scent of sadness, of dark matter, coming from her? Agnes buries her face in the child's warm neck and inhales. Is it her? Is her child, her girl, under threat from some dark, gathering force?

Susanna squeals, surprised at this attention, saying, Mamma, Mamma, fastening her arms around Agnes's neck. Her arms, Agnes can feel, are not long enough to go right around her, so they grip with their fierce fingers to Agnes's shoulders.

Agnes sniffs her as a dog follows a trail, with both nostrils, as if sucking up her daughter's essence. She smells the pear-blossom hint of Susanna's skin, the warm hair, the scent of bedclothes and meal. Nothing else.

She lifts her daughter's diminutive round form, saying, will they find a slice of bread, a cup of milk, and she is thinking about the new baby, curled small as a nut inside her, and how Susanna will love it, how they will play together, how it will be a Bartholomew for her, a friend and companion and ally, always. Will it be a boy or a girl? Agnes asks herself and, strangely, can locate no sense of the answer.

With Susanna at her feet, she cuts a slice of bread and slathers it with honey. Susanna sits on her lap now, at the table, because Agnes wants her close, wants her right there, in case this smell, this darkness, should try to come near. And Agnes talks, to keep her daughter distracted, to keep her safe from the world. The child is listening to the stream of talk coming from Agnes's mouth, hooking out the words she knows, to shout them loud: bread, cup, foot, eye.

They are singing a song together, about birds nesting and bees humming, when Susanna's father comes down the stairs, into the room. Agnes is aware of him lifting a cup, filling it with water from the pitcher, of him drinking it, then another and another. He walks around them and slumps into a chair opposite.

Agnes looks at him. She feels herself breathe in, then out, in, out, like a tree filling with wind. The sour, damp smell is back. It is stronger. It is right here before them. It drifts off him, like smoke, collecting above his head in a grey-green cloud. He pulls it with him, this odour, as if he is enveloped in its mist. It seems to exude from his skin.

Agnes examines her husband. He looks the same. Or does he? His face, under his beard, is sallow, parchment pale. His eyes seem hooded and have purplish shadows under them. He stares out of the window, and yet doesn't. He seems not to see anything before him. His other hand, resting on the table between them, is filled with empty air. He is like the picture of a man, canvas thin, with nothing behind it; he is like a person whose soul has been sucked out of him or stolen away in the night.

How can this have happened, right under her nose? How can he have fallen into this state, without warning, without her seeing the signs? Were there signs? She tries to think. He has been sleeping more than usual, it is true, and spending more time out in the evenings, at taverns with his friends. It has been a long time since he read to her, at night, by candlelight, in their bed – she cannot remember the last time he did this. Have they been speaking together, as they used to, beside the fire at night? She thinks they have, perhaps less than usual. But she is busy, with the child, with the house, with her garden, with callers at the window, and he has been carrying on with his afternoons of tutoring and mornings of running errands for his father. Life has been sweeping them all along together, in step, she had thought. And now this.

Susanna is still singing, clapping her hands together. Her knuckles are dimpled, each one, indented on the bone. The song goes round and round, the same four notes, the same drone of sounds, round and round. It evidently does not please him because he winces and covers one ear with a hand.

Agnes frowns. She thinks about the baby, there in her belly, curled in water, listening to all that is going on, breathing in this foul air; she thinks about the warm weight of Susanna on her lap; she thinks about this cloud of grey and rot coming off her husband.

Is this marriage, this child, their life together causing his malaise? Is it their home in this apartment that is draining the life out of him in this way? She has no idea. The thought fills her with panic. How can she tell him about the new child in her belly while he is in this state? It might only worsen his melancholy and she cannot bear to see her news greeted with sorrow, with anything less than rapture.

She says his name. No response. She says it again. He raises his chin and looks at her: his face is horrifying to her.

Grey, puffy, beard straggly and unkempt. How did he get like this? How did it happen? How can she not have noticed this change coming? What is it she has not seen, or chosen not to see?

'Are you ill?' she asks him.

'Me?' he says, and it seems to take him a long time to hear her, to articulate a response. 'No. Why do you ask?'

'You do not look well.'

He sighs. He rubs a hand over his brow, his eyes. 'Do I not?' he says.

She stands, shifting Susanna to her hip. She touches his forehead, which feels clammy and cool, like the skin of a frog. He twists irritably out of her grasp, waving away her hand.

'All's well,' he says, and his words are heavy, as if he is spitting out pebbles as he speaks. 'Don't fuss.'

'What ails you?' she says. Susanna is kicking her legs, trying to turn her mother's face towards her, telling her she needs to sing.

'Nothing,' he says. 'I'm tired. That is all.' He stands, scraping the chair against the floor. 'I'm going back to bed.'

'Why don't you eat?' Agnes asks, trying to shush Susanna, bouncing her up and down. 'Some bread? Honey?'

He shakes his head. 'I'm not hungry.'

'Remember your father wanted you to go early to—'

He interrupts her, with a curt wave of his hand. 'Tell him to send Gilbert. I'll not go anywhere today.' He heads for the stairs, dragging his feet across the floor, pulling the misty smell after him, like a ream of old, unwashed cloth. 'I need to sleep,' he says.

Agnes watches him go up the stairs, pulling himself up by

the rail. She turns to look into the round, dark, wise eyes of her daughter.

'Sing, Mamma,' is Susanna's advice.

In the still of the night, she whispers to him, asks him what is wrong, what is on his mind, can she help him? She puts her hand to his chest, where she feels his heart tap against her palm, over and over, over and over, as if asking the same question and getting no answer.

'Nothing,' is what he replies.

'It must be something,' she says. 'Can you not say?'

He sighs, his chest lifting and falling under her hand. He fidgets with the sheet edge, rearranges his legs. She feels the scrape of his shin against hers, the restless tug of the sheet. The bed-curtains are close around them, forming a cave where the two of them lie together, with Susanna asleep on the pallet, arms flung wide, her mouth pursed, hair plastered to her cheeks.

'Is it . . .' she begins, ' . . . are you . . . do you wish we had not . . . wed? Is that it?'

He turns to her, for what feels like the first time in many days, and his face is pained, aghast. He presses his hand down on top of hers. 'No,' he says. 'Never. How could you say such a thing? You and Susanna are all I live for. Nothing else matters.'

'What is it, then?' she says.

He lifts her fingers, one by one, to his lips, kissing their tips. 'I don't know,' he says. 'Nothing. A heaviness of spirit. A melancholy. It's nothing.'

She is just falling into sleep, when he says, or seems to say, 'I am lost. I have lost my way.'

He moves towards her, then, and grips her round the waist, as if she is drifting away from him, into huge, tidal waters.

Over the next while, she observes him carefully, in the manner of a doctor watching a patient. She sees how he cannot sleep at night but then cannot rouse himself in the morning. How he rises at midday, groggy, whey-faced, his mood flat and grey. The smell off him is worse then, the sour, rank scent soaked into his clothing, his hair. His father comes to the door, shouting and bawling, telling him to stir himself, to put in a day's work. She sees how she, Agnes, must remain calm, steady, must make herself bigger, in a way, to keep the house on an even keel, not to allow it to be taken over by this darkness, to square up to it, to shield Susanna from it, to seal off her own cracks, not to let it in.

She sees how he drags his feet and sighs when he goes off to teach his pupils. She watches him stare out of the window when his brother Richard returns from school. She sees the way he sits at table with his parents, a scowl on his face, his hand toying with the food, with the plate. She sees him reach for the ale pitcher when his father praises Gilbert's handling of a certain worker at the tannery. She sees Edmond come and stand at his side and lay his head on his sleeve; the boy has to butt him with his forehead several times before his brother realises he is there. She sees the absent, weary way he lifts the child to his lap. She sees Edmond stare intently into his brother's face, a small hand pressed to each stubbled cheek. She sees that Edmond, alone, is the only other person who notices that something is amiss with him.

She sees how her husband starts in his seat if the cat leaps on the table, if the door slams in a breeze, if a plate is put down too roughly. She sees the way John snaps at him, sneers, invites Gilbert to join in with this. You are useless, she hears John say to him, when he spills ale on the tablecloth. Can't even pour your own ale, eh, eh, Gilbert, did you see?

She sees the cloud above him grow darker, gather its horrible rank strength. She wants to reach across the table then, to lay her hand on his arm. She wants to say, I am here. But what if her words are not enough? What if she is not enough of a salve for his nameless pain? For the first time in her life, she finds she does not know how to help someone. She does not know what to do. And, anyway, she cannot take his hand, not here, not at this table. There are plates and cups and candlesticks between them, and Eliza is standing now to clear the meat dish and Mary is trying to feed Susanna cuts of meat that are too large for her. There is so much to do in a family of this size, so much to see to, so many people needing so many different things. How easy is it, Agnes thinks, as she lifts the plates, to miss the pain and anguish of one person, if that person keeps quiet, if he keeps it all in, like a bottle stoppered too tightly, the pressure inside building and building, until – what?

Agnes doesn't know.

He drinks too much, late into the night, not out with his friends, but sitting at the table in the bedchamber. He cuts feather after feather into quills, but none is quite right, he says. One is too long, another too short, a third too thin for his fingers. They split or scratch the page or blur and spot. Is it too much to ask for a man to have a working quill? Agnes wakes one night to hear him shout this, hurling the whole lot at the wall, ink pot and all, making Susanna wail. She doesn't recognise him, then, holding her screaming child to her side: his livid face, his dishevelled hair, his yelling mouth, the splash of ink, like a black island, on the wall.

In the morning, as he lies sleeping, she ties Susanna to her back and walks the path to Hewlands, stopping on the way to gather feathers, the heads of poppies, sprays of nettles.

She finds Bartholomew by following a noise of repetitive thudding. He is at the nearest fold, swinging a hammer on to the top of a fence post, driving it into the earth: thwack, crack. He is making enclosures for the new lambs. She knows that he could have told one of the others to do this job but he is a good fencer: his height, his extraordinary strength, his unswerving, unstinting approach to a task.

As she approaches, he lets the hammer fall to his feet. He waits, mopping at his face, watching her as she walks towards him.

'I brought you this,' Agnes says, holding out a hunk of bread and a packet of the cheese she makes herself, in the outhouse in Henley Street, straining ewe's milk through muslin.

Bartholomew nods, accepts the food, takes a bite and chews, all without taking his eyes from Agnes's face. He lifts the corner of Susanna's bonnet and passes a finger over her sleeping cheek. Then his eyes are pulled back to Agnes. She smiles at him; he continues to chew.

'Well?' is the first thing he says.

'It is,' Agnes begins, 'no great matter.'

Bartholomew rips the crust off the bread with his teeth. 'Tell me.'

'It is merely . . .' Agnes shifts the weight of Susanna '. . .

he doesn't sleep. He stays awake all night and then cannot rise. He is sad and sullen. He will not speak, except to argue with his father. There is a terrible heaviness about him. I do not know what to do.'

Bartholomew considers her words, just as she knew he would, his head on one side, his gaze focused on something in the distance. He chews, on and on, the muscles in his cheeks and temples tensing and tensing. He slides the remainder of the bread and cheese into his mouth, still saying nothing. When he has swallowed, he exhales. He bends. He picks up his hammer. Agnes stands to one side, out of range of his swing.

He sends two blows down on top of the post, both true and straight. The post seems to shudder and flinch, drawing into itself. 'A man,' he says, then strikes another blow, 'needs work.' He swings the hammer again, brings it down on the post. 'Proper work.'

Bartholomew tests the post with a hand and finds it steady. He moves along to the next, already loosely dug into the soil. 'He is all head,' he says, swinging his hammer, 'that one. All head, with not much sense. He needs work to steady him, to give him purpose. He can't go on this way, an errand-boy for his father, tutoring here and there. A head like his, he'll run mad.'

He puts a hand to the post, which doesn't seem to his liking, because he takes the hammer to it again, once, twice, and the post is driven further in.

'I hear it said,' Bartholomew mutters, 'that the father is free with his fists, particularly with your Latin Boy. Is that true?'

Agnes sighs. 'I have not seen it with my own eyes but I don't doubt it.'

Bartholomew is about to swing the hammer but checks himself. 'Has he ever lost his temper with you?'

'Never.'

'And the child?'

'No.'

'If he ever raises a hand to either of you,' Bartholomew begins, 'if he even tries, then—'

'I know,' Agnes cuts in, with a smile. 'I don't think he would dare.'

'Hmm,' Bartholomew mutters. 'I should hope not.' He flings down the hammer and walks over to his pile of posts, stacked in a heap. He selects one, weighs it in his hand, holds it up and looks along it, to check its line.

'It would be hard,' he says, without looking at her, 'for a man to live in the shadow of a brute like that. Even if it was in the house next door. Hard to draw breath. Hard to find your path in life.'

Agnes nods, unable to speak. 'I had not,' she whispers, 'realised how bad it was.'

'He needs work,' Bartholomew says again. He hoists the post to his shoulder and comes up to her. 'And perhaps a distance between him and his father.'

Agnes looks away, down the path, at the dog, lying in the shade, pink rag of a tongue unrolled.

'I have been thinking,' she begins, 'that it might interest John to set up elsewhere. In London.'

Bartholomew raises his head, narrows his eyes. 'London,' he repeats, rolling the word over his tongue.

'To extend his business there.'

Her brother pauses, rubs at his chin. 'I see,' he says. 'You mean that John might send someone to the city, for a while. Someone he trusts. A son perhaps.'

Agnes nods. 'Just for a while,' she says.

'You would go with him?'

'Of course.'

'You would leave Stratford?'

'Not at first. I would wait until he was settled, with a house, and then I would follow him, with Susanna.'

Brother and sister regard each other. Susanna, on Agnes's back, stirs, gives a small sob, then settles back to sleep.

'London is not so far away,' Bartholomew says.

'True.'

'Many go there, to find work.'

'Again, true.'

'There might be opportunities to be found there.'

'Yes.'

'For him. For the business.'

'I think so.'

'He might find a position for himself. Away from his father.'

Agnes reaches out and touches the cut end of the post Bartholomew is holding, tracing a finger around and around the circles there.

'I don't think John would listen to a woman in this matter. If an associate were to put the idea in his head – someone with an interest in his business, with a stake – so as to make it look like John's idea in the first place, then . . .'

'The notion would take hold.' Bartholomew finishes for her. He rests his hand on her arm. 'What about you?' he says in a low voice. 'You would not mind if he . . . went ahead of you? It could take some time for him to establish himself.'

'I would mind,' she says. 'Very much. But what else can I do? He cannot continue like this. If London could save him from this misery, it is what I want.'

'You would come back here,' he jerks his thumb towards Hewlands, 'in the meantime, you and Susanna, so that—'

Agnes shakes her head. 'Joan would never take to the idea. And there will be more of us soon.'

Bartholomew frowns. 'What are you saying? There will be another child?'

'Yes. By winter's end.'

'Have you told him?'

'Not yet. I will hold off, until all is arranged.'

Bartholomew nods at her, then gives her one of his rare, wide smiles, putting his powerful arm around her shoulders. 'I shall seek out John. I know where he drinks. I'll go there tonight.'

gnes is sitting on the floor by the pallet, next to Judith, a cloth in her hand. She has been there all night: she will not rise, she will not eat, she will not sleep or rest. It is everything Mary can do to get her to drink a little. The heat from the fire is so great that Agnes's cheeks have scarlet spots upon them; strands of hair have escaped from her coif to write themselves in damp scribbles on her neck.

As Mary watches, Agnes dips the cloth into the bowl of water and wipes Judith's brow, her arms, her neck. She murmurs some words to her daughter, something soft and soothing.

Mary wonders if the child hears her. Judith's fever has not broken. The bubo in her neck is so large, so taut, it may burst. And then all will be lost. The girl will die. Mary knows this. It may be tonight, in the deepest dark, because that is the most dangerous time for the sick. It may be tomorrow or even the day after. But come it will.

There is nothing they can do now. Just as three of her own daughters were taken, two when they were just babies, Judith will go from them. They will not have her any more.

Agnes is gripping the child's limp fingers, Mary sees, as if she is trying to tether her to life. She would keep her here, haul her back, by will alone, if she could. Mary knows this urge – she feels it; she has lived it; she is it, now and for ever. She has been the mother on the pallet, too many times, the woman trying to hold on, to keep a grip on her child. All in vain. What is given may be taken away, at any time. Cruelty and devastation wait for you around corners, inside coffers, behind doors: they can leap out at you at any moment, like a thief or brigand. The trick is never to let down your guard. Never think you are safe. Never take for granted that your children's hearts beat, that they sup milk, that they draw breath, that they walk and speak and smile and argue and play. Never for a moment forget they may be gone, snatched from you, in the blink of an eye, borne away from you like thistledown.

Mary feels tears gathering in her eyes, feels her throat closing over. The sight of Judith's hair, still plaited, the line of her jaw and neck. How can it be that she will no longer exist? That, before too long, she and Agnes will be washing this body, combing out that plait, readying her for burial? Mary turns briskly, taking up a pitcher, a cloth, a plate, anything, moving them to the table and back again.

Eliza, who is seated at the table, her chin in her hand, whispers, 'I should write. Don't you think so, Mamma?'

Mary glances at the pallet, where Agnes has her head bowed, almost as if in prayer. All day, Agnes has refused to let Eliza write to Judith's father. All will be well, she has kept saying, as she ground up herbs, with increasingly frantic movements, as she tried to get Judith to swallow tinctures and tisanes, as she rubbed ointments into her skin. We mustn't alarm him. It is not necessary.

Mary turns back to Eliza and gives her a quick, single nod. She watches as Eliza goes to a cupboard and takes out ink, paper and quill; her brother keeps them there for when he is at home. She sits down at the table and dips her quill into the ink and, hesitating for just a moment, writes.

Dear Brother,

I am sorrie to tel you that Judith, your daughter, is
verie sick. We belief she has not manie hours left to
her. Plea/e come bak to us, if you can. And make hast.

God /peed to you, dearest brother.

Your loving sister,

Eliza

Mary melts the sealing-wax over a candle; she sees Agnes
watching as they drip it on to the folded page. Eliza writes the
address of her brother's lodgings on the front, then Mary takes
up the letter and goes next door with it, to her own house. She
will find a coin, open a window, call to whoever is in the street
to take it to the inn on the road out of Stratford and ask the
innkeeper to convey it, fast as he can, to London, to her son.

Not long after Mary leaves to find a coin, to hail a passer-by,
Hamnet drifts to the surface of sleep. He lies for a while under
the sheet, wondering why nothing feels right, why the world
feels as though it has slanted slightly, why he feels so dry of
mouth, so heavy of heart, so sore in the head.

He looks one way in the dark room and sees his parents'
bed: empty. He looks the other and sees the pallet where his
sisters sleep. Only one body is under the covers and then he
remembers: Judith is sick. How could he have forgotten?

He lurches upright, pulling the bedclothes with him, and
makes two discoveries. His head is filled with pain, like a bowl
brimful of scalding water. It is a strange, confusing kind of
pain – it drives out all thought, all sense of action. It saturates
his head, spreading itself to the muscles and focus of his eyes;

it tinkers with the roots of his teeth, with the byways of his ears, the paths of his nose, the very shafts of his hair. It feels enormous, significant, bigger than him.

Hamnet crawls from the bed, dragging the sheet with him, but no matter. He needs to find his mother: amazing how strong this instinct is, even now, as a great lad of eleven. He recalls this sensation, this urge – just – from when he was much younger: the driving need to be with his mother, to be under her gaze, to be by her side, close enough to be able to reach out and touch her, because no one else would do.

It must be near dawn because the new light of day is seeping into the rooms, thin and pale as milk. He makes it down the stairs, which seem to lurch and sway in front of him, one step at a time. He has to turn to face the wall because everything around him is in motion.

Downstairs is the following scene: his aunt Eliza is asleep at the table, her head resting on her arms. The candles have burnt out, drowned in pools of themselves. The fire is reduced to a heap of idling ashes. His mother is bent forward, her head on the pallet, asleep, a cloth gripped in her hand. And Judith is looking right at him.

'Jude,' he says, or tries to say, because his voice doesn't seem to be working. It rasps; it prickles; it seems unable to get out of his dry and raw throat.

He drops to his knees and crawls along the straw to reach her.

Her eyes glitter with a strange, silvery light. She is worse: he can see this. Her cheeks are sunken, white, her lips cracked and bloodless, the swellings in her neck red and shining. He comes to crouch next to his twin, careful not to wake his mother. His hand finds hers; their fingers twine together.

He sees Judith's eyes roll back in her head, once, twice. Then they open wide and slide towards him. It seems to take her a great deal of effort.

Her lips curve upwards in what might be a smile. He feels a pressure on his fingers. 'Don't cry,' she whispers.

He feels again the sensation he has had all his life: that she is the other side to him, that they fit together, him and her, like two halves of a walnut. That without her he is incomplete, lost. He will carry an open wound, down his side, for the rest of his life, where she had been ripped from him. How can he live without her? He cannot. It is like asking the heart to live without the lungs, like tearing the moon out of the sky and asking the stars to do its work, like expecting the barley to grow without rain. Tears are appearing on her cheeks now, like silver seeds, as if by magic. He knows they are his, falling from his eyes on to her face, but they could just as easily be hers. They are one and the same.

'You shall be well,' she murmurs.

He grips her fingers in anger. 'I shall not.' He passes his tongue over his lips, tasting salt. 'I'll come with you. We'll go together.'

Again, the flicker of a smile, the pressure of her fingers. 'Nay,' she says, his tears glistening on her face. 'You shall stay. They need you.'

He can feel Death in the room, hovering in the shadows, over there beside the door, head averted, but watching all the same, always watching. It is waiting, biding its time. It will slide forward on skinless feet, with breath of damp ashes, to take her, to clasp her in its cold embrace, and he, Hamnet, will not be able to wrest her free. Should he insist it takes him too? Should they go together, just as they always have?

Then the idea strikes him. He doesn't know why he hadn't thought of it before. It occurs to Hamnet, as he crouches there, next to her, that it might be possible to hoodwink Death, to pull off the trick he and Judith have been playing on people since they were young: to exchange places and clothes, leading people to believe that each was the other. Their faces are the same. People remark on this all the time, at least once a day. All it takes is for Hamnet to put on Judith's shawl or for her to don his hat; they will sit at the table like that, eyes lowered, smiles concealed, and their mother will place a hand on Judith's shoulder and say, Hamnet, can you bring in the wood? Or their father might come into a room and see what he thinks is his son, dressed in a jerkin, and ask him to conjugate a verb in Latin, only to discover it is his daughter, hiding her laughter, revelling in the illusion, and she will push aside the door to reveal the real son, hidden away.

Could he pull off their trick, their joke, just once more? He thinks he can. He thinks he will. He glances over his shoulder at the tunnel of dark beside the door. The blackness is depthless, soft, absolute. Turn away, he says to Death. Close your eyes. Just for a moment.

He slides his hands underneath Judith, one palm under her shoulders, the other under her hips, and he shunts her sideways, towards the fireplace. She is lighter than he expected; she rolls to her side and her eyes open a crack as she rights herself. She watches, frowning, as he lays himself down in the dip her body has made, as he takes her place, as he smooths his hair down, on either side of his face, as he pulls the sheet up over both of them, tucking it under their chins.

They will look, he is sure, the same. No one will know which is which. It will be easy for Death to make a mistake, to take him in her place.

She is stirring beside him, trying to sit up. 'Nay,' she is saying again. 'Hamnet, nay.'

He knew she would know straight away what he was doing. She always does. She is shaking her head, but is too weak to raise herself from the pallet. Hamnet holds the sheet fast over both of them.

He breathes in. He breathes out. He turns his head and breathes into the whorls of her ear; he breathes in his strength, his health, his all. You will stay, is what he whispers, and I will go. He sends these words into her: I want you to take my life. It shall be yours. I give it to you.

They cannot both live: he sees this and she sees this. There is not enough life, enough air, enough blood for both of them. Perhaps there never was. And if either of them is to live, it must be her. He wills it. He grips the sheet, tight, in both hands. He, Hamnet, decrees it. It shall be.

usanna, shortly before her second birthday, sits in a basket on the floor of her grandmother's parlour, her legs crossed, her skirts billowing up around her, filled with air. She holds a wooden spoon in each hand and with these she paddles as fast as she can. She is sculling down the river. The current is fast and weaving. Weeds waft and unravel. She has to paddle and paddle to stay afloat – if she stops, who knows what may happen? Ducks and swans drift alongside her, seemingly serene and unruffled, but Susanna knows that their webbed feet are working, working beneath the water. No one but she can see these animals. Not her mother, who stands at the window, her back to the room, scattering seed on the sill. Not her grandmother, who sits at the table, her workbox open in front of her. Not her father, who is a pair of legs, encased in dark stockings, pacing from one wall to another. The soles of his shoes scuff and thud on the surface of Susanna's river. He walks past a duck, through a swan, across a bank of reeds. Susanna wants to tell him to be careful, to check if he can swim. She has a vision of her father's head – dark, like his stockings – disappearing beneath the brownish-green lapping waters. She feels her throat clutch, her eyes sting at the thought.

She looks up at her father and sees that he has stopped pacing. His legs are still, straight, a pair of tree trunks. He is standing in front of his mother, who is still sewing, her needle disappearing and reappearing through the fabric. It looks to Susanna like a fish, a slender silver one, a minnow perhaps or a grayling, leaping out of the water and diving back down, leaping out, diving down, and she is thinking about her river again when she realises that her grandmother has slammed down her sewing, has stood up, has begun to shout at Susanna's father, right up into his face. Susanna watches, aghast, spoon-paddles poised. She takes in this unusual sight, presses it into her mind: her grandmother, face distorted by anger, her hand gripping the arm of her son; her father wresting his arm from her grip, speaking in a low and menacing tone; then her grandmother gesturing towards Susanna's mother, rapping out her name – said by her grandmother so that it sounds like *Annis* – making her mother turn around. Her mother's dress is stuffed out at the front with another baby. A brother or sister for you, she has been told. Her mother is also holding a squirrel on her arm. Can this be true? Susanna knows it is. The animal's tail flares red as a flame in the sunlight coming through the glass. It scampers up her mother's sleeve, to nestle under her cap, next to the hair, which Susanna is sometimes permitted to unravel, to brush, to plait.

Her mother's face is serene. She contemplates the parlour, the grandmother, the man, the child in the boat-basket. She strokes the squirrel's tail; Susanna feels a pull, a longing to do the same, but the squirrel will never let her come near. Her mother strokes the tail and shrugs at whatever is being said to her. She gives a vague smile and turns away, lifting the squirrel down from her shoulder and letting it escape out of the open casement.

Susanna watches all this. The ducks and swans swim closer and closer, crowding in.

* * *

Mary stitches and stitches, the needle rising from the seam and falling into it. She hardly knows what she is doing but she can see that, as she listens to what her son is saying, her stitches are getting bigger, clumsier, and this annoys her in a specific way because she is known for her needlework – she is, she knows it. She tries to keep her head, tries to remain calm, but her son is saying that he has no doubt this plan will work, that he will be able to expand John's business in London. Mary can barely contain her rage, her scorn. Her daughter-in-law is contributing nothing to this discussion, of course, but merely standing at the window, making half-witted noises into the air.

There is a reddish, rat-faced squirrel that lives in a tree outside the house: Agnes likes to feed and pet it, from time to time. Mary cannot for the life of her understand why, and she has told her daughter-in-law that it must not enter the house, heaven knows what diseases and plagues it might carry, but Agnes will not listen. Agnes never listens. Not even now, when her husband is proposing to leave the house, to run away, to hide, when what he really ought to be doing is falling on his knees and begging forgiveness, from his mother, who took him and his bride and her swollen belly into her own house not three years ago, from his father who, with God as their witness, has his faults but always tries to do his best by his family. Not-listening is Agnes's customary state.

She cannot look at her son; she cannot look at her daughter-in-law, standing there, her belly swollen once more, fussing over that damn squirrel in her hands, as if nothing of any consequence is happening here.

John treats Agnes as a simpleton, a rural idiot. He nods at her, if he passes her in the house or sees her at table. How are

we today, Agnes? he will say, as if to a child. He will look upon
her mildly, if she brings a tangle of filthy roots out of her pocket,
or opens her hands to show them a collection of shining acorns.
He tolerates her eccentricities, her night-time wanderings, her
sometimes dishevelled appearance, the daft imaginings and
predictions she on occasion comes out with, the various animals
and other creatures she brings into the house (a newt, which
she put in the water pitcher, a featherless dove, which she
nursed back to full health). If Mary complains to him as they
lie in bed at night, he pats her hand and says, Let the girl alone.
She's from the country, remember, not from the town. At which
Mary could say three things: Agnes is no girl. She is a woman
who enticed a much younger boy, our boy, into marriage for
the worst possible reason. And: You forgive her too much, and
only because of that dowry of hers. Don't think I don't see this.
And: I am also from the country, brought up on a farm, but
do I run about the place in the night and bring wild animals
into the house? No, I do not. Some of us, she will sniff to her
husband, know how to conduct ourselves.

'It would help matters,' her son is saying, airily, insistently,
'help all of us, to expand Father's business like this. It's an
inspired idea of his. God knows things in this town have
become difficult enough for him. If I were to take the trade
to London, I am certain I might be able to—'

Before even realising that her patience has slipped out from
under her, like ice from under her feet, she is up, she is
standing, she is gripping her son by the arm, she is shaking
it, she is saying to him, 'This whole scheme is nothing but
foolishness. I have no idea what put this notion into your
father's head. When have you ever shown the slightest interest

in his business? When have you proved yourself worthy of this kind of responsibility? London, indeed! Remember when we sent you to fetch those deerskins in Charlecote and you lost them on the way back? Or the time you traded a dozen gloves for a book? Remember? How can you and he even consider taking business to London? You think there are no glovers in London? They'll eat you alive, soon as look at you.'

What she really wants to say is, Don't go. What she really wants is for him to be able to unpick this marriage to this scullion with wildness running in her veins, for him never to have seen her, this woman from the forest whom everybody said was a strange, unmarriageable sort. Why would she have set her sights on Mary's son, who had no job, no property? She wishes she had never come up with the scheme to send her son as tutor to that farm by the forest: if she could go back and undo that, she would. Mary hates having this woman in her house, the way she can appear in the room without being heard, the way she looks at you, right into you, right through you, as if you are nothing but water and air to her, the way she croons and sings to the child. What she really wants is for her son never to have got wind of John's plan to branch out into London. The thought of the city, its crowds, its diseases, stops the breath in her chest.

'Agnes,' she says, as her son irritably pulls away his arm, 'surely you agree with me. He cannot go. He cannot just walk away like this.'

Agnes turns at last, from the window. She is still holding, Mary is incensed to see, the squirrel in her hands. Its tail slides and slips through her fingers; its eyes, gold beads pierced with black, fix themselves on Mary. Beautiful fingers, Agnes has, Mary is pained to notice. Tapering, white, slender. Agnes is, Mary is forced to admit, a striking woman. But it is an unsettling, wrong sort of beauty: the dark hair is ill-matched with the golden-green eyes, the skin whiter than milk, the teeth evenly spaced but pointed, like a fox's. Mary finds she cannot look at her daughter-in-law for long, she cannot hold her gaze. This creature, this woman, this elf, this sorceress, this forest sprite – because she is that, everyone says so, Mary knows it to be true – bewitched and ensnared her boy, lured him into a union. This, Mary can never forgive.

Mary appeals to Agnes now. Surely, on this, they may be united. Surely, her daughter-in-law will come down on her side in this matter, the task of keeping him with them, at home, safe, where they can see him.

'Agnes,' Mary says, 'we are in agreement, are we not? These are foolish plans with no basis in sense. He must stay here, with us. He should be here, when this baby is born. His place is with you, with the children. He must get down to work, here, in Stratford. He cannot take off like this. Can he? Agnes?'

Agnes lifts her head and her face is visible for a moment, beneath her cap. She smiles, her most enigmatic, maddening smile, and Mary feels a falling in her chest, sees her mistake, sees that Agnes is never going to side with her.

'I see no reason,' Agnes says, in her light, fluting voice, 'to keep him against his will.'

Fury swarms into Mary's throat. She could strike the woman, no matter that she is with child. She could take this needle and drive it into the white flesh of her, flesh that her son has touched and taken and kissed and everything else. The thought of it makes Mary sick, makes her stomach heave, the idea of her boy, her child, and this creature.

She gives an inarticulate noise, half sob, half scream. She hurls her needlework to the floor and stamps away from the table, away from her work, away from her son, stepping over the child, who is sitting in a basket by the hearth, two kitchen spoons in her hands.

It does not escape her notice, as she makes her way towards the passage, that Agnes and her son start to laugh, softly at first, then more loudly, shushing each other, their footsteps sounding on the flags, walking towards each other, no doubt.

Weeks later, Agnes walks through the streets of Stratford, her hand hooked into her husband's arm. The greatness of her belly prevents her from walking too fast; she cannot draw enough breath into her chest because the baby is taking up more and more room. She can sense her husband trying to move slowly for her, can sense his muscles quivering with the effort of suppressing his innate need for exertion, for motion, for speed. It is, for him, like trying to hold off from drinking when you are ravaged with thirst. He is ready to be gone: she sees this. There has been much preparation, much argument, many arrangements to be made, letters to write, bags to pack, clothes that Mary must wash and wash again herself; nobody else is allowed. There are samples of gloves that John must oversee, then package and unpack and repackage.

And now the moment has arrived. Agnes conjugates it: he is going, he will be gone, he will go. She has put these circumstances together; she has set it in motion, as if she were the puppeteer, hidden behind a screen, gently pulling on the strings of her wooden people, easing and guiding them on where to go. She asked Bartholomew to speak to John, then waited for John to speak to her husband. None of this would have happened if she hadn't got Bartholomew to plant the idea in John's head. She has created this moment – no one else – and yet, now it is happening, she finds that it is entirely at odds with what she desires.

What she desires is for him to stay at her side, for his hand to remain in hers. For him to be there, in the house, when she brings this baby into the world. For them to be together. What she desires, though, does not matter. He is going. She is, however secretly, sending him away.

His pack is bound and tied upon his back. More boxes of goods will be sent after him when he is settled. His boots are cleaned and polished; she has massaged grease into their seams, to keep out the damp of London streets.

Agnes casts a sideways glance at him. His profile is set, his beard trimmed and oiled (she did this herself, too, last night, stroking the blade against the leather strop, then taking its lethal edge to the skin of her beloved – such trust, such submission). His eyes are lowered: he doesn't want to greet people or talk for long. His hand is tight over hers, his fingers pressing down hard. He is eager to get under way. To get this over. To embark.

He is talking about a cousin he will visit in London, how the cousin has secured a room for him.

'Is it by the river?' she hears herself say, even though she knows the answer: he has told her all this before. It seems important that they keep talking, about nothing of great significance. The people of Stratford are all around them. Watching, observing, listening. It is important, for him, for her, for the family, for the business, that they appear harmonious, in step, in accord. That their very bearing refute the rumours going around: they cannot live together; John's business is failing; he is leaving for London because of some kind of disgrace.

Agnes lifts her chin a little higher. There is no disgrace, says the straightness of her back. There is no problem in our marriage, says the proud, outward curve of her middle. There is no failing in the business, say her husband's shining boots.

'It is,' he says. 'And not far from the tanneries, I believe. So I shall be able to view them, for Father, and establish which is the best.'

'I see,' she says, even though she has a distinct feeling that he shall not be in the gloving business for long.

'The river,' he continues, 'is said to have dangerous tides.'

'Oh?' she says, even though she has heard him telling this to his mother.

'It is crucial, my cousin says, each time you cross to secure an experienced boatman.'

'Indeed.'

He talks on, about the different shores of the river, the landing stages, how certain times of day are safer than others. She pictures a thick, wide river, twisted with lethal currents, studded with tiny vessels, like a garment sewn with beads. She pictures one of these vessels, containing her husband, swept downstream, his dark head uncovered, his clothes filled with river-drink, streaked with mud, his boots brimming with silt. She has to shake her head, grip her fingers to the solidity of his arm, to rid herself of this. It is not true, it will not be true; it is just her mind playing tricks on her.

She walks with him as far as the posting inn, him talking now about lodgings, about how he will be back before she knows it, how he will think of her, of Susanna, every day. He will secure a dwelling for all of them there, in London, as soon as he can and they may all live together again, by and by. There, by the milestone with one arrow towards 'London' (she knows this word, the large, confident stroke of the L, the rounded os, like a pair of eyes, the repeated arch of the *n*), they stop.

'You will write?' he says, his face creasing. 'When the time comes?' Both his hands reach towards her and cup the lower curve of her stomach.

'Of course,' she says.

'My father,' he gives a rueful smile, 'is hoping for a boy.'

'I know.'

'But I do not mind. Boy or girl. Maid or lad. It is all one to me. As soon as I get word, I shall make arrangements to come and fetch you all. And then we shall be together, in London.'

He holds her close, as close as he can, with the swell of the child between them, his arms around her. 'Do you have no feeling?' he whispers into her ear. 'No sense this time? Of what it will be?'

She leans her head into him, close to the opening of his shirt. 'No,' she says, and she is aware of the puzzlement in her voice. It has come as a surprise to her that she has been unable to picture or divine the child she is carrying: girl or boy, she cannot tell. She is receiving no definite signs. She dropped a knife from the table the other day and it fell pointing towards the fire. A girl, then, she thought. But later the same day she found herself spooning the pap of an apple, sharp, pleasingly crisp, into her mouth and she thought: A boy. It is altogether confusing. Her hair is dry and crackles when she brushes it, which means a girl, but her skin is soft, her nails strong, which means a boy. A male peewit flew into her path the other day but then a female pheasant came squawking out of the bushes.

'I cannot tell,' she says. 'And I don't know why. It—'

'You must not worry,' he says, putting a hand on either side of her face and lifting it up so that they are looking into each other's eyes. 'All shall be well.'

She nods, dropping her gaze.

'Have you not always said you will have two children?'

'I have,' she says.

'Well, then. Here,' he rests a palm against her, 'is the second. Ready and waiting. All shall be well,' he says again. 'I know it.'

He kisses her, full on the mouth, then draws back to regard her. She pulls her face into a smile, catching herself hoping that some of the town may be watching. There, she thinks, as she cups her hand against his cheek, and there, as she touches her fingers to his hair. He kisses her again, for longer this time. Then he sighs, cradling the back of her head, his face buried in her neck.

'I shan't go,' he mutters, but she feels the pull and stretch of the words, how he says them, but at the same time they peel away from his real feelings.

'You shall,' she says.

'I shan't.'

'You must.'

He sighs again, his breath rustling in the starch of her coif. 'Perhaps I shouldn't be leaving you now, while you are . . . I think perhaps—'

'It must be,' she says, and touches her fingers to the canvas of his pack from which, she knows, he has removed some of the glove samples his father has given him, and replaced them with books and papers. She gives him a wry half-smile. Perhaps he catches her knowledge of this act, perhaps not.

'I have your mother and your sister,' she continues, pressing her hand to his luggage, 'and your whole family. Not to mention my own. You need to go. You will find us a new home in London and we will join you there, as soon as we can.'

'I don't know,' he murmurs. 'I hate to leave you. And what if I fail?'

'Fail?'

'What if I can't find work there? What if I can't expand the business? What if—'

'You won't fail,' she says. 'I know it.'

He frowns and looks at her more carefully. 'You know it? What do you know? Tell me. Have you a sense of something? Have you—'

'Never mind what I know. You must go.' She pushes at his chest, putting air and space between them, feeling his arms slide off her, disentangling them. His face is crumpled, tense, uncertain. She smiles at him, drawing in breath.

'I won't say goodbye,' she says, keeping her voice steady.

'Neither will I.'

'I won't watch you walk away.'

'I'll walk backwards,' he says, backing away, 'so I can keep you in my sights.'

'All the way to London?'

'If I have to.'

She laughs. 'You'll fall into a ditch. You'll crash into a cart.'

'So be it.'

He darts forward, catches her to him and kisses her once. 'That's for you,' he says, then kisses her again. 'That's for Susanna.' And again, 'And that's for the baby.'

'I shall be sure to deliver it,' she says, trying to keep the smile on her face, 'when the time comes. Now go.'

'I'm going,' he says, walking away from her, still facing her. 'It doesn't feel like leaving, if I walk like this.'

She flaps her hands. 'Go,' she tells him.

'I'm going. But I shall be back before you know it to fetch you all.'

She turns away before he reaches the bend in the road. It will take him four days to reach London, less if he is picked up along the way by a willing farmer with a cart. She will encourage him to go but she will not watch him leave.

She walks back, more slowly, the way she came. How odd it feels, to move along the same streets, the route in reverse, like inking over old words, her feet the quill, going back over work, rewriting, erasing. Partings are strange. It seems so simple: one minute ago, four, five, he was here, at her side; now, he is gone. She was with him; she is alone. She feels exposed, chill, peeled like an onion.

There is the stall they passed earlier, piled high with tin pots and cedar shavings. There is the woman they saw, still making her decision, holding two pots in her hands, weighing them, and how can she still be there, how can she still be engaged in the same activity, in the choosing of a pot, when such a change, such a transformation has occurred in Agnes's life? Her very world has cloven in two, and here is the same dog, dozing in a doorway. Here is a young woman, tying up clothing into bundles, just as she was doing when they passed. Here is her neighbour, a man with grizzled hair and a yellowish tinge to his thin face (he will not last the year, Agnes thinks, the fact flitting through her mind like a swallow across a sky), giving her a grave nod as he walks by. Can he not see, can he not read that life as she knows it is over, that he is gone?

The baby gives a swift, shrugging movement, pressing a palm, a foot, a shoulder against the wall of skin. She places a hand there – a hand outside, next to the hand inside – as if nothing has changed, as if the world is just as it was.

liza's letter is taken by a lad from a few houses along: he was up and out, walking down Henley Street before dawn because he has been sent by his father to see to a cow in calf on the far side of the river. Mary hailed him from the window, gave him the letter, with instructions to take it to the posting inn, pressing a coin into his hands.

The boy tucks it into his sleeve, not before examining the slanted scrawl on the front. He has never learnt to read so it is meaningless to him but, all the same, he likes the loops, the shapes, the dark cross-hatchings of ink, like the marks made when branches are shaken against an iced-over window-pane.

He takes it to the inn near the bridge, then continues on to his cow, which still hasn't calved and stares at him with large and what seem to the boy frightened eyes, jaws grinding cud. Later that morning the innkeeper hands it, with others, to a grain merchant, who is riding that day to London.

Eliza's letter to her brother travels in the leather satchel of the grain merchant as far as Banbury. From there, it is taken by cart to Stokenchurch, and it lands at the door of the lodgings. The landlord squints at it, holding it up to the sunlight, which enters his passageway at a slant. His eyesight is poor. He sees the name of his lodger, who yesterday left for Kent. The theatres are closed, because of the plague, by order of the court, and so the lodger and his company of players have taken themselves off to tour nearby towns, places where it is permitted to gather in a crowd.

The landlord must wait for his son to come back from some business in Cheapside. When he does – grumpily, because the person he was due to meet did not arrive and it rained heavily and the son is wet to the skin – it is several hours before he gets out ink and quill, takes the letter from the mantel, and painstakingly, tongue wedged in the corner of his mouth, writes the address of the inn in Kent, where the lodger told them he would be staying.

The letter is then passed from hand to hand, to an inn in the outskirts of the city, where it waits for someone travelling to Kent – in this instance, a man pushing a cart, sat upon by a woman and a dog and a chicken.

When the letter reaches him, he – lodger, brother, husband, father and, here, player – is standing in a guildhall in a small town on the eastern fringes of Kent. The hall smells of cured meat, of boiled beets; there is a heap of farming implements and sacking in the corner; narrow blades of light enter the space from high, mildew-spotted windows.

He is leaning back, regarding these weak beams of light, reflecting on how they meet each other halfway across the hall, creating archways of light, and how they give the whole space an underwater feel, as if he and the rest of the company are fish, swimming about in the gloomy depths of a greenish pond.

A small child – a boy, he supposes – darts in, barefoot, bareheaded, ragged of smock, scrofulous of complexion, and calls out an approximation of his name, in an assertive, reedy voice, waving a letter aloft, as if it were a flag.

'It is I,' he says wearily, holding out his hand. It will be a demand for money, a complaint, an edict from a patron. 'Hear this,' he says to his colleagues, who are milling aimlessly on the raised dais, as if, he thinks, they aren't putting on a performance in less than three hours, as if nothing in particular is happening here in this dusty hall. 'You will need to count your paces from left to right, like so,' he demonstrates, walking towards the shoeless child, 'or else one of you will fall offstage and into the audience. It is smaller than we are used to, but used to it we must be.' He comes to a halt in front of the child. Strangely colourless hair and wide-set eyes. A sore on the bottom lip. Fingernails rimmed with filth. Six or seven years of age, perhaps more.

He tweaks the letter from the child's grip. 'For me?' he says, sliding his fingers into his purse and extracting a coin. 'And for you.' He flips the coin into the air between them. Instantly, the child is animated, his scrawny body leaping into life.

He laughs, turning on his heel, pulling at the red seal, stamped slightly off-centre with his family's insignia. He registers his sister's hand before he lifts his head. Onstage, the young lad is pacing stiffly towards the older actor, edging around the rim of the dais, as if the floor beneath were awash with boiling lead.

'Good God,' he roars, his voice stretching at the wooden struts, the skin of plaster on the walls. He knows how to throw his voice, how to expand it so it becomes the sound of a giant. The actors freeze, mouths agape. 'We have only a few hours before this hall will be filled with the good people of Kent. Are you meaning to give them a circus? Do we intend to make them laugh or are we putting on a tragedy? Look to it or we won't be eating tomorrow.'

He cracks the page he is holding against the air, stares at them a moment longer, for effect. It seems to have worked. The young lad looks to be on the verge of tears, twisting his fingers into his costume. He turns, to hide his smile, then glances down at the letter.

'Dear brother,' he sees. And 'verie sick', and 'your daughter'. 'Plea ſe come bak to us,' it says: 'not manie hours left to her.'

It seems hard to breathe, suddenly. The air in the hall is as hot as a furnace, with particles of chaff. He feels his chest labouring in and out, but no air seems to be reaching him. He stares at the page, reading the words once, twice. The whiteness of the paper seems to pulse, stark and glaring, one moment, then recede behind the black strokes of the letters. He sees for a moment his daughter, her face lifted up to look at him, her hands clasped together, her eyes fixed on his. He wants to loosen his clothes; he wants to tear off his fastenings. He must get out, he must leave this building.

With the letter gripped in his fist, he rushes at the door, pushes his weight against it. Outside, the colours accost his eyes: the glancing lapis sky, the virulent green of the verge, the creamy blossoms of a tree, the pink kirtle of a woman leading a nag along the road. On either side of the animal's flanks are woven baskets. It is immediately obvious to him that one basket is much heavier than the other: the baskets are uneven, dragging down on one side.

Even up that load, he wants to yell at her, much as he just yelled at the players inside the hall. But he doesn't have the breath. His lungs are still heaving in and out, his heart hammering now in his ribcage, hammering, hesitating, hammering once more. His vision seems to shimmer at its edges, the pale tree blossoms wavering, as if seen through a fire's heat.

Verie sick, he thinks, not manie hours left.

He wants to tear down the sky, he wants to rip every blossom from that tree, he wishes to take a burning branch and drive that pink-clad girl and her nag over a cliff, just to be rid of them, to clear them all out of his way. So many miles, so much road stands between him and his child, and so few hours left.

He is conscious of a hand on his shoulder, a face near his, another hand gripping his arm. Two of his friends are there, saying, What, what is the matter, what has happened? One of them, Heminge, is trying to take the letter from his hand, peeling back his fingers, and he will not let it go, he will not. For someone else to read those words might make them true, make them come to pass. He is shrugging the men off, both of them, all of them, because here are more of them, his players, crowding round him, but somehow he feels the gritted ground under his knees and the voice of his friend, Heminge, is reading the words of the letter aloud. Hands are patting his shoulders now; he is being assisted to his feet. Someone is telling someone else to run for a horse, any horse, that they must get him to Stratford as soon as possible. Go, Heminge is urging the young boy who was, not so long ago, nervous of the drop at the edge of the stage, go and fetch a horse. The young boy takes off down the road, dirt flying up from his heels, his costume – a ridiculous thing of brocade and velvet, made to cast the illusion of a woman on the form of a lad – flapping about him.

He watches him go, peering through the thicket of legs surrounding him.

owards the end of Agnes's second pregnancy, Mary is watchful. She doesn't let Agnes alone for long. She has noticed her daughter-in-law's middle getting larger and larger, rounder than seems possible. She has seen Agnes secreting certain items in a sack under the table: cloths, scissors, twine, packets of herbs and dried rinds. Her appearance is astonishing, as if she is smuggling pumpkins inside her gown. I don't know how she's still walking, John mumbled one night, as they lay, curtained tight inside their bed. How does she stay standing?

Mary keeps an eye on her, and instructs Eliza and the servants to do the same. She will not permit this grandchild – a boy, they are all hoping – to be born in a bush, like poor Susanna. But that, she consoles herself, was before they fully understood the extent of Agnes's eccentricities and ways.

'The minute she asks you to take care of Susanna, the minute you see her reaching for that sack, let me know,' Mary hisses to the serving girl. 'The very minute. Do you hear me?'

The girl nods, eyes wide.

Agnes is warming honey over the fire, into which she plans to stir extract of valerian and tincture of chickweed. She dips a spoon into it and pushes it one way, then the other, watching it slide over and around the wooden tip. It is beginning to surrender to the heat, losing its stiffness, easing and loosening into liquid, changing one form for another. She is thinking about the letter that arrived from her husband earlier in the week. She has asked Eliza to read it to her twice and she wants to ask her to read it again today, as soon as she can find her. In it, he told Agnes that he has obtained a contract to make gloves for players at a theatre: Agnes had to ask Eliza to go back and read these words again, so that she was sure she understood, to point them out on the paper, so she could recognise them again, later. Players. Theatre. Gloves. Such gloves they need, Eliza had read haltingly, a frown on her face, as she made out the unfamiliar words. Long gauntlets for fighting, fine gloves with jewels and beads for kings and queens and scenes in court, soft gloves for ladies but the size must necessarily be bigger on these for they are to fit the hands of young stage boys.

So much to mull over in this letter. It has taken Agnes days to absorb all the detail; she has run the words over and over inside her head, she has traced them with a finger, and now she has them down to memory. Jewels and beads. Scenes in court. The hands of young stage boys. And soft gloves for ladies. There is something in the way he has written all this, in such lingering detail, in the long passage about these gloves for the players that alerts Agnes to something. She is not yet sure what. Some kind of change in him, some alter- ation or turning. Never has he written so much about so little: a glove contract. It is just a contract, like many others, so why, then, does she feel like a small animal, hearing something far off?

She is leaning over to pick up the chickweed tincture and is about to add it to the honey, drop by slow drop, when she feels an odd yet familiar tensing in her lower abdomen. A drawing down, a clenching: insistent, particular. She pauses.

It cannot be that. It is too soon. There is still at least another moon to reach fullness before the baby will be born. It must be a false pain, one of those that warns the body of what is to come. She straightens up, using the fireplace for support. Her belly is so big – so much bigger than last time – that she is in danger of toppling into the flames.

She grips the mantel, watching with an unaccustomed detachment as her knuckles turn white. What is happening? She had meant to ask Eliza – today or tomorrow – to write to him, to ask him to return to them. She would like him here for the birth, she has decided. She would like to lay eyes on him again, to take his hand, before this child makes it into the world. She wants to look into his face, to find out what is happening in his life, to ask him about these gloves for kings and queens and players. She wants, she realises, as she stands at the fire, to check that he is the same as he ever was, whether London has altered him unrecognisably.

She pulls in a breath: the sweet, floral scent of the honey, the acrid valerian, the sour musk of chickweed. The pain, instead of easing off, intensifies. She is aware of her centre tightening, as if an iron band is being placed around her. No false pain, this. It will squeeze her and squeeze her, until her body yields up this baby. It may be hours, it may be days: she finds she cannot get a sense of how long. Agnes lets out her breath, slowly, slowly, one hand on the fireplace. She was not expecting this. There was no sign.

She'd thought she had time to get word to him. But now there is no time. This is too soon. She knows this. Yet she also knows that a pain like this cannot be argued with, cannot be got around.

Agnes turns to face the room. Everything around her looks suddenly different, as if she has never seen it before, as if she doesn't daily wipe and polish this table, those chairs, sweep these flagstones, beat the dust from that wall hanging and the rug. Who lives here, in this narrow room, with leaded windows at the end and long shelves of pots and powders? Who put those wands of hazel into a jug, so that their tight buds would yield up early their bright, creased leaves?

Certainties have deserted her. Nothing is as she thought it was. She'd thought she had more time; she'd thought this baby would come much later, but it seems not. She, who has always known, always sensed what will happen before it happens, who has moved serenely through a world utterly transparent, has been wrongfooted, caught off guard. How can this be?

Agnes touches her stomach, as if to communicate with the child inside. Very well, she wants to say to it, what must be shall be. You shall be heard. I will get ready for you.

She has to hurry. She has to get out of this house as quickly as she can. She will not birth this baby here, under this roof. Mary has her eye on her, she knows. She will need to be quick, quiet, wily. She will need to leave now.

Beside her, Susanna is crouching on the floor, holding her doll by its leg, exclaiming to herself.

'Come,' Agnes says to her, aiming for a tone of brisk cheer. She holds out her hand. 'Let's go and find Eliza, shall we?'

Susanna, lost in her game with the upside-down doll, is astonished to see the hand of an adult drop down from above. One moment, there was a doll and the doll was a person who could fly, except her wings could not be seen, and she, Susanna, could also fly and she and the doll were taking to the skies, among the birds, up above the trees. And now there is this: a hand.

She tips back her face and sees her mother looming over her, all stomach, with a faraway face, saying something about Eliza, about going.

Susanna's face pulls in and she frowns. 'No,' she says, curling both hands around the leg of her doll.

'Please,' says her mother, and her voice doesn't sound as it usually does. It is pinched and tight, like an outgrown smock.

'No,' Susanna says again, angry now, because her sense of the game is evaporating, drifting away, with all this talking from above. 'No-no-no!'

'Yes,' Agnes is saying, and Susanna is astonished to feel herself lifted off her feet, the hearthrug falling away from her, the fire whisking past her, as she is carried, without ceremony, out of the room, away from her doll, which has fallen to the floor, through the door and down the path to the washhouse, where the maid is standing, scrubbing at something in a bowl.

'Here,' Agnes says, thrusting the roaring child into her arms. 'Can you take her to Eliza?' She leans in and kisses Susanna on the cheek, then the forehead, then the cheek again. 'Sorry, my darling. I'll be back. Very soon.'

Agnes goes quickly, very quickly, up the path, reaching her hearth just as the next pain comes. There is no question, now, of what is happening. She remembers it all from last time, except somehow this feels different. It is fast, it is early, it is insistent. She is not yet where she needs to be, in the forest, alone, with the trees over her head. She is not alone. She is still here, in the town, in the apartment. There is not a moment to lose. Ah-ah-ah, she hears herself pant. She grips the back of a chair until it passes. Then she makes her way across the room to the table, where she has left her bag.

She hooks her fingers around the strap and is at her front door in seconds, manoeuvring herself through, stepping out. Just before she shuts it, she listens for a moment, then nods, satisfied: Susanna's wails have stopped, which means she must be in the presence of her aunt.

She is setting out across the street, pausing to let a horse pass by, when someone falls into step beside her. She turns to see Gilbert, her brother-in-law, next to her, grinning.

'Going somewhere?' he says, raising his eyebrows.

'No,' Agnes says, panic beating, like a pulse, against her brow. She has to get to the forest, she must. If she is made to stay here, she doesn't know what will happen. It won't bode well. Something will go wrong. She is so certain of this fact, while unable to explain why. 'I mean, yes. To . . .' She tries to focus on Gilbert but his face, his beard, looks blurry and indistinct. She is struck, once again, by how unlike his brother he is. 'To . . .' she casts around for a plausible place '. . . the bakery.'

He clamps his hand around her elbow. 'Come,' he says.

'Where?'

'Back to the house.'

'No,' she says, pulling her elbow away. 'I won't. I'm going to the bakery and you – you must let me go. You mustn't stop me.'

'Yes, I must.'

'No, you must not.'

At this point, Mary comes hurrying up, out of breath. 'Agnes,' she says, taking her other arm, 'you are to come back to the house. We have everything ready. You needn't worry.' And then, out of the corner of her mouth, to Gilbert: 'Go for the midwife.'

'No,' Agnes is shouting now, 'let me go.' How can she explain to these people that she cannot remain here, she cannot birth the child in this way? How can she make them understand the dread that has been filling her, ever since she heard the words of that letter?

Agnes is taken, half carried, half dragged, not to her own narrow slip of a house, but to theirs, through their wide door, down the passage and up the narrow stairs. A door is pushed open, and through she sails, her ankles held together, like a criminal, like a lunatic.

She can hear a voice saying, No, no, no; she can sense a pain coming for her, the way it's possible to feel a raincloud approaching before seeing it. She wants to stand, to crouch, so that she is ready for it, prepared, able to face it down, but someone is pressing her shoulders back to a bed. Another person is gripping her forehead. The midwife is there, lifting her skirts, saying she must look, that the men must leave, that only the women may stay.

All Agnes wants is the green of a forest. She craves the dappled, animate pattern of light on ground, the merciful shade of a leaf-canopy, the not-quite-quiet, the repeating seclusion of trunks, disappearing into the distance. She will not make it to the forest. There is not enough time now. The doors of this house are too many, she knows this.

If only he had been here. He would have been able to hold them off. He would have listened to her pleas, in that way he has, of leaning towards someone, as if drinking in their words.

He would have made sure she reached the forest, that she wasn't forced to come in here. What has she done? Why did she send him away? What will become of them, separated in this way, with him dealing and bargaining for theatre silver, making gloves for the hands of lads to give the illusion of ladies, with her locked and barred in this room, so far away, with no one to take her part? What has she done?

Agnes pushes them off her, climbs out of bed. She walks, instead of a stitched, lapsing path through trees, from wall to wall, and back again. It is hard to order and command her thoughts. She would like a moment to herself, alone, without pain, so that she can think clearly about everything. She wrings her hands. She can hear herself, or someone, wailing, Why did I do it? She doesn't know what 'it' refers to. This room, she knows, is where her husband was born – and his brothers and sisters, even those little dead ones. He took his first breath here, within these drapes, near this window.

It is to him she speaks, in her disordered mind, not the trees, not the magic cross, not the patterns and markings of lichen, not even to her mother, who died while trying to give birth to a child. Please, she says to him, inside the chamber of her skull, please come back. I need you. Please. I should never have schemed to send you away. Make sure this child has safe passage; make sure it lives; make sure I survive to care for it. Let us both come through this. Please. Let me not die. Let me not end up cold and stiff in a bloodied bed.

Something is wrong, off, out of place. She doesn't know what. It is like listening to an instrument with one untuned string: the grating sense that all is not as it should be. It is all too fast, too soon. She had no sense of this coming. She is in the wrong place. He is in the wrong place. She may not make it, she may not. Her mother may, this very moment, be calling her to that place from which people never return.

The midwife and Mary have their hands on her now: they are guiding her to a stool, except it's not a proper stool. It is blackened oiled wood, three-legged, splay-footed, with a basin beneath and an empty seat – just a gaping hole. Agnes doesn't like it, doesn't take to that absent seat, that vacancy, so she rears back, she wrenches her arms from their grasp. She will not sit on the black stool.

That letter. What was different about that letter? It wasn't the detail, it wasn't the list of gloves needed. Was it the mention of long gloves for ladies? Is she bothered, hooked by the mention of ladies? She doesn't think so. It was the feeling that came off the page. The glee that rose up, like steam, between the words he had written. It feels wrong that the two of them are so far away from each other, so separated. While he is deciding what length of glove, what manner of beading, what embroidery would best suit a player king, she is clenched by agony and about to die.

She will die, she thinks. What other reason can there be for her having no sign that any of this would happen? That she is about to die, to pass on, to leave this world. She will never see him, never see Susanna again.

Agnes takes to the floor, felled by this presentiment. Never again. She braces herself with her palms flat to the boards, her legs folded either side of her, crouched. If death is to come, let it be quick, she prays. Let the child within her live. Let him come back and be with his children. Let him think kindly of her, always.

The midwife is plucking at her sleeve, but Mary seems to have given up trying to entice her to the stool. Agnes will not be led; she feels that Mary knows this by now. Mary sits down on the hateful stool and holds out a muslin cloth, ready to catch the baby.

The theatre, he had written, was in a place called Shoreditch; Eliza had had to sound out the word, letter by letter, to get the sense of it. 'Shore', she had said, and then 'ditch'. Shore-ditch? Agnes had repeated. She pictured the bank of a river, silted, reed-frilled, a place where yellow flags might grow, and birds would nest, and then a ditch, a treacherously slippery sloped hole, with muddy water in the bottom. 'Shore' and then 'ditch'. The first part of the word a nice-sounding sort of place, the latter part horrible. How can there be a ditch at a shore? She had started to ask Eliza, but Eliza was reading on, describing a play he had watched there, while waiting for the man with the glove contract, about an envious duke and his faithless sons.

The midwife is huffing, getting down on the floor, fussing with her skirts and apron, saying she will need extra pay, that her knees aren't up to this. She near-flattens herself to the rug and peers upwards.

'It'll soon be over,' is her verdict. 'Bear down,' she says, a touch brusquely.

Mary puts a hand to Agnes's shoulder, the other to her arm. 'There now,' she mutters. 'Soon be over.'

Agnes hears their words from a great distance. Her thoughts are brief now, snipped short, pared back to the bone. Husband, she thinks. Gloves. Players. Beads. Theatre. Envious duke. Death. Think kindly. She is able to form the realisation, not in words, perhaps, but in a sensation, that he sounded not different in that letter but returned. Back to himself. Restored. Better. Returned.

She watches, with a kind of detached fascination, as something domed appears between her legs. She curls her head under, into herself, to see it. The crown of a head easing from her, turning, twisting, slick, like a water creature, a shoulder, a long back, beaded with spine. The midwife and Mary catch it between them, Mary saying, a boy, a boy, and Agnes sees her husband's chin, his mouth in a pout; she sees her father's fair hair, once again, growing in a peak on this brow; she sees the long, delicate fingers of her mother; she sees her son.

Agnes and the boy are on the bed, the child feeding, his tiny fist curled possessively at his mother's breast. She would feed him before anything, before washing herself, she said. She has insisted that the cord and caul be wrapped and bound in cloth; she raised her head to watch, as Mary and the midwife carried out this task. She will, she tells them, bury it under a tree when the child has passed his first month. The midwife is collecting her tools, packing her sack, folding a sheet, emptying a bowl from the window. Mary is sitting on the bed, saying to Agnes that she must let her swaddle the baby, it is the right thing to do, that all her babies were swaddled and look how they turned out, great strong lads, all of them, and Eliza too, and Agnes is shaking her head. No swaddle, thank you, she is saying, and the midwife is smiling to herself in the corner, because she attended Mary in her last three births and found her a great deal more pleased with herself than she ought to be.

The midwife, swirling a cloth around a bowl, has to bow her head because this daughter-in-law, a strange girl by all accounts, is a match for Mary. She can see that. She would be prepared to bet all her pennies (hidden in an earthen jar behind the daub of her cottage, which no living person knows) that this baby will wear no swaddling clothes.

Something makes her turn, wet cloth in hand. When she is telling the story, to a dozen or so townspeople later, she will say that she doesn't know why she turned: she just did. Midwife's intuition, she will say later, tapping her finger to her nose.

Agnes is upright in bed, one hand pressed to her middle; with the other, she still holds the baby to her breast.

'What is it?' Mary says, rising from the bed.

Agnes shakes her head, then doubles up again, with a low moan.

'Give me the boy,' Mary says, holding out her arms. Her face is alarmed, but tender. She wants that child, the midwife sees, despite everything, despite her own eight children, despite her age. She wants that baby, wants to feel it up against her, to hold its parcelled, dense warmth.

'No,' Agnes says, through clenched teeth, her body curled into itself. Her expression is bewildered, stretched, frightened. 'What is happening?' she whispers, in the hoarse, fearful voice of a child.

The midwife steps forward. She puts a hand to the girl's belly and presses down. She feels the skin tightening, pulling into itself. She lifts the skirts and peers upwards. There it is: the wet curve of a second head. It is unmistakable.

'It's starting again,' she says.

'What do you mean?' Mary asks, with her slightly imperious air.

'She's starting again,' the midwife repeats. 'There's another one coming.' She pats Agnes's leg. 'You're having twins, my girl.'

Agnes takes this news in silence. She lies back in the bed, clutching her son, exhausted, grey-faced, her limbs slack, her head bowed. The only sign of the pains is a whitening of her face, a pursing of her lips. She allows them to take the baby and to tuck it into the cradle by the fire.

Mary and the midwife stand on either side of the bed. Agnes stares up at them, her eyes wide and glassy, her face ghastly white. She raises a finger and points, first at Mary, then at the midwife.

'Two of you,' she rasps out.

'What did she say?' the midwife says to Mary.

Mary shakes her head. 'I'm not sure.' Then she addresses the girl: 'Agnes, come to the stool. It is ready. It is here. We shall help you. The time has come.'

Agnes is gripped by a pain, her body twisting first one way, then the next. Her fingers snatch at the sheet, pulling it from the mattress, and she presses it to her mouth. The cry that escapes her is ragged and muffled.

'Two of you,' she mutters again. 'Always thought it would be my children, standing at the bed, but it turns out that it was you.'

'What was that?' the midwife says, disappearing once again under the hem of Agnes's shift.

'I've no idea,' Mary says, more brightly than she feels.

'She's raving,' the midwife says, with a shrug. 'Doesn't know where she is. It takes some like that. Well,' she says, hauling herself upright again, 'this baby is coming, so we need to get her up off that bed.'

Between them, gripping her under each arm, they get Agnes up. She permits them to lead her out of bed to the stool and she slumps down on it without a murmur. Mary stands behind Agnes, propping up her limp form.

After a while, Agnes begins to speak, if the sounds and disjointed words could be called that. 'I should never . . .' she mutters, and her voice is no more than a whisper, gulping for air '. . . I should never . . . I got it wrong . . . He's not here . . . I cannot—'

'You can,' the midwife says, from her position on the floor. 'And you will.'

'I cannot . . .' Agnes grips Mary's arm, her face wet, her eyes wide, glittering, unseeing, willing her to understand '. . . you see, my mother died . . . and . . . and I sent him away . . . I cannot—'

'You—' the midwife begins, but Mary interrupts her.

'Hold your tongue,' she snaps. 'Attend to your work.' She cups her hand around Agnes's bloodless face. 'What is it?' she whispers.

Agnes looks at her and her flecked eyes are pleading, scared. Mary has never seen this look on her face before.

'The thing is . . .' she whispers '. . . it was me . . . I sent him away . . . and then my mother died.'

'I know she did,' Mary says, moved. 'You won't, though. I am sure of it. You are strong.'

'She . . . she was strong.'

Mary grips her hand. 'You will be fine, you'll see.'

'But the problem . . .' Agnes says '. . . is that . . . I should never . . . I should never have . . .'

'What? What should you never have done?'

'I should never have sent him . . . to . . . to London . . . It was wrong . . . I should—'

'It wasn't you,' Mary says soothingly. 'It was John.'

Agnes's head, lolling on its neck, snaps round to face her. 'It was me,' she mutters, teeth clenched.

'It was John,' Mary insists.

Agnes shakes her head. 'I shan't make it through,' she gasps. She grips Mary by the hand, her fingers pressing painful spots into the flesh. 'Will you take care of them? You and Eliza. Will you?'

'Take care of who?'

'The children. Will you?'

'Of course, but—'

'Don't let my stepmother take them.'

'Certainly not. I would never—'

'Not Joan. Anyone but Joan. Promise me.' Her expression is maddened, drained, her fingers clamped into Mary's hand. 'Promise me you'll look after them.'

'I promise,' Mary says, frowning, staring into the face of her daughter-in-law. What has she seen? What does she know? Mary is chilled, discomforted, her skin crawling with horror. She refuses, for the main part, to believe what people say about Agnes, that she can see people's futures, she can read their palms, or whatever it is she does. But now, for the first time, she has a sense of what people mean. Agnes is of another world. She does not quite belong here. The thought, however, of Agnes dying, in front of her, fills her with despair. She cannot let that happen. What would she say to her son?

'I promise,' she says again, looking her daughter-in-law right in the eye. Agnes lets go of her hand. Together, they look down at the dome of her belly, at the shoulders of the midwife, below.

The second labour is short, fast and difficult. The pains come without interval, on and on, and Mary can see that Agnes, like a swimmer going under, cannot catch her breath in between. Her screams, by the end, are ragged, hoarse, desperate. Mary holds her, her own face wet with tears. She begins to form, in her head, the words she will say to her son. We tried our best. We did everything we could. In the end, we couldn't save her.

When the baby emerges, it is clear to them all that the death they have been dreading is not Agnes's after all. The baby is grey in colour, the cord tight around its neck.

No one says anything as the midwife eases the body out with one hand and catches it in the other. A girl child, half the size of the first, and silent. Eyes shut tight, fists curled, lips pursed, as if in apology.

The midwife unloops the cord quickly, deftly, and turns the little doll upside-down. She lands a slap on its bottom, once, twice, but nothing. No noise, no cry, no flicker of life. The midwife raises her hand a third time.

'Enough,' says Agnes, holding out her arms. 'Let me have her.'

The midwife mumbles about how she should not look on it, how it is bad luck. It is best, she says, you don't see it. She will take it away, she says, and make sure it gets a decent burial.

'Give her to me,' Agnes says, and goes to rise from the stool.

Mary steps forward and takes the child from the midwife. Its face is perfect, she thinks, and the image of its brother's

– the same brow, the same line of jaw and cheek. It has eyelashes and fingernails and is still warm.

Mary hands the tiny form to Agnes, who takes it and holds it to her, cradling the head in her palm.

The room is silent.

'You have a beautiful boy,' the midwife says, after a moment. 'Let's bring him here and you may feed him.'

'I will fetch him,' Mary says, starting towards the cradle.

'No, I will,' says the midwife, crossing before her, stepping into her path.

Annoyed, Mary pushes at her shoulder. 'Out of my way. I will fetch my grandson.'

'Mistress, I need to say that—' The midwife is squaring up to her, but she never finishes her sentence because from behind them comes a thin, spiralling cry.

They both turn, in unison.

The child in Agnes's arms, the girl, is wailing, arms rigid with outrage, her minute form rinsing itself pink as she draws in air.

Two babies, then, not one. Agnes tells herself this as she lies in bed, curtains drawn against the sharp draughts.

It is by no means certain, in those first few weeks, whether the girl-child will survive. Agnes knows this. She knows it in her mind, in her bones, in her skin, right down to her heart. She knows in the way her mother-in-law tiptoes into the room and peers at the children, sometimes putting a quick hand to their chests. She sees it in the way Mary urges John to take the babies to be churched: she and John wrap the infants in blanket after blanket, then tuck them into their clothing and hurry to the priest. Mary bursts back into the house a while later, with the air of a woman who has completed a race, outrun an enemy, holding out the smaller of the twins towards her, saying, There, it is done, here she is.

Agnes may not sleep, it seems. She may not rise from the bed. She may not have a hand spare or empty. One or both of the babies will need to be held at any given moment. She will feed one, then the other, then the first again; she will feed them both at once, heads meeting in the centre of her chest, their bodies podded under each of her arms. She feeds and feeds and feeds.

The boy, Hamnet, is strong. This she has known since the moment she first saw him. He latches on with a definite and sure force, sucking with great concentration. The girl, Judith, needs to be encouraged on to the breast. Sometimes, when her mouth is opened for her and the breast placed inside it, she looks confused, as if unsure what she is meant to do. Agnes must stroke her cheek, tap her chin, run a finger along her jaw, to remind her to suck, to sup, to live.

Agnes's concept of death has, for a long time, taken the form of a single room, lit from within, perhaps in the middle of an expanse of moorland. The living inhabit the room; the dead mill about outside it, pressing their palms and faces and fingertips to the window, desperate to get back, to reach their people. Some inside the room can hear and see those outside; some can speak through the walls; most cannot.

The idea that this tiny child might have to live out there, on the cold and misted moor, without her, is unthinkable. She will not let her pass over. It is always the smaller twin who is taken: everybody knows this. Everyone, she can tell, is waiting, breath held, for this to happen. She knows that for the girl child, the door leading out of the room of the living is ajar; she can feel the chill of the draught, scent that icy air. She knows that she is meant to have only two children but she will not accept this. She tells herself this, in the darkest hours of the night. She will not let it happen; not tonight, not tomorrow, not any day. She will find that door and slam it shut.

She keeps the twins tucked into bed, on either side of her; she has one breathing in one ear and one in the other. When Hamnet wakes, with a creaking cry, to feed, Agnes rouses Judith. Feed, little one, she whispers to her, time to feed.

She fears her foresight; she does. She remembers with ice-cold clarity the image she had of two figures at the foot of the bed where she will meet her end. She now knows that it's possible, more than possible, that one of her children will die, because children do, all the time. But she will not have it. She will not. She will fill this child, these children, with life. She will place herself between them and the door leading out, and she will stand there, teeth bared, blocking the way. She will defend her three babes against all that lies beyond this world. She will not rest, not sleep, until she knows they are safe. She will push back, fight against, undo the foresight she has always had, about having two children. She will. She knows she can.

When her husband comes, there is a moment when he doesn't recognise her. He is looking for his handsome, full-lipped wife, standing by her pots and pestle, but he finds instead, prostrate on the bed, a waif, half crazed with sleeplessness and determination and single-minded purpose. He finds a woman worn thin with feeding, with grey-ringed eyes, with a face desperate and focused. He finds two babies with the same inscrutable face, one double the size of the other.

He takes them in his hands; he meets their steady gazes; he looks into their identical eyes; he arranges them, head to foot, upon his knee; he watches as one takes the thumb of the other into its mouth and sucks upon it; he sees that the pair have led a life together that began before anything else. He touches their heads with both of his palms. You, he says, and you.

She can tell, even through her dazed exhaustion, even before she can take his hand, that he has found it, he is fitting it, he is inhabiting it – that life he was meant to live, that work he was intended to do. It makes her smile, there on the bed, to see him stand so tall, his chest thrown wide, his face clear of worry and frustration, to inhale his scent of satisfaction.

They still believe, as they sit together in the birthing room, that she will join him in London soon, that she will bring the three children to the city and they will live there together. They believe that this is shortly to happen. She is already planning what to pack and take with them. She is telling Susanna that soon they will live in a big city and she will see houses and boats and bears and palaces. Will the babies come with us? Susanna asks, with a sidelong glance at the cradle. Yes, Agnes says, hiding her smile.

He has already looked at houses; he is saving money to buy a place for them. He has envisaged taking Susanna on his shoulders to look at the river, bringing them all to the playhouse. He has imagined his new friends looking with wistful envy at his wife's dark eyes and slender gloved wrists, at the pretty heads of his children. He pictures a kitchen with two cradles, his wife bending over the fire, a yard at the back where they might keep hens or rabbits. It will just be the five of them, perhaps more in time: he permits himself this thought. No one else. No family next door. No brothers or parents or in-laws bursting into the place at odd hours. Nobody at all. Just them, this kitchen, these cradles. He can almost smell this kitchen: the beeswax on the table surface, the curdled-milk smell of the babies, the starch of the laundry. His wife will hum to herself as she works, the babes will gurgle and chatter, Susanna will be out at the back, talking to the rabbits, examining their liquid eyes, their sleek fur, and he will sit at his hearth, surrounded by his family, not cramped into a lodging room, writing letters that take four days to reach them. He will no longer lead this double life, this split existence. They will be there, with him; he will need only to raise his head to see them. He will be alone no more in the big city: he will have a firmer foothold there, a wife, a family, a house. With Agnes there, beside him, who knows what may be possible for him?

Neither he nor his wife, as they sit in the room with their tiny babies, knows that this plan will never come off. She will never bring the children to join him in London. He will never buy a house there.

The girl child will live. She will grow from a baby to an infant to a child, but her hold on life will remain tenuous, frail, indefinite. She will suffer convulsions, her limbs shaking and trembling, fevers, congestion of the chest. Her skin will flush with rashes, her lungs will labour to draw in air. If the other two children get a head cold, she will be seized by an ague. If they have a cough, she will be racked by wheezing.

Agnes will delay their departure for London by a few months: until she is well, she asks Eliza to write to him. Until spring comes. Until the heat of summer is over. When the winds of autumn are past. When the snow has melted.

Judith is two, her mother staying awake with her each night, steaming bowls of pine and clove inside the bed-curtains, so that she may breathe, so that the blue fades from her lips, and she might sleep, before it is apparent to everyone that the move to London will never take place. The child's health is too fragile. She would never survive the city.

The father will visit them, during plague season, when the playhouses are closed. He has given up selling gloves, hawking his father's wares, severing himself entirely from the business. He now works only in the playhouses. He watches one night as his wife walks the floor with the girl; she has a distemper of the stomach.

She is a preternaturally beautiful child, even to the indifferent observer, with clear blue eyes and soft, celestial curls. She fixes her gaze, over her mother's shoulder as they walk from one side of the room to the other, on her father. Silent tears edge down her cheeks and she grips her mother's shift in both hands. He looks back at her steadily. He clears his throat. He tells his wife that he has decided to spend the money he has saved, not on a house in London but on some land just outside Stratford. It will bring in good rent, he tells her. He stands, as if to square up to this decision, to this new future.

In the birthing room, with the tiny twins on his lap, a hand curled around each of their heads, he says to Agnes that he believes her foresight, her prophecy about two children was false. Or, rather, that it was a sense of the twins' coming. It meant, he says, still gazing at his pair of babies, that she would have twins. Susanna and then twins.

His wife is silent. When he looks at the bed, he sees she has fallen asleep, as if all she was waiting for was for him to arrive, to take the babies on to his lap, to cradle their heads in his hands.

gnes startles awake, her head jerking up, her lips and tongue in the middle of forming a word; she isn't sure what it would have been. She had been dreaming about wind, a great invisible force whipping her hair from side to side, tugging at the clothes on her body, hurling dust and grit into her face.

She looks down at herself. She isn't in bed but seems to be half sitting, half slumped on the edge of a pallet, still in her gown. She has a cloth in one hand. It is damp, creased, warmed in the cradle of her palm. Why is she holding it? Why is she sitting like this, asleep?

It comes to her in a rush, as if a gust of wind from her dream is crossing the room. Judith, the fever, the night.

Agnes lurches to her feet. Has she been sleeping? How could she have slept? She shakes her head, once, twice, as if trying to rid herself of slumber, of the dream. The room is profoundly dark: it is the deepest part of the night, the most lethal hour. The fire is almost out, just a rubble of red embers, the candle spent. She feels about her desperately, blindly: there is a limb, under a sheet, a knee, an ankle. Agnes gropes upwards and encounters a wrist and two hands clasped together. The flesh, under her touch, is hot. Which, she tells herself, as she turns and begins scrabbling in the coffer for a candle, is good, very good, because it means that Judith is still alive.

It is good, she is telling herself, it is good, as she seizes the cool waxy column of a candle and holds its wick to an ember. If there is life, there is hope.

The candlewick catches, the flame guttering, nearly vanishing, then gathering strength. A circle of light appears around Agnes's outstretched arm, and widens out, pushing back the darkness.

There is the fireplace, the mantel. There are Agnes's slippers and her shawl, fallen to the floor. There is the pallet and there are Judith's feet, poking up under the sheet; there are her legs, her knees, and there is her face.

Agnes covers her mouth when she sees it. The skin is so pale as to be almost colourless; the eyelids are half open, with the eyes rolled up under the lids. Her lips, white and cracked, are open and she is taking tiny half-sips of air.

Still with her hand over her mouth, Agnes looks down upon her daughter. The part of her that has attended the sick, the ailing, the convalescents, the malingerers, the grieving, the mad, thinks: It will not be long. The other part of her, which nursed and tended and cared and petted and fed and clothed and embraced and kissed this child, thinks: This cannot be, this cannot happen, please, not her.

Agnes bends to touch her forehead, to take her pulse, to try to give her some ease, and as she does so, the candle reveals a sight so peculiar, so unexpected that it takes a moment for Agnes to understand what she is seeing.

The first thing she registers is that Judith's hand is not, as she first thought, clasping her other hand. It is entwined with another's. There is someone on the pallet with Judith, another body, another – as strange as it seems – Judith. There are two Judiths, curled up together, in front of the dying fire.

She blinks. She shakes herself. It is Hamnet, of course. He has come down in the night and squeezed himself on to the pallet next to his twin. And there he lies, in peaceful, deep sleep, next to her, holding her hand.

Agnes regards the scene, candle held aloft. She will think back to this moment later, and ask herself when she knew all was not as she'd thought it was. When did she notice? What was it that alerted her?

There is her daughter, very sick indeed, lying on her back, her face blanched by fever, and there is her son, curled next to her, his arm around her. And yet there is something not right about that arm. Agnes stares at it, mesmerised. It is Hamnet's arm and yet it is not.

She switches her gaze to the hand it holds, Judith's hand, and sees that the fingernails of this one are stained with something black. Almost like ink.

And when, Agnes asks herself, does Judith use ink?

A strange, dementing confusion starts up inside her, like the buzz of a hundred bees. She darts forward and, pushing the candle into a stick on the hearth, places her hands on her children.

Her son, a healthy colour, is next to the fire, and her daughter is on the other side of the pallet. But here, tucked into Hamnet's neck, her fingers find the long plait belonging to Judith. And here are Hamnet's wrists, protruding from Judith's smock, with the crescent-shaped scar he got from a sickle when he was young. It is Hamnet's shorter hair that is dark with the sweat of Judith's fever; it is Judith who is sleeping the untroubled sleep of the well.

Agnes cannot understand what she sees. Can she be dreaming? Is this some nightly apparition? She yanks back the sheet covering them and looks at them, lying there. The feet of the sick child reach further down the mattress. The taller child is the one who is sick.

It is Hamnet, not Judith.

At that moment, perhaps feeling the cold air, the eyes of the smaller twin open and fix themselves on her, standing there above them with the sheet in her hands.

'Mamma?' the child says.

'Judith?' Agnes whispers, because she still cannot believe what her eyes are telling her.

'Yes,' the child says.

Hamnet cannot know about the horse hired for his father. He will never know that his father's friend secured a mare for him, a beast with a temper, a fiery eye, a muscled shoulder and a coat that shone like a conker.

He has no idea that his father is, even now, making his way as fast as this ill-tempered mare will carry him, stopping only for water and as much food as he can find in the minutes he allows himself. From Tunbridge to Weybridge, then on to Thame. He swaps horses in Banbury. He is thinking only of his daughter, how he must narrow down the miles between them, he must make it home, he must hold her in his arms, he must look upon her once more, before she passes into that other realm, before she breathes her last.

His son, though, knows nothing of this. None of them does. Not Susanna, who has been sent to her mother's physick garden at the back of the house to collect roots of gentian and lovage for a poultice. Not Mary, who is scolding the maid in the cookhouse because the girl has been weeping and wailing all afternoon about how she wants to go home, how she needs to see her mother. Not Eliza, who is explaining to a woman who has come to the window hatch that Agnes cannot speak with her today, or tomorrow, but perhaps come back next week. And not Agnes herself, who crouches by the pallet with her back to the window.

Judith, her child, her daughter, her youngest born, is seated in a chair. Agnes still cannot believe it. Her face is pallid but her eyes are bright and alert. She is thin and weak, but she opens her mouth for broth, she fixes her gaze on her mother.

Agnes is pulled in two, as she sits beside her son, holding on to his shivering body. Her daughter has been spared; she has been delivered back to them, once again. But, in exchange, it seems that Hamnet may be taken.

She has given him a purgative, she has fed him jelly of rosemary and mint. She has given him all that she gave Judith, and more. She has placed a stone with a hole beneath his pillow. Several hours ago, she called for Mary to bring the toad and she has bound it to his stomach with linen.

None of it has pulled him back; none of it has restored him. She feels her hope for him begin to leak from her, like water from a punctured bucket. She is a fool, a blind idiot, the worst kind of simpleton. All along, she thought she needed to protect Judith, when it was Hamnet who was destined to be taken. How could Fate be so cruel in setting her such a trap? To make her concentrate on the wrong child so that it could reach out, while she was distracted, and snatch the other?

She thinks of her garden, of her shelves of powders, potions, leaves, liquids, with incredulity, with rage. What good has any of that been? What point was there to any of it? All those years and years of tending and weeding and pruning and gathering. She would like to go outside and rip up those plants by their roots and fling them into the fire. She is a fool, an ineffectual, prideful fool. How could she ever have thought that her plants might be a match for this?

Her son's body is in a place of torture, of hell. It writhes, it twists, it buckles and strains. Agnes holds him by the shoulders, by the chest, to keep him still. There is, she is starting to see, nothing more she can do. She can stay beside him, comfort him as best she can, but this pestilence is too great, too strong, too vicious. It is an enemy too powerful for her. It has wreathed and tightened its tendrils about her son, and is refusing to surrender him. It has a musky, dank, salty smell. It has come to them, Agnes thinks, from a long way off, from a place of rot and wet and confinement. It has cut a swingeing path for itself through humans and beasts and insects alike; it feeds on pain and unhappiness and grief. It is insatiable, unstoppable, the worst, blackest kind of evil.

Agnes does not leave his side. She swabs his brow, his limbs with the damp cloth. She packs salt in the bed with him. She lays a posy of valerian and swans' feathers on his chest, for comfort, for solace. Hamnet's fever climbs and climbs, the buboes swell tighter and tighter. She lifts his hand, which is a grim blue-grey along its side, and presses it to her cheek. She would try anything, she would do anything. She would open her own veins, her own body cavity, and give him her blood, her heart, her organs, if it would do the slightest good.

His body sweats, its humours expressing outwards through the skin, as if emptying itself.

Hamnet's mind, however, is in another place. For a long

time, he could hear his mother and his sisters, his aunt and his grandmother. He was aware of them, around him, giving him medicines, speaking to him, touching his skin. Now, though, they have receded. He is elsewhere, in a landscape he doesn't recognise. It is cool here, and quiet. He is alone. Snow is falling, softly, irrevocably, on and on. It piles up on the ground around him, covering paths and steps and rocks; it weighs down the branches of trees; it transforms everything into whiteness, blankness, stasis. The silence, the cool, the altered silver light of it is something more than soothing to him. He wants only to lie down in this snow, to rest himself; his legs are tired, his arms ache. To lie, to surrender himself, to stretch out in this glistening, thick white blanket: what relief it would give him. Something is telling him that he must not lie down, he must not give in to this desire. What could it be? Why shouldn't he rest?

Outside his body, Agnes is speaking. She is trying to apply the poultice to the swellings in his neck and armpits but he is trembling so much that the mixture will not stay in place. She is saying his name, over and over again. Eliza is scooping up Judith in her arms and taking her to the opposite end of the room. Judith is letting out a hoarse whistling noise, kicking against the clutches of her aunt. Anyone, Eliza is thinking, who describes dying as 'slipping away' or 'peaceful' has never witnessed it happen. Death is violent, death is a struggle. The body clings to life, as ivy to a wall, and will not easily let go, will not surrender its grip without a fight.

Susanna watches her brother, convulsing by the hearth, watches her mother fussing around with her useless paste and bandages. She would like to snatch them from her hands and hurl them at the wall and say, Stop, leave him be, let him alone. Can you not see it is too late for that? Susanna presses fierce fists to her eyes. She cannot look any more; she cannot bear it.

Agnes is whispering, Please, please, Hamnet, please, don't leave us, don't go. Near the window, Judith is struggling, asking to be placed next to him on the pallet, saying she needs him, she must speak to him, let her go. Eliza holds her, saying, There, there, to her, but has no idea what she means by that. Mary is kneeling at the end of the pallet, holding on to one of his ankles. Susanna is leaning her forehead into the plaster of the wall, her hands over her ears.

All at once, he stops shaking and a great soundlessness falls over the room. His body is suddenly motionless, his gaze focused on something far above him.

Hamnet, in his place of snow and ice, is lowering himself down to the ground, allowing his knees to fold under him. He is placing first one palm, then the other, on to the crisp, crystalline skin of snow, and how welcoming it feels, how right. It is not too cold, not too hard. He lies down; he presses his cheek to the softness of the snow. The whiteness of it is glaring, jarring to his eyes, so he closes them, just for a moment, just enough, so he may rest and gather his strength. He is not going to sleep, he is not. He will carry on. But he needs to rest, for a moment. He opens his eyes, to reassure himself the world is still there, and then lets them close. Just for now.

Eliza rocks Judith, tucking the child's head under her chin, and mutters a prayer. Susanna's face is turned towards her brother, her wet cheek to the wall. Mary crosses herself, gripping

Agnes's shoulder. Agnes bends forward to touch her lips to his forehead.

And there, by the fire, held in the arms of his mother, in the room in which he learnt to crawl, to eat, to walk, to speak, Hamnet takes his last breath.

He draws it in, he lets it out.

Then there is silence, stillness. Nothing more.

II

I am dead:
Thou livest;
. . . draw thy breath in pain,
To tell my story

Hamlet, Act V, scene ii

room. Long and thin, with flags fitted together, smoothed to a mirror. A group of people are standing in a cluster near the window, turned towards each other, in hushed conference. Cloths have been draped over the panes, so there is little light, but someone has propped open the window, just a crack. A breeze threads through the room, stirring the air inside it, toying with the wall drapes, the mantel-cloth, carrying with it the scent of the street, dust from the dry road, a hint of a pie baking somewhere nearby, the acrid sweetness of caramelising apple. Every now and again the voices of people passing by outside catapult odd words into the room, severed from sense, small bubbles of sound released into the silence.

Chairs are tucked into place around the table. Flowers stand upright in a jar, petals turned back, pollen dusting the table beneath. A dog asleep on a cushion wakes with a start, begins to lick its paw, then thinks better of it and subsides back into slumber. There is a pitcher of water on the table, tailed by a cluster of cups. No one drinks. The people by the window continue to murmur to each other; one reaches out and clasps the hand of another; this person inclines their head, the white, starched top of their coif displayed to the rest.

They glance towards the end of the room, where the fireplace is, again and again, then turn back to each other.

A door has been lifted from its hinges and placed on two barrels by the fireplace. A woman is sitting beside it. She is motionless, back bent, head lowered. It is not immediately apparent that she even breathes. Her hair is disarrayed and falls in strands around her shoulders. Her body is curved over, her feet tucked under, her arms outstretched, the nape of her neck exposed.

Before her is the body of a child. His bared feet splay outwards, his toes curled. The soles and nails still bear the dirt so recently accrued from life: grit from the road, soil from the garden, mud from the riverbank, where he swam not a week ago with his friends. His arms are by his sides, his head turned slightly towards his mother. His skin is losing the appearance of the living, becoming parchment white, stiff and sunken. He is dressed, still, in his nightshirt. His uncles were the ones to unhinge the door and bring it into the room. They lifted him, gently, gently, with careful hands, with held breath, from the pallet where he died to the hard wooden surface of the door.

The younger uncle, Edmond, had wept, tears blurring his sight, which was, for him, a relief because he found it too painful to look into the still features of his brother's dead son. This is a child whom he has known and seen every day of his short life, a child whom he taught to catch a wooden ball, to pick fleas from a dog, to whittle a pipe from a reed. The older uncle, Richard, did not cry: instead his sadness passed over into anger – at the grim task they had been bidden to do, at the world, at Fate, at the fact that a child could fall ill and then be lying there dead. The anger made him snap at Edmond whom he thought wasn't taking enough of the boy's weight, not holding the legs as firmly as he should have done, by the knees and not the ankles, fumbling the job, messing it up.

Both uncles leave soon afterwards, exchanging a few words with the people in the room, then finding excuses of work, of errands to run, of places they must go.

In the room there are mostly women: the boy's grandmother, the baker's wife, who is godmother to the boy, the boy's aunt. They have done all they can. Burnt the bedding and the mattress and the straw and the linens. Aired the room. Put the twin girl to bed upstairs, for she is still weak, still unwell, although making a good recovery. They have cleaned the room, sprinkling lavender water around it, letting in the air. They have brought a white sheet, strong thread, sharp needles. They have said, in respectful and quiet voices, that they will help with the laying out, that they are here, that they will not leave, that they are ready to begin. The boy must be prepared for burial: there is no time to lose. The town decrees that any who die of the pestilence must be buried quickly, within a day. The women have communicated this to the mother, in case she is not aware of the ruling, or has forgotten it, in her grief. They have placed bowls of warm water and cloths beside the mother and cleared their throats.

But nothing. She does not respond. She does not raise her head. She does not listen or even seem to hear suggestions to start the laying out, the washing of the body, the stitching of the shroud. She will not look at the bowls of water, instead letting them cool beside her. She did not glance at the white bolt of the sheet, folded into a neat square, placed at the foot of the door.

She will only sit, her head bent, one hand touching the boy's inert, curled fingers, the other his hair.

Inside Agnes's head, her thoughts are widening out, then

narrowing down, widening, narrowing, over and over again. She thinks, This cannot happen, it cannot, how will we live, what will we do, how can Judith bear it, what will I tell people, how can we continue, what should I have done, where is my husband, what will he say, how could I have saved him, why didn't I save him, why didn't I realise it was he who was in danger? And then, the focus narrows, and she thinks: He is dead, he is dead, he is dead.

The three words contain no sense for her. She cannot bend her mind to their meaning. It is an impossible idea that her son, her child, her boy, the healthiest and most robust of her children, should, within days, sicken and die.

She, like all mothers, constantly casts out her thoughts, like fishing lines, towards her children, reminding herself of where they are, what they are doing, how they fare. From habit, while she sits there near the fireplace, some part of her mind is tabulating them and their whereabouts: Judith, upstairs. Susanna, next door. And Hamnet? Her unconscious mind casts, again and again, puzzled by the lack of bite, by the answer she keeps giving it: he is dead, he is gone. And Hamnet? The mind will ask again. At school, at play, out at the river? And Hamnet? And Hamnet? Where is he?

Here, she tries to tell herself. Cold and lifeless, on this board, right in front of you. Look, here, see.

And Hamnet? Where is he?

With her back to the door, she faces the fireplace, which is filled only with ashes, held in the fragile shape of the log they once were.

She is aware of people arriving and leaving, via the door to the street, and the door out to the yard. Her mother-in-law,

Eliza, the baker's wife, the neighbour, John, some other people she cannot place.

They speak to her, these people. She hears words and voices, murmured mostly, but she doesn't turn around. She doesn't raise her head. These people, walking in and out of her house, pushing speech and utterances towards her ears, are nothing to do with her. They offer nothing she wants or needs.

One of her hands rests on her son's hair; the other still grips his fingers. These are the only parts of him that are familiar, that still look the same. She allows herself to think this.

His body is different. Increasingly so, as the day wears on. It is as if a strong wind – the one from her dream, she believes – has lifted her son off the ground, battered him against rocks, whirled him around a cliff, then set him back down. He is misused, abused, marked, maltreated: the illness has ravaged him. For a while after he died, the bruises and black marks spread and widened. Then they stopped. His skin has turned to waxy tallow, the bones standing up beneath. The cut above his eye, the one she has no idea how he came by, is still livid and red.

She regards the face of her son, or the face that used to belong to her son, the vessel that held his mind, produced his speech, contained all that his eyes saw. The lips are dry, sealed. She would like to dampen them, to allow them a little water. The cheeks are stretched, hollowed by fever. The eyelids are a delicate purplish-grey, like the petals of early spring flowers. She closed them herself. With her own hands, her own fingers, and how hot and slippery her fingers had felt, how unmanageable the task, how difficult it had been to put her fingers – trembling and wet – over those lids, so dear, so known, she could draw them from memory if someone were to put a stick of charcoal in her hand. How is anyone ever to shut the eyes of their dead child? How is it possible to find two pennies and rest them there, in the eye sockets, to hold down the lids? How can anyone do this? It is not right. It cannot be.

She grips his hand in hers. The heat from her own skin is giving itself to his. She can almost believe that the hand is as it was, that he still lives, if she keeps her eyes away from that face, from that never-rising chest and the inexorable stiffness invading this body. She must grip the hand tighter. She must keep her hand on the hair, which feels as it always did: silken, soft, ragged at the ends where he tugs it as he studies.

Her fingers press into the muscle between Hamnet's thumb and forefinger. She kneads the muscle there, gently, in a circular motion, and waits, listens, concentrates. She is like her old kestrel, reading the air, listening out, waiting for a signal, a sound.

Nothing comes. Nothing at all. Never has she felt this before. There is always something, even with the most mysterious and private of people; with her own children, she found always a clamour of images, noise, secrets, information. Susanna has begun to hold her hands behind her back when near to her mother, so aware is she that Agnes can find out whatever she wants in this way.

But Hamnet's hand is silent. Agnes listens; she strains. She tries to hear what might be under the silence, behind it. Could there be a distant murmur, some sound, a message, perhaps, from her son? A sign where he is, a place she might find him? But there is nothing. A high whine of nothing, like the absence of noise when a church bell falls silent.

Someone, she is aware, has arrived next to her, crouching down, touching her arm. She doesn't need to look to know it's Bartholomew. The breadth and weight of that hand. The heavy tread and shuffle of his boots. The clean scent of hay and wool.

Her brother touches her dry cheek. He says her name, once, twice. He says he is sorry, he is heart sore. He says no one would have expected this. He says he wishes it could have been otherwise, that he was the best of boys, the very best, that it is a terrible loss. He places his hand over hers.

'I will see to the arrangements,' he murmurs. 'I've dispatched Richard to the church. He will make sure that all is prepared.' He breathes in and she can hear, in that breath, all that has been said around her. 'The women are here, to help you.'

Agnes shakes her head, mute. She curls a single finger into the dip of Hamnet's palm. She remembers examining his palm, and Judith's, when they were babes, lying together in the crib. She had uncurled their miniature fingers and traced the lines she found. How remarkable had seemed the creases of their hands: just like hers, only smaller. Hamnet had a definite deep groove through the middle of his palm, like the stroke of a brush, denoting a long life; Judith's had been faint, uncertain, petering out, then restarting in another place. It had made her frown, made her raise the curled fingers to her lips, where she kissed them, again and again, with a fierce, almost angry love.

'They can . . .' Bartholomew is saying '. . . lay him out. Or they can be with you while you do it. Whichever you prefer.'

She holds herself very still.

'Agnes,' he says.

She uncurls the fingers of Hamnet's hand and peers at the palm. The fingers are not noticeably stiffer than before, most definitely not. There it is, the long, strong line of life, coursing from the wrist to the base of the fingers. It is a beautiful line, a perfect line, a stream through a landscape. Look, she wants to say to Bartholomew. Do you see that? Can you explain this?

'We must prepare him,' Bartholomew says, tightening his grip on hers.

She presses her lips together. If they were alone, she and Bartholomew, maybe then she could risk letting out some of the words jamming up her throat. But as it is, the room so full of silent people, she cannot.

'He must be buried. You know this. The town will come to take him if we do not.'

'No,' she says. 'Not yet.'

'Then when?'

She bows her head, turning away from him, back to her son.

Bartholomew shifts his weight. 'Agnes,' he says, in a low voice so that, maybe, no one else can hear them, although they will be listening, Agnes knows. 'It is possible that word may not have reached him. He would come, if he knew. I know he would. But he would not find it amiss if we were to go ahead. He would understand the necessity of it. What we must do is send another letter and in the meantime—'

'We will wait,' she gets out. 'Until tomorrow. You may tell the town that. And I will lay him out. No one else.'

'Very well,' he says, and stands up. She sees him look at Hamnet, watches his eyes travel from the bare and blackened feet of his nephew, all the way to his ravaged face. Her brother's mouth presses itself into a line and he closes his eyes briefly. He makes the sign of the cross. Before he turns away, he reaches out and rests his hand on the boy's chest, just above where his heart used to beat.

A task to be done, and she will do it alone.

She waits until evening, until everyone has left, until most people are in bed.

She will have the water at her right hand and she will sprinkle a few drops of oil into it. The oil will resist, refuse to mix with the water, and will instead resolve itself into golden circles on the surface. She will dip and rinse the cloth.

She begins at the face, at the top of him. He has a wide forehead and his hair grows up from the brow. He had, of late, begun to wet it in the morning, to try to get it to lie flat, but the hair would not listen. She wets it now but it still does not listen, even in death. You see, she says to him, you cannot change what you are given, cannot bend or alter what is dealt to you.

He gives no answer.

She wets her hands in the water and then draws her fingers through his hair; she finds flecks of lint, a teasel, a leaf from a plum tree. These, she lays aside, on a plate: flotsam from her boy. She combs with her fingers until the hair is clean. May I, she asks him, take a lock from you? Would you mind?

He gives no answer.

She takes a knife, the one she finds so useful for prising kernels from fruit – she bought it from a gypsy she met in the lane one day – and takes a skein of hair at the back of his head. The knife severs the strands easily, as she knew it would. She holds up the hair. Light yellow at the end, bleached by the summer sun, darkening to near-brown at the roots. She lays it carefully next to the plate.

She wipes his forehead, his closed eyes, his cheeks, his lips, the open wound on his brow. She clears the shell-whorls of both ears, the soft stem of neck. She would wash the fever from him, draw it from his skin, if she could. The nightshirt must be cut from him, so she runs the gypsy's knife down each arm, along the chest.

She is dabbing the cloth, gently, so gently, over the bruised and swollen armpits, when Mary comes in.

She stands in the doorway, looking down at the boy. Her face is wet, her eyes swollen. 'I saw the light,' she says, in a cracked voice. 'I was not sleeping.'

Agnes nods towards a chair. Mary was with her when Hamnet came into the world; she may stay to see him out of it.

The candle is flaring and burning high, illuminating the ceiling and leaving the edges of the room in shadow. Mary sits in the chair; Agnes can see the white of her nightgown hem.

She dips the cloth, she washes, she dips it again. A repetitive motion. She runs her fingers over the scar on Hamnet's arm where he fell from a fence at Hewlands, over the puckered knot from a dog bite at a harvest fair. The third finger of his right hand is calloused from gripping a quill. There are small pits in the skin of his stomach from when he had a spotted pox as a small child.

She washes his legs, his ankles, his feet. Mary takes the bowl, changes the water. Agnes washes the feet again, and dries them.

The two women look at each other for a moment, then Mary picks up the folded sheet, holding a corner in each hand. The sheet unravels, opens like an enormous flower, its petals wide, and Agnes is faced with its startling blank white expanse. The brightness of it is star-like, unavoidable, in this dark room.

She takes it. She presses her face to it. It smells of juniper, of cedar, of soap. Its nap is soft, enveloping, forgiving.

Mary helps her to lift Hamnet's legs and then his torso, to slide the sheet under him.

Hard to fold him in. Hard to lift the sheet's corners and cover him, smother him in its whiteness. Hard to think, to know, that she will never again see these arms, these knuckles, these shins, that thumbnail, that callus, this face, after this.

She cannot cover him the first time. She cannot do it the second. She takes the sheet, she drapes it over him, she removes it. Does it again. Removes it again. The boy lies, unclothed, washed clean, in the centre of the sheet, hands folded on his chest, chin tilted upwards, eyes shut fast.

Agnes leans on the edge of the board, breathing hard, the fabric gripped in her hands.

Mary watches. She reaches over the body of the boy to touch Agnes's hand.

Agnes looks at her son. The birdcage ribs, the interlaced fingers, the round bones of the knees, the still face, the corn-coloured hair, which has dried now, standing up from his brow, as it always does. His physical presence has always been so strong, so definite, unlike Judith's. Agnes has always known if he enters a room, or leaves it: that unmistakable clatter of feet, that passage of air, the heavy thud as he sits down on a chair. And now she must give up this body, submit it to the earth, never to be seen again.

'I cannot do it,' she says.

Mary takes the sheet from her. She tucks it one way, over his legs, then the other, over his chest. Some part of Agnes registers, in the deft way she performs this task, that she has done it before, many times.

Then, together, they reach up to the rafters. Agnes selects rue, comfrey, yellow-eyed chamomile. She takes purple lavender and thyme, a handful of rosemary. Not heartsease, because Hamnet disliked the smell. Not angelica, because it is too late for that and it did not help, did not perform its task, did not save him, did not break the fever. Not valerian, for the same reason. Not milk thistle, for the leaves are so spiny and sharp, enough to pierce the skin, to bring forth drops of blood.

She tucks the dried plants into the sheet, nestles them next to his body, where they whisper their comfort to him.

Next is the needle. Agnes threads it with thick twine. She begins at the feet.

The point is sharp; it punctures the weave of the cloth and slides out the other side. She keeps her eyes on her work, the drawing together of the sheet, to make a shroud. She is a sailor, stitching a sail, preparing a boat that will carry her son into the next world.

She has reached the shins when something makes her lift her head. There is a figure standing at the bottom of the stairs. Agnes's heart clenches like a fist, she almost cries out, There you are, have you come back, but then she sees it is, in fact, Judith. The same face, but this one is alive, stricken, trembling.

Mary starts up from her chair, saying, Back to bed, now, come, you must sleep, but Agnes says, No, let her stay.

She puts down the needle, carefully, because it must not prick him, even now, and holds out her arms. Judith leaves the stairs, she steps into the room, she hurls herself against her mother, pressing her face into her apron, saying something about kittens, and something else about sickness, about changing places, about it being her fault, and then sobs tear through her, gale winds through a tree.

Agnes says to her: It is no fault of yours. None at all. The fever came for him and there was nothing we could do. We must bear it the best we can. Then she says: Do you want to see him?

Mary arranges the sheet so that Hamnet's face is uncovered. Judith comes to stand beside him, looking down, her hands drawn up, clenched into themselves. Her expression melds from disbelief to timidity to pity to grief and back again.

'Oh,' she says, drawing in breath. 'It is really him?'

Agnes, standing next to her, nods.

'It doesn't look like him.'

Agnes nods again. 'Well, he is gone.'

'Gone where?'

'To . . .' she inhales a deep, almost steady breath '. . . to . . . Heaven. And his body is left behind. We have to take care of it the best we can.'

Judith puts out a hand and touches the cheek of her twin.

Tears course down her face, chasing each other. She has always cried such enormous tears, like heavy pearls, quite at odds with the slightness of her frame. She shakes her head, hard, once or twice. Then she says, 'Will he never come back?'

And Agnes finds she can bear anything except her child's pain. She can bear separation, sickness, blows, birth, depriva- tion, hunger, unfairness, seclusion, but not this: her child, looking down at her dead twin. Her child, sobbing for her lost brother. Her child, racked with grief.

For the first time, the tears come for Agnes. They fill her eyes without warning, blur her vision, pouring forth to run down her face, her neck, soaking her apron, running between her clothes and her skin. They seem to come not just from her eyes but from every pore of her body. Her whole being longs for, grieves for her son, her daughters, her absent husband, for all of them, when she says, 'No, my love, he will never come again.'

The milky, uncertain light of dawn is reaching into the room. Agnes is making the final stitches in the shroud, tucking it in at his shoulder, neatening the edges near his knees. Mary has emptied the bowls, wrung out the cloths, swept the loose leaves and buds from the floor. Judith has her cheek against the cloth near his shoulder. Susanna has come in from next door and she sits next to her sister, head lowered.

They have made him ready, between them. He is clean and set for burial, parcelled in white cloth.

Agnes finds that her mind rears back, like a horse refusing a ditch, when she thinks of the grave. She can think forward

to walking with him to church – Bartholomew and perhaps
Gilbert and John will carry him; she can picture the priest
blessing the body. But the lowering of him into the ground,
into a dark pit, never to be seen again, she cannot think about.
She cannot imagine. She cannot possibly permit this to happen
to her child.

She is, for the third or fourth time, trying to thread her
needle – she needs to stitch the sheet over his face, she must,
it needs to be done – but the twine is thicker than she is used
to, and frayed, and will not go through the eye of the needle,
however many times she aims. She is wetting the end in her
mouth when there comes a thudding at the door.

She raises her head. Judith whimpers, looks up. Mary turns
from the fireplace.

'Who could that be?' she says.

Agnes puts down the needle. All four of them stand. The
knocking comes again: a row of sharp raps.

For a wild moment, Agnes believes that something has
come to her house, again, to take her other children, to take
her boy, before she is ready, before she has him fully prepared.
It is too early in the morning for it to be a mourner or a
neighbour, come to pay their final respects, or for the town
officials to snatch away the body. It must be some spectre,
some wraith, come calling at their door. But for whom?

Again, the sound comes: a thudding, a rapping. The door
leaps on its hinges.

'Who's there?' Agnes calls out, her voice bolder than she
feels.

The latch lifts, the door swings open, and there, suddenly,
is her husband, stepping in under the lintel, his clothes and

head all wetted and dark with rain, his hair streaked to his cheeks. His face is sleepless, crazed, his skin pale. 'Am I too late?' he says.

Then his eye falls upon Judith, who is standing by the candle, and a smile breaks out across his features.

'You,' he says, striding across the room, holding out his arms. 'You are here, you are well. I was worried – I couldn't rest – I came as soon as I heard but now I see that—'

He stops, pulled up short. He has seen the board, the shroud, the bundled figure.

He looks around at them, one by one. His face is fearful, confused. Agnes can see him ticking them off. His wife, his mother, his elder daughter, his younger daughter.

'No,' he says. 'Not . . . ? Is it . . . ?'

Agnes looks at him and he looks back at her. She wants, more than anything, to stretch this moment, to expand the time before he knows, to shield him from what has happened for as long as she can. Then she gives a swift, single, downward nod.

The sound that comes out of him is choked and smothered, like that of an animal forced to bear a great weight. It is a noise of disbelief, of anguish. Agnes will never forget it. At the end of her life, when her husband has been dead for years, she will still be able to summon its exact pitch and timbre.

He moves quickly across the room and pulls back the cloth. And there is his son's face before him, a blue-white lily-flower, eyes sealed shut, lips pursed, as if the boy is displeased, unimpressed by what has taken place.

The father cups a hand to the son's chill cheek. His fingers hover, trembling, over the bruise on his brow. He says, No, no, no. He says, God in Heaven. And, then, crouching low, over the boy, he whispers: How did this happen to you?

His women gather round, putting their arms around him, pulling him close.

So it is the father who carries Hamnet for burial. He hoists the board aloft, balanced on his outstretched arms, his son held before him, wrapped in a white shroud, with flowers and blooms around his body.

Behind him is Agnes, holding Susanna's hand on one side, and Judith's on the other. Judith is carried by Bartholomew; she tucks her face into his neck and her tears run down to soak his shirt. Mary and John, Eliza and the brothers follow after, along with Joan, Agnes's siblings, and the baker and his wife.

The father bears him, unaided, along Henley Street, tears and sweat streaming down his face. Towards the crossroads, Edmond breaks free of the mourners and goes to his brother's side. Together, they take the board between them, the father the head and Edmond the feet.

The neighbours, the townsfolk, the people on the streets step aside when they see the silent procession. They put down their tools, their bundles, their baskets. They edge backwards, to the sides of the streets, clearing the way. They take off their hats. If they are holding children, they clutch them a little closer, when they see the glover's son walk by with his dead and shrouded boy. They cross themselves. They call out words of comfort, of sorrow. They send up a prayer – for the boy, for the family, for themselves. Some of them weep. Some exchange whispers about the family, the glover, the airs his wife puts on, how everyone thought the glover's son would amount to nothing, what a wastrel he had always seemed, and now look at him – a man of consequence in London, it is said, and there he goes, with his richly embroidered sleeves and shining leather boots. Who would have thought it? Is it really true that he makes all that money from the playhouse? How can that be? All of them, though, look with sadness at the covered body, at the stricken face of the mother, walking between her daughters.

For Agnes, the walk to the graveyard is both too slow and too fast. She cannot bear the rows and rows of peering eyes, raking over them, sealing an image of her son's shrouded body inside their lids, thieving that essence of him. These are people who saw him every day, passing by their doors, below their windows. They exchanged words with him, ruffled his hair, exhorted him to hurry if he was late for the school bell. He played with their children, darted in and out of their houses and shops. He carried messages for them, petted their dogs, stroked the backs of their cats as they slept on sunny window-sills. And now their lives are carrying on, unchanged, their dogs still yawning by the fireplaces, their children still whining for supper, while he is no more.

So she cannot bear their gaze, cannot meet their eyes. She doesn't want their sympathy and their prayers and their murmured words. She hates the way the people part to let them past and then, behind them, regroup, erasing their passage, as if it were nothing, as if it never were. She wishes to scratch the ground, perhaps with a hoe, to score the streets beneath her, so that there will forever be a mark, for it always to be known that this way Hamnet came. He was here.

Too soon, too quickly, they are nearing the graveyard, they are through the gate, they are walking between the lines of yew trees, studded with their soft, scarlet berries.

The grave is a shock. A deep, dark rip in the earth, as if made by the careless slash of a giant claw. It is over at the far side of the graveyard. Just beyond it, the river is taking a slow, wide bend, turning its waters in another direction. Its surface is opaque today, braided like a rope, rushing always onwards.

How Hamnet would have loved this patch of ground. She observes herself forming this thought. If he could have chosen, if he were here, next to her, if she could turn to him and ask him, she is sure he would have pointed at this very spot: next to the river. He was ever one for water. She has always had a terrible time keeping him from weed-filled banks, from the dank mouths of wells, from stinking drains, from sheep-soiled puddles. And, now, here he will be, sealed in the earth for eternity, by the river.

His father is lowering him in. How can he do that, how is it possible? She knows that it has to be, that he is only doing what he must, but Agnes feels she could not perform this task. She would never, could never, send his body into the earth like that, alone, cold, to be covered over. Agnes cannot watch, she cannot, her husband's arms straining, his face twisted and clenched and gleaming, Bartholomew and Edmond stepping forward to help. Someone is sobbing somewhere. Is it Eliza? Is it Bartholomew's wife, who lost a baby herself not so long ago? Judith is whimpering, Susanna clutching her by the hand, so Agnes misses the moment, she misses seeing her son, the shroud she sewed for him, disappearing from view, entering the dark black river-sodden earth. It was there one moment, then she dipped her head to look at Judith, and then it was gone. Never to be seen again.

It is even more difficult, Agnes finds, to leave the grave-yard, than it was to enter it. So many graves to walk past, so many sad and angry ghosts tugging at her skirts, touching her with their cold fingers, pulling at her, naggingly, piteously, saying, Don't go, wait for us, don't leave us here. She has to clutch her hem to her, fold her hands inwards. A strangely difficult idea, too, that she entered this place with three chil-dren and she leaves it with two. She is, she tells herself, meant to be leaving one behind here, but how can she? In this place of wailing spirits and dripping yew trees and cold, pawing hands?

Her husband takes her arm as they reach the gate; she turns to look at him and it is as if she has never seen him before, so odd and distorted and old do his features seem. Is it their long separation, is it grief, is it all the tears? she wonders, as she regards him. Who is this person next to her, claiming her arm, holding it to him? She can see, in his face, the cheekbones of her dead son, the set of his brow, but nothing else. Just life, just blood, just evidence of a pumping, resilient heart, an eye that is bright with tears, a cheek flushed with feeling.

She is hollowed out, her edges blurred and insubstantial. She might disintegrate, break apart, like a raindrop hitting a leaf. She cannot leave this place, she cannot pass through this gate. She cannot leave him here.

She gets hold of the wooden gatepost and grips it with both hands. Everything is shattered but holding on to this post feels like the best course of action, the only thing to do. If she can stay here, at the gate, with her daughters on one side of her and her son on the other, she can hold everything together.

It takes her husband, her brother and both of her daughters to unpeel her hands, to pull her away.

Agnes is a woman broken into pieces, crumbled and scattered around. She would not be surprised to look down, one of these days, and see a foot over in the corner, an arm left on the ground, a hand dropped to the floor. Her daughters are the same. Susanna's face is set, her brows lowered in something like anger. Judith just cries, on and on, silently; the tears leak from her and will, it seems, never stop.

How were they to know that Hamnet was the pin holding them together? That without him they would all fragment and fall apart, like a cup shattered on the floor?

The husband, the father, paces the room downstairs, that first night, and the one after. Agnes hears him from the bedroom upstairs. There is no other sound. No crying, no sobbing, no sighing. Just the scuff-thud, scuff-thud of his restless feet, walking, walking, like someone trying to find their way back to a place for which they have lost the map.

'I did not see it,' she whispers, into the dark space between them.

He turns his head; she cannot see him do this, but she can hear the rustle and crackle of the sheets. The bed-curtains are drawn around them, in spite of the relentless summer heat.

'No one did,' he says.

'But *I* did not,' she whispers. 'And I should have. I should have known. I should have seen it. I should have understood that it was a terrible trick, making me fear for Judith, when all along—'

'Ssh,' he says, turning over, laying an arm over her. 'You did everything you could. There is nothing anyone could have done to save him. You tried your best and—'

'Of course I did,' she hisses, suddenly furious, sitting up, wrenching herself from his touch. 'I would have cut out my heart and given it to him, if it would have made any difference, I would have—'

'I know.'

'You don't know,' she says, thumping her fist into the mattress. 'You weren't here. Judith,' she whispers, and tears are slipping from her eyes, now, down her cheeks, dripping through her hair, 'Judith was so ill. I . . . I . . . was so intent on her that I wasn't thinking . . . I should have paid more attention to him . . . I never saw what was coming . . . I always thought she was the one who would be taken. I cannot believe that I was so blind, so stupid to—'

'Agnes, you did everything, you tried everything,' he repeats, trying to ease her back into the bed. 'The sickness was too strong.'

She resists him, curling into herself, wrapping her arms around her knees. 'You weren't here,' she says again.

He goes out into the town, two days after they buried him. He must speak to a man who leases fields from him, must remind him of the debt.

He steps out from the front door and finds that the street

278

is full of sunlight, full of children. Walking along, calling to each other, holding their parents' hands, laughing, crying, sleeping on a shoulder, having their mantles buttoned.

It is a sight past bearing. Their skin, their skulls, their ribs, their clear, wide eyes: how frail they are. Don't you see that? he wants to shout to their mothers, their fathers. How can you let them out of your houses?

He gets as far as the market, and then he stops. He turns on his heels, ignoring the greeting, the outstretched hand of a cousin, and goes back.

At the house, his Judith is sitting by the back door. She has been set the task of peeling a basket of apples. He sits down beside her. After a moment, he reaches into the basket and hands her the next apple. She has a paring knife in her left hand – always her left – and she peels the skin from it. It drips from the blade in long, green curls, like the hair of a mermaid.

When the twins were very small, perhaps around their first birthday, he had turned to his wife and said, Watch.

Agnes had lifted her head from her workbench.

He pushed two slivers of apple across the table to them. At exactly the same moment, Hamnet reached out with his right hand and gripped the apple and Judith reached out with her left.

In unison, they raised the apple slices to their lips, Hamnet with his right, Judith with her left.

They put them down, as if with some silent signal between them, at the same moment, then looked at each other, then picked them up again, Judith with her left hand, Hamnet with his right.

It's like a mirror, he had said. Or that they are one person split down the middle.

Their two heads uncovered, shining like spun gold.

He meets his father, John, in the passageway, just as his father is stepping out of the workshop.

The two men pause, each staring at the other.

His father puts up a hand to rub at the bristles on his chin. His Adam's apple bobs uncomfortably up and down as he swallows. Then he gives something halfway between a grunt and a cough, sidesteps his son, and retreats back into the workshop.

Everywhere he looks: Hamnet. Aged two, gripping the edges of the window ledge, straining to see out into the street, his finger outstretched, pointing to a horse passing by. As a baby, tucked with Judith into a cradle, neat as two loaves. Pushing open the front door with too much force as he returns from school, leaving a mark on the plaster that makes Mary exclaim and scold. Catching a ball in its hoop, over and over again, just outside the window. Lifting his face from his schoolwork to his father to ask about a tense in Greek, his cheek stained with a smear of chalk in the shape of a comma, a pause. The sound of his voice, calling from the back yard, asking, Will someone come and look because a bird has landed on the back of the pig.

And his wife so still and silent and pale, his elder daughter so furious with the world, lashing and lashing at them with an angry tongue. And his younger girl just cries; she puts her head down on the table or stands in a doorway or lies in bed and weeps and weeps, until he or her mother, putting their arms about her, beg her to leave off or she will make herself sick.

And the smell of leather, of whittawing, of hides, of singed fur: he cannot get away from it. How did he spend all those years in this house? He finds he cannot breathe the sour air here, now. The knock at the window, the demands of people wanting to buy gloves, to look at them, to try them on their hands, to endlessly discuss beading and buttons and lace. The ceaseless conversation, back and forth, over this merchant and that, this whittawer, that farmer, that nobleman, the price of silk, the cost of wool, who is at the guild meetings and who isn't, who will be alderman next year.

It is intolerable. All of it. He feels as though he is caught in a web of absence, its strings and tendrils ready to stick and cling to him, whichever way he turns. Here he is, back in this town, in this house, and all of it makes him fearful that he might never get away; this grief, this loss, might keep him here, might destroy all he has made for himself in London. His company will descend into chaos and disorder without him; they will lose all their money and disband; they might find another to take his place; they won't prepare a new play for the coming season, or they will and it will be better than anything he could ever write, and that person's name will be across the playbills and not his, and then he will be kicked out, replaced, not wanted any more. He might lose his hold on all that he has built there. It is so tenuous, so fragile, the life of the playhouses. He often thinks that, more than anything, it is like the embroidery on his father's gloves: only the beautiful shows, only the smallest part, while underneath is a cross-hatching of labour and skill and frustration and sweat. He needs to be there, all the time, to ensure that what is underneath happens, that all goes to plan. And he longs, it is true, for the four close walls of his lodging, where no one else ever comes, where no one looks for him or asks for him or speaks to him or bothers him, where there is just a bed, a coffer, a desk. Nowhere else can he escape the noise and life and people around him; nowhere else is he able to let the world recede, the sense of himself dissolve, so that he is just a hand, holding an ink-dipped feather, and he may watch as words unfurl from its tip. And as these words come, one after another, it is possible for him to slip away from himself and find a peace so absorbing, so soothing, so private, so joyous that nothing else will do.

He cannot give this up, cannot stay here, in this house, in this town, on the edges of the glove business, not even for his wife. He sees how he may become mired in Stratford for ever, a creature with its leg in the jaws of an iron trap, with his father next door, and his son, cold and decaying, beneath the churchyard sod.

He comes to her and says he must leave. He cannot stay away from his company for long. They will need him: they will be returning soon to London and they must ready themselves for the new season. Other playhouses would be only too glad to see theirs go under; the competition, especially at the start of the season, is fierce. There are many preparations to be made and he needs to be there to see all is done right. He cannot leave it to the other men. No one else can be relied upon. He has to leave. He is sorry. He hopes she understands.

Agnes says nothing as he delivers this speech. She lets the words wash over and around her. She continues to let the slops fall from a basin into the pig trough. Such a simple task: to hold aloft a basin and let its contents fall. Nothing more is required of her than to stand here, leaning on the swine wall.

'I will send word,' he says, behind her, and she starts. She had almost forgotten he was there. What was it he had been saying?

'Send word?' she repeats. 'To whom?'

'To you.'

'To me? Why?' She gestures down at herself. 'I am here, before you.'

'I meant I will send word when I have reached London.'

Agnes frowns, letting the last of the slops fall. She recalls, yes, a moment ago, he had been talking of London. Of his friends there. 'Preparations' had been the word he used, she believes. And 'leave'.

'London?' she says.

'I must leave,' he says, with a hint of crispness.

She almost smiles, so ridiculous, so fanciful is the notion. 'You cannot leave,' she says.

'But I must.'

'But you cannot.'

'Agnes,' he says, with full-blown irritation now. 'The world does not stand still. There are people waiting for me. The season is about to begin and my company will return from Kent any day now and I must—'

'How can you think of leaving?' she says, puzzled. What must she say to make him understand? 'Hamnet,' she says, feeling the roundness of the word, his name, inside her mouth, the shape of a ripe pear. 'Hamnet died.'

The words make him flinch. He cannot look at her after she has spoken them; he bows his head, fixing his gaze on his boots.

To her, it is simple. Their boy, their child, is dead, barely cold in his grave. There will be no leaving. There will be staying. There will be closing of the doors, the four of them drawing together, like dancers at the end of a reel. He will remain here, with her, with Judith, with Susanna. How can there be any such talk of leaving? It makes no sense.

She follows his gaze, down to his boots, and sees there, beside his feet, his travelling bag. It is stuffed, filled, like the belly of an expectant woman.

She points at it, mutely, unable to speak.

'I must go . . . now,' he mutters, stumbling over his words, this husband of hers who always speaks in the way a stream runs fast and clear over a steep bed of pebbles. 'There is . . . a trade party leaving today for London . . . and they have . . . a spare horse. It is . . . I need to . . . that is, I mean . . . I shall take your leave . . . and will, in good time, or rather, shall—'

'You will leave now? Today?' She is incredulous, turning from the wall to face him. 'We need you here.'

'The trade party . . . I . . . that is . . . It is not possible for them to wait and . . . it is a good opportunity . . . so that I may not be travelling alone . . . You don't like me to make the journey alone, remember . . . You yourself have said so . . . many times . . . so then—'

'You mean to go now?'

He takes the swine bowl from her and puts it on the wall, taking both her hands in his. 'There are many who rely on me in London. It is imperative that I return. I cannot just abandon these men who—'

'But you may abandon us?'

'No, of course not. I—'

She pushes her face right up to his. 'Why are you going?' she hisses.

He averts his eyes from hers but does not let go of her hands. 'I told you,' he mutters. 'The company, the other players, I—'

'Why?' she demands. 'Is it your father? Did something happen? Tell me.'

'There is nothing to tell.'

'I don't believe you.' She tries to withdraw her hands from his grasp but he will not let go. She twists her wrists one way and then the other.

'You speak of your company,' she says, into the space between their faces, which is so narrow they must be breathing each other's breath, 'you speak of your season and your preparation, but none of these is the proper reason.' She struggles to free her hands, her fingers, so that she may grip his hand; he knows this and will not let her. That he prevents her makes her livid, incensed, red-hot with such fury as she has not felt since she was a child.

'It is no matter,' she pants, as they struggle there, beside the guzzling swine. 'I know. You are caught by that place, like a hooked fish.'

'What place? You mean London?'

'No, the place in your head. I saw it once, a long time ago, a whole country in there, a landscape. You have gone to that place and it is now more real to you than anywhere else. Nothing can keep you from it. Not even the death of your own child. I see this,' she says to him, as he binds her wrists together with one of his hands, reaching down for the bag at his feet with the other. 'Don't think I don't.'

Only when he has shouldered his bag does he let go. She shakes her hands, the wrists scored and reddened, rubbing her fingers against the marks of his grip.

He is breathing hard as he stands two paces away from her. He crushes his cap in his hand, avoiding her eye.

'You will not bid me farewell?' she says to him. 'You will walk away without bidding me goodbye? The woman who bore your children? Who nursed your son through his final breath? Who laid him out for burial? You will walk away from me, without a word?'

'Look after the girls,' is all he says, and this smarts like the slender but sharp prick of a needle. 'I will send word,' he says again. 'And hope to return to you again before Christmas.'

She turns away from him towards the swine. She sees their bristly backs, their flapping ears, hears their satisfied gruntings.

He is suddenly there, behind her. His arms circle her waist, turn her around, pull her towards him. His head is next to hers: she smells the leather of his gloves, the salt of his tears. They stand like this, together, unified, for a moment, and she feels the pull towards him that she always does and always has, as if there is an invisible rope that circles her heart and ties it to his. Our boy was made, is what she thinks, of him and of her. They made him together; they buried him together. He will never come again. There is a part of her that would like to wind up time, to gather it in, like yarn. She would like to spin the wheel backwards, unmake the skein of Hamnet's death, his boyhood, his infancy, his birth, right back until the moment she and her husband cleaved together in that bed to create the twins. She would like to unspool it all, render it all back down to raw fleece, to find her way back, to that moment, and she would stand up, she would turn up her face to the stars, to the heavens, to the moon, and appeal to them to change what lay in wait for him, to plead with them to devise a different outcome for him, please, please. She would do anything for this, give anything, yield up whatever the heavens wanted.

Her husband holds her close as she clasps him with both arms, despite everything, just as she did that night, his body fitted to hers. He breathes in and out, into the curved side of her coif, as if he might speak, but she doesn't want the words, has no need of them. She sees, over his shoulder, that travelling bag of his, at his feet.

There will be no going back. No undoing of what was laid out for them. The boy has gone and the husband will leave and she will stay and the pigs will need to be fed every day and time runs only one way.

'Go, then,' she says, turning from him, pushing him away, 'if you are going. Return when you can.'

She discovers that it is possible to cry all day and all night. That there are many different ways to cry: the sudden outpouring of tears, the deep, racking sobs, the soundless and endless leaking of water from the eyes. That sore skin around the eyes may be treated with oil infused with a tincture of eyebright and chamomile. That it is possible to comfort your daughters with assurances about places in Heaven and eternal joy and how they may all be reunited after death and how he will be waiting for them, while not believing any of it. That people don't always know what to say to a woman whose child has died. That some will cross the street to avoid her merely because of this. That people not considered to be good friends will come, without warning, to the fore, will leave bread and cakes on your sill, will say a kind and apt word to you after church, will ruffle Judith's hair and pinch her wan cheek.

It is hard to know what to do with his clothes.

For weeks, Agnes cannot move them from the chair where he left them before taking to bed.

A month or so after burial she lifts the breeches, then puts them down. She fingers the collar of his shirt. She nudges the toe of his boot so that the pair are lined up, side by side.

Then she buries her face in the shirt; she presses the breeches to her heart; she inserts a hand into each boot, feeling the empty shapes of his feet; she ties and unties the necklines; she pushes buttons into holes and out again. She folds the clothes, unfolds them, refolds them.

As the fabric runs through her fingers, as she puts each seam together, as she flaps out the creases in the air, her body remembers this task. It takes her back to the before. Folding his clothes, tending to them, breathing in his scent, she can almost persuade herself that he is still here, just about to get dressed, that he will walk through the door at any moment, asking, Where are my stockings, where is my shirt?, worrying about being late for the school bell.

She and Judith and Susanna sleep together in the curtained bed, without discussing the matter: the girls' truckle is never pulled out but remains tucked away. She draws the curtains tight around the three of them. She tells herself that nothing can get them, nothing will come in through the windows or down the chimney. She stays awake most of the night, listening for the knock and keen of bad spirits trying to find a way in. She puts her arms around her slumbering daughters. She wakes often, during the night, to check them for fevers, swellings, strange colorations of the skin. She switches sides, from time to time, throughout the night, so that she lies between Judith and the outside world, and then Susanna. Nothing will get past her this time. She will be waiting. Nothing will come to take her children. Never again.

Susanna says she will pass the night next door, with her grandparents. I cannot sleep here, she says, avoiding her mother's eye. There's too much shifting about.

She gathers her nightcap, her gown, and leaves the room, her skirts gathering the dust mice that have collected on the floor.

Agnes cannot see the point of sweeping the floor. It just gets dirty again. Cooking food seems similarly pointless. She cooks it, they eat it and then, later on, they eat more.

*

The girls go next door for their meals; Agnes doesn't stop them.

To walk by his grave every Sunday is both a pain and a pleasure. She wants to lie there so that her body covers it. She wants to dig down with her bare hands. She wants to strike it with a tree branch. She wants to build a structure over it, to shield it from the wind and the rain. Perhaps she would come to live in it, there, with him.

God had need of him, the priest says to her, taking her hand after the service one day.

She turns on him, almost snarling, filled with the urge to strike him. I had need of him, she wants to say, and your God should have bided His time.

She says nothing. She takes her daughters' arms and walks away.

She has a dream that she is in the fields at Hewlands. It is dusk and the earth is bare and dug into deep furrows. Ahead of her is her mother, bending to the soil and straightening up. When Agnes gets closer she sees that her mother is sowing tiny pearl-white teeth in the ground. Her mother doesn't turn or pause as Agnes approaches, just smiles at her, then carries on dropping milk teeth into the ground, one after another.

Summer is an assault. The long evenings, the warm air wafting through the windows, the slow progress of the river through the town, the shouts of children playing late in the street, the horses flicking flies from their flanks, the hedgerows heavy with flowers and berries.

Agnes would like to tear it all down, rip it up, hurl it to the wind.

Autumn, when it comes, is terrible too. The sharpness on the air, early in the morning. The mist gathering in the yard. The hens fussing and murmuring in their pen, refusing to come out. The leaves crisping at their edges. Here is a season Hamnet has not known or touched. Here is a world moving on without him.

Letters come, from London. Susanna reads them aloud. They are briefer, Agnes notices, when she examines them later, not quite covering one page, his script looser, as if written in haste. They don't speak of the playhouse, of the audiences, of the performances, of the plays he writes. None of this. Instead, he tells them of the rain in London and how it soaked his stockings last week, how his landlord's horse is lame, how he met a lace-seller and bought them all a handkerchief, each with a different edging.

She knows better than to look out of the window at the hour school begins and ends. She keeps herself busy, head averted. She will not go out at this time.

Every golden-haired child in the street puts on his gait, his aspect, his character, making her heart leap, like a deer. Some days, the streets are full of Hamnets. They walk about. They jump and run. They jostle each other. They walk towards her, they walk away from her, they disappear around corners.

Some days she doesn't go out at all.

The lock of his hair is kept in a small earthenware jar above the fire. Judith has sewn a silk pouch for it. She drags a chair to the mantel when she thinks no one is looking and gets it down.

The hair is the same colour as her own; it might have been cut from her own head; it slips like water through her fingers.

What is the word, Judith asks her mother, for someone who was a twin but is no longer a twin?

Her mother, dipping a folded, doubled wick into heated tallow, pauses but doesn't turn around.

If you were a wife, Judith continues, and your husband dies, then you are a widow. And if its parents die, a child becomes an orphan. But what is the word for what I am?

I don't know, her mother says.

Judith watches the liquid slide off the ends of the wicks, into the bowl below.

Maybe there isn't one, she suggests.

Maybe not, says her mother.

Agnes is upstairs. She is sitting at the desk where Hamnet kept his collection of pebbles in four pots. He liked to tip them out periodically and sort them in different ways. She is peering into each pot, observing that the last time he arranged them, he did so by colour, not size and—

She looks up to see her daughters standing before her. Susanna has a basket in one hand, a knife in the other. Judith stands behind her, holding a second basket. They are both wearing a rather severe expression.

'It is time,' Susanna says, 'to gather rosehips.'

It is something they do every year, at this time, just as summer tips towards autumn, scouring the hedgerows, filling their baskets with the hips that swell and grow in the wake of the petals. She has taught them, these daughters of hers, how to find the best ones, to split them with a knife, to boil them up, to make a syrup for coughs and chest colds, to see them all through the winter.

This year, though, the hips' ripeness and their brazen colour are an insult, as are the blackberries turning purple, the elder tree's darkening berries.

Agnes's hands, curled around the pebble pots, feel enfeebled, useless. She doesn't think she is able to grip the knife, to grasp the thorned stems, to pluck the waxy-skinned hips. The idea of harvesting them, bringing them home, stripping off their leaves and stems, then boiling them over a fire: she doesn't think she can do that at all. She would rather lie down in her bed and pull the blankets over her head.

'Come,' says Susanna.

'Please, Mamma,' says Judith.

Her daughters press their hands to her face, to her arms; they haul her to her feet; they lead her down the stairs, out into the street, talking all the while of the place they have seen, filled with rosehips, they tell her, simply filled. She must come with them, they say; they will show her the way.

The hedgerows are constellations, studded with fire-red hips.

*

When they were first married, he took her out one night into the street and it was passing strange, to be there, the place so quiet, so black, so empty.

Look up, he had said to her, standing behind her and putting his arms around her, his hands coming to rest on the curve of her stomach. She leant back her head so that it lay propped on his shoulder.

Balanced on the tops of the houses was a sky scattered with jewels, pierced with silver holes. He had whispered into her ear names and stories, his finger outstretched, pulling shapes and people and animals and families out of the stars.

Constellations, he had said. That was the word.

The baby that was Susanna turning over in her belly, as if listening.

Judith's father writes to say that business is good, that he sends his love, that he won't be home until after winter because the roads are bad.

Susanna reads the letter aloud.

His company are having a great success with a new comedy. They took it to the Palace and the word was that the Queen was much diverted by it. The river in London is frozen over. He is looking to buy more land in Stratford, she finishes. He has been to the wedding of his friend Condell; there had been a wonderful wedding breakfast.

There is a silence. Judith looks from her mother, to her sister, to the letter.

A comedy? her mother asks.

*

It is not easy to be alone in a house like this, Judith finds. There will always be someone bustling in on you, someone calling your name, a person on your heels.

There is a place that was always hers and Hamnet's, when they were small, a wedge-shaped gap between the wall of the cookhouse and that of the pig-pen: a narrow opening, just possible to squeeze yourself through, if you turned sideways, and then a widening three-corner space. Room enough for two children to sit, legs outstretched, backs to the stone wall.

Judith takes rushes from the floor of the workshop, one by one, hides them in the folds of her skirt. She slips through the gap when no one is looking and weaves the rushes into a roof. The kittens, who are cats now, slink in after her, two of them, with identical striped faces and white-socked feet.

Then she may sit there, hands folded, and let him come, if he will.

She sings to herself, to the cats, to the rush roof above her, a string of notes and words, toora-loora-tirra-lirra-ay-ay-ayee, sings on and on, until the sound finds the hollow place within her, finds it and pours into it, filling it and filling, but of course it will never be full because it has no shape and no edge.

The cats watch her, with their implacable green eyes.

Agnes stands in the market with four other women, a tray of honeycombs in her hands. Her stepmother, Joan, is among them. One of them is complaining, telling of how her son refuses to accept an apprenticeship she and her husband have arranged for him, how he shouts if they try to talk to him about it, how he says he will not go, they cannot make him. Even when, the woman says, her eyes popping wide, his father beats him.

Joan leans forward to tell of how her youngest son refuses to rise from his bed in the morning. The other women nod and grumble. And in the evening, she says, her face in a grimace, he will not get into it, stamping around the house, stirring the fire, demanding food, keeping everyone else awake.

Another woman answers with a story about how her son will not stack the firewood in the way she likes, and her daughter has refused an offer of marriage, and what is she to do with children like that?

Fools, Agnes thinks, you fools. She keeps several hand-widths between herself and her stepmother. She stares down into the repeating shapes of the honeycomb. She would like to shrink herself down to the size of a bee and lose herself among them.

'Do you think,' Judith says to Susanna, as they push shirts, shifts and stockings under the surface of the water, 'that Father doesn't come home because of . . . my face?'

The washhouse is hot, airless, full of steam and soap bubbles. Susanna, who hates laundry more than any other task, snaps, 'What are you talking about? He does come home. He comes home all the time. And what has your face to do with anything?'

Judith stirs the laundry pot, poking at a sleeve, a hem, a stray cap. 'I mean,' she says quietly, without looking at her sister, 'because I resemble him so closely. Perhaps it is hard for Father to let his eye rest upon me.'

Susanna is speechless. She tries to say, in her usual tone, don't be ridiculous, what utter nonsense. It is true, though, that it has been a long time since their father came to them. Not since the funeral. No one says this aloud, however; no one mentions it. The letters come, she reads them. Her mother keeps them on the mantel for a few days, taking them down every now and again, when she thinks no one is watching. And then they vanish. What she does with them after that, Susanna doesn't know.

She looks at her sister, looks at her carefully. She lets the laundry plunger fall into the pot, and puts a hand on each of Judith's small shoulders. 'People who don't know you so well,' Susanna says, examining her, 'would say you look the same as him. And the resemblance between you both is . . . was . . . remarkable. It was hard to believe, at times. But we who live with you see differences.'

Judith looks up at her, wonderingly.

Susanna touches her cheek with a trembling finger. 'Your face is narrower than his. Your chin is smaller. And your eyes are a lighter shade. His were more flecked. He had more freckles than you. Your teeth are straighter.' Susanna swallows painfully. 'Father will know all these things, too.'

'Do you think so?'

Susanna nods. 'I never . . . I never confused the two of you. I always knew which was which, even when you were babies. When you used to play those games, the two of you, swapping clothes or hats, I always knew.'

There are tears now, sliding out of Judith's eyes. Susanna lifts a corner of her apron and wipes them away. She sniffs and turns back to the pot, seizing the plunger. 'We should get back to this. I think I hear someone coming.'

*

Agnes searches for him. Of course she does. In the nights and nights and weeks and months after he dies. She expects him. Sits up nights, a blanket around her shoulders, a candle burning itself up beside her. She waits where his bed used to be. She seats herself in his father's chair, placed on the very spot he died. She goes out into the frost-gilded yard and stands under the bare plum tree and speaks aloud: Hamnet, Hamnet, are you there?

Nothing. No one.

She cannot understand it. She, who can hear the dead, the unspoken, the unknown, who can touch a person and listen to the creep of disease along the veins, can sense the dark velvet press of a tumour on a lung or a liver, can read a person's eye and heart like some can read a book. She cannot find, cannot locate the spirit of her own child.

She waits in these places, she keeps her ear tuned, she sifts through the sounds and wants and disgruntlements of other, noisier, beings, but she cannot hear him, the only one she wants to hear. There is nothing. Just silence.

Judith, though, hears him in the swish of a broom against the floor. She sees him in the winged dip of a bird over the wall. She finds him in the shake of a pony's mane, in the smattering of hail against the pane, in the wind reaching its arm down the chimney, in the rustle of the rushes that make up her den's roof.

She says nothing, of course. She folds the knowledge into herself. She closes her eyes, allows herself to say silently, inside her mind, I see you, I hear you, where are you?

*

Susanna finds it hard to be in the apartment. The unused pallet propped against the wall. The clothes kept on the chair, the empty boots beneath. The pots of his stones that no one is allowed to touch. The curl of his hair kept on the mantel.

She moves her comb, her shift, her gown next door. She takes up the bed that was once her aunts'. Nothing is said. She leaves her mother and sister to their grief and moves in above the workshop.

Agnes is not the person she used to be. She is utterly changed. She can recall being someone who felt sure of life and what it would hold for her; she had her children, she had her husband, she had her home. She was able to peer into people and see what would befall them. She knew how to help them. Her feet moved over the earth with confidence and grace.

This person is now lost to her for ever. She is someone adrift in her life, who doesn't recognise it. She is unmoored, at a loss. She is someone who weeps if she cannot find a shoe or overboils the soup or trips over a pot. Small things undo her. Nothing is certain any more.

Agnes bolts her casement, closes her door. She doesn't answer the knocks that come in the evening or the early morning.

If people stop her in the street, with questions about sores, gum swellings, deafness, a rash on the legs, heartache, coughs, she shakes her head and walks on.

She lets the herbs grow grey and crisp, no longer waters her physick garden. The pots and jars on her shelf become covered in a layer of pale dust.

It's Susanna who gets a damp rag and wipes the jars, who

takes down the desiccated and useless herbs from the rafters and feeds them into the fire. She doesn't fetch the water herself but Agnes hears her instructing Judith to carry a pot, once a day, to the small patch of earth, on the other side of the henhouse, where the medicinal plants grow. Ensure all are watered, Susanna calls after Judith's retreating back. Agnes listens, realising that she's adopting her grandmother's voice, the one Mary uses for the serving girls.

Susanna is the one to shred the marigold petals into vinegar, to mash and add honey. She is the one to ensure the mixture is shaken every day.

Judith begins to lift the window latch when people knock. She speaks with the person outside, standing on tiptoe to hear them. Mamma, Judith will say, it is a washerwoman from down by the river. A man from outside town. A child on behalf of his mother. An old woman from the dairy. Will you see them?

Susanna won't answer the knocks, but watches and listens and gestures to Judith if someone comes to the window.

Agnes refuses for a while. She shakes her head. She waves off her daughters' entreaties. She turns back to the fire. But when the old woman from the dairy comes for a third time, Agnes nods. The woman comes in, takes up her place in the big wooden chair with the worn arms, and Agnes listens to her tales of aching joints, a phlegmy chest, a mind that skids and slips, forgetting names, days, tasks.

Agnes rises and goes to her worktable. She brings her pestle and mortar out of the cupboard. She does not allow herself to think that last time she used this it was for him; the last time she held this pestle in her fingers, felt its cold weight, was then, just before, and how useless it was, that it did no good. She doesn't think these things at all, as she breaks up sharp stems of rosemary, for blood to the head, comfrey and hyssop.

She hands the old dairywoman the packet. Three times a day, she tells her: a sprinkling in hot water. Drink when cool.

She will not take the coins the woman tries to give her, fumblingly, hesitatingly, but she pretends not to see the wrapped cheese left on the table, the bowl of thick cream.

Her daughters show the woman out, saying goodbye. Their voices are like bright birds, taking wing, swooping around the room and out into the skies.

How is it these children, these young women came from her? What relation do they bear to the small beings she once nursed and dandled and washed? More and more, her own life seems strange and unrecognisable to her.

Sometime past midnight, Agnes stands in the street, a shawl around her. She was woken by footsteps, light, fast ones, with a familiar tittuping rhythm.

She was pulled from sleep by a sense of feet approaching her window, by a definite feeling that someone was outside. And so here she is, alone in the street, waiting.

'I'm here,' she says aloud, turning her head first one way, then the other. 'Are you?'

At that very moment her husband is sitting under the same sky, in a skiff rounding a bend in the river. They are travelling upstream but he can sense that the tide is turning; the river

seems confused, almost hesitant, trying to flow in two directions at once.

He shivers, pulling his cloak around himself more tightly
(he will catch a chill, he hears a voice inside his head chide,
a soft voice, a caring voice). The sweat from earlier has cooled,
sitting uneasily and clammily between his skin and the wool
of his clothes.

Most of the company are asleep, stretching themselves out
in the bottom of the boat and lowering their hats over their
faces. He does not sleep; he never can on these evenings, the
blood still hurtling through his veins, his heart still galloping,
his ears still hearing the sounds and roars and gasps and
pauses. He longs for his bed, for the enclosed space of his
room, for that moment when his mind will fall silent, when
his body will realise it is over and that sleep must come.

He huddles into himself as he sits on the hard board of the
boat, watching the river, the sliding by of the houses, the dip
and sway of lights on other vessels, the shoulders of the boatman
as he wrestles the craft through trickier currents, the dripping
lift of the oars, the white scarf of breath that streams from
his mouth.

The Thames has thawed now (he had told them it was
frozen in his last letter); they can reach the Palace once more.
He sees, again, for a moment, the vista of eyes beyond the
edge of the stage, beyond the world that encases him and his
friends, blurred by candle flames. The faces watching him, at
these moments, are colours smeared with a wet brush. Their
shouts, their applause, their avid expressions, their open
mouths, their rows of teeth, their gazes that would drink him
up (if they could, but they cannot, for he is covered, protected

in a costume, like a whelk in a shell – they may never see the real him).

He and his friends have just performed a historical play, about a long-dead king, at the Palace. It has proved, he has found, a subject safe for him to grapple with. There are, in such a story, no pitfalls, no reminders, no unstable ground to stumble upon. When he is enacting old battles, ancient court scenes, when he is putting words into the mouths of distant rulers, there is nothing that will ambush him, tie him up and drag him back to look on things he cannot think about (a wrapped form, a chair of empty clothes, a woman weeping at a piggery wall, a child peeling apples in a doorway, a curl of yellow hair in a pot). He can manage these: histories and comedies. He can carry on. Only with them can he forget who he is and what has happened. They are safe places to stow his mind (and no one else on stage with him, not one of the other players, his closest friends, will know that he finds himself looking out, every evening, over the watching crowd, in search of a particular face, a boy with a slightly crooked smile and a perpetually surprised expression; he scans the audience minutely, carefully, because he still cannot fathom that his son could just have gone; he must be somewhere; all he has to do is find him).

He covers first one eye, then the other, turning to regard the city. It is a game he can play. One of his eyes can only see what is at a distance, the other what is close by. Together they work so that he may see most things, but separated; each eye sees only what it can: the first, far away, the second, close up.

Close up: the interlocking stitches of Condell's cape, the lapped wooden rim of the boat, the whirlpool drag of the oars.

Far away: the frozen glitter of stars, shattered glass on black silk, Orion forever hunting, a barge cutting stolidly through the water, a group of people crouching at the edge of a wharf – a woman, with several children, one almost as tall as the mother (as tall as Susanna now?), the smallest a baby in a cap (three, he'd had, such pretty babies, but now there are only two).

He switches eyes, with a quick movement, so that the woman and her children, night-fishing (so close to the water, too close, surely), are no more than indistinct shapes, meaningless strokes of a nib.

He yawns, his jaw cracking with a sound like a breaking nutshell. He will write to them, perhaps tomorrow. If he has time. For there are the new pages to be done, the man from across the river to see; the landlord must be paid; there is a new boy to try out for the other has grown too tall, his voice trembling, his beard coming in (and such a secret, private pain it is, to see a boy growing like that, from lad to man, effortlessly, without care, but he would never say that, never let on to anyone else how he avoids this boy, never speaks to him, how he hates to look upon him).

He throws off his cloak, suddenly hot, and shuts both eyes. The roads will be clear now. He knows he should go. But something holds him back, as if his ankles are tethered. The speed of his work here – from writing to rehearsing to staging and back to writing again – is so breathless, so seamless, it is quite possible for three or four months to slip past without him noticing. And there is the ever-present fear that if he were to step off this whirling wheel, he might never be able to get on it again. He might lose his place; he has seen it happen to others. But the magnitude, the depth of his wife's grief for their son exerts a fatal pull. It is like a dangerous current that, if he were to swim too close, might suck him in, plunge him under. He would never surface again; he must hold himself separate in order to survive. If he were to go under, he would drag them all with him.

If he keeps himself at the hub of this life in London, nothing can touch him. Here, in this skiff, in this city, in this life, he can almost persuade himself that if he were to return, he would find them as they were, unchanged, untrammelled, three children asleep in their beds.

He uncovers his eyes, lifts them to the jumbled roofs of houses, dark shapes above the flexing, restless surface of the river. He shuts his long-sighted eye and stares down the city with an imperfect, watery gaze.

Susanna and her grandmother sit in the parlour, cutting up bed sheets and hemming them into washcloths. The afternoon drags by; with every piercing of the cloth and the easing through of the thread, Susanna tells herself she is a few seconds closer to the end of the day. The needle is slippery in her fingers; the fire is burning low; she feels slumber approach, then back off, approach again.

Is this what it feels like to die, to sense the nearness of something you can't avoid? The thought falls into her head from nowhere, like a drop of wine into water, colouring her mind with its dark, spreading stain.

She shifts in her seat, clears her throat, bends closer over her needle.

'Are you quite well?' her grandmother asks.

'Yes, thank you,' Susanna says, without looking up. She wonders how much longer they will be hemming cloths: they have been at it since midday and there seems to be no end in sight. Her mother was here, for a while, and Judith, too, but her mother disappeared next door with a customer who wanted a cure for ulcers, and Judith had drifted off to do whatever it is she does. Talk to stones. Draw indecipherable shapes with her left hand, in chalk, on the floors. Collect the feathers fallen from the dovecote and weave them together with string.

Agnes steps into the room behind them.

'Did you give him a cure?' Mary asks her.

'I did.'

'And did he pay you?'

Without moving her head, Susanna sees, from the corner of her eye, her mother shrug and turn towards the window. Mary sighs and stabs her needle through the cloth she is holding.

Agnes remains at the window, one hand on her hip. The gown she is wearing is loose on her this spring, her wrists narrow, her fingernails bitten down.

Mary, Susanna knows, is of the opinion that grief is all very well in moderation, but there comes a time when it is necessary to make an effort. She is of the opinion that some people make too much of things. That life goes on.

Susanna sews. She sews and sews. Her grandmother asks her mother, Where is Judith, how are the serving girls getting along with the washing, is it raining, doesn't it seem that the days are getting longer, was it not kind of their neighbour to return that runaway fowl?

Agnes says nothing, just keeps on looking out of the window.

Mary talks on, of the letter they received from Susanna's father, how he is about to take the company on tour again, that he had a chest cold – caught from river fumes – but is now recovered.

Agnes gives a sharp intake of breath, turning to them, her face alert, strained.

'Oh,' Mary says, putting her hand to her cheek, 'you frightened me. Whatever is—'

'Do you hear that?' Agnes says.

All three pause, listen, their heads cocked.

'Hear what?' Mary asks, her brows beginning to knit.

'That . . .' Agnes holds up a finger '. . . There! Do you hear it?'

'I hear nothing,' Mary snaps.

'A tapping.' Agnes strides to the fireplace, presses a hand to the chimney breast. 'A rustling.' She leaves the fireplace and moves to the settle, looking up. 'A definite noise. Can't you hear it?'

Mary allows a long pause. 'No,' she says. 'It's likely nothing more than a jackdaw come down the chimney.'

Agnes leaves the room.

Susanna grips the cloth in one hand, the needle in the other. If she just keeps on making stitches, over and over, of equal size, perhaps all this will pass.

Judith is in the street. She has Edmond's dog with her; it lies in the sun, one paw raised up, while she weaves green ribbon into the long hair of its neck. It looks up at her trustingly, patiently.

The sun is hot on her skin, the light in her eyes, which is perhaps why she doesn't notice the figure coming down Henley Street: a man, walking towards her, hat in his hand, a sack slung on his back.

He calls her name. She lifts her head. He waves. She is running towards him before she even says his name to herself, and the dog is leaping along beside her, thinking that this is much more fun that the ribbon game, and the man has caught her in his arms and swung her off the ground, saying, My little maid, my little Jude, and she cannot catch her breath for laughing, and then she thinks she has not seen him since—

'Where have you been?' she is saying to him, suddenly furious, pushing him away from her, and somehow she is crying now. 'You've been gone such a long time.'

If he sees her anger, he doesn't show it. He is lifting his sack from the ground, scratching the dog behind his ears, taking her by the hand and pulling her towards the house.

'Where is everyone?' he booms, in his biggest, loudest voice.

A dinner. His brothers, his parents, Eliza and her husband, Agnes and the girls all squeezed together around the table. Mary has beheaded one of the geese, in his honour – the honking and shrieking were terrible to hear – and now its carcass lies, dismantled and torn, between them all.

He is telling a story involving an innkeeper, a horse and a millpond. His brothers are laughing, his father is pounding the table with his fist; Edmond is tickling Judith, making her squeal; Mary is remonstrating with Eliza about something; the dog is leaping for scraps thrown to it by Richard, barking in between. The story reaches a climax – something to do with a gate left open, Agnes isn't sure what – and everybody roars. And Agnes is looking at her husband, across the table.

There is something about him, something different. She cannot put her finger on what. His hair is longer, but that's not it. He has a second earring in his other ear, but that's not it. His skin shows signs of the sun and he is wearing a shirt she hasn't seen before, with long, trailing cuffs. But it is none of these things.

Eliza is talking now and Agnes glances towards her for a moment, then back at her husband. He is listening to whatever Eliza is saying. His fingers, shining with goose fat, toy with a crust on his plate. How the goose complained and then shrieked, Agnes thinks, and then ran for a moment, headless, as if sure it could get away, could change its fate. Her husband's face is eager as he listens to his sister; he is leaning forward slightly. He has one arm around Judith's chair.

It's a whole year, almost, that he's been away. Summer has come again and it is almost the anniversary of their son's death. She does not know how this can be, but it is so.

She stares at him, stares and stares. He has come back among them, embracing them all, shouting for them, pulling gifts from his bag: hair combs, pipes, handkerchiefs, a hank of bright wool, a bracelet for her, in hammered silver, a ruby at the clasp.

The bracelet is finer than anything she has ever owned. It has intricate circling etchings in its slippery surface and a raised setting for the stone. She cannot imagine what it must have cost him. Or why he would spend money on it, he who never wastes a penny, who has been so careful with his purse ever since his father lost his fortune. She fiddles with it, spinning it round and round, as she sits at the table, across from her husband.

The bracelet, she realises, has something bad coming off it, like steam. It was too cold, at first, gripping her skin with an icy, indifferent embrace. Now, though, it is too hot, too tight. Its single red eye glowers up at her with baleful intent. Someone unhappy, she knows, has worn it, someone who dislikes or resents her. It is steeped in bad luck, bad feeling, polished with it to a dull lustre. Whoever it used to belong to wishes her harm.

Eliza sits, smiling now, as she finishes speaking. The dog has settled itself beside the open window. John is seizing the ale and refilling his cup.

Agnes looks at her husband and suddenly she sees it, feels it, scents it. All over his body, all over his skin, his hair, his face, his hands, as if an animal has run over him, again and again, leaving tiny pawmarks. He is, Agnes realises, covered in the touches of other women.

She looks down at her plate, at her own hands, her own fingers, at their roughened tips, at the whorls and loops of her fingerprints, at the knuckles and scars and veins of them, at the nails she cannot stop herself gnawing the minute they emerge. For a moment, she believes she may vomit.

Grasping the bracelet, she draws it off her wrist. She looks at the ruby, holds it close to her face, wondering what it has seen, where it has come from, how it came into her husband's possession. It is a deep interior red, a drop of frozen blood. She raises her eyes and her husband is looking straight at her.

She puts the bracelet down on the table, holding his gaze. For a moment, he seems confused. He glances at the bracelet, then at her, then back; he half rises, as if he might speak. Then the blood rushes to his face, his neck. He lifts a hand, as if to reach out for her, then lets it drop.

She stands, without speaking, and leaves the room.

He comes to find her that evening, just before sunset. She is out at Hewlands, tending her bees, pulling up weeds, cutting the blooms off chamomile flowers.

She sees him approach along the path. He has taken off his fine shirt, his braided hat, and is wearing an old jerkin that he keeps hanging on the back of their door.

She doesn't watch him as he walks towards her; she keeps her head averted. Her fingers continue to pluck at the yellow-faced flowers, picking them, then dropping them into a woven basket at her feet.

He stands at the end of the row of bee skeps.

'I brought you this,' he says. He holds out a shawl in his hands.

She turns her head to look at it for a moment, but doesn't say anything.

'In case you were cold.'

'I'm not.'

'Well,' he says, and he places it carefully on top of the nearest skep. 'It's here if you need it.'

She turns back to her flowers. Picks one bloom, two blooms, three blooms, four.

His feet come nearer, scuffing through the grass, until he stands over her, looking down. She can see his boots out of the corner of her eye. She finds herself seized by a passing urge to pierce their toes. Over and over, with the tip of her knife, until the skin beneath is nicked and sore. How he would howl and leap about.

'Comfrey?' he says.

She cannot think what he means, what he is talking about. How dare he come here and speak to her of flowers? Take your ignorance, she wants to say to him, and your bracelets and your shining, fancy boots back to London and stay there. Never come back.

He is gesturing, now, at the flowers in her basket, asking are they comfrey, are they violas, are they—

'Chamomile,' she manages to say, and her voice, to her ears, sounds dull and heavy.

'Ah. Of course. Those are comfrey, are they not?' He points at a clump of feverfew.

She shakes her head and she is struck by how dizzy it makes her feel, as if the slight movement might topple her over into the grass.

'No,' she gestures with fingers stained a greenish-yellow, 'those.'

He nods vigorously, seizes a spear of lavender in his fingers, rubs it, then lifts his hand to his nose, making exaggerated appreciation noises.

'The bees are thriving?'

She gives a single, downward nod.

'Yielding much honey?'

'We've yet to find out.'

'And . . .' he sweeps an arm towards Hewlands farmhouse '. . . your brother? He is well?'

She lifts her face to look at him, for the first time since he arrived. She cannot continue this conversation for a single moment longer. If he says one more thing to her about flowers, about Hewlands, about bees, she doesn't know what she will do. Invert her knife into his boots. Push him backwards into the bee skep. Run from him, to Hewlands, to Bartholomew or to the dark green haven of the forest and refuse to come out again.

He holds her frank gaze for the count of a breath, then his eyes skitter away.

'Can't look me in the eye?' she says.

He rubs at his chin, sighs, lowers himself shakily to the ground beside her, and holds his head in his hands. Agnes lets the knife slip from her hands. She doesn't think she can trust herself to keep holding it.

They sit like that, together, but facing away from each other, for some time. She will not, she tells herself, be the first to speak. Let him decide what should be said, since he is so skilled with words, since he is so fêted and celebrated for his pretty speeches. She will keep her counsel. He is the one who has caused this problem, this breach in their marriage: he can be the one to address it.

The silence swells between them; it expands and wraps itself around them; it acquires shape and form and tendrils, which wave off into the air, like the threads trailing from a broken web. She senses each breath as it enters and leaves him, each shift as he crosses his arms, as he scratches an elbow, as he brushes a hair from his brow.

She stays quite still, with her legs folded beneath her, feeling as if a fire smoulders within her, consuming and hollowing out what is left there. For the first time, she feels no urge to touch him, to put her hands on him: quite the opposite. His body seems to give off a pressure that pushes her away, makes her draw into herself. She cannot imagine how she will ever put her hand where another woman's has been. How could he have done it? How could he leave, after the death of their son, and seek solace in others? How could he return to her, with these prints on him?

She wonders how he could go from her to another. She cannot imagine another man in her bed, a different body, different skin, different voice; the thought would sicken her. She wonders, as they sit there, if she will ever touch him again, if perhaps they shall always be apart now, if there is someone in London who has ensnared his heart and keeps it for her own. She wonders how he will tell her all this, what words he will choose.

Beside her, he clears his throat. She hears him inhale, about to speak, and she readies herself. Here it comes.

'How often do you think of him?' he says.

For a moment, she is taken aback. She had been expecting an account, an explanation, perhaps an apology, for what she knows has occurred. She was bracing herself for him to say, We cannot go on like this, my heart belongs to another, I shall not return again from London. Him? How often does she think of him? She cannot think to whom he refers.

Then she realises what he means and she turns to look at him. His face is obscured by his folded arms, his head hanging down. It is an attitude of abject grief, of sorrow, of such utter sadness that she almost rises to go and put her arms around him, to comfort him. But she recalls that she may not, she cannot.

Instead, she watches a swallow swoop down to skim the

tops of the plants, searching for insects, then lift up towards the trees. Beside them, the trees inflate and exhale, their leaf-heavy branches shuddering in the breeze.

'All the time,' she says. 'He is always here and yet, of course,' she presses a fist against her breastbone, 'he is not.'

He doesn't reply but when she steals a glance at him, she sees he is nodding.

'I find,' he says, his voice still muffled, 'that I am constantly wondering where he is. Where he has gone. It is like a wheel ceaselessly turning at the back of my mind. Whatever I am doing, wherever I am, I am thinking: Where is he, where is he? He can't have just vanished. He must be somewhere. All I have to do is find him. I look for him everywhere, in every street, in every crowd, in every audience. That's what I am doing, when I look out at them all: I try to find him, or a version of him.'

Agnes nods. The swallow circles around and comes back, as if it has something of importance to tell them, if only they could understand. Its cheek flashes scarlet, its head purple-blue, as it passes. Across the surface of the pot of water beside her, a series of clouds roll by, indifferent and slow.

He says something in a subdued, hoarse voice.

'What was that?' she says.

He says it again.

'I didn't hear you.'

'I said,' he says, lifting his head – she sees that his face is scored with tears, 'that I may run mad with it. Even now, a year on.'

'A year is nothing,' she says, picking up a fallen chamomile bloom. 'It's an hour or a day. We may never stop looking for him. I don't think I would want to.'

He reaches out across the space between them and seizes her hand, crushing the flower between their palms. The dusty, pollen-heavy scent fills the air. She tries to pull away but he holds her fast.

'I am sorry,' he says.

She pulls at her wrist, trying to wrest it from his grasp. His strength, his insistence surprises her.

He says her name, with a questioning lilt. 'Did you hear me? I am sorry.'

'For what?' she mutters, giving her arm one last, futile tug, before letting it fall limp in his grasp.

'For everything.' He sighs unevenly, shakily. 'Will you never come to live in London?'

Agnes looks at him, this man who has imprisoned her hand, this father of her children, and shakes her head. 'We cannot. Judith would never survive it. You know that.'

'She might.'

There is a distant sound of bleating, carried on the wind. Both of them turn their heads towards it.

'Would you take that risk?' Agnes says.

He says nothing, but holds her hand between both of his. She twists her hand inside his until it is facing upwards and she grips the muscle between his thumb and forefinger, looking right at him. He gives a faint smile but doesn't pull away. His eyes are wet, lashes drawn into spikes.

She presses the muscle, presses and presses, as if she might draw juice from it. She senses mostly noise, at first: numerous voices, calling in loud and soft and threatening and entreating tones. His mind is crammed with a cacophony, with strife, with overlapping speech and cries and yells and yelps and whispers, and she doesn't know how he stands it, and there are the other women, she can feel them, their loosened hair, their sweat-marked handprints, and it sickens her but she keeps holding on, despite wanting to let go, to push him away, and there is also fear, a great deal of fear, of a journey, something about water, perhaps a sea, a desire to seek a faraway horizon, to stretch his eyes to it, and beneath all this, behind it all, she finds something, a gap, a vacancy, an abyss, which is dark and whistling with emptiness, and at the bottom of it she finds something she has never felt before: his heart, that great, scarlet muscle, banging away, frantic and urgent in its constancy, inside his chest. It feels so close, so present, it's almost as if she could reach out and touch it.

He is still looking at her when she releases her grip. Her hand nestles, inactive, inside his.

'What did you find?' he says to her.

'Nothing,' she replies. 'Your heart.'

'That's nothing?' he says, pretending to be outraged. 'Nothing? How could you say such a thing?'

She smiles at him, a faint smile, but he snatches her hand to his chest.

'And it's your heart,' he says, 'not mine.'

He wakes her that night as she is dreaming of an egg, a large egg, at the bottom of a clear stream; she is standing on a bridge, looking down at it, at the currents, which are forced around its contours.

The dream is so vivid that it takes her a minute to come to, to realise what is happening, that her husband is gripping her tightly, his head buried in her hair, his arms wound about her waist, that he is saying he is sorry, over and over again.

She doesn't reply for a while, doesn't respond to or return his caresses. He cannot stop. The words flow from him, like water. Like the egg, she lies unmoving in their currents.

Then she brings up a hand to his shoulder. She senses the hollow, the cave, made by her palm as it rests there. He takes the other hand and presses it to his face; she feels the resisting spring of his beard, his insistent and assertive kisses.

He will not be stopped, diverted; he is a man intent on one destination, on one action. He yanks and pulls at her shift, bunching its folds and lengths in his hand, swearing and blaspheming with the effort, until he has parted her from it, until she is laughing at him, then he covers her with himself and will not let her go; she feels herself as a separate being, a body apart, dissolve, until she has no idea, no sense of whose skin is whose, which limb belongs to whom, whose hair it is in her mouth, whose breath leaves and enters whose lips.

'I have a proposal,' he says afterwards, when he has shifted himself to lie beside her.

She has a strand of his hair between her fingers and she twists and twists it. The knowledge of the other women had receded during the act, pulled away from her, but now they are back, standing just outside the bed-curtains, jostling for space, brushing their hands and bodies against the fabric, sweeping their skirts on the floor.

'A marriage proposal?' she says.

'It is,' he says, kissing her neck, her shoulder, her chest, 'I fear, a little late for that and besides – ow! My hair, woman. Do you mean to separate it from my head?'

'Perhaps.' She gives it a further tweak. 'You would do well to remember your marriage. From time to time.'

He raises his head from her and sighs. 'I do. I will. I do.' He smooths the skin of her face with his fingers. 'Do you wish to hear my proposal or not?'

'Not,' she says. She has a perverse desire to thwart whatever it is he is about to say. She will not let him off so easily, will not let him think it is all as meaningless to her as it is to him.

'Well, stop your ears if you don't want to hear it because I'm going to speak whether I have your permission or not. Now—'

She begins to move her hands to her ears but he holds them fast, in one of his.

'Let go,' she hisses.

'I shan't.'

'Let go, I tell you.'

'I want you to listen.'

'But I don't want to.'

'I thought,' he says, releasing her hands and drawing her close to him, 'that I would buy a house.'

She turns to look at him but they are enclosed in darkness, a thick, absolute, impenetrable dark. 'A house?'

'For you. For us.'

'In London?'

'No,' he says impatiently, 'Stratford, of course. You said you would rather stay here, with the girls.'

'A house?' she repeats.

'Yes.'

'Here?'

'Yes.'

'Have you money for a house?'

She hears him smile beside her, hears his lips cleaving away from his teeth. He takes her hand and kisses it between each word. 'I have. And more besides.'

'What?' She pulls her hand away. 'Is this true?'

'It is.'

'How can that be?'

'You know,' he says, flopping back on the mattress, 'it is always a pleasure for me to be able to surprise you. An unaccustomed, rare pleasure.'

'What do you mean?'

'I mean,' he says, 'that I don't think you have any idea what it is like to be married to someone like you.'

'Like me?'

'Someone who knows everything about you, before you even know it yourself. Someone who can just look at you and divine your deepest secrets, just with a glance. Someone who can tell what you are about to say – and what you might not – before you say it. It is,' he says, 'both a joy and a curse.'

She shrugs. 'None of these things I can help. I never—'

'I have money,' he interrupts, with a whisper, his lips brushing her ear. 'A lot of money.'

'You have?' She sits up in amazement. She had grasped that his business was flourishing but this is still news to her. She thinks fleetingly of the costly bracelet, which she has since covered with ashes and bone fragments, wrapped in hide, and buried by the henhouse. 'How did you come by this money?'

'Don't tell my father.'

'Your father?' she repeats. 'I – I won't, of course, but—'

'Could you leave this place?' he asks. His hand comes to rest on her spine. 'I want to take you and the girls out of here, to lift you all up and to plant you somewhere else. I want you away from all . . . this . . . I want you somewhere new. But could you leave here?'

Agnes considers the thought. She turns it this way and that. She pictures herself in a new house, a cottage perhaps, a room or two, somewhere on the edge of town, with her daughters. A patch of land, for a garden; a few windows looking out over it.

'He is not here,' she says eventually. This stills the hand on her back. She tries to keep her voice even but the anguish leaks out of the gaps between words. 'I have looked everywhere. I have waited. I have watched. I don't know where he is but he isn't here.'

He pulls her back towards him, gently, carefully, as if she is something he might break, and draws the blankets over her.

'I will see to it,' he says.

The person he asks to broker the purchase is Bartholomew. He cannot, he writes in a letter to him, ask any of his brothers as they might bring his father into it. Will Bartholomew help him in this?

Bartholomew considers the letter. He places it on his mantelpiece and glances at it, now and then, as he eats his breakfast.

Joan, agitated by the letter's appearance at their door, walks back and forth across the room, asking what is in it, is it from 'that man', as she refers to Agnes's husband? She demands to know, it is only right. Does he want to borrow money? Does he? Has he come to a bad end in London? She always knew he would. She had him pegged for a bad sort from the day she first laid eyes on him. It still grieves her that Agnes threw away her chance on a good-for-nothing like him. Is he asking to borrow money from Bartholomew? She hopes Bartholomew isn't for a minute considering lending him anything at all. He has the farm to think of, and the children, not to mention all his brothers and sisters. He really should listen to her, Joan, on this matter. Is he listening? Is he?

Bartholomew continues to eat his porridge in silence, as if he can't hear her, his spoon dipping and rising, dipping and rising. His wife becomes nervous and spills the milk, half on the floor and half on the fire, and Joan scolds her, getting down on her hands and knees to mop up the mess. A child starts to cry. The wife tries to fan the fire back to life.

Bartholomew pushes the remainder of his breakfast away from him. He stands, Joan's voice still twittering away behind him, like a starling's. He claps his hat to his head and leaves the farmhouse.

He walks over the land to the east of Hewlands, where the ground has become boggy of late. Then he comes back.

His wife, his stepmother and his children gather round him again, asking, Is it bad news from London? Has something happened? Joan has, of course, examined the letter, which has been passed from hand to hand in the farmhouse, but neither she nor Bartholomew's wife can read. Some of the children can but they cannot decipher the script of their mysterious uncle.

Bartholomew, still ignoring the women's questions, takes

out a sheet of paper and a quill. Painstakingly, he dips into the ink and, with his tongue held firmly between his teeth, he writes back to his brother-in-law and says, yes, he will help.

Several weeks later, he goes to find his sister. He looks for her first at the house, then at the market, and then at a cottage where the baker's wife directs him – a small dark place on the road out by the mill.

When Bartholomew pushes open the door, she is applying a poultice to the chest of an elderly man lying on a rush mat. The room is dim; he can see his sister's apron, the white shape of her cap; he can smell the acrid stink of the clay, the damp of the dirt floor and something else – the overripe stench of sickness.

'Wait outside,' she says to him softly. 'I'll be there in a moment.'

He stands in the street, slapping his gloves against his leg. When she appears at his side, he begins to walk away from the door of the sick man.

Agnes looks at him as they proceed towards the town; he can feel her reading him, assessing his mood. After a moment or two, he reaches across and takes the basket from her arm. A brief glance into it reveals a cloth parcel, with some kind of dried plant sticking out of it, a bottle with a seal, some mushrooms and a half-burnt candle. He suppresses a sigh. 'You shouldn't go into places like that,' he says, as they approach the marketplace.

She straightens her sleeves but says nothing.

'You shouldn't,' he says again, knowing all the while that he is wasting his breath. 'You need to look to your own health.'

'He's dying, Bartholomew,' she says simply. 'And he has no one. His wife, his children. All dead.'

'If he's dying, why are you trying to cure him?'

'I'm not.' Her eyes flash as she looks at him. 'But I can ease his passage, take away his pain. Isn't that what we all deserve, in our final hour?'

She puts out a hand and tries to take back her basket but Bartholomew won't let go.

'Why are you in such an ill humour today?' she says.

'What do you mean?'

'It's Joan,' she says, finally giving up her pointless struggle for the basket and fixing him with a gimlet gaze, 'is it not?'

Bartholomew inhales, moving the basket to his other hand so it is out of Agnes's reach, once and for all. He hasn't come here to talk about Joan but it was foolish of him to think that Agnes wouldn't notice his gloom. There had been an argument over breakfast with his stepmother. He has been saving money for years to extend the farmhouse, to put on an upper floor and further rooms at the back – he is weary of sleeping in a hall with endless children, a gurning stepmother and various beasts. Joan has been obstructive about the plan from the start. This place was good enough for your father, she cried, as she served the porridge this morning, why isn't it good enough for you? Why must you raise the thatch, take the roof from over our heads?

'Do you want my advice?' Agnes asks.

Bartholomew shrugs, his mouth set.

'With Joan, you must pretend,' Agnes says, as they come in sight of the first stalls of the marketplace, 'that what you want isn't what you want at all.'

'Eh?'

Agnes pauses to examine a row of cheeses, to greet a woman in a yellow shawl, before walking on.

'Let her believe you've changed your mind,' she says, as she weaves ahead of him, in and out of the market crowds. 'That you don't want to rebuild the hall. That you think it's too much bother, too costly.' Agnes throws him a look from over her shoulder. 'I promise you, within a week, she will be saying that she thinks the hall has become too crowded, that more rooms are needed, that the only reason you aren't building them is because you're too lazy.'

Bartholomew considers this as they reach the far side of the market. 'You think that will work?'

Agnes allows him to catch up with her, so that they are once again walking side by side. 'Joan is never content and she cannot rest if others are. The only thing that pleases her is making others as unhappy as she is. She likes company in her perpetual dissatisfaction. So hide what will make you happy. Make her believe you want its opposite. Then all will be as you wish. You'll see.'

Agnes is just about to turn towards Henley Street, when Bartholomew catches her elbow and tucks her arm into his, easing her down a different street, towards the Guildhall and the river.

'Let us walk this way,' he says.

She hesitates for a moment, giving him a quizzical look, then silently relents.

They pass by the windows of the grammar school. It is possible to hear the pupils chanting a lesson. A mathematical formula, a verb construction, a verse of poetry, Bartholomew cannot tell what it is. The noise is rhythmic, fluting, like the cries of distant marsh birds. When he glances at his sister, he sees her head is bent, her shoulders hunched inwards, as if she is protecting herself from hail. The grip on his arm tells him that she wishes to cross the street, so they do.

'Your husband,' Bartholomew says, as they wait for a horse to pass, 'wrote to me.'

Agnes raises her head. 'He did? When?'

'He instructed me to buy a house for him and—'

'Why didn't you tell me?'

'I'm telling you now.'

'But why didn't you tell me before now, before I—'

'Do you want to see it?'

She presses her lips together. He can tell that she wants to say no, but is simultaneously filled with curiosity.

She opts to shrug, affecting indifference. 'If you like.'

'No,' Bartholomew says, 'if you like.'

She shrugs again. 'Perhaps another day, when—'

Bartholomew reaches out with his free hand and points to a building across the road from where they are standing. It is an enormous place, the biggest in the town, with a wide central doorway, three storeys stacked on top of each other, and arranged on a corner, so that the front of it faces them, the side stretching away from them.

Agnes follows the direction of his pointing finger. He watches her look at the house. He watches her glance at either side of it. He watches her frown.

'Where?' she says.

'There.'

'That place?'

'Yes.'

Her face is puckered with confusion. 'But which part of it?
Which rooms?'

Bartholomew puts down the basket he is holding and rocks
back on his heels before he says, 'All of them.'

'What are you saying?'

'The whole house,' he says, 'is yours.'

The new house is a place of sound. It is never quiet. At night
Agnes walks the corridors and stairs and chambers and
passageways, her feet bare, listening out.

In the new house, the windows shudder in their frames. A
breath of wind turns a chimney into a flute, blowing a long,
mournful note down into the hall. The click of wooden wainscots settling for the night. Dogs turning and sighing in their
baskets. The small, clawed feet of mice skittering unseen in
the walls. The thrashing of branches in the long garden at the
back.

In the new house, Susanna sleeps at the furthest end of
the corridor; she locks her door against her mother's nocturnal
wanderings. Judith has the chamber next to Agnes's; she skims
over the surface of sleep, waking often, never quite reaching
the depths. If Agnes opens the door, just the sound of the
hinges is enough to make her sit up, say, Who's there? The
cats sleep on her blankets, one on either side of her.

In the new house, Agnes is able to believe that if she were
to walk down the street, across the marketplace, up Henley
Street and in through the door of the apartment, she would
find them all as they were: a woman with two daughters and
a son. It would not be inhabited by Eliza and her milliner

husband, not at all, but by them, as they ought to be, as they would be now. The son would be older now, taller, broader, his voice deeper and more sure of itself. He would be sitting at the table, his boots on a chair, and he would be talking to her – how he loved to talk – about his day at school, things that the master had said, who was whipped, who was praised. He would be sitting there and his cap would be hanging behind the door and he would say he was hungry and what was there to eat?

Agnes can let this idea suffuse her. She can hold it within herself, like wrapped and hidden treasure, to be taken out and polished and admired when she is alone, when she walks the new, enormous house at night.

She sees the garden as her terrain, her domain; the house is so large an entity, attracting so much comment and admiration and envy, questions about her husband and what he does, how is his business and is it true he is often at court? People are attracted and repelled by the house, all at once. Since her husband bought it, people have been unable to stop talking about it. They express surprise to her face, but behind her back, she knows what is said: how could he have done it, he always was such a useless hare-brain, soft in the head, his gaze up in the clouds, where did such money come from, was he dealing illegally out there in London, no surprise if he was, given what manner of a man his father was, how can money like that have come from working in a playhouse? It's not possible.

Agnes has heard it all. The new house is a jam pot, pulling flies towards it. She will live in it but it will never be hers.

Outside its back door, though, she can breathe. She plants

a row of apple trees along the high brick wall. Two pairs of pear trees on either side of the main path, plums, elder, birch, gooseberry bushes, blush-stemmed rhubarb. She takes a cutting from a dog-rose growing by the river and cultivates it against the warm wall of the malthouse. She puts in a rowan sapling near the back door. She fills the soil with chamomile and marigold, with hyssop and sage, borage and angelica, with wormwort and feverfew. She installs seven skeps at the furthest edge of the garden; on warm July days it is possible to hear the restless rumble of the bees from the house.

She turns the old brewhouse into a room where she dries her plants, where she mixes them, where people come, in through the side gate, to ask for cures. She orders a larger brewhouse, the biggest in town, to be built at the back of the house. She clears the old well in the courtyard. She makes a knot garden, with box hedges in an interlocking grid, their vacancies filled with purple-headed lavender.

The father comes home to the new house twice, sometimes three times a year. He is home for a month in the second year they live in the house. There have been food riots in the city, he tells them, with apprentices marching on Southwark and pillaging shops. It is also plague season again in London and the playhouses are shut. This is never said aloud.

Judith notes the absence of this word during his visits. She notes that her father loves the new house. He walks around it, with slow, lingering steps, looking up at the chimneys and lintels, shutting and opening each door. If he were a dog, his tail would be constantly wagging. He is to be seen out in the courtyard, early in the morning, where he likes to pull up the first water from the well and take a drink. The water here, he says, is the freshest, most delicious he has ever tasted.

Judith sees, too, that for the first few days her mother will not look at him. She steps aside if he comes close; she leaves the room if he enters.

He trails her, though, when he is not shut inside his chamber, working. Into the brewhouse, around the garden. He hooks a finger into her cuff. He comes to stand next to her in the outhouse while she works, ducking his head to see under her cap. Judith, crouching in the chamomile path, on the pretext of weeding, sees him pick a basket of apples and offer them, with a smile, to her mother. Agnes takes it without a word and puts it aside.

After a few days, however, there will be a kind of thawing. Her mother will permit his hand to drop to her shoulder as he passes her chair. She will humour him, in the garden, answering his constant enquiries as to what is this flower, and this, and what is it used for? She listens as, holding an ancient-looking book, he compares her names for the plants to those in Latin. She will prepare a sage elixir for him, a tea of lovage and broom. She will carry it up the stairs, into the room where he is bent over his desk, shutting the door after her. She will take his arm when they walk together out in the street. Judith will hear laughter and talk from the outhouses.

It's as if her mother needs London, and all that he does there, to rub off him before she can accept him back.

Gardens don't stand still: they are always in flux. The apple trees stretch out their limbs until their crowns reach higher than the wall. The pear trees fruit the first year, but not the second, then again the third. The marigolds unfold their bright petals, unfailingly, every year, and the bees leave their skeps to skim over the carpet of blooms, dipping into and out of the petals. The lavender bushes in the knot garden grow leggy and woody, but Agnes will not pull them up; she cuts them back, saving the stems, her hands heavy with fragrance.

Judith's cats have kittens and, in time, those kittens have kittens. The cook tries to seize them for drowning but Judith will have none of it. Some are taken to live at Hewlands, others at Henley Street, and others throughout the town, but even so, the garden is filled with cats of various sizes and ages, all with a long, slender tail, a white ruff and leaf-green eyes, all lithe and sinewy and strong.

The house has no mice. Even the cook has to admit that there are advantages to living alongside a dynasty of cats.

Susanna grows taller than her mother. She assumes charge of the house keys; she wears them on a hook at her waist. She keeps the account book, pays the servants, oversees what goes in and out of her mother's cure trade and the burgeoning brewing and malt business. If people fail to pay, she sends one of her uncles round to their door. She corresponds with her father about income, investment, rent accruing from his properties, which tenants have not paid up and which are late with payment. She advises him on how much money to send and how much to keep in London; she lets him know if she hears of a field or a house or a plot of land for sale. She takes it upon herself, at her father's bidding, to buy furniture for the new house: chairs, pallets, linen chests, wall hangings, a new bed. Her mother, however, refuses to give up her bed, saying it was the bed she was married in and she will not have another, so the new, grander bed is put in the room for guests.

Judith stays close to her mother, keeping in her orbit, as if proximity to her guarantees something. Susanna doesn't know what. Safety? Survival? Purpose?

Judith weeds the garden, runs errands, tidies her mother's workbench. If her mother asks her to run and fetch three leaves of bay or a head of marjoram, Judith will know exactly where they are. All plants look the same to Susanna. Judith spends hours with her cats, grooming them, communicating with them in a language of crooning, high-pitched entreaties. Every spring she has kittens to sell; they are, she tells people, excellent mousers. She has the kind of face, Susanna thinks, that people believe: those wide-set eyes, the sweet, quick smile, the alert yet guileless gaze.

All this activity in the garden sets Susanna's teeth on edge; she keeps mostly to the house. The plants that require endless weeding and tending and watering, the infernal bees that drone and sting and zoom into your face; the callers who arrive and depart all day, through the side gate: it drives her to distraction.

She makes an effort, once a day, to teach Judith her letters. She has promised her father that she will do this. Dutifully, she calls her sister in from the back and makes her sit in the parlour, with an old slate in front of them. It is a thankless task. Judith squirms in her seat, stares out of the window, refuses to use her right hand, saying it feels all wrong, picks at a loose thread in her hem, doesn't listen to what Susanna is saying and, when she does, becomes distracted halfway through by a man shouting about cakes in the street. Judith refuses to grasp the letters, to see how they merge together into sense, wonders if there could be a trace of something Hamnet wrote on this slate, cannot remember from day to day which is an *a* and which a *c*, and how is she to tell the difference between a *d* and a *b*, for they look entirely the same to her, and how dull it all is, how impossible. She draws eyes and mouths in all the gaps in the letters, making them into different creatures, some sad, some happy, some winsome. It takes a year for Judith to reliably produce a signature: it is a squiggled initial, but upside down and curled like a pig's tail. Eventually, Susanna gives up.

When she complains to their mother, about how Judith will not learn to write, will not help with the accounts, will not take some responsibility for the running of the house, Agnes gives a slight smile and says, Judith's skills are different from yours but they are skills just the same.

Why, Susanna thinks, stamping back inside the house, does no one see how difficult life is for her? Her father away and never here, her brother dead, the whole house to see to, the servants to watch. And she must take all this on while living with two . . . Susanna hesitates at the word 'half-wits'. Her mother is not a half-wit, just not like other people. Old-fashioned. A countrywoman. Set in her ways. She lives in this place as if it were the house she was born in, a single hall surrounded by sheep; she behaves, still, like the daughter of a farmer, traipsing about the lanes and fields, gathering weeds in a basket, her skirts wet and filthy, her cheeks flushed and sunburnt.

Nobody ever considers her, Susanna thinks, as she climbs the stairs to her chamber. Nobody ever sees her trials and tribulations. Her mother out in the garden, up to her elbows in leaf mulch, her father in London, acting out plays that people say are extremely bawdy, and her sister somewhere in the house, singing a winding song of her own devising in her breathy, fluty voice. Who will come to court her, she demands of the air, as she flings open the door and lets it slam behind her, with a family like this? How will she ever escape this house? Who would want to be associated with any of them?

Agnes watches the child drop from her younger daughter, as a cloak from a shoulder. She is taller, slender as a willow strip, her figure filling out her gowns. She loses the urge to skip, to move quickly, deftly, to skitter across a room or a yard; she acquires the freighted tread of womanhood. Her features become more defined, the cheekbones rising, the nose sharpening, the mouth turning into the mouth it needs to be.

Agnes looks at this face; she looks and looks. She tries to see Judith for who she is, for who she will be, but there are moments when all she is asking herself is: Is this the face he would have had, how would this face have been different on a boy, how would it look with a beard, with a male jaw, on a strapping lad?

Night-time in the town. A deep, black silence lies over the streets, broken only by the hollow lilt of an owl, calling for its mate. A breeze slips invisibly, insistently through the streets, like a burglar seeking an entrance. It plays with the tops of the trees, tipping them one way, then the other. It shivers inside the church bell, making the brass vibrate with a single low note. It ruffles the feathers of the lonely owl, sitting on a rooftop near the church. It trembles a loose casement a few doors along, making the people inside turn over in their beds, their dreams intruded upon by images of shaking bones, of nearing footsteps, of drumming hoofs.

A fox darts out from behind an empty cart, moving sideways along the dark and deserted street. It pauses for a moment, one foot held off the ground, outside the Guildhall, near the school where Hamnet studied, and his father before him, as if it has heard something. Then it trots on, before swerving left and vanishing into a gap between two houses.

The land here was once a marsh – damp, watery, half river and half earth. To build houses, the people had first to drain the land, then lay down a bed of rushes and branches to buoy up the buildings, like ships on a sea. In wet weather, the houses remember. They creak downwards, pulled by ancient recall; wainscots crack, chimney breasts fracture, doorways loosen and rupture. Nothing goes away.

The town is quiet, its breath held. In an hour or so, the dark will begin to weaken, light will rise and people will wake in their beds, ready – or not – to face another day. Now, though, the townspeople are asleep.

Except for Judith. She is coming along the street, wrapped in a cloak, the hood covering her head. She goes past the school, where the fox was until a moment ago; she doesn't see it but it sees her, from its hiding place in an alleyway. It watches her with widened pupils, alarmed by this unexpected creature sharing its nocturnal world, taking in her mantle, her quick-stepping feet, the hurry in her gait.

She crosses the market square quickly, keeping close to the buildings, and turns into Henley Street.

A woman had come to see her mother in the autumn, seeking something for her swollen knuckles and painful wrists. She was, she told Judith when she opened the side gate to her, the midwife. Her mother seemed to know the woman; she gave her a long look, then a smile. She had taken the woman's hands in her own, turning them gently over. Her knuckles were lumpen, purple, disfigured. Agnes had wrapped comfrey leaves around them, binding them with cloth, then left the room, saying she would fetch some ointment.

The woman had placed her bandaged hands on her lap. She stared at them for a moment, then spoke, without looking up.

'Sometimes,' she had said, apparently to her hands, 'I have to walk through the town late at night. Babies come when they come, you see.'

Judith nodded politely.

The woman smiled at her. 'I remember when you came. We all thought you wouldn't live. But here you are.'

'Here I am,' Judith murmured.

'Many a time,' she continued, 'I've been coming along Henley Street, past the house where you were born, and I've seen something.'

Judith stared at her for a moment. She wanted to ask what, but also dreaded the answer. 'What have you seen?' she blurted out.

'Something, or perhaps I should say someone.'

'Who?' Judith asked, but she knew, she knew already.

'Running, he is.'

'Running?'

The old midwife nodded. 'From the door of the big house

to the door of that dear little narrow one. As clear as anything. A figure, it is, running like the wind, as if the devil himself is at its back.'

Judith felt her heart speed up, as if she were the one condemned to run for eternity along Henley Street, not him.

'Always at night,' the woman was saying, passing one hand over the other. 'Never during the day.'

And so Judith has come, every night since, slipping out of the house in the dark hours, to stand here, waiting, watching. She has said nothing of this to her mother or Susanna. The midwife chose to tell her, and her only. It is her secret, her connection, her twin. There are mornings when she can feel her mother looking at her, observing her tired, drawn face, and she wonders if she knows. It wouldn't surprise her. But she doesn't want to speak to anyone else about it, in case it never comes true, in case she can't find him, in case he doesn't appear to her.

In the narrow house, these days, in the room where Hamnet died, shaking and convulsing all over, the fever's poison coursing through him, there are many millinery heads, all facing the door, a crowd of silent, wooden, featureless observers. Judith watches this door; she stares and stares at it.

Please, is what she is thinking. Please come. Just once. Don't leave me here like this, alone, please. I know you took my place, but I am only half a person without you. Let me see you, even if only for the last time.

She cannot imagine how it might be, to see him again. He would be a child and she is now grown, almost a woman. What would he think? Would he recognise her now, if he were to pass her in the street, this boy who will for ever remain a boy?

Several streets away, the owl leaves its perch, surrendering itself to a cool draught, its wings silently breasting the air, its eyes alert. To it, the town appears as a series of rooftops, with gullies of streets in between, a place to be navigated. The massed leaves of trees present themselves as it flies, the stray wisps of smoke from idle fires. It sees the progress of the fox, which is now crossing the street; it sees a rodent, possibly a rat, traversing a yard and disappearing down into a pit; it sees a man, sleeping in the doorway of a tavern, scratching at a fleabite on his shin; it sees coneys in a cage at the back of someone's house; horses standing in a paddock near the inn; and it sees Judith, stepping into the street.

She is unaware of the owl, skimming the sky above her. Her breath comes into her body in ragged, shallow bursts. She has seen something. A flicker, a hint, a motion, imperceptible, but there, unmistakably. It was like the passage of a breeze through corn, like the glancing of a reflection off a pane, when you pull the window towards you – that unexpected streak of light passing through the room.

Judith crosses the road, her hood falling from her head. She stands outside her former home; she paces from its door to that of her grandparents. The very air feels coalescent, charged, as it does before a thunderstorm. She shuts her eyes. She can feel him. She is so sure of this. The skin on her arms and neck shrinks and she is desperate to reach out, to touch him, to take his hand in hers, but she dares not. She listens to the roar of her pulse, her ragged breathing and she knows, she hears, underneath her own, another's breathing. She does. She really does.

She is shaking now, her head bowed, her eyes shut tight.

The thought that forms inside her head is: I miss you, I miss you, I would give anything to have you back, anything at all.

Then it is over, the moment passing. The pressure drops like a curtain. She opens her eyes, puts her hand up to the wall of the house to steady herself. He is gone, all over again.

Mary, early in the day, opening the front door to let out the dogs into the street, finds a person in front of the house, slumped and crouched, head on knees. For a moment, she believes it is a drunkard, collapsed there during the night. Then she recognises the boots and hem of her granddaughter, Judith.

She fusses and clucks around her, brings the half-frozen child in, calling for blankets and hot broth, for Lord's sake.

Agnes is out the back, bending over her plant beds, when the serving girl appears, saying that her stepmother, Joan, has come to call.

It is a wild and stormy day, the wind gusting down into the garden, finding a way up and over the high walls to blast down on them all, hurling handfuls of rain and hail, as if enraged by something they have done. Agnes has been out there since dawn, tying the frailer plants to sticks, to buttress them against the onslaught.

She pauses, clutching the knife and twine, and peers at the girl. 'What did you say?'

'Mistress Joan,' says the girl again, her face screwed up, one hand holding on her cap, which the wind seems determined to rip from her head, 'is waiting in the parlour.'

Susanna is running along the path, head down, barrelling

towards them. She is shouting something at her mother but the words are lost, whirled away, up to the skies. She gestures towards the house, first with one hand, then the other.

Agnes sighs, considers the situation for a moment longer, then slides the knife into her pocket. It will be something to do with Bartholomew, or one of the children, the farm, these improvements to the hall; Joan will be wanting her to intercede and Agnes will have to be firm. She doesn't like to get involved in things that go on at Hewlands. Doesn't she have her own house and family to see to?

The minute she gets inside the house, Susanna starts to pluck at her cap, at her apron, at the hair that has escaped its moorings. Agnes waves her away. Susanna trails her along the passage and through the hall, whispering that she can't possibly receive visitors looking like that, and doesn't she want to go and restore her appearance, Susanna will see to Joan, she promises.

Agnes ignores her. She crosses the hall with a firm, quick tread and pushes open the door.

She is met by the sight of her stepmother, sitting very upright in Agnes's husband's chair. Opposite her is Judith, who has placed herself on the floor. There are two cats in her lap and three others circling her, lavishly rubbing themselves along her sides and back and hands. She is talking, with uncharacteristic fluency, about the different cats and their names, their food preferences and where they elect to sleep.

Agnes happens to know that Joan has a particular dislike of cats – they steal her breath and make her itch, she has always said – so she is suppressing a smile as she comes into the room.

'. . . and, most surprising of all,' Judith is saying, 'this one is the brother of that one, which you wouldn't think, would you, if you saw them at a distance, but up close, you'll see that their eyes are exactly the same colour. Exactly. Do you see?'

'Mmm,' says Joan, her hand pressed over her mouth, standing to greet Agnes.

The two women meet in the middle of the room. Joan takes her stepdaughter by the upper arms with a grip that is resolute and swift. Her eyes flutter closed as she plants a kiss on her cheek; Agnes resists the urge to pull herself away. They ask each other how do they do, are they well, are the families well?

'I fear,' Joan says, as she returns to her seat, 'I have interrupted you in . . . some task or other?' She looks pointedly down at Agnes's muddied apron, her dirt-encrusted hem.

'Not at all,' Agnes replies, taking a seat, putting a hand to Judith's shoulder, in passing. 'I've been at work in the garden, trying to save some of the plants. Whatever brings you to town in such fearsome weather?'

Joan seems momentarily wrong-footed by the question, as if she hadn't been prepared to be asked. She smooths the folds of her gown, presses her lips together. 'A visit to a . . . a friend. A friend who is unwell.'

'Oh? I am sorry to hear that. What is the matter?'

Joan waves her hand. 'It is but a trifle . . . a mere cold on the chest. Nothing to be—'

'I would gladly give your friend a tincture of pine and elder. I have some freshly made. Very good for the lungs, especially over the winter and—'

'No need,' Joan says hastily. 'I thank you, but no.' She clears her throat, looking around the room. Agnes sees her eyes light on the ceiling, the mantel, the fire-irons, the painted drapes on the walls, which feature a design of forests, leaves, dense branches punctuated by leaping deer: a gift from her husband, who had them made up in London. Agnes's recent and unexpected wealth bothers Joan. There is something unbearable to her about the sight of her stepdaughter living in so fine a house.

As if following her train of thought, Joan says, 'And how is your husband?'

Agnes regards her stepmother for a moment, before replying: 'Well, I believe.'

'The theatre still keeps him in London?'

Agnes laces her hands together in her lap and gives Joan a smile before she nods.

'He writes to you often, I suppose?'

Agnes feels a slight adjustment inside her, a minute sensation, as if a small, anxious animal is turning itself around. 'Naturally,' she says.

Judith and Susanna, however, give her away. They turn their heads to look at her, quickly, too quickly, like dogs awaiting a signal from their master.

Joan, of course, doesn't miss this. Agnes sees her stepmother lick her lips, as if tasting something good, something sweet on them. She thinks again of what she said to Bartholomew, years ago, in the marketplace: that Joan likes company in her perpetual dissatisfaction. How is Joan hoping to bring her down now? What information has she that she will wield, like a sword, to slash though this house, this room, this place she and her daughters inhabit, trying to live as best they can in the presence of such enormous, distracting absences? What does Joan know?

The truth is that Agnes's husband hasn't written for several months, save a short letter assuring them he is well, and another, addressed to Susanna, asking her to secure the purchase of another field. Agnes has told herself, and the girls, that nothing is amiss, that he will be busy, that sometimes letters go astray on the road, that he is working hard, that he will be home before they know it, but still the thought has gnawed at her. Where is he and what is he doing and why has he not written?

Agnes crosses her fingers, burying them in the folds of her apron. 'We heard from him a week or so ago. He was telling us that he is very busy, they are preparing a new comedy and—'

'His new play is of course not a comedy,' Joan cuts across her. 'But you knew that, I expect.'

Agnes is silent. The animal inside her flexes itself restlessly, starts to scrape at her innards with its needling claws.

'It's a tragedy,' Joan continues, baring her teeth in a smile. 'And I am certain he will have told you the name of it. In his letters. Because of course he would never call it that without telling you first, would he, without your by-your-leave? I'm sure you've seen the playbill. He probably sent you one. Everyone in town is talking about it. My cousin, who came back from London yesterday, brought it. I'm sure you have one but I carried it with me, just the same, for you.'

Joan stands and crosses the room, a ship in full sail. She drops a curled paper into Agnes's lap.

Agnes eyes it, then takes it with two fingers and flattens it against her mud-splattered apron. For a moment, she cannot tell what she is looking at. It is a printed page. There are many letters, so many, in rows, grouped into words. There is her husband's name, at the top, and the word 'tragedie'. And there, right in the middle, in the largest letters of all, is the name of her son, her boy, the name spoken aloud in church when he was baptised, the name on his gravestone, the name she herself gave him, shortly after the twins' birth, before her husband returned to hold the babies on his lap.

Agnes cannot understand what this means, what has happened. How can her son's name be on a London playbill? There has been some odd, strange mistake. He died. This name is her son's and he died, not four years ago. He was a child and he would have been a man but he died. He is himself, not a play, not a piece of paper, not something to be spoken of or performed or displayed. He died. Her husband knows this, Joan knows this. She cannot understand.

She is aware of Judith leaning over her shoulder, of her saying, What, what is it? and of course she cannot read the letters, cannot string them together to make sense to her – strange that she cannot recognise the name of her own twin – and she is aware of Susanna holding steady the corner of the playbill; her own fingers are trembling, as if caught in the wind from outside, just long enough for her to read it. Susanna tries to tweak it from her grasp but Agnes isn't letting go, there is no way she's letting go, not of that piece of paper, not of that name. Joan is looking at her, open-mouthed, taken aback at the turn her visit has taken. She was evidently underestimating the effect of the playbill, had no idea it might produce such a reaction. Agnes's daughters are ushering Joan from the room, saying that their mother isn't quite herself, Joan should return another time, and Agnes is able, despite the playbill, despite the name, despite everything, to hear the false concern in Joan's voice as she bids them all goodbye.

Agnes takes to her bed, for the first time in her life. She goes to her chamber and she lies down and will not get up, not for meals, not for callers, not for sick people who knock at the side door. She doesn't undress but lies there, on top of the blankets. Light streams in through the latticed windows, pushing itself into cracks in the bed-curtains. She keeps the playbill folded between her hands.

The sounds of the street outside, the noises of the house, the footsteps of the servants coming up and down the corridor, the hushed tones of her daughters all reach her. It is as if she is underwater and they are all up there, in the air, looking down on her.

At night, she rises from her bed and goes outside. She sits between the woven, rough sides of her skeps. The humming, vibrating noises from within, beginning just after dawn, seem to her the most eloquent, articulate, perfect language there is.

Susanna, scorched with rage, sits down at her desk-box with a blank sheet of paper. How could you? she writes to her father. Why would you, how could you not tell us?

Judith carries bowls of soup to her mother's bed, a posy of lavender, a rose in a vase, a basket of fresh walnuts, their shells sealed up.

*

The baker's wife comes. She brings rolls, a honey cake. She affects not to notice Agnes's appearance, her untended hair, her etched and sleepless face. She sits on the edge of the bed, settling her skirts around her, takes Agnes's hand in her warm, dry grip and says: he always was an odd one, you know that. Agnes says nothing but stares up at the tapestry roof of her bed. More trees, some with apples studding their branches.

'Do you not wonder what is in it?' the baker's wife asks, ripping off a hunk of the bread and offering it to Agnes.

'In what?' Agnes says, ignoring the bread, barely listening.

The baker's wife pushes the strip of bread between her own teeth, chews, swallows, tears off another shred before answering: 'The play.'

Agnes looks at her, for the first time.

To London, then.

She will take no one with her, not her daughters, not her friend, not her sisters, none of her in-laws, not even Bartholomew.

Mary declares it madness, says Agnes will be attacked on the road or murdered in her bed at an inn along the way. Judith begins to cry at this and Susanna tries to hush her, but looks worried all the same. John shakes his head and tells Agnes not to be a fool. Agnes sits at her in-laws' table, composed, hands in her lap, as if she can't hear these words.

'I will go,' is all she says.

Bartholomew is sent for. He and Agnes take several turns around the garden. Past the apple trees, past the espaliered pears, through the skeps, past the marigold beds, and round again. Susanna and Judith and Mary watch from the window of Susanna's chamber.

Agnes's hand is tucked into the crook of her brother's arm. Both their heads are bowed. They pause, briefly, beside the brewhouse for a moment, as if examining something on the path, then continue on their way.

'She will listen to him,' says Mary, her voice more decisive than she feels. 'He will never permit her to go.'

Judith brings her fingers up to the watery pane of glass. How easy it is to obliterate them both with a thumb.

When the back door slams, they rush downstairs but there is only Bartholomew in the passage, placing his hat on his head, preparing to leave.

'Well?' Mary says.

Bartholomew lifts his face to look at them on the stairs.

'Did you persuade her?'

'Persuade her in what?'

'Not to go to London. To give up this madness.'

Bartholomew straightens the crown of his hat. 'We leave tomorrow,' he says. 'I am to secure horses for us.'

Mary is saying, 'I beg your pardon?' and Judith is starting to weep again and Susanna clasping her hands together, saying, 'Us? You will go with her?'

'I shall.'

The three women surround him, a cloud wrapping itself around the moon, peppering him with objections, questions, entreaties, but Bartholomew breaks free, steps towards the door. 'I will see you tomorrow, early,' he says, then steps out into the street.

Agnes is a competent if not committed horsewoman. She likes the beasts well enough but finds being aloft a not altogether comfortable experience. The ground rushing by makes her feel giddy; the shift and heave of another being beneath her, the squeak and squeal of saddle leather, the dusty, parched scent of the mane mean she is counting down the hours she must spend on horseback, before she reaches London.

Bartholomew insists that the road via Oxford is safer and faster; a man who trades in mutton has told him this. They ride through the gentle dips and heights of the Chiltern Hills, through a rainstorm and a smattering of hail. In Kidlington, her horse becomes lame so she changes to a piebald mare with narrow hips and a flighty way of high-stepping if they come across a bird. They pass the night at an inn in Oxford; Agnes barely sleeps for the sound of mice in the walls and the snores of someone in the room next door.

Towards mid-morning on the third day of riding, she sees first the smoke, a grey cloth thrown over a hollow. There it is, she says to Bartholomew, and he nods. As they move closer, they hear the peal of bells, catch the scent of it – wet vegetable, animal, lime, some other things Agnes cannot name – and see its vast sprawl, a broken clutter of a city, the river winding through it, clouds pulling up threads of smoke from it.

They ride through the village of Shepherd's Bush, the name of which makes Bartholomew smile, and past the gravel pits of Kensington and over the brook at Maryburne. At the Tyburn hanging-tree, Bartholomew leans down from his saddle to ask the way to the parish of St Helen's, in Bishopsgate. Several people walk by without answering him, a young man laughs, skittering off into a doorway on bare, cut feet.

On towards Holborn, where the streets are narrower and blacker; Agnes cannot believe the noise and the stench. All around are shops and yards and taverns and crowded doorways. Traders approach them, holding out their wares – potatoes, cakes, hard crab-apples, a bowl of chestnuts. People shout and yell at each other across the street; Agnes sees, she is sure, a man coupling with a woman in a narrow gap between buildings. Further on, a man relieves himself into a ditch; Agnes catches sight of his appendage, wrinkled and pale, before she averts her gaze. Young men, apprentices, she supposes, stand outside shops, entreating passers-by to enter. Children still with first teeth are wheeling barrows along the road, calling out their contents, and ancient men and women sit with gnarled carrots, shelled nuts, loaves laid out around them.

The scent of cabbage-heads and burnt hide and bread dough and filth from the street fills her nose as she guides her horse, both hands gripping the reins. Bartholomew reaches over to seize the bridle, so that they won't become separated.

Thoughts begin to cram into Agnes's head as she rides close to her brother: what if we can't find him, what if we get lost, what if we don't find his lodgings by nightfall, what shall we do, where should we go, shall we secure rooms now, why did we come, this was madness, my madness, it is all my fault.

When they reach what they believe is his parish, Bartholomew asks a cake-seller to direct them to his lodgings. They have it written out, on a piece of paper, but the cake-seller waves it away from her, with a gap-toothed smile, telling them to go that way, then this, then straight on, then sharp sideways past the church.

Agnes grips the reins of her horse, sitting straighter in her saddle. She would do anything to be able to get down, for their journey to be at an end. Her back aches, her feet, her hands, her shoulders. She is thirsty, she is hungry, and yet now she is here, now she is about to see him, she wants to pull on the bridle of her horse, turn it around, and head directly back to Stratford. What had she been thinking? How can she and Bartholomew just arrive on his doorstep? This was a terrible idea, a dreadful plan.

'Bartholomew,' she says, but he is ahead of her, already dismounting, tying his horse to a post, and walking up to a door.

She says his name again, but he doesn't hear her because he is knocking at the door. She feels her heart pound against her bones. What will she say to him? What will he say to them? She can't remember now what it was she wanted to ask him. She feels again for the playbill in her saddlebag and glances up at the house: three or four storeys, with windows uneven and stained in places. The street is narrow, the houses leaning towards each other. A woman is propped against her doorway, staring at them with naked curiosity. Further down, two children are playing a game with a length of rope.

Strange to think that these people must see him every day, as he comes to and fro, as he leaves the house in the morning. Does he exchange a word with them? Does he ever eat at their homes?

A window opens above them; Agnes and Bartholomew look up. It is a girl of nine or ten, her hair neatly parted on either side of her sallow face, carrying an infant on her hip.

Bartholomew speaks the name of her husband and the girl shrugs, jiggling the now crying infant. 'Push the door,' she says, 'and go up the stairs. He's up in the attic.'

Bartholomew indicates, with a jerk of his head, that she must go and he will stay in the street. He takes the bridle of her horse as she slides down.

The stairs are narrow and her legs tremble as she climbs, from the long ride or the peculiarity of it all, she doesn't know, but she has to haul herself up by the rail.

At the top, she waits for a moment, to catch her breath. There is a door before her. Panelled wood with knots flowing through it. She reaches out a hand and taps it. She says his name. She says it again.

Nothing. No answer. She turns to look down the stairs and almost goes down them. Perhaps she doesn't want to see what lies beyond this door. Might there be signs of his other life, his other women? There may be things here she does not want to know.

She turns back, lifts the latch and steps in. The room has a low ceiling slanting inwards at all angles. There is a low bed, pushed up against the wall, a small rug, a cupboard. She recognises a hat, left on top of a coffer, the jerkin lying on the bed. Under the light of the window there is a square table, with a chair tucked beneath. The desk-box on top of it is open and she can see a pen-case, inkwell and pen-knife. A collection of quills is lined up next to three or four table-books, bound by his hand. She recognises the knots and stitching he favours. There is a single sheet of paper in front of the chair.

She doesn't know what she expected but it wasn't this: such austerity, such plainness. It is a monk's cell, a scholar's study. There is a strong sense in the air, to her, that no one else ever comes here, that no one else ever sees this room. How can the man who owns the largest house in Stratford, and much land besides, be living here?

Agnes touches her hand to the jerkin, the pillow on the bed. She turns around, to take it all in. She walks towards the desk and bends over the sheet of paper, the blood hammering at her head. At the top, she sees the words:

My dear one –

She almost rears back, as if burnt, then she sees, on the next line:

Agnes

There is nothing more, just four words, then a blank.

What would he have written to her? She presses her fingers to the empty space on the page, as if trying to glean what he might have said, had he been able. She feels the grain of the paper, the sun-warmed wood of the table; she runs her thumb across the letters forming her name, feeling the minute indentations of his quill.

She is startled by a call, a cry. She straightens up, lifting her hand from the page. It is Bartholomew, shouting her name.

She crosses the room, she moves through the door, and descends the stairs. Her brother is waiting for her at the open door. He says that the woman in the house over the street has told him they won't find Agnes's husband at home, that he won't be back until nightfall.

Agnes glances over at the woman, who is still leaning against her doorframe. She shakes her head at Agnes. 'You won't find him here, I tell you. Look for him at the playhouse, if you want him.' She points with her arm. 'Over the river. Yonder. That's where he'll be.'

She ducks back inside her house and bangs the door.

Agnes and Bartholomew regard each other for a moment. Then Bartholomew goes to fetch the horses.

The neighbour in the doorway is right: he is, as she predicted, at the playhouse.

He is standing in the tiring house, just behind the musicians' gallery, at a small opening that gives out over the whole theatre. The other actors know this habit of his and never store their costumes or props there, never take up the space around that window.

They think he stands there to watch the people as they arrive. They believe he likes to assess how many are coming, how big the audience will be, how much the takings.

But that is not why. To him, it is the best place to be, before a performance: the stage below him, the audience filling the circular hollow in a steady trickle, and the other players behind him, transforming themselves from men to sprites or princes or soldiers or ladies or monsters. It is the only place to be alone in such a crowd. He feels like a bird, above the ground, resting on nothing but air. He is not of this place but above it, apart from it, observing it. It brings to mind, for him, the wind-hovering kestrel his wife used to keep, and the way it would hold itself in high currents, far above the tree tops, wings outstretched, looking down on all around it.

He waits, with both hands on the lintel. Beneath him, far beneath him, people are gathering. He can hear their calls, their murmurings, the shouts, the greetings, demands for nuts or sweetmeats, arguments that brew up quickly, then die away.

From behind him comes a crash, a curse, a burst of laughter. Someone has tripped on someone else's feet. There is a ribald joke about falling, about maidenheads. More laughter. Someone else comes running up the stairs, asking, Has anyone seen my sword, I've lost my sword, which of you whoreson dogs have taken it?

Soon, he will need to disrobe, to take off the clothes of daily life, of the street, of ordinariness, and put on his costume. He will need to confront his image in a glass and make it into something else. He will take a paste of chalk and lime and spread it over his cheeks, his nose, his beard. Charcoal to darken the eye sockets and the brows. Armour to strap to his chest, a helmet to slot over his head, a winding sheet to place about his shoulders. And then he will wait, listening, following the lines, until he hears his cue, and then he will step out, into the light, to inhabit the form of another; he will inhale; he will say his words.

He cannot tell, as he stands there, whether or not this new play is good. Sometimes, as he listens to his company speak the lines, he thinks he has come close to what he wanted it to be; other times, he feels he has entirely missed the mark. It is good, it is bad, it is somewhere in between. How does a person ever tell? All he can do is inscribe strokes on a page – for weeks and weeks, this was all he did, barely leaving his room, barely eating, never speaking to anyone else – and hope that at least some of these arrows will hit their targets. The play, the complete length of it, fills his head. It balances there, like a laden platter on a single fingertip. It moves through him – this one, more than any other he has ever written – as blood through his veins.

The river is casting its frail net of mist. He can scent it on the breeze, its dank and weed-filled fumes wafting towards him.

Perhaps it is this fog, this river-heavy air, he doesn't know, but the day feels ill to him. He is filled with an unease, a slight foreboding, as if something is coming for him. Is it the performance? Does he feel something will be amiss with it? He frowns, thinking, running over in his head any moments that might feel un-rehearsed or ill-prepared. There is not one. They are ready and waiting. He knows this because he himself pushed them through it, over and over again.

What is it, then? Why does he have this feeling that something approaches him, that some kind of reckoning awaits him, so that he must be constantly glancing over his shoulder?

He shivers, despite the heat and closeness of the room. He moves his hands through his hair, tugs on the hoops through his ears.

Tonight, he decides, out of nowhere, he will return to his room, straight away. He will not go drinking with his friends. He will go directly to his lodgings. He will light a candle, he will sharpen a quill. He will refuse to go to a tavern with the rest of the company. He will be firm. He will remove their hands from his arms, if they try to drag him. He will cross over the river, go back to Bishopsgate and write to his wife, as he has been trying to, for a long time. He will not avoid the matter in hand. He will tell her about this play. He will tell her all. Tonight. He is certain of it.

Halfway across the bridge, Agnes thinks she cannot go on. She isn't sure what she expected – a simple arch, perhaps, of wood, over some water – but it wasn't this. London Bridge is like a town in itself, and a noxious, oppressive one at that. There are houses and shops on either side, some jutting out over the river; these buildings overhang the passage so that, at times, it is completely dark, as if they have been plunged into night. The river appears to them in flashes, between the buildings, and it is wider, deeper, more dangerous than she had ever imagined. It flows beneath their feet, beneath the horses' hoofs, even now, as they make their way through this crowd.

From every doorway and shop, vendors call and yell at them, running up with fabric or bread or beads or roasted pigs' trotters. Bartholomew pulls his bridle away from them, with a curt gesture. His face, when Agnes looks at it, is as expressionless as ever, but she can tell he is as disquieted by all this as she is.

'Perhaps,' she mutters to him, as they pass what appears to be a heap of excrement, 'we should have taken a boat.'

Bartholomew grunts. 'Maybe, but then we might have—' He breaks off, the words disappearing before he can speak them. 'Don't look,' he says, glancing upwards, then back at her.

Agnes widens her eyes, keeping them on his face. 'What is it?' she whispers. 'Is it him? Have you seen him? Is he with someone?'

'No,' Bartholomew says, stealing another glance at whatever it is. 'It's . . . Never mind. Just don't look.'

Agnes cannot help herself. She turns in her saddle and sees: drooping grey clouds pierced by long poles, shuddering in the breeze, topped by things that look, for a moment, like stones or turnips. She squints at them. They are blackened, ragged, oddly lumpish. They give off, to her, a thin, soundless wail, like trapped animals. Whatever can they be? Then she sees that the one nearest her seems to have a row of teeth set into it. They have mouths, she realises, and nostrils, and pitted sockets where eyes once were.

She lets out a cry, turns back to her brother, her hand over her mouth.

Bartholomew shrugs. 'I told you not to look.'

When they reach the other side of the river, Agnes leans into her saddlebag and pulls out the playbill Joan gave her.

There, again, is the name of her son and the black letters, arranged in their sequence, shocking as it was the first time she saw it.

She turns it away from her, gripping it tightly in her hand, and waves it at the next person who comes near the flank of her horse. The person – a man with a pointed brushed beard and cape thrown back from his shoulders – indicates a side-street. Go that way, he says, then left, then left again, and you shall see it.

She recognises the playhouse from her husband's description: a round wooden place next to the river. She slides from her horse's back, and Bartholomew takes the reins, and her legs feel as if they have lost their bones somewhere along the way. The scene around her – the street, the riverbank, the horses, the playhouse – seems to waver and swing, coming in and out of focus. Bartholomew is speaking. He will, he says to her, wait for her here; he will not move from this spot until she comes back. Does she understand? His face is pushed up very close to hers. He appears to be waiting for some response, so Agnes nods. She steps away from him, in through the large doors, paying her penny.

As she comes through the high doorway, she is greeted by the sight of row upon row of faces, hundreds of them, all talking and shouting. She is in a tall-sided enclosure, which is filling with people. There is a stage jutting out into the gathering crowd, and above them all, a ceiling of sky, a circle containing fast-moving clouds, the shapes of birds, darting from one edge to the next.

Agnes slides between shoulders and bodies, men and women, someone holding a chicken beneath their arm, a woman with a baby at her breast, half-hidden by a shawl, a man selling pies from a tray. She turns herself sideways, steps between people, until she gets herself as close as she can to the stage.

On all sides, bodies and elbows and arms press in. More and more people are pouring through the doors. Some on the ground are gesturing and shouting to others in the higher balconies. The crowd thickens and heaves, first one way, then the next; Agnes is pushed backwards and forward but she keeps her footing; the trick seems to be to move with the current, rather than resist it. It is, she thinks, like standing in a river: you have to bend yourself to its flow, not fight it. A group in the highest tier of seats is making much of the lowering of a length of rope. There is shouting and hooting and laughter. The pie-man ties to its end a laden basket and the people above begin to haul it up towards them. Several members of the crowd leap to snatch it, in a playful or perhaps hungry fashion; the pie-man deals each of them a swift, cracking blow. A coin is thrown down by the people above and the pie-man lunges to catch it. One of the men he has just hit gets to it first and the pie-man grabs him around the throat; the man lands a punch on the pie-man's chin. They go down, hard, swallowed by the crowd, amid much cheering and noise.

The woman next to Agnes shrugs and grins at her with blackened, crooked teeth. She has a small boy on her shoulders. With one hand, the child grips his mother's hair, and with the other, he holds what to Agnes looks like a lamb's shank bone, gnawing at it with sated, glazed indifference. He regards her with impassive eyes, the bone between his small, sharp teeth.

A sudden, blaring noise makes Agnes jump. Trumpets are sounding from somewhere. The babble of the crowd surges and gathers into a ragged cheer. People raise their arms; there is a scattering of applause, several cheers, some piercing whistles. From behind Agnes, comes a rude noise, a curse, a yelled exhortation to hurry up, for Lord's sake.

The trumpets repeat their tune, a circling refrain, the final note stretched and held. A hush falls over the crowd and two men walk on to the stage.

Agnes blinks. The fact that she has come to see a play has somehow drifted away from her. But here she is, in her husband's playhouse, and here is the play.

A pair of actors stand upon a wooden stage and speak to each other, as if no one is watching, as if they are completely alone.

She takes them in, listening, attentive. They are nervous, jittery, glancing about themselves, gripping their swords. Who's there? one of them shouts to the other. Unfold yourself, the other shouts back. More actors arrive on the stage, all nervous, all watchful.

The crowd around her, she cannot help but notice, is entirely still. No one speaks. No one moves. Everyone is entirely focused on these actors and what they are saying. Gone is the jostling, whistling, brawling, pie-chewing mass and in its place a silent, awed congregation. It is as if a magician or sorcerer has waved his staff over the place and turned them all to stone.

Now that she is here and the play has begun, the strangeness and detachment she felt during the journey, and while she stood in his lodgings, rinses off her, like grime. She feels ready, she feels furious. Come on then, she thinks. Show me what you've done.

The players on the stage mouth speeches to each other. They gesture and point and mince back and forth, gripping their weapons. One says a line, then another, then it is the first's turn. She watches, baffled. She had expected something familiar, something about her son. What else would the play be about? But this is people in a castle, on a battlement, debating with each other over nothing.

She alone, it seems, is exempt from the sorcerer's spell. The magic has not touched her. She feels like heckling or scoffing. Her husband wrote these words, these exchanges, but what has any of this to do with their boy? She wants to shout to the people on the stage. You, she would say, and you: you are all nothing, this is nothing, compared to what he was. Don't you dare pronounce his name.

A great weariness seizes her. She is conscious of an ache in her legs and hips, from the many hours on horseback, of her lack of sleep, of the light, which seems to sting her eyes. She hasn't the strength or the inclination to put up with this press of bodies around her, with these long speeches, these floods of words. She won't stand here any longer. She will leave and her husband will never be any the wiser.

Suddenly, the actor on stage says something about a dreaded sight, and a realisation creeps over her. What these men are seeking, discussing, expecting is a ghost, an apparition. They want it, and yet they fear it, too, all at the same time.

She holds herself very still, watching their movements, listening to their words. She crosses her arms so that no one around her may touch or brush against her, distracting her. She needs to concentrate. She doesn't want to miss a sound.

When the ghost appears, a collective gasp passes over the audience. Agnes doesn't flinch. She stares at the ghost. It is in full armour, the visor of the helmet drawn down, its form half-hidden by a shroud. She doesn't listen to the bluster and bleating of frightened men on the battlements of the castle. She watches it through narrowed lids.

She has her eye on that ghost: the height, that movement of the arm, hand upturned, a particular curl of the fingers, that roll of the shoulder. When he raises the visor, she feels not surprise, not recognition, but a kind of hollow confirmation. His face is painted a ghastly white, his beard made grey; he is dressed as if for battle, in armour and helmet, but she isn't fooled for a moment. She knows exactly who is underneath that costume, that disguise.

She thinks: Well, now. There you are. What are you up to?

As if her thoughts have been beamed to him, from her mind to his, through the crowds – calling out now, shouting warnings to the men on the battlements – the ghost's head snaps around. The helmet is open and the eyes peer out over the heads of the audience.

Yes, Agnes tells him, here I am. Now what?

The ghost leaves. It seems not to have found whatever it was seeking. There is a disappointed murmur from the audience. The men onstage keep talking, on and on. Agnes shifts her feet, raising herself on tiptoe, wondering when the ghost will return. She wants to keep him in her sights, wants him to come back; she wants him to explain himself.

She is craning past the head and shoulders of a man in front when she accidentally treads on the toes of the woman next to her. The woman lets out a small yelp and lurches sideways, the child on her shoulders dropping his lamb bone. Agnes is apologising, catching the elbow of the woman to steady her, and bending to retrieve the bone, when she hears a word from the stage that makes her straighten up, makes the bone slide from her fingers.

Hamlet, one of the actors said.

She heard it, as clear and resonant as the strike of a distant bell.

There it is again: Hamlet.

Agnes bites her lip until she tastes the tang of her own blood. She grips her hands together.

They are saying it, these men up there on the stage, passing it between them, like a counter in a game. Hamlet, Hamlet, Hamlet. It seems to refer to the ghost, the dead man, the departed form.

To hear that name, out of the mouths of people she has never known and will never know, and used for an old dead king: Agnes cannot understand this. Why would her husband have done it? Why pretend that it means nothing to him, just a collection of letters? How could he thieve this name, then strip and flense it of all it embodies, discarding the very life it once contained? How could he take up his pen and write it on a page, breaking its connection with their son? It makes no sense. It pierces her heart, it eviscerates her, it threatens to sever her from herself, from him, from everything they had, everything they were. She thinks of those poor heads, their bared teeth, their vulnerable necks, their frozen expressions of fear, on the bridge, and it is as if she is one of them. She can feel the shiver of the river, their bodiless sway and dip, their voiceless and useless regret.

She will go. She will leave this place. She will find Bartholomew, mount that exhausted horse, ride back to Stratford and write a letter to her husband, saying, Don't come home, don't ever come back, stay in London, we are done with you. She has seen all she needs to see. It is just as she feared: he has taken that most sacred and tender of names and tossed it in among a jumble of other words, in the midst of a theatrical pageant.

She had thought that coming here, watching this, might give her a glimpse into her husband's heart. It might have offered her a way back to him. She thought the name on the playbill might have been a means for him to communicate something to her. A sign, of sorts, a signal, an outstretched hand, a summons. As she rode to London, she had thought that perhaps now she might understand his distance, his silence, since their son's death. She has the sense now that there is nothing in her husband's heart to understand. It is filled only with this: a wooden stage, declaiming players, memorised speeches, adoring crowds, costumed fools. She has been chasing a phantasm, a will-o'-the-wisp, all this time.

She is gathering her skirts, pulling her shawl about her, getting ready to turn her back on her husband and his company, when her attention is drawn by a boy walking on to the stage. A boy, she thinks, unknotting and reknotting her shawl. Then, no, a man. Then, no, a lad – halfway between man and boy.

It is as if a whip has been snapped hard upon the skin. He has yellow hair which stands up at the brow, a tripping, buoyant tread, an impatient toss to his head. Agnes lets her hands fall. The shawl slips from her shoulders but she doesn't stoop to pick it up. She fixes her gaze upon this boy; she stares and stares as if she may never look away from him. She feels the breath empty from her chest, feels the blood curdle in her veins. The disc of sky above her seems at once to press down on her head, on all of them, like the lid of a cauldron. She is freezing; she is stiflingly hot; she must leave; she will stand here for ever, on this spot.

When the King addresses him as 'Hamlet, my son,' the words carry no surprise for her. Of course this is who he is. Of course. Who else would it be? She has looked for her son everywhere, ceaselessly, these past four years, and here he is.

It is him. It is not him. It is him. It is not him. The thought swings like a hammer through her. Her son, her Hamnet or Hamlet, is dead, buried in the churchyard. He died while he was still a child. He is now only white, stripped bones in a grave. Yet this is him, grown into a near-man, as he would be now, had he lived, on the stage, walking with her son's gait, talking in her son's voice, speaking words written for him by her son's father.

She presses a hand to either side of her head. It is too much: she isn't sure how to bear it, how to explain this to herself. It is too much. For a moment, she thinks she may fall, disappear beneath this sea of heads and bodies, to lie on the compacted earth, to be trampled under a hundred feet.

But then the ghost returns and the boy Hamlet is speaking with it: he is terrified, he is furious, he is distraught, and Agnes is filled by an old, familiar urge, like water gushing into a dry streambed. She wants to lay hands on that boy; she wants to fold him in her arms, comfort and console him – she has to, if it is the last thing she does.

The young Hamlet on stage is listening as old Hamlet, the ghost, is telling a story about how he died, a poison coursing through his body, 'like quicksilver', and how like her Hamnet he listens. The very same lean and tilt of the head, the gesture of pressing a knuckle to the mouth when hearing something he doesn't immediately comprehend. How can it be? She doesn't understand it, she doesn't understand any of it. How can this player, this young man, know how to be her Hamnet when he never saw or met the boy?

The knowledge settles on her like a fine covering of rain, as she moves towards the players, threading her way through the packed crowds: her husband has pulled off a manner of alchemy. He has found this boy, instructed him, shown him, how to speak, how to stand, how to lift his chin, like this, like that. He has rehearsed and primed and prepared him. He has written words for him to speak and to hear. She tries to imagine these rehearsals, how her husband could have schooled him so exactly, so precisely, and how it might have felt when the boy got it right, when he first got the walk, that heartbreaking turn of the head. Did her husband have to say, Make sure your doublet is undone, with the ties hanging down, and your boots should be scuffed, and now wet your hair so it stands up, just so?

Hamlet, here, on this stage, is two people, the young man, alive, and the father, dead. He is both alive and dead. Her husband has brought him back to life, in the only way he can. As the ghost talks, she sees that her husband, in writing this, in taking the role of the ghost, has changed places with his son. He has taken his son's death and made it his own; he has put himself in death's clutches, resurrecting the boy in his place. 'O horrible! O horrible! Most horrible!' murmurs her husband's ghoulish voice, recalling the agony of his death. He has, Agnes sees, done what any father would wish to do, to exchange his child's suffering for his own, to take his place, to offer himself up in his child's stead so that the boy might live.

She will say all this to her husband, later, after the play has ended, after the final silence has fallen, after the dead have sprung up to take their places in the line of players at the edge of the stage. After her husband and the boy, their hands joined, bow and bow, facing into the storm of applause. After the stage is left deserted, no longer a battlement, no longer a graveyard, no longer a castle. After he has come to find her, forcing his way through the crowds, his face still streaked with traces of paste. After he has taken her by the hand and held her against the buckles and leather of his armour. After they have stood together in the open circle of the playhouse, until it was as empty as the sky above it.

For now, she is right at the front of the crowd, at the edge of the stage; she is gripping its wooden lip in both hands. An arm's length away, perhaps two, is Hamlet, her Hamlet, as he might have been, had he lived, and the ghost, who has her husband's hands, her husband's beard, who speaks in her husband's voice.

She stretches out a hand, as if to acknowledge them, as if to feel the air between the three of them, as if wishing to pierce the boundary between audience and players, between real life and play.

The ghost turns his head towards her, as he prepares to exit the scene. He is looking straight at her, meeting her gaze, as he speaks his final words:

'Remember me.'

Author's Note

This is a work of fiction, inspired by the short life of a boy who died in Stratford, Warwickshire, in the summer of 1596. I have tried, where possible, to stick to the scant historical facts known about the real Hamnet and his family, but a few details – names, in particular – have been altered or elided over.

Most people will know his mother as 'Anne' but she was named by her father, Richard Hathaway, in his will, as 'Agnes' and I decided to follow his example. Some believe that Joan Hathaway was Agnes's mother, while others argue she was her stepmother; there is little evidence to support or discredit either theory.

Hamnet's sole surviving paternal aunt was called not Eliza but Joan (as was the eldest sister who predeceased her); I took the liberty of changing it because the doubling up of names, while common in parish records of the time, can be confusing for readers of a novel.

There were guides at Shakespeare's Birthplace Trust who told me that Hamnet, Judith and Susanna grew up in their grandparents' house in Henley Street; others seemed certain that they would have lived in the little adjoining property. Either way, the two households would have been closely linked but I chose to opt for the latter.

Lastly, it is not known why Hamnet Shakespeare died: his burial is listed but not the cause of his death. The Black Death or 'pestilence', as it would have been known in the late sixteenth century, is not mentioned once by Shakespeare, in any of his plays or poetry. I have always wondered about this absence and its possible significance; this novel is the result of my idle speculation.

Acknowledgements

Thank you, Mary-Anne Harrington.

Thank you, Victoria Hobbs.

Thank you, Jordan Pavlin.

Thank you, Georgina Moore.

Thank you, Hazel Orme, Yeti Lambregts, Amy Perkins, Vicky Abbott, and all at Tinder Press.

Thank you to the staff at Shakespeare's Birthplace Trust, and the guides at Holy Trinity Church, Stratford, who were unfailingly generous and patient in the face of numerous questions.

Thank you, Bridget O'Farrell, for the loan of a kitchen table.

Thank you, Charlotte Mendelson and Jules Bradbury, for herbal and plant advice.

The following books were invaluable during the writing of this novel: *The Herball or General Historie of Plantes* by John Gerard, 1597 (arranged by Marcus Woodward, © Bodley Head, 1927); *Shakespeare's Restless World* by Neil McGregor (Allen Lane, 2012); *A Shakespeare Botanical* by Margaret Willes (Bodleian Library, 2015); *The Book of Faulconrie or Hauking* by George Turberville (London, 1575); *Shakespeare's Wife* by Germaine Greer (Bloomsbury, 2007); *Shakespeare* by Bill Bryson (Harper Press, 2007); *Shakespeare: The Biography* by

Peter Ackroyd (Vintage, 2006); *How To Be a Tudor* by Ruth Goodman (Penguin, 2015); *1599: A Year in the Life of William Shakespeare* by James Shapiro (Faber & Faber, 2005); and the website Shakespeare Documented, shakespearedocumented. folger.edu/

Special thanks are due to Mr Henderson, in whose English class, in 1989, I first heard about the existence of Hamnet. I hope he will rate this book as 'not bad'.

Thank you, SS, IZ and JA.

And thank you, Will Sutcliffe, for everything.

To Write a House

amnet is a book I've been wanting to write for a long time. Every once in a while, I would make an optimistic start: do some research, fill a notebook, go to a library, write a few pages, perhaps pin some maps to the wall. And then I would swerve away from it, towards another project, another book, putting all my notes back in the cupboard.

It's always possible to find more reasons not to write a book than to actually write one.

At last count, I have produced three books instead of writing *Hamnet*: all were set upon with relief. I'd found a valid distraction! No one could say I wasn't writing a book; I just wasn't writing the one I had promised I would.

About three years ago, as I was going through the final edit for *I Am, I Am, I Am*, I gave myself a talking-to. I had to stop circling around this idea once and for all; I either had to knuckle down and write about this sixteenth-century boy or forget about him. I squared up to myself: come on then, now or never.

I read through what I already had and quite quickly

realised that I had started the story in the wrong place, from the wrong point of view. So I opened a new document and began again, with a clear image in my head: a boy coming down a staircase.

I wrote a string of words describing this. The heat of the August day, the sound of his boots on the treads, his anxiety about his twin sister, who is ill. I felt the low thrum of excitement you get when you think you might finally be on the right track. My fingers were tap-tapping away. Then the boy gets to the bottom of the stairs and he stumbles and—

Here I stopped. I lifted my hands from the keyboard.

The floor he falls on: what kind of floor was it? I pondered this for a moment. What were Elizabethan floors made of? Wooden boards, compacted dirt, tile, carpet – what?

I had no idea. I couldn't picture it. I had stumbled, just like the boy on my initial page. I stood up and thumbed through my shelf of research books. Nothing. I trawled the internet. It could tell me what material lined the floors of Tudor palaces, but this was a house in a small English market town.

I sat at my desk, staring at my screen, at the signalling cursor, at my curtailed paragraph. There was nothing for it, I knew. It was time to get myself to Stratford.

To walk into the Shakespeare family house on Henley Street, Stratford-upon-Avon, is an astonishing experience.

That the place exists at all, for it to have survived the intervening four hundred years, seems nothing short of miraculous. You move through the doors, the rooms, you gaze out of the criss-cross leaded windows and you ask yourself: how can this still be here?

Shakespeare, for all his extraordinary output of plays and poetry, left a very scant paper trail. There are only a handful of documents with which to trace his life. We can delve into his plays and poetry and try to extrapolate the workings of his mind, but to locate the man himself is a tricky, amorphous task.

There are so many gaps in his biography, so many mysteries, so many unanswered questions about the son of a glover who came to be the world's most revered playwright. To be able to simply buy a ticket and wander through the rooms where he grew up, then, is a gift like no other.

You enter, not through the door the family would have used, but through the side via what initially seemed to me to be a kind of antechamber. You pass through this into the parlour, which has a cavernous fireplace and wall hangings and would, in the sixteenth century, have held a four-poster bed for the use of guests. From there, you reach the hall, where the family ate their meals. Then there is the passage and, beyond that, John Shakespeare's glove workshop, with a vending window on to the street.

I've always had a fascination for writers' homes. If ever

I'm in a place where there is a museum-house, I will make a point of going. I've wandered among Tolstoy's mirrors and lamps, examined Lorca's desk, I've stood in the room where Charlotte Brontë died, I've peered out of the windows of Beatrix Potter's study, sniffed for traces of Plumtree's Potted Meat in the James Joyce tower, and contemplated Keats' tree.

The house in Henley Street, however, is quite another experience, partly because it's so extraordinarily old and strange, and partly because, well, it's *him*. The man on whose shoulders we all stand, whose words have woven themselves into our very language, whose plays continue to reveal the hidden layers and inner workings of human-kind.

Usually, when you create a house in a novel, it's a gradual and piecemeal process. You might purloin a staircase from somewhere you used to live and perhaps tack that to a kitchen from a half-remembered holiday cottage. You might borrow a window-box or garden border from the home of your best friend at primary school. Or you might make up the whole thing. The outlook from the front door could well be a place where you once went to a party in your twenties. It's a Frankensteinian process, writing a house. You walk about it like a visitor at night, fumbling your way in the dark-ness, groping for light switches, discovering rooms and cupboards you had no idea were there.

Except this time, the house where I would set my novel already existed, and had done for almost half a millennium, and I was standing in the middle of it. It's hard to convey how odd this felt, to find the location for your soon-to-be-written story, ready and waiting for you.

I made my first circuit in a daze: through the parlour and the hall, along the passage, into the workshop, up into the chambers, the birth room, and down again. I paused at the final step of the staircase, running my hand along the panelling, looking up, looking down.

Flagstones. Here was my answer. Here was what I'd travelled three hundred miles to see. The floor in this house, at the bottom of the stairs, was flagstones, fitted together like jigsaw pieces. Should someone stumble and fall here, it would hurt.

I came out through the back door, into what would have been the yard, where the cook- and washhouses would have stood, but was now filled with Spanish schoolchildren watching two caped actors declaiming the Romeo and Tybalt fight scene.

Then I went round again, this time with more focus. I took photographs of practically everything I saw – floors, windows, doorways, chimney flues, sills – I drew maps of the layout, I asked the guides approximately ninety questions each and wrote down everything they said, not caring if they thought me slightly crazed.

The guide in the anteroom on the side of the house

told me that Shakespeare's three children would have grown up in the big house with their grandparents. Another guide, standing by the velvet ropes across the hall, told me that Shakespeare and his wife would have moved into the side apartment and the children would have grown up there.

'It's obvious,' he said to me. 'John Shakespeare had built the apartment in a gap between his house and the next – it makes sense that the young married couple would have been given it.'

'So you think Hamnet died not in the big house but in the side apartment?' I asked.

He nodded. 'I think so.'

I went outside to the street and looked up at the latticed windows of the side apartment. Was I looking at the place where eleven-year-old Hamnet took his final breath? Was this the doorway he was carried out of, on his way to burial? Was what I originally took to be an anteroom in fact the main focus of Hamnet's short life? I allowed my eyes to pass across to the big house. Or was it behind one of these windows that he died?

Impossible to tell, of course: the only two documented facts about Hamnet Shakespeare are the parish records of his baptism and then his burial. There is the stupendous echo of his name in the title and protagonist of his father's play, but all we can be sure of is that he was born and that he died.

What I did know, as I stood there in Henley Street, was that this was the place where he grew up, where he learned to walk and talk and run and play. He would have come in and out of these doors every day of his life; he would have eaten his meals in the hall, with the rest of the family; he would have been sent out of the house on errands; he would have played in this street with his sisters, and walked along it on his way to school; he would have been carried down it, on his final journey.

Back at home, I printed out all the photographs and stuck them up around my desk. I studied my plans of the houses. I kept up my book-based research but I interleaved it with research of a more physical, tactile kind.

To better inhabit and understand the life of Hamnet's mother, I dug a patch of ground and planted a garden of Elizabethan medicinal plants. I went on a herbal medicine course and learned how to macerate stems, dry petals, mash leaves into a poultice, create tinctures, make elixirs, how to cure a cough with elderberries and ease stiff joints with comfrey leaves. I flew a kestrel in a damp and rainy wood, watching the dip and flight of its wings. I picked up one of its shed feathers and added it to my pinboard. I made bread, according to a sixteenth-century recipe, leaving it to prove in an earthenware pot, and tried to imagine doing this two or three times, every single day. I searched along riverbanks for hagstones and tied them through their holes with herbs, and hung them up at the front and back doors of my house, in the hope that they might ward off evil spirits and illness. I wanted to understand the labour of these tasks, how they felt, the hope and fear imbued in each, how they might change a person.

And, of course, I wrote. Visiting Stratford was, it seemed, the catalyst I needed. I could picture the house now, and its rooms and floors and furniture. I knew how it would sound in windy weather and in rain. I could see how the sun would slant in on bright mornings. I could walk along the street and across the marketplace in my mind. Most importantly of all, I could picture the procession of a flower-laden bier, all the way to that churchyard next to the river.

Maggie O'Farrell,
Edinburgh, 2020

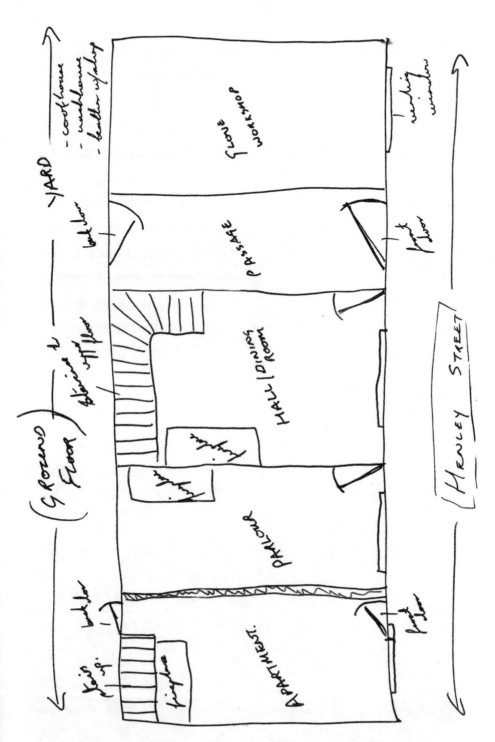

Maggie's own map of the ground floor, Shakespeare's Birthplace Trust

Shakespeare's Birthplace, Henley Street, Stratford

© Alicia G. Monedero/Shutterstock

Dining room, Shakespeare's Birthplace

© Mark Andrews/Alamy

The apartment,
Shakespeare's Birthplace

Parish Register, Holy Trinity Church,
Stratford-upon-Avon: Baptism Entry for
Hamnet and Judith Shakespeare, 2nd February 1585

20 Jone daughter to Erasius Mitheles
20 Jone daughter to John Robines
25 Elizabeth daughter to Richard Gritton
26 John sonne to John Wheeler
January 3 ffrancis daughter to James Allen
5 daughter to William Raynold
6 John sonne to John Trowte
13 Anne daughter to John Shewarde
14 John sonne to John Pittes
15 Richard a Bastard of Mr phillip Moxes servant
21 Thomas sonne to Mr Thomas Raynold
21 William sonne to Edward Williams
February 2 Hamnet & Judeth sonne & daughter to william Shakspere
3 Margret daughter to Hugh piggette
10 John sonne to John ffisher
11 Thomas sonne to Richard Taylor
14 Richard sonne to John Elsome
21 Mary & Jone daughters to John Goodyeare
28 George sonne to Georges Carles
March 6 Josias sonne to Adrian Young
6 Margery daughter to John Hudsonne
14 Anne daughter to william Parsons
14 Richard sonne to Richard Dowles
14 John sonne to Humfrey Heldar
14 Katherine daughter to Thomas Henshaw

Ric Byfield
Abramizyd ...
James ... clerk

Parish Register, Holy Trinity Church, Stratford-upon-Avon: Burial Entry for Hamnet Shakespeare, 11th August 1596

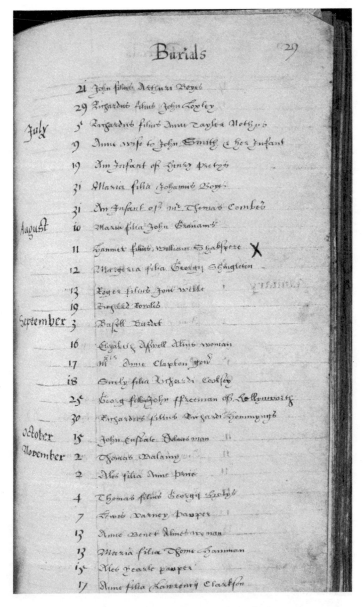

By kind permission of the Shakespeare Birthplace Trust